MARQUE OF CAINE

BAEN BOOKS by CHARLES E. GANNON

The Terran Republic Series
Fire with Fire
Trial by Fire
Raising Caine
Caine's Mutiny
Marque of Caine
Endangered Species (forthcoming)

The Starfire Series
(with Steve White)
Extremis
Imperative
Oblivion

The Ring of Fire Series
(with Eric Flint)
1635: The Papal Stakes
1636: Commander Cantrell in the West Indies
1636: The Vatican Sanction

**To purchase any of these titles in e-book form,
please go to www.baen.com.**

MARQUE OF CAINE

CHARLES E. GANNON

MARQUE OF CAINE

This is a work of fiction. All the characters and events portrayed in this book are fictional, and any resemblance to real people or incidents is purely coincidental.

Copyright © 2019 by Charles E. Gannon

All rights reserved, including the right to reproduce this book or portions thereof in any form.

A Baen Books Original

Baen Publishing Enterprises
P.O. Box 1403
Riverdale, NY 10471
www.baen.com

ISBN: 978-1-4814-8409-1

Cover art by Bob Eggleton
Map by Randy Asplund

First printing, July 2019

Distributed by Simon & Schuster
1230 Avenue of the Americas
New York, NY 10020

Library of Congress Cataloging-in-Publication Data

Names: Gannon, Charles E., author.
Title: Marque of caine / Charles E. Gannon.
Description: Riverdale, NY : Baen, [2019] | Series: The Terran Republic series | "A Baen Books Original"—Title page verso.
Identifiers: LCCN 2019006251 | ISBN 9781481484091 (trade pb)
Subjects: | GSAFD: Science fiction.
Classification: LCC PS3607.A556 M37 2019 | DDC 813/.6—dc23 LC record available at https://lccn.loc.gov/2019006251

Pages by Joy Freeman (www.pagesbyjoy.com)
Printed in the United States of America

10 9 8 7 6 5 4 3 2 1

With deep and enduring appreciation for my friend and editor, Toni Weisskopf, whose support and skill made this novel better in every conceivable way.

And as always, with thanks and love to my whole family (my wife Andrea and living children Connor, Kyle, Alexandra, and Pierce), who cheered me on through this lengthy endeavor.

CONTENTS

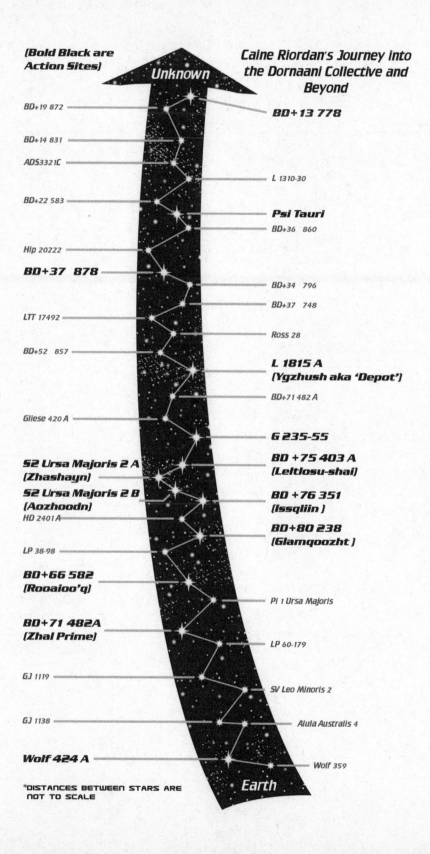

[Bold Black are Action Sites]

Caine Riordan's Journey into the Dornaani Collective and Beyond

Unknown

BD+19 872

BD+13 778

BD+14 831

ADS 3321C

L 1310-30

BD+22 583

Psi Tauri

BD+36 860

Hip 20222

BD+37 878

BD+34 796

BD+37 748

LTT 17492

Ross 28

BD+52 857

**L 1815 A
(Ygzhush aka 'Depot')**

BD+71 482 A

Gliese 420 A

G 235-55

**S2 Ursa Majoris 2 A
(Zhashayn)**

**BD +75 403 A
(Leitlosu-shai)**

**S2 Ursa Majoris 2 B
(Aozhoodn)**

**BD +76 351
(Issqliin)**

HD 2401 A

**BD+80 238
(Glamqoozht)**

LP 38-98

**BD+66 582
(Rooaioo'q)**

Pi 1 Ursa Majoris

**BD+71 482A
(Zhal Prime)**

LP 60-179

GJ 1119

SV Leo Minoris 2

GJ 1138

Alula Australis 4

Wolf 424 A

Wolf 359

Earth

*DISTANCES BETWEEN STARS ARE NOT TO SCALE

PART ONE

Earth and Environs
June–July 2123

IN SUA PATRIA

Propheta in sua patria honorem non habet
(The prophet hath no honor in his own country)

Chapter One

Caine Riordan watched the hull of the eighteen-foot sloop recede. "Pretty strong headwind in the Narrows today, son."

Seventeen-year-old Connor Corcoran looked over his shoulder as he stowed the pole he'd used to push off from Oualie New Dock. He smiled, a hint of indulgence in the expression. "There's a pretty strong headwind in the Narrows *every* day, Dad."

"Dad": hearing that never gets old. Caine smiled back. "Fair enough. But it's a lot trickier tackling it solo."

Connor stood to the tiller, his smile widening as the boat drifted back and the breeze started toying with the telltales. "As you've told me. Every time I've tackled it on my own. With you in the boat."

Yes, with me in the boat. Where I can intervene. Help you. Save you, if it comes to that. But Caine forced himself to simply raise his hand and wave. "Have fun, Connor."

"I will. And Dad?" Connor had to raise his voice a little to be heard across the widening gap. He was making ready to swing away from the dock.

"What is it?"

"You're going to keep your promise, right?"

Caine sighed. "I gave you my word. I will not watch. You are on your own." Riordan checked his wristlink, which was offline. As it had been since the day they had arrived on the island of Nevis almost two years ago. "I'll meet you back here at three PM."

3

Connor cupped a theatrical hand to his ear. "What's that you said? Four o'clock?"

Riordan replied in a loud, flat tone. "Three PM. As agreed."

"You are a killjoy, Dad."

"I love you too, Connor."

Who waved, and—with the eager agility of seventeen-year-olds everywhere—leaped to the tasks that would aim the sloop's prow out toward the cerulean waters of the leeward Caribbean.

Riordan decided that seeing the boat out of Oualie Bay wasn't "watching." It was just part of saying farewell. *Okay, a very* long *farewell.* Caine squinted against the midmorning sunlight bouncing up from the bleached dock planks, eyes tracking the sloop's filling, dwindling sails. Finally, its red-tipped masthead disappeared behind the northern headland. He turned and walked slowly back to his car.

"Car" was a pretty grand term for the cramped, motorized box. It was adequate for Nevis, though: the round island's only major artery for vehicles was a thirty-three-kilometer coastal ring-road. Riordan slipped into the driver's seat, activated the electric motor, and tapped the "reverse trip" tab on the dashboard's faded screen. The weathered vehicle began rolling forward, angling toward the low eastern hills that mounted toward Nevis' central volcanic peak.

As it reached the coast road, the electric motor was still an atonal whine: just one of the many ways the car was showing its age. Which was probably greater than Riordan's forty years. But the car had two decisively redeeming features: it was reliable and it was nondescript. And of the two features, its unremarkable appearance among the island's other worn vehicles was the most important.

In order to remain unfound, Riordan had made every aspect of their existence on Nevis as commonplace as possible. Their house was modest and not in a particularly desirable part of the island, yet not so remote that it spawned the speculations and aura of mystery associated with truly secluded homes. They used local currency, forwarded by off-shore agents who sent any extraordinary requirements in an unnumbered crate. Both father and son shopped in the local market at Brick Kiln, visited the larger stores in Charlestown once or twice a month.

As the car swung onto the long, scrub-bracketed stretch of road that paralleled the Narrows and ran past Amory Air Terminal, its engine's two-toned whine finally settled into a normal monotone hum. Riordan glanced to his left—surely a mere glance did not constitute "watching" Connor—to see if the sloop's sail had appeared yet.

Nothing. Not too surprising, given that the headwinds were brisk in the small channel between Nevis and the larger island of St. Kitts to the north. Connor would spend a lot of time tacking back and forth across that breeze before getting through the windward mouth and into the open ocean.

Caine sighed, sat back. The roadside scrub was now interspersed with elephant grass and sandy flats. The towering cone of Mt. Nevis started brightening, murky gray transforming to rich green as the sun bathed it more fully. A kilometer marker flashed by, then another.

Riordan resisted the temptation to look in the rearview mirror or instruct the car to slow down. *There's nothing to worry about. He's piloted through the Narrows at least twenty times. Hell, he's a better sailor than I am. Ought to be; he came to it earlier.*

A moment later, his resolve forgotten, Caine glanced in the rearview mirror. Back where the leeward mouth of the strait spilled the waters of the Atlantic into the Caribbean, he glimpsed a flash of white over the cars parked at the air terminal: the upper corner of the sloop's mainsail.

Riordan breathed out slowly. And along with the air in his lungs, he expelled the high, hard knot of worry that had been lodged in his chest ever since leaving the dock. Not because he had any misgivings about Connor's skills or calm in a crisis. Nothing as defined or finite as that. No, this was the same fear that awakened Caine in the quiet, solid darkness of the tropical nights, body covered in sweat. No matter which images of battle and carnage came to haunt him, no matter which specific terror rose up through them, the lessons they rehearsed were always the same:

There's no such thing as certainty.

Control is an illusion.

Death and destruction descend the moment you forget to watch for them.

That was what two years of intermittent war had taught him. And once you learned those lessons, you didn't just remember them: you lived them, moment to moment.

He didn't have anything as severe as full-blown PTSD. The interludes of combat had been sharp but short-lived, with long reprieves in between: not the constant repetition that shapes new reflexes, molds new behaviors. But its impact upon him was no less real. Dawn no longer brought easy presumptions of personal safety, or even human dominance. Now, he and the rest of humanity saw each dawn as being the potential harbinger of a disorienting new reality—just the way it had been four years ago.

On that morning early in April 2119, humanity had awakened into a universe in which it was comfortingly, and safely, alone. By nightfall, news of ancient ruins on Delta Pavonis Three had been leaked and supplanted the universe's vast emptiness with anticipations of a cosmos populated by past or present exosapients.

Just six months later, the grim sequelae of that revelation shook Earth out of its last semicomplacent slumber. Alien invaders fell from the sky, seized Indonesia as both leverage and as a beachhead, and crippled the globe's power grid to ensure their mastery. And over the many months that followed, as Caine crept through both terrestrial and alien undergrowth on missions to reclaim some of the autonomy humanity had lost, he learned and relearned the prime lesson common to all these shocks:

That all assumptions, like all plans, are never more than a second away from a catastrophic collision with reality.

Riordan snapped his eyes away from the rearview mirror that he had stopped seeing, focused on the road that he knew better than his own face by now. After the fighting was over, Caine believed he had made his peace with the unpredictable imminence of death and disaster, a specter that could not be dismissed, only managed. During long months between the stars, there had been ample opportunity to confront it, to work through it, however unevenly and imperfectly.

But now things were different.

His eyes drifted back to the rearview mirror: he could see more of the sloop's mainsail, and now some of its jib as well. *It was easier when my fear was only for myself, and for others who had come into harm's way of their own volition. But now, it's my son. My only son. My only family.*

The faces of Riordan's parents flitted through his mind; they were both gone, and he had been their only child. Connor's mother Elena was untold scores of light-years away, frozen on the edge of death in an alien cold-cell: mortally wounded, so far as human surgeons were concerned. Right here, right now, all Caine had was Connor.

The sails of the sloop continued their uneven progress, disappeared behind the Air Terminal's main building.

Riordan looked away, tried to see the road ahead instead of Connor's face. Two years ago, he had not known the boy outside of a few pictures. Now, this young man was one of the two stars around which Caine's world revolved. And with Elena out of reach in the unresponsive Dornaani Collective, Riordan's impulses toward family, protectiveness, and love had all fixed upon Connor. A tendency against which he fought, lest the boy—no, *young man*—begin to feel smothered, and so, compelled to recoil from the relationship which had developed between them.

And which had changed Riordan's life in ways he could not have foreseen.

The car plunged into a cut traversing a small stand of palms; the Narrows were no longer visible.

Connor Corcoran glanced at the telltales. Their already-weak flutter was stilling, becoming more of a tremble. He'd have to tack back soon.

He glanced at Amory Air Terminal, looked for the sun-bleached green car in which he'd learned to drive. Not in the parking lot. Not in the pull-off at the overlook, either. He smiled. Dad was as good as his word. As ever. In fact, the harder it was for him to keep a promise, the more meticulously he did so.

That was one of the first things he'd noticed about his father when he met him just over two years ago, in the summer of 2121. Monday, August 18, 2:32 PM, to be exact. Connor smiled into the sun. Not that he had made a special note of it or anything. After all, it had just been a matter of meeting his father for the first time.

Mom had never spoken much about Caine Riordan, and there were almost no pictures of him, not until Connor was in his teens. The few to be found were mostly in wonky news and political websites. Not crazy conspiracy outlets—well, not *many* of those—but it certainly wasn't the kind of journalism that reached mainstream audiences. It struck Connor as strange: Caine Riordan seemed to be kind of famous, but only with people who either followed, or were themselves, political insiders.

Mom didn't say anything about his father when more pictures started emerging in 2119, but she did start acting oddly. She became cautious around Uncle Trevor, Grandma, and particularly his late grandad's old friend, "Nuncle" Richard. It was as if she had started to suspect them of keeping some kind of secret but couldn't be sure of which ones were in on it, or what it was about.

Connor brought the sloop around. The sun angled back toward his eyes; his goggles darkened until they reached the photochromatic shading he had preset. The sloop was picking up speed nicely once again.

Shortly after Caine Riordan's pictures started resurfacing, Mom had gone on one of her longer field trips. Only when she returned a few months later did Connor learn, along with the rest of the world, that actually, she had gone to meet with aliens. But his mother had a more personal revelation for him: she had not only served with his father on that mission, but learned that his memory was damaged, that he didn't remember her. At all.

However, the rest of the Corcoran clan not only considered Caine Riordan's memory loss genuine, but proof that he had been forcibly abducted shortly after meeting Elena. Connor watched and listened carefully but never detected any sign that his mom, or even his hyper-protective Uncle Trevor, blamed this Riordan guy. For anything. But they didn't want to talk about it much, either. Especially Grandma, who seemed more rattled by the news of Riordan's sudden reappearance than anyone else. So, with Connor's entire family avoiding any conversations that might have answered his growing questions, he reconciled himself to the probability that, once the initial shock blew over, there'd be plenty of opportunities to get to the bottom of what was keeping them all so reticent on the topic of Caine Riordan.

Except it was just about then that aliens came plummeting out of the sky, dropping nuclear bombs on Hainan and Montevideo while blacking out most of the world with EMP strikes. In the middle of which, his mom went missing. Then Uncle Trevor and Nuncle Richard went totally off the grid as well. That left Connor with his grandma, just like all the other times when Mom had been away on field research. As if being thirteen wasn't difficult and unsettling enough on its own.

A set of rogue swells started buffeting the sloop. Connor eased his hold on the tiller, rolled with the last half of them, spared a long, sweeping glance at the coastline of Nevis. Nope: no green car pulled off on the side of the road or even hidden in the shade of the clumps of palms that edged down toward the water. Connor nodded to himself, was grateful that his dad was truly letting him do this on his own.

To his surprise, Connor discovered that made him a little bit sad.

One hundred and twenty meters beyond Charlestown's much-repaired concrete pier, the crew of a medium-sized freighter emerged from various hatches, blinking into the sun, stretching and complaining. These were typical morning rituals, as much a part of life aboard the SS *Golden Hold* as its dilapidated engines, cranky anchor windlass, and wheezing water condensers. The crew accepted all these defects, and more, with the genial grumpiness of sailors who serve on a hull that will never be the pride of any owner or flag and who prefer it that way.

They started the day with a bit of extra grousing, since, according to their place in the cargo transfer rota, they should have been able to approach the wharf immediately. But an equally unimpressive ship that had been docked there the previous night— SS *Grouper*, also of Bahamian registry—was still tied to the bollards, unloading the last of her old-fashioned wooden crates. It was a particularly satisfying catalyst for griping, because both the hands and officers of the *Golden Hold* could participate equally in blaming another ship for preventing them from doing work that they really did not want to do anyhow. Thus, camaraderie and apathy were happily conjoined.

Only one of the crew emerged from a superstructure hatch that faced away from the sun, on the leeward side of the freighter. He checked up and down the walkway that followed the protective wall of the gunwale. No one in sight: the rest of the crewmembers were leaning over the rail on the brightly lit windward side, competing to think up the most original jeers that could be tossed in the general direction of the *Grouper*.

The crewman ducked back into the shadowed hatchway, an oval inkblot surrounded by a wash of less absolute darkness. He reemerged with a small crate, walked it to the rear starboard corner of the superstructure, pried off the top, removed his new watch, detached a small disk from its back, and squeezed it before tossing it inside the container.

A small red LED glowed at the disk's center as it disappeared into the crate's lightless maw.

Chapter Two

Riordan put his hand on the dashboard to steady himself. Two klicks past Amory Air Terminal, the road degenerated so rapidly that driving at the speed limit was inadvisable. Unfortunately, the car only knew what it was told by the island's static database: Nevis had neither the budget nor the demand for a self-updating roadnet.

The car bumped and jostled through one small village after another, none more than a kilometer apart. Locals recognized the car, waved casually. Caine returned the greeting.

Upon entering a cluster of slightly more modern buildings—Brick Kiln—the car swerved to the right, exiting the main road just before reaching the "Old Town": dusty, cramped streets hemmed in by stone buildings. The car climbed up the narrow lane rapidly. Riordan overrode the automatic controls, took the wheel. The road surface here was not just annoying, it was dangerous.

Slaloming around the worst of the holes, Riordan was glad for the distraction: easier not to think about what Connor might be doing. But at least the sloop, if no more modern than Nevis' electric and ethanol-powered cars, was an excellent ship. The well-maintained unipiece hull was almost forty years old, the alloy masts about half that. The radar and radio were sturdy, if basic, as were the sails. The only truly modern feature was the "ray-grabber" cabin roof that was, despite appearances, one big, high-efficiency solar panel. On days like today, it kept a steady current flowing into the flat-form battery that resembled a drop ceiling affixed to the small cabin's overhead.

The Slimline Janus outboard was not quite as modern, but that, too, was preferable so as not to attract undue attention. Massing only thirty kilos, it was a dual-operation motor, able to switch between the high performance of gasoline and the endurance of electricity at a moment's notice. That had proven extremely handy when the weather turned unexpectedly as it had on one of their earliest trips to the barren island-butte known as Redonda. They'd had no choice but to try to beat the storm back to Nevis: there was no bay or mooring on the uninhabited rock spur. By saving the gasoline to fight the tougher currents and prestorm swells on the forty-kilometer return trip, they got the sloop to safety before the rain and wind arrived to knock down trees and take the odd roof or two.

The narrow road straightened, the gradient easing. Up ahead, Caine glimpsed the muted sheen of their house's solar shingles, checked his wristlink. Not quite ten AM. Enough time for a quick hike to the small rise known as Mount Butler, a fast descent into the rainforest behind it, and then a leisurely northward return through the ravine that separated the knobby hill from the skirts of Mount Nevis.

Beyond the Narrows, Connor tacked away from Nevis toward St. Kitts, but more specifically, toward Booby Island. A one-hundred-meter hump of stone and tenacious bushes, even a shallow draft sloop had to take care while slipping between the hull-gutting rocks that surrounded it. Once ashore, Connor would eat his lunch and take advantage of the island's isolation, as he and his father habitually did, to get in some quick target practice.

It was perfect for handguns. A short scramble up into the rocks and you were invisible among the gnarled branches. The reports were swallowed by the swift current's constant susurration and the bash and spray of unruly swells.

Connor scanned the horizon: a few fishing boats, back beyond the leeward mouth of the channel and heading in the opposite direction. As usual, Booby Island meant privacy. Which, for both father and son, also meant safety.

Connor, like many of his generation, did not take safety for granted. Not anymore. But unlike the generations that would follow, he remembered a time when you never gave a thought to the basic security of your existence. You just got up and started your day.

Then the aliens invaded. Even after they were kicked off Earth, Connor struggled against the fear that his family would never really be safe again. His mom had been badly wounded during the Battle of Jakarta—so badly that other, friendly aliens had to take her away for advanced care. Trevor and Nuncle Richard left Indonesia to chase the invaders back to their own worlds. News tended to be sparse, vague, and even contradictory. What was manifestly obvious, however, was that, except for his grandma, his whole family had been swallowed up by the war. Hell, even Caine Riordan, his ostensible father, was gone.

Uncle Trevor didn't come back for almost eight months. Nuncle Richard didn't come back for almost a year and was gone again after a few weeks. And Mom never came back at all. But, a year and a half later, Uncle Trevor showed up on Grandma's doorstep with confidential news: Caine Riordan had finally returned. When asked if he wanted to meet his father, glib, voluble fifteen-year-old Connor discovered that, for the first few minutes, the only reply he could muster was a series of emphatic nods.

However, that meeting didn't take place right away. Certain of Earth's governments, particularly those of the Developing World Coalition bloc, wanted to bring Riordan to trial. For what reason, and on what charges, was never particularly clear. Politicians and reporters flung around various terms: dereliction of duty, disobeying orders, mutiny, even treason on one or two occasions. But in the end, Caine was either exonerated or whitewashed, because they were willing to let him go. And so Connor finally met his father.

As Connor approached Booby Island he turned increasingly into the breeze, slowing the sloop by instinct. Which was fortunate, because only half of his mind was on the boat; the other was on all the changes that had occurred since that first meeting.

He smiled, looked around: bright sun, blue water, and the calming sounds of the sea. A father who did not push, but led by example. Who had effectively homeschooled him for the past two years. Not by lecturing, but by enticing him from question to question, by finding what Connor loved most and creating projects that integrated and engaged those passions. And who was always ready to listen, always ready with a smile, or, eventually, a hug.

Connor tossed the small anchor over the side. For fifteen

years, he hadn't known his father at all. For the last two, he'd spent almost every waking and sleeping hour near him.

All things being equal, it had been worth the wait.

Five seconds after the crewman left the crate on the afterdeck of the *Golden Hold*, a discus-sized quadrotor drone emerged from its square, dark mouth. Sensors spun, examined. It moved to the taffrail, scouting the parts of the ship that were in its line of sight, and then the watery reaches astern. It rose slightly and sent a millisecond tight-beam signal back along the path it had flown.

A larger drone, more than half a meter across, rose out of the crate, propellers buzzing far more audibly than its partner's. It made for the taffrail, passed the smaller drone and, once over open water, dropped sharply. It leveled off only two meters above the low swells, its chromaflage skin shading toward a dark gray-blue. An unaided human eye would have been at pains to pick it out.

The other drone kept observing the ship until the larger one was within a hundred meters of Charlestown. Then it, too, went over the stern and dropped closer to the waves, rushing to catch up to its larger partner and seeking for the transponder signal that it had been programmed to discover amidst the wash of other transmissions cluttering the local wavelengths.

Catching a faint fragment of the target signal, the drones angled toward the Narrows and locked on to a course that would swing around the north slopes of Mount Nevis until it reached the jungle ravines on its windward side.

Caine's car bumped and creaked up his steep driveway, the engine's labors diminishing once it crested the lip of the carport.

Up the stairs to the single-story house two steps at a time, physical key into the front door, and then Riordan was moving briskly for the kitchen. Specifically, to the refrigerator for a bottle of water. Hikes into Nevis' rain-forested volcanic slopes were strenuous, not low-impact strolls.

The bottle misted over as soon as it came out of the fridge, prompting Caine to glance at the brass weather clock on his way to the whitewashed veranda. The humidity wasn't too bad. Better than the water-beaded bottle had made him anticipate.

But, as Riordan stepped outside to test it for himself, he had to admit that his concern with the humidity was more a matter of habit than anything else. Upon arriving two years ago, he'd been trepidatious about walks in the jungle. By one PM, the air felt more like something you drank rather than breathed, summoning memories that had been burned into his lungs and his mind. Three and a half years ago, he had struggled to keep up with Indonesian insurgents in Java. A year after that, he had almost died of xenospore-induced asthma on a planet of the very alien Slaasriithi.

But now, miraculously, his wind was better than ever and seemed to improve with each passing week. So had the ease with which he got through an increasing number of calisthenics, a moderate weight-lifting regimen, and morning swims in the ocean. Maybe it was the climate. Maybe it was his own home cooked food. Maybe it was the slower pace of life in the Caribbean. But in almost every way, he felt more vigorous and energetic than he had in ten years. Or maybe, he thought with a smile, that's just another benefit of being relaxed, of being happy.

Of being a father.

Riordan popped the bottle's top, took a long drink. Preemptive hydration remained a requirement, no matter how fit he felt, no matter how promising the weather was. And he'd never seen finer than today's: still no clouds in the sky and still a cool breeze in the foothills.

He sipped again, stared down the long slope at the buildings of Brick Kiln. Some of the roofs were solar shingle, others refurbished solar panels, and no small number were still corrugated steel that winked and shimmered in the sun. Like the cracked and creased road that ran between those shiny-topped houses, nothing much had changed there since well before humanity had dodged its first extraplanetary threat forty years ago: the Doomsday Rock.

Riordan smiled at the contrast between the town and the Consolidated Terran Republic's futurist projections and imagery. Like every new state before it, the CTR depicted the coming decades as those which would finally usher in a world of ubiquitous plenty, tidiness, and sleek new machinery.

The reality, both now and historically, was that whatever the future held, change was always uneven in distribution and irregular in timing. Plenty still varied along social lines. Tidiness was transient. And slick new technology labored alongside worn machines that were older than their operators.

Happily, that made Nevis a great place to hide. Although it was well-wired, many devices were still analog instead of digital, or even manual instead of electric. Only a modest number of its machines actively exchanged data, little of which was useful to the netcrawling search bots that could seek out a disappeared person's electronic scent like so many computerized bloodhounds. The island had cameras in all the places that required them— the banks, the clinic, the two police stations, the small medical school, cargo holding areas, and the Air Terminal—but almost none on the roadways or in the shops. And if you spent cash rather than electronic credits, your online footprint remained practically invisible.

Riordan sealed the water bottle, slipped it into a cargo pocket as he made for his bedroom. Time to change into a lighter, looser shirt.

As he entered, he caught a glimpse of himself in the mirror. No worry wrinkles, no dark rings under his eyes. It was nice to start each day without looking over your shoulder for the people who were surely looking for you.

The small drone pulled ahead of the larger one, angling northeast, well away from Charlestown. They kept low as they neared the stretch of sand that marked the northern end of Pinney's Beach. Less spectacular and far from tourist amenities, it was the most likely place to come ashore undetected. An alarmed seagull watched the drones hum over the whitecaps, cross ten meters of coral powder beach, then five meters of dune grass and driftwood before disappearing into the dark beneath the palms.

Once concealed, the drones' twinned trajectories bent northward, courting the shadows as they flew up the smooth, tree-cluttered slope. Skirting the small villages of Vaughans and Jessup's Village, they held course until their altimeters indicated they were two hundred meters above sea level.

The larger drone's onboard navigation program paused for a millisecond as its positional confirmation routine kicked in. Both drones' sensors measured fixed emission sources and expected visual landmarks, compared results, established that the first overground waypoint had been reached. Second stage navigation and evasion parameters were accessed. Self-learning processes were initiated. Statistically significant operational variables—weather,

EM activity levels, change in expected frequency of human or vehicular encounters—were assessed, deemed negligible.

Satisfied that all approach protocols were nominal, the larger drone emitted a single, coded millisecond ping. After two seconds, an even more brief, and heavily encoded signal pinged back: the target's transponder. It was active, and its general directionality placed it well within the engagement footprint of the primary scenario.

With the discus now back in the lead, the two drones altered course. Whereas before they had been heading on a mostly straight line for the volcanic cone at the approximate center of Nevis, now they began to maneuver around it in a slow clockwise curve that kept them between 200 and 220 meters above sea level.

Driven by a ceaseless cascade of numbers, of digital measurements and directions, there was nothing in the drone's processing that would have been vaguely familiar to a human's sensory perception of the world. However, if a programmer had been there to translate the data stream, the plan was simple enough. Taking Mount Nevis as the face of a clock, the two drones were starting from the nine-o'clock position and sweeping around until they got to one o'clock: the coordinates of Waypoint Two.

Once there, they would be in range to commence terminal operations.

Chapter Three

JUNE 2123
NEVIS, EARTH

As Riordan finished buttoning his shirt, his wristlink chirped: a pending text message. Prefixed with a secure code he had only seen four times since arriving on Nevis. He authorized delivery, frowned as he read:

> Antigua InterIsland Holidays:
> The ultimate experience!

Riordan ignored the rest of the advertising copy; it was meaningless window-dressing. Instead, he double-checked the origination code: it had not come from the off-shore agents' secure number on St. Kitts, but rather from the remote hub on Antigua. More importantly, the code phrases were authentic.

Specifically, "Antigua InterIsland Holidays" was the online business shell in which Caine's protectors back in DC housed a direct comm link to him. The second line—"The Ultimate Experience!"—referred to his imminent death, not a unique island tour. The protocol triggered by that phrase required Riordan to presume himself completely compromised. He could not even trust the two agents on St. Kitts.

Reacting more than thinking, Caine started down the standard action list. Item number one: alert Connor.

But Riordan stopped his index finger in mid jab. No. This was Ultimate Experience, the only condition that necessitated a reassessment of all security breach SOPs. Because if the breach was the result of an intel leak, then the enemy was almost certainly waiting for Caine to follow his assigned game plan.

Meaning that was precisely what he must not do. Alerting Connor would bring him back early, which was more likely to endanger than protect him; he was almost certainly not a target. But if the threat force *expected* Caine to signal him first, then—

Riordan took two long steps back into the kitchen, extracted his small go-kit from the hollowed-out heater. He opened it, pocketed the small liquimix pistol and scooped up the three micro drones. He brought up his wristlink's emergency command screen, touched it to the first microdrone, tapped a preset code that would have it follow the road directly to the air terminal. Riordan made one change. Instead of the drone emitting Caine's transponder code, the drone was now set to imitate Connor's. Riordan launched it. Humming, the tiny drone sped out to the veranda and dove out of sight toward the road.

The next two drones didn't need any modifications to their preset routines. He set the first one loose from the front door, ran down to the car with the other. He opened the driver-side door, rolled down the windows, turned on the engine, tapped the dashboard, selected "regular destinations." He chose the long route to Charlestown—twenty-two kilometers—and stepped back as the vehicle started driving itself down the hill. Illegal, of course, but he'd be happy to answer for it later. If he was still alive.

Patting his pocket to make sure the water bottle hadn't fallen out, Caine made for the trees at the double-quick.

As the two drones from the *Golden Hold* reached the twelve-o'clock position of their partial circumnavigation of Mount Nevis, their sensors registered three new transponders, all transmitting mission-critical codes.

One signal was not the target's code. It belonged to the target's child and was useful only as an ancillary indicator. It might be co-located with, or close to, the target itself. But in this case, the child's signal was moving north on the main road, away from the other three. Whether it was heading for the air terminal, Charlestown, or some other destination was immaterial to locating the actual target. However, it did trigger a recalculation of the mission's completion parameters and a drastically reduced timeframe. With the ancillary signal moving away from the target, there was a significantly increased likelihood that the child was attempting to summon reinforcements for the target. The mission had to be completed before that was accomplished.

However, the far greater challenge to the drones' self-learning systems was to assess how and why the original target transponder had suddenly transformed into three separate but identical signals, which were now moving on entirely different trajectories. One was apparently following the main road south at vehicular speed, directly away from the projected engagement zone. It was too early to calculate possible destinations or determine if this was simply a diversion.

The second signal was moving at human speed, but heading due east, either down to the small community designated as Brick Kiln or beyond it to the rocky Atlantic coastline and the wind turbines arrayed along it. Again, the destination could not yet be projected and diversionary movement was certainly a possibility.

The third signal was making slower progress in the opposite direction, heading toward Mount Nevis on a highly irregular course. This made it an excellent candidate for being the actual target: the movement was typical of humans, not machines. On the other hand, since there were now three identical signals moving in different directions, scenario algorithms indicated near certainty that the target was aware of the impending attack. It might have had time to program an automated device to mimic human movement. Data on the tactical sophistication and inventiveness of the target multiplied the likelihood of him employing such a ruse.

Probabilities and odds were integrated and compared, assets measured. It took an inordinately long time—almost two whole seconds—for the drones to arrive at their optimal response.

As they drew within five hundred meters of the original engagement zone, the discus-sized drone activated its three sub-drones, each about the size of a clay pigeon. The discus slowed, giving them a stable launch platform as they rose up. One buzzed eastward, chasing the transponder signal heading for the coast. The other two joined the larger drone, which swerved southward in pursuit of the signal wending its way through the jungle. All variables considered, it had the highest probability of being the actual target, which, along with the difficult terrain, warranted the extra assets. The discus itself swung to follow the main road southward. Chasing a vehicle while remaining in contact with the larger drone required its superior speed, endurance, and transmitter.

Riordan was gratified that he was not panting yet, even though he had pressed himself hard for the first fifteen minutes.

Still moving, he sipped from the water bottle, replaced it, and veered off his accustomed route, taking a game trail to the west. So much for this morning's refreshing hike in the woods; now, it was a run through the jungle. He recalled a song by that name, played by one of the cryogenically suspended Vietnam War veterans that his team had found and rescued during the mission to the Hkh'Rkh colony world of Turkh'saar. The chorus of the song felt particularly appropriate, just now.

The game trail ended after fifty meters, reducing his progress to a slow, stumbling trot. The tall, thin tree trunks were thick around him, the stone-littered ground slimy with moisture and rotting leaves.

But this short cut reduced the distance by two-thirds and there were no clear sight lines. The region's occasional hikers stayed on the trails, so they didn't create new paths or gaps in the foliage. Whoever or whatever might be following Riordan would be hard put to follow, let alone keep up with, him.

Unless, of course, they had the codes that could dupe his surgically implanted transponder into emitting a ping: then they'd find him no matter where he went. Which made it all the more important that he reached the ravine before they reached him.

Up ahead, he could hear the distant chatter of a thin watercourse falling over rocks. He sprint-stumbled toward it.

The large drone and its two small scouts halted in front of a wall of tree trunks. The subdrones would certainly be able to weave their way forward, but it was impassable for the larger one. As a group, they reversed out of the dead end: the third one that had stymied them since the target's transponder had moved off known trails. The large drone's considerable self-learning program—mislabeled its "brain" by overenthusiastic academics and the journalists who believed them—analyzed the problem.

The crucial variable was the uncertainty of navigational

outcome. The position of the target's transponder was well-established; the trees did nothing to block the ping-backs. Standard algorithms had initially recommended a straight-line intercept, relying upon forward-looking radar scans to detect and follow vectors where the foliage was less dense. Unfortunately, the jungle continued to thicken and radar penetrated less than fifty meters. Each time, what started out as a comparatively clear path slowly became impassable.

At this rate, statistical analysis indicated that the target would reach the other side of the island before the drones effected intercept. And if the target's child—whose signal was now nearing the air terminal—was seeking assistance, he would surely find and return with it long before then. That mission-failure condition would immediately trigger the drone's self-destruct protocol, thereby minimizing forensically useful evidence.

The big drone's self-learning analytics ran through higher-risk intercept options. Rise and maneuver to a point directly above the target, then attempt to descend through the jungle canopy? Contraindicated. Despite increasing the risk of detection by both local law enforcement and any target-friendly assets that might be in covert overwatch, the vertical assault option still did not guarantee success. Observational data was indeterminate regarding the canopy's obstructive characteristics, but radar showed it to be unpromisingly thick. Any significant delay during descent would certainly give the target ample opportunity to detect the drone's audio signature and possibly inflict damage while it was vulnerable.

The self-learning system went further outside its optimal mission parameters and engaged less conventional subroutines: heuristic learning, historical examples, human prediction algorithms. All analyses produced the same result: return to the trail. It was the longer route by a factor of three, but its unobstructed flight path would allow the drone to eventually overtake the target. The only drawback was increased risk of detection by other humans—the risk variable that weighed most heavily against any autonomous departures from the precoded scenarios.

But no other option promised comparable speed and efficacy, and the risk was no worse than a pop-up attempt to effect an overhead intercept.

The two subdrones reversed, sped back toward the trail that

twisted through the jungle like a serpent. The large drone followed at a distance of twenty meters.

Riordan had not come this way often enough to recall the subtle differences in the trees that signified he was nearing his goal. A surge in daylight—sudden and bright—triggered a shielding reflex with his hand. It put him off balance just as he remembered that the small clearing was a half step below the jungle floor. He tumbled forward.

A faint sulfur stink hit his nostrils as his chest and cheek hit the slimy mud. *Might as well get used to both.* He pushed up on his arms, looked around. No sign of pursuit. The trail here was more overgrown than before: the hiking traffic had been low and the sightlines were more limited than usual. All to his advantage.

Riordan rose and looked across the small clearing, where a crevice almost bisected a wedge of volcanic rock that pushed through the foliage. It was the cavemouth he'd been heading for: a tapering spearhead of black shadow, two meters from base to tip.

Moving from rock to rock to avoid the mud, Caine quickly crossed to and entered the cave, tapping his wristlink three times for maximum illumination. As on his prior visits, the mud had pooled back into the cave itself. The morning run-off from Nevis carried dirt down the slopes and kept the ground wet.

The light from his wristlink picked out the walls' most jagged protrusions: every inch was rough and irregular, like most of the island's volcanic vents. He smiled.

Dimming his light, he felt for and located a short left-hand switchback tunnel that was more like a hidden alcove. He shone the light higher, saw the small natural ledge he'd found twenty months ago. Riordan reached up cautiously. It was a little close to the entrance for bats, but you could never be sure...

Fortunately, his fingertips brushed against smooth, dry plastic, not leathery wings and sharp teeth. Pulling down the bag, Riordan inspected its seal: still tight.

The contents—mostly communications gear—showed no sign of water damage. They had been left behind at the house that Richard Downing's family used to own, just a few miles further south on the ring road. It was also where Elena's brother Trevor had linked up with the ops team that he had led to Indonesia. Needing to travel light, they had left behind a small stash of equipment, the location of which Trevor had shared just before Caine began his voluntary exile on Nevis.

Caine had excavated the gear his first week there, but much of it had already been discovered by the implacable foe of all hidden tropical caches: water. Half of the electronics were ruined, as were the two handguns that might have proven handy. But spec ops teams carried lots more than guns and radios, and enough of the equipment had survived that Caine resolved to hide it in a safer, higher, drier place.

Just in case.

As Connor climbed down Booby Island's stony northern flank, he heard a faint high-pitched growl cutting through the rising and falling surges of the windward surf. He scanned the sky directly over St. Kitts: nothing. But when he widened his sweep to the ocean, he detected a small dark blot far to the west, coming around the leeward bluff known as Nags Head. The blot grew larger, but did not move to the right or left.

Which meant it was heading straight for Booby Island.

Connor turned and swiftly clambered back up into the gnarled trees, the midday sweat suddenly cool on his body, the grip of the sloop's pistol slick in his hand.

As the main drone and its two small reconnaissance platforms neared the target's transponder, they slowed: the signal was coming from a mass of what seemed to be solid rock. One of the subdrones swung wide and flanked the volcanic spur that protruded into the clearing. Ladar scans confirmed the AI's conjecture: there was a cave opening.

The main drone updated and assessed the summative operational situation. The discus-sized drone that had followed the signal heading south indicated that although it was slowly gaining on its target, it might not effect intercept before draining its battery.

The third subdrone was still tracking the signal that was now following Nevis' rocky eastern coastline. There, the difficulty was not speed but unexpected terrain obstructions—obstructions that the target was courting to frustrate and extend the pursuit.

But it was precisely that similarity between those two targets— that they were attempting to evade, rather than elude—which suggested that the signals were emanating from decoys. A human would not settle for evasion or mere delay. A human's survival instinct required nothing less than complete escape or complete concealment. Which meant that the signal in the cave was almost certainly the one emanating from the actual target.

The large drone advanced its subdrones to further assess the environment: the cave mouth was large enough to admit a human easily. Scanning the internal layout from outside was impossible without a sophisticated densitometer, a device many times the mass and volume of the drone itself. The geographic feature into which the cave penetrated was otherwise solid rock, rising up a further three meters and terminating in a wildly overgrown shelf that was itself an extrusion of the larger, higher slopes of volcanic rock. If there was any means of flying upward to achieve vertical descent into the cave, ladar scans did not reveal it.

The drone's AI chewed at the problem, quickly reduced it to a single operational option. Send a subdrone into the cave to acquire a 3-D ladar rendering of the layout, and, in the course of doing so, attempt to close with the source of the transponder signal. The main drone would follow relatively close behind. If the target emerged to destroy the subdrone or flee, it would be eliminated. The other subdrone would maintain a rear watch and remain in reserve as a potential replacement for the first subdrone.

Obedient to the main drone's summons, the lead quadrotor abandoned its fruitless survey of the overgrown upslope ledge and made for the cave mouth.

Chapter Four

Riordan peered closely into the cracked corner-checking mirror. Although the combo goggles from his stash were half-broken—the thermal imaging was busted—the light intensification enabled him to see a small object float into the cave. Drifting only ten centimeters above the rough floor, it edged forward, swiveling slowly.

As Riordan watched it work, he kept the mirror in close contact with the surrounding stone. The drone was evidently creating a 3-D map of the cave. Too small to be an attack element but, whether another drone or humans were in charge of the operation, that command element had wisely decided not to enter the cave blind. Yet, the little quadrotor's sensors were a heavy load for its small fans, which suggested a comparatively short range and limited battery life. Its home platform, whether carried by a human operator or mounted on a larger drone, was probably nearby.

However, humans would have been hard pressed to arrive here so quickly. Even if they had a fix on Caine's transponder, the trail leading to it often branched in counter-instinctual directions. Pursuers on foot would have had to guess the correct turn every time in order to be here already. But drones were fast enough that they would have been able to have guess incorrectly several times and still be on site by now. So, the proximal elements of the pursuit were likely to be purely automated.

Furthermore, the movements of the drone suggested a machine controller. Every action, no matter how small, was precise: no wobble, no lingering or reversing to inspect an unusual feature. Machine controllers never reassessed what they had already assessed, just as following a "hunch" was not within the scope of their processors.

As the little quadrotor crept further into his mirror-reflected field of vision, Caine refined his hypotheses. Autonomous strike assets were also likely when an enemy's highest priority was anonymity. And whoever wanted to kill Caine was probably even more determined to remain unimplicated.

That decided Riordan. He couldn't be sure he was only facing automatons, but that was the safest bet. He activated his pistol's smartgun attachment, then squeezed the remote control actuator he held snugged between his left thumb and the mirror's handle.

The instant he did so, the quadrotor spun, its sensor cluster swinging away from the rear of the cave where Caine was located. Now fixed on the alcove from which Caine had retrieved the bag, the little drone moved forward, inspecting that section of the rough wall.

Riordan leaned out, gave his smartgun a look at its target, selected the image of the quadrotor as soon as it was highlighted in the scope, and squeezed the trigger. The gun did not fire until Caine had aligned it with its designated target, at which point the weapon fired twice. The impacts bounced the drone off the wall, showering pieces as it fell.

Riordan ducked back into his cramped space, raised the mirror again to watch for a reaction, noticed blood rolling down toward his wrist. *Damn it.* His self-inflicted forearm wound was still dripping, some of it spilling to the ground. Hopefully, it would blend into the patches of thin mud that had collected in the low points of the floor.

Because there wasn't anything Caine could do about it now.

The main drone's AI registered all the relevant information at once: the sound of a firearm; the abrupt termination of the datafeed from the subdrone in the cave; and its last, fragmentary detection of a small gap in the left-hand cave wall.

Priorities altered immediately. The last subdrone was pulled off rearguard duty and sent into the tunnel at maximum speed. Secondary contingencies to deal with the possibility of the target escaping from the cave or the arrival of his allies were dismissed. A swiftly mounted attack would ensure that the target could not flee, and any inbound allies would arrive too late. However, in the event that they materialized sooner than anticipated, the self-destruct circuit was brought to readiness.

The second subdrone swept into the cave, skimmed above the debris that had been its partner, and then went high as it drew abreast of the fractionally scanned alcove. It was almost certainly the source of the attack, since that was definitely the source of the transponder signal. The large drone slowly entered the cave behind the smaller one, its more powerful fans filling the narrow space with a steady current of deeper sound.

The subdrone's audio sensors reported the concomitant drop in discriminative acuity and edged forward until it was able to look into the craggy recess at a shallow angle: nothing. The alcove curved away from opening, doubled back in the direction of the entrance. The subdrone would have to advance further to get a good look inside.

As it started to do so, a human voice emanated from the alcove. It was faint, almost a whisper. Direction-finding confirmed that it was colocated with the transponder signal. There was also a brief, frequency-jumping radio emission from further within the cave, consistent with a highly compressed communications burst. Possibly a remote signaling device of some kind.

The AI assessed: the transponder signal from within the alcove was so proximal that the target's elimination was virtually ensured. Only final confirmation and a firing solution were required. The large drone sent the smaller one forward to acquire a target lock, then followed, accelerating, hastening to close the distance and bring its weapons to bear.

The subdrone turned the corner, scanned in all spectra.

The sound of the human voice was emanating from what appeared to be a wadded shirt on the cave floor. A playback device was hidden in the folds of fabric, which, combined with the noise from the larger drone, had compromised audio reception enough to momentarily cause the voice to be mistaken for a living, rather than recorded, human. Wires ran away from the crumpled shirt to the radio-controlled actuator that had triggered the playback remotely. Completing the ruse, the target's transponder signal was emanating not from a human body, but from a waist-high hollow just behind the playback unit. A close scan revealed that the transponder was wedged into a crevice and was covered in a dark fluid. Split-second analysis confirmed what the AI simultaneously conjectured: based on color, reflectivity, and projected viscosity, the liquid was blood.

Crammed in alongside the transponder was a handgun slaved to another remote activation unit. The AI spent .001 seconds matching the firearm to a corresponding file image: a Unitech ten-millimeter liquimix pistol. An enhanced model capable of five-round bursts and fitted with a smartgun targeting system. At this range, if the weapon was loaded with armor piercing rounds, its mission-kill probability on the large drone was eighty-five percent or greater. The AI did not detect any mechanism capable of adjusting the weapon's aimpoint, but a definitive scan would take another half second. Too long.

Mission preservation algorithms took over. A port opened in the drone's undercarriage. Two minirockets flashed into the alcove, detonated sharply.

At the same instant, the subdrone detected sounds of movement at the far end of the cave. Turning swiftly, it spotted a faint and mostly hidden thermal signature leaping upward.

The AI, busy reassessing the tactical scenario, ran a heuristic analysis of how the new movement might be causally related to the events leading to the detection and destruction of the decoy in the alcove. Integrated result: the actual target had excised its transponder to use as bait, and had somehow hidden itself from thermal sensors in a very small crevice at the rear of the cave, from which it was now attempting a vertical exit. However, if the main drone closed on the target, the improved sensor results would ensure a clean lock on the target, despite its curiously degraded IR signature.

The large drone rotated, revved its rotors to close at maximum speed—

—just as it detected another high-compression radio burst from the back of the cave. Having two prior samples for comparison, identification was almost instantaneous: the encryption was military grade.

Overhead, as if in response to that radio burst, something with a low electric current activated.

Already speeding forward, the drone's AI correlated the new data and projected the logical endpoint of the chain of events in which it was now trapped. There was no time left to establish a lock on the target. The only options now were:

Command One: fire all remaining fourteen-millimeter missiles using preliminary target solution.

Command Two: engage self-destruct.

The electric impulse carrying those instructions reached the drone's weapon control circuits the same moment that the plastic explosive concealed in an overhead crevice detonated.

Connor leaned farther back into the brush as the slowing aircar's throaty rush up-dopplered into a two-toned roar. Between boughs, he watched the vehicle's four thrusters roll through a sharp attitude change; the two at the rear pivoted ninety degrees into VTOL mode, the front pair snapped forward 135 degrees into counterthrust. The aircar shuddered to a halt. One of the three silhouettes in its open passenger compartment swept Booby Island with multispectral binoculars.

Clutching his pistol, Connor knew, even as he threw himself back behind a boulder, that he had reacted a second too late. If he had seen the binoculars, its thermal imaging and motion sensors had certainly seen him. He snapped the safety off, experienced a sharp longing for his dad, but thought about only one thing: surviving.

The thrusters quieted considerably. Then a shout: "Connor?"

It wasn't surprising that these men knew his name—there had been nothing uncertain about their approach—but he was shocked to recognize the voice. Was that Uncle Trevor? No. Couldn't be. It was probably some kind of trick...

"Connor, it's me, Uncle Trevor. I'll come to you, if you want."

"How do I know it's really you?"

"Want me to tell you what we had for Thanksgiving three years ago?"

Connor swore silently. *Damn it, even I don't remember that.*

"Or maybe you want me to tell you the dish I bring every year that everyone secretly hates. Even you."

"Hey, I never said—"

"I wasn't born yesterday, Connor. I know when I'm being patronized."

Connor closed his eyes. Whoever they were, they had a high-powered and very expensive government aircar, were probably armed to the teeth with the latest milspec weapons, and outnumbered him at least three to one. He, on the other hand, had a decent civilian handgun, a couple of auspiciously placed trees and rocks to hide behind, and no idea what the hell was going on. He risked a peek around the other side of the rock.

If the guy who saw and waved at him wasn't his uncle, then either Connor was hallucinating or someone had created a clone of Trevor just to trick him. Yeah, right. Connor stood up.

Trevor waved both arms, his sudden smile actually glinting in the sun. He gestured for the driver to boost the fans, which pushed the aircar up the slope until it was hovering just below Connor's hiding place. Trevor waved for him to hop down into the vehicle.

Connor grabbed his gear, took his uncle's extremely firm hand—*damn, he's strong!*—and took a long step down into the car. "Uncle Trevor, what the hell is going—?"

"We've got to find your father." Trevor tapped the driver, pulled Connor down, pointed to the four-point straps. "Harness up. We're moving."

Connor barely had time to get the unfamiliar buckles done before the aircar leaped forward. "Moving where? Why?"

"You've been found, both of you." Trevor had a carbine with him: a short-barreled version of the standard military shoulder arm, the CoBro eight-millimeter liquimix. He snapped it over to full automatic. "We don't know how they did it, but given the timing, our bet is that there's a leak in our intelligence services. That's why there are only the three of us here; we know we can trust each other. The guy driving is my pal, Chief Petty Officer Cruz, and this gentleman is Associate Director Gray Rinehart."

Associate Director of what? Connor wondered, but he was too worried about his father to follow that any further. "Is Dad okay? Where is he?"

Trevor ran his hand through his hair: the speed-amplified breeze caught it, made it look like a lion's mane in a wind tunnel. "That's the trouble. He could be in any one of three, maybe four, places."

"Huh?"

"Just as we were lifting to pick you up, Caine's transponder... well, it multiplied. There are three identical copies of his transponder signal on the grid right now and we don't know which is his."

"How is that possible?"

Trevor sighed. "We gave him three decoys before you came here. In case he had to confuse someone who was trying to track him. We had just entered St. Kitts' airspace when two extra transponder signals showed up—and an extra one of yours, too. So your dad clearly got our message that your cover is blown and you're in danger."

Connor thought for a moment. "Can you show me where the transponders are?"

Trevor glanced at Rinehart, who shrugged and tilted a polarized palmtop toward Connor.

Connor studied it briefly. "These signals: can you show me their prior movement?"

Rinehart raised an eyebrow, adjusted the view: flashing lines showed the path of each transponder.

Connor nodded, pointed at the one that had traveled the least. "That's Dad."

"How do you know?"

"The one that's way to the south is just stupid. Dad wouldn't get into the car to drive around the island. If the enemy has drones, they could downlook and kill him the same way a hawk gets a rabbit—couldn't they?"

Trevor and Rinehart exchanged looks that became furtive smiles. "That sounds about right. And the other one, to the east of your house?"

"I know that part of the coast. You have to be a goat to move around down there. From a map, it looks like you could walk it. And you could if you're both lucky and suicidal. But most likely, you're just going to fall or get washed out to sea by one of the bigger waves. After you get bounced around on the jagged volcanic rocks, that is. But this signal"—he pointed at the transponder icon that had moved part of the way to Mount Nevis—"that's on the path where we go hiking. Or running, if Dad decides to make our day particularly miserable. And at that exact spot, there are caves. *Lots* of caves."

Trevor tapped the driver on the shoulder. "Site three. Maximum thrust."

"Sir," muttered Cruz, "that speed is way above local limits. We're going to become real high profile, real fast."

"Yeah, and that's a real shame. Redline it, Carlos."

A flock of seagulls scattered out of their way, startled and perhaps envious of the wedge-shaped aircar which left them behind as if they were suspended motionless in midair.

Chapter Five

JUNE 2123
NEVIS, EARTH

Connor saw it the same moment the others in the aircar did: twinned plumes of gray smoke rising up from the northeastern skirts of Mt. Nevis. One was much heavier and thicker.

Rinehart cleared his throat. "Those are right on top of the transponder signal."

Trevor glanced at him. "Bio register?"

Rinehart frowned. "No data. Either the connection has been disrupted or that part of the transponder is malfunctioning."

Connor felt his stomach harden and sink. "Or Dad could be—"

Trevor did not let him finish. "No. That's not what the null signal means. It means that the transponder is either out of contact with your dad, or its ability to detect ongoing life-signs has been ruined."

"You mean, like what would happen if his arm was blown off?"

Gray Rinehart looked away as Trevor shook his head. "There's no reason to think that."

Connor's weight was suddenly pushing against the straps on his chest: Cruz was slowing, lest he overshoot the twin columns of smoke.

Rinehart adjusted the settings on his palmtop's tracking program, frowned. "The transponder signal should be stronger by now."

Trevor looked over his shoulder. "Unless he's still in a cave."

Rinehart nodded. "In which case, it's time to go spelunking."

They were dropping down toward the source of the smoke.

Connor saw that the larger plume was curling up out of the cave he and Dad had nicknamed the Mud Hole. The smaller plume was emerging from the tangle of bushes and vines that capped it like a thatch of wild hair.

Cruz glanced back as they pulled close enough to touch the immense volcanic slab that housed the cave. "If you want to go spelunking, sirs," he yelled over the thrusters, "you may have to rappel down. There's no place large enough for me to land."

"That won't be necessary, Chief," a more distant voice shouted. *Dad's voice!*

A mud-coated figure stood up from the tangled growth atop the spur as the aircar's engines settled into the hoarse rush of low-power hover.

Gun at the ready, Trevor leaped from the aircar to where Caine stood. Connor made to follow, but Riordan held up a hand. "Better that I come on board." Dad had spoken loudly, but slowly, evenly: the way he did when counseling caution. Connor looked over the side of the car: a missed jump here could easily result in broken bones. A lot of them. Still . . .

His father must have seen the look on his face. "C'mon, son, be sensible. Reporting for Plebe Summer with your leg in a cast is no way to start at the Academy, is it?"

Connor took a deep breath. He hated it when his dad got overprotective. He hated it even more when he was right. But by the time Cruz had snugged the aircar a little closer and everyone was on board, all he really cared about was that his dad was alive.

As Caine buckled in, Trevor stared hard at his bloodied left arm, started reaching under his seat for a medkit. Riordan shook his head. "It'll wait." He smiled. "It's self-inflicted."

Trevor raised an eyebrow. "The transponder?"

Caine shrugged. "As long as it was in me, I was in their crosshairs."

Connor goggled. "So you just cut it out?"

Caine smiled. "Sorry to lessen your opinion of me, son, but there was no 'just' about it. It hurt like hell."

"But you did it."

"You would, too." *I just hope you never have to do anything like it.* He turned to Trevor. "That block of C-8 and bag of decommissioned equipment you left at the safe house saved my life. The remote controllers and actuators got their killer drone looking the wrong way at the right moment."

Cruz whistled. "Sir, you are one ballsy—uh, nervy gambling man."

"What do you mean, Carlos?"

"Well, in order to come after you, they had to know where you were, right, sir? So how could you be sure they didn't know about the equipment cache?"

Trevor smiled. "Because it was totally off the books, Cruz. Only Richard Downing and I knew it was there. I told Caine about it just before he came down."

Connor turned to look at his father, eyes wide. "And you never told *me* about it?"

Caine shrugged. "You were never going to be at the Mud Hole when it mattered."

"What do you mean?"

Trevor nodded approvingly. "Your dad means that if he had time enough to get to the cave, then he had time enough to make sure you were safe before going there. No matter who or what might come after him."

"What you're really saying is that you wanted to stash me away somewhere while they swooped in and killed you."

Caine reached across the aircar, put both hands on his son's shoulders. He did not speak immediately. Then: "What I wanted was for you to be out of harm's way. I've had too many people become 'collateral damage' because they were near me when the hammer came down." He pushed aside the nightmares in which he not only lost his son, but was the cause of it. "Not you, too, Connor." *Not like your mother.* "Not you."

Connor's eyes told Riordan that his son had read his thoughts—right before the young, tanned arms reached out to rest on Caine's shoulders. Connor squeezed them tightly for a long moment, then shook them. "Damn it, Dad. You make me crazy."

"That's part of my job as a parent. If I read the manual correctly."

Trevor was staring back at the receding plumes. "That's a lot of smoke, even for a C-8 charge."

Riordan nodded. "The drone must have triggered its self-destruct device. Almost got me, too." He ran his hand along several gashes on his left calf and ankle.

Gray Rinehart studied them sagely. "From spalled rock?"

"Yep. Chips came flying up that old fumarole pretty hard."

Rinehart shrugged, unconcerned. "If there's anything that needs to be removed, it shouldn't be too deep. But we'll need to clean you up, first."

Connor smiled. "Yeah, Dad, you look like you were rolling in the mud."

Riordan smiled back. "That's because I was."

Trevor scanned Caine from head to toe. "Old expedient against IR and thermal imaging." He nodded approvingly. "Limited effectiveness, but better than nothing."

Caine returned the nod absently, leaned back into the seat, finally felt his body begin to relax, worried it might start shaking, instead. He concentrated on external sensations: the sun, the sky, the breeze. "I just wish I had some ideas about who's behind this attack and why."

Rinehart looked at Trevor. "We might be able to shed some light on that."

Trevor nodded. "There are two possible reasons, and they might be linked. First, this month's message from Bannor raised a flag."

Connor was looking from face to face. "Bannor? The Green Beret who worked for Dad?"

Caine smiled softly. "I wouldn't put it quite that way, son. Let's say I enjoyed the benefit of his advice because I had the dubious benefit of rank."

Trevor let out a long-suffering sigh. "Okay, okay: even I won't give you grief about your rank anymore. It may have been a political assignment, but in the end, you earned it. And then some. And yes, Connor, Bannor Rulaine was your dad's XO on several operations."

"And now Bannor's in trouble?"

Trevor seemed uncertain how to respond. Caine stepped in. "He and the rest of my team couldn't risk returning after our last mission. They, and the humans we found stranded on Turkh'saar, were both politically hot."

Connor frowned. "How hot?"

"Nuclear. The odds were good that the people we rescued would 'disappear,' and that my team would wind up in secure facilities for years. Or longer. So they all went into hiding."

"While you risked a firing squad by coming back?"

"Connor, things were never going to come to that."

Trevor looked away. Gray Rinehart stared at Caine from under silvery brows.

Riordan ignored their dubiety. "Anyhow, it seems that Bannor's most recent status report indicates—but only to Trevor and me—that they are all in imminent danger of being discovered."

Connor shook his head. "Wait a minute. You once told me that Bannor and all those other people made a deal with Nuncle Richard and the government. Well, a bunch of governments. And now one of those governments is breaking that deal?"

"Looks like it." Riordan turned toward Trevor. "Is that why I got the Ultimate Experience signal?"

Connor blinked. "The what?"

Rinehart leaned back, blew out his cheeks. "A few of us in IRIS—the Institute for Reconnaissance, Intelligence, and Security—set up a back channel to keep your father apprised of any changes in his security status."

"You mean, if someone was coming to kill him?"

Rinehart had the good grace to look sheepish. "Pretty much. At any rate, the group which oversees that back channel reports only to Director Sukhinin and to me. No one else knows it exists."

"Which, theoretically, keeps it from being compromised or infiltrated," Trevor expanded, nodding.

Connor frowned. "So, because Bannor sent a message that someone was breaking the deal, the deal-breakers sent someone to kill *Dad*?"

Caine shook his head. "There's got to be more to it than that. Firstly, good luck to anyone trying to monitor the updates we get from Bannor. If you don't know what to look for, or where, you'd have no idea that there's any communication coming from him at all.

"Secondly, even if they knew your Uncle Trevor was the one compiling Bannor's updates, that still wouldn't tell them where I am." He studied Trevor's face, then Rinehart's. "So the 'other possible reason' your uncle mentioned must be something that not only revealed where I am, but caused someone with that information to decide I had to be taken off the game board."

Trevor looked down, then nodded. When he looked back up, his face had become unreadable. "The Dornaani have sent a message. About Elena." He looked at Connor. "They're the ones who have your mom in surgical cryostasis. And now they want to talk to your dad."

Caine forgot his resolve to remain relaxed. "When? Where?"

Before Trevor could answer, Connor angrily spat out a question of his own. "Wait. You mean someone here on Earth wants to keep us from getting Mom back? Who the hell would—?"

"Calm, now." Rinehart's voice was avuncular yet firm. "We won't find out by shouting about it."

"Okay, so how *are* we going to find out?"

Caine looked up, realizing what Rinehart had already deduced. "By determining who knew that I would be notified about the message from the Dornaani."

Rinehart nodded. "So you understand."

Caine nodded back. "I think so. Word of the Dornaani contact reached you through official channels. Which means it was seen by lots of other people, many of whom knew it would be relayed to me. And one of them learned that the final destination of the message was here on Nevis. So although killing me *could* be an attempt to preempt my meeting the Dornaani, it's just as likely that whoever attacked me today already wanted me dead. This was just the first time they had actionable intelligence."

Rinehart nodded. "Whether you've been on their hit list for years or just a few days, we can't say. But we do know this: the Dornaani message was addressed to the Proconsul of the Consolidated Terran Republic. It was coded top secret ultra and bounced down to the Commonwealth bloc's foreign office, to the U.S. State Department, and then finally to us in IRIS."

"Since you are nominatively my warders."

Rinehart nodded. "Which means the leak is almost certainly in IRIS. None of the upstream organizations have any information about your whereabouts."

Trevor's face had become expressive again. "For an intel organization, IRIS seems to have a lot of leaks."

Riordan leaned forward. "When do I meet the Dornaani, and where?"

"*If* you go to meet them, you'll be rendezvousing with a ship of theirs. It will be at a border system in a few months."

"*If?*" shouted Connor. "*If* he's goes? And what about me? I should be goi—!"

"Connor." Riordan waited until the only sounds in the aircar were the hoarse rush of the thrusters and the flapping of wind-slapped collars and sleeves. "Connor," he repeated, "even if I was willing to let you miss early admission to the Naval Academy, I doubt the Dornaani would allow this to be a family outing. And as far as *my* going is concerned"—Riordan turned back to Rinehart—"I suspect my next stop is D.C. and another set of hearings. Isn't it?"

Rinehart's smile was very faint and very rueful. "There's a rhetorical question if I ever heard one."

"Look," said Trevor, leaning toward Caine, "there's going to be a lot of sympathy for you. For Elena. And this is the first contact we've had about her in over three years. This is what we've all been waiting for."

As Riordan heard those words, he lost the ability to control his thoughts. *Elena. I might be able to get closer to you. Elena.*

Rinehart looked over at him. "And you'll be the first human to visit the Dornaani Collective, to see how they live."

Riordan knew his answering grin was, at best, crooked. "Somehow, Gray, first contact has lost whatever appeal it held for me." Riordan had never wanted the job. He had fallen into it. And just like quicksand, it had proven almost impossible to get out of.

Gray Rinehart shrugged. "Still, the stakes don't get much higher than this."

Caine saw Elena's face. "No, they truly don't." He took a moment to watch the leeward coast of St. Kitts flash past, the gulls wheeling, the waves obliterating themselves in white explosions against the rocks. "The Dornaani message: did it come from Alnduul?"

"It did."

Riordan nodded: another reason for hope. "What else did Alnduul say?"

"That he has answers to all your questions."

Caine smiled. "Alnduul underestimates the magnitude of my curiosity."

Cruz banked gently to the right and began down toward St. Kitts' air terminal, putting the wind fully in their faces.

Chapter Six

Connor checked his wristlink, then surveyed the private dining room overlooking the Chesapeake. He had been in this restaurant, the Bosun's Chair, at least fifty times and it never changed. But somehow, it felt different. After almost two years on Nevis, everything on the mainland seemed impossibly loud, impossibly hasty, and now, impossibly far removed from the dangers at large in the world.

Less than a week ago, he had awakened early, excited to sail through the Narrows on his own, a rite of passage for a kid who had grown up safe and sound—and was eager not to be. What he got instead was a glimpse into the darker world beneath that safe and sound one, a world from which one never really returns.

Connor's turning gaze wound up on his dad, who was watching him from three seats away. They shared a smile, one that Connor had to work at keeping happy. Attending the Academy was all he had wanted for three years, but being separated from his dad—that was hard to imagine now. Just as it was hard to imagine that he had ever felt differently, sitting in this very room, waiting to meet his father for the very first time, and certain—*certain*—that this late-come parent would never be more to him than an amiable interloper in his real family. And yet, a few months later, Connor decided to accompany this apparently friendly and forthright man into incognito exile. Because it was either that or never get to really know his father.

Who proved to be patient, persistent, good-natured, deeply interested in Connor's dreams, and who, above all, radiated parental love like a wood stove: steady, warm, utterly reliable. But now Dad was being whisked away, just like his mother and grandfather had been.

Connor sighed and rose. His father did the same. Time to go.

He started toward Caine wishing there was some way to both spend another year with his father and still move forward into adulthood.

But that was not the way of things.

As Riordan stood, Trevor caught his eye, made exaggerated pointing motions toward the door and then his wristlink. Riordan nodded, turned back toward Connor with as bright a smile as he could muster. "Your Uncle Trevor is eager to get you to your induction party."

Connor's lips crinkled upward. "Well, he ranks me, so I guess I'd better step lively."

Riordan gathered his son into a wide-armed hug. "I'm going to miss you, Connor. Very much."

Connor's voice was muffled in his shoulder. "I'm going to miss you too, Dad."

Riordan nodded. "I'd ask you to call every week and promise I'd do the same, but I don't think they have comm service where I'm going." Riordan managed to keep his smile from crumbling.

Connor's dimmed. "It's okay, Dad. Just find Mom and bring her home. Nothing else matters. Except that you stay safe."

"I will. I love you, son."

"I love you too, Dad."

Riordan watched Connor walk out the wharfside door, his Uncle Trevor on one side, his grandmother Patrice Corcoran on the other.

From the tap-room behind him, feet shuffled closer. Caine didn't have to look to know who it was: the two security operatives who'd been sent by IRIS.

"Yes," Riordan said, "I'm ready to leave."

"Actually, Mr. Riordan, we're here to tell you that Mr. Downing has been waiting to speak with you."

Riordan turned, looked at the guards. The woman reminded him of a panther; the man, a Kodiak bear. "I thought I was traveling *with* Mr. Downing."

"Change of plans, sir. You're being sequestered in different locations."

Riordan nodded, wondered at the significance of the change, entered the tap-room.

Richard Downing was sitting in one of the dark wood booths, his eyes fixed on a tall glass of seltzer in front of him. His own two minders were waiting at the far end of the bar, close to the door. Caine's took stools at the other end. They may have exchanged faint nods.

Riordan slid into the facing booth. "Hello, Richard."

Downing looked up, startled. Three years ago, he had been impossible to surprise. "Caine. Good to see you."

"And it's good to see you, too." Except it wasn't good to see Richard, not looking like this: bags under his eyes, his face gray, his slender six-foot two-inch frame almost gaunt.

Downing smiled sadly. "You have always been a poor liar, Caine." He sipped his seltzer. "I just wanted to say good luck in the days to come."

"And you as well. I've heard they're dragging you into sequestration again, too. Why?"

Downing shrugged. "Not really sure. Wouldn't be surprised if they want to use me as a watchdog, to alert them when you fail to tell the truth." He laughed. "If so, they certainly do not understand our prior arm's-length working relationship. Particularly when it comes to whatever contact arrangements you made with your old crew."

Riordan shrugged. "I have nothing to tell them now that I didn't two years ago."

Downing raised an uncertain palm. "Or this might simply be another opportunity for the new Procedural Compliance Directorate to demonstrate their power in IRIS, to spank the Old Guard all over again. Don't make that face, Caine. They're all from the Developing World Coalition, so they will take every opportunity to exert, and thereby reinforce, their authority."

Riordan leaned back, discovered he needed to change the subject. "So, what about you? What comes next?"

"I suspect they're going to take another run at putting my head on a pike, too."

"How? By trotting out the same unsupported accusations and fabricated evidence?"

Downing's smile was rueful. "Oh, I'm sure they can dress up the leftovers well enough to claim it's a new dish. They just need to create a strong enough whiff of impropriety and insubordination to ensure that I become a political liability to the powers-that-be. A month after they're done having at me, I'll be sent packing. Quietly. With apologies and a poorly attended retirement party."

Riordan frowned. Downing was no choir boy. But to watch him get cashiered for finally—*finally*—putting people before pragmatism? For ensuring the safety of Caine's crew and the "Lost Soldiers" they'd rescued from Turkh'saar? No. Not acceptable.

Caine made sure his voice was casual. "So what if we could trick the DWC flacks into thinking that you were on their side? Or, at least, that you were willing to throw me under the bus to appease them?" As he spoke, Riordan shifted in his seat until the guards fell within his peripheral vision: neither pair were properly positioned to use directional eavesdropping devices.

Downing had looked up sharply. "'Throw you under the bus?' What on earth are you talking about, Riordan?"

"What if, after they're done grilling me to no avail, you were able to tell them *how* Bannor informed me that their agents were closing in on my old crew and the Lost Soldiers?"

Richard became very still. "Caine, I appreciate the offer, but I doubt it would help me. More importantly, once they know how Bannor is communicating to you, they'd backtrack along those data streams to find him and probably the Lost Soldiers."

"No, they won't, because there are no data streams left to backtrack."

Downing's eyes widened. "Of course. When Bannor used the channel to send a message to *your* attention, it also meant he was shutting it down."

Riordan nodded. "And Bannor immediately began relocating everyone."

Richard smiled. "So there's no way to reestablish contact."

"Precisely. But the inquisitors won't know that. They'll think you're giving them viable intelligence, a channel they can monitor." Riordan leaned back. "Now, are you interested?"

"To coin a phrase, I'm all ears." Downing had pretty big ears.

Riordan smiled. "So here's how we managed it. Bannor posted anonymous content on various sites and blogs every month. None of it had anything to do with us. They were weather reports, travel logs, hotel and travel reviews. The only meaningful parts were descriptions of the weather or night skies, all of which directly or indirectly indicated positions of moons or planets.

"If every one of those astronomical details were correct for that location and that date, it meant no one was closing in on the hiding place of the Lost Soldiers and the others."

Downing nodded, smiling. "But an error meant that he and the Lost Soldiers were in imminent danger of discovery. And that you, personally, were to be alerted. Well done, Commodore. And"—his voice dropped—"thank you, Caine. It's always good to have a trump card."

Downing's minders glanced at their wristlinks, then out at the street, then started toward the booth.

Richard stood. "I suppose this is goodbye. I hope we'll see each other again. And if you have to start a war to bring Elena back, I shall gladly serve in that army. Here's my hand on it."

Caine shook Downing's hand, nodded at the fierce, almost agonized resolve in the other's worn face, and watched as he made for the exit, a stick-figure framed by dusk-dimmed windows.

Chapter Seven

A moment after the glass door closed behind Downing and his guards, another silhouette approached it and entered at a brisk walk: Commander Lorraine Phalon.

Physically, she was the opposite of Richard Downing. He was made of long straight lines where she was rounded; he was slender where she was sturdy. And whereas Downing had been ready to smile, Phalon's face currently signaled a predisposition not to.

Caine put out his hand at the same moment she did. "It's good to see you again, Commander Phalon."

"Likewise, Commodore." She scanned him quickly. "Life in the Caribbean seems to agree with you, sir."

"It's a marked improvement over being grilled in windowless conference rooms." He noticed the rank insignia on her lower sleeve, cocked an eyebrow. "I see congratulations are in order. A full commander now. Evidently speaking on my behalf didn't get you blackballed."

She might have been on the verge of smiling. "I might have been, but Admiral Silverstein had my back. And yours. He made it clear that he would tender his resignation before bowing to political pressure. Which never came: the buck stopped on President Liu's desk, and she tossed it right back at the interbloc politicos. Pissed off the Traditionalist faction in Beijing no end, sir."

Riordan waved off the honorific. "I take it you are my official escort."

44

Phalon's expression became pinched. "I do not have that sad honor, sir. But we do have a moment to talk about what's in store for you. May I?"

Riordan indicated the opposite seat. As she slid into spot Downing had vacated, Riordan's two minders sat a little straighter.

Commander Phalon folded her hands. Caine wondered if such long fingernails were within regs for the JAG's office, to say nothing of the color. "The hearings on your request to enter Dornaani space will be run by politicos from the Developing World Coalition. Who aren't any bigger fans of IRIS, or of you, than they were two years ago."

Riordan shrugged. "Can't say I blame them, even though I understand why IRIS couldn't include them, initially."

"No disagreement, sir, but that's all high-level politics. Way beyond my pay grade."

Riordan smiled. "These days, *everything* is beyond my pay grade." He sat straighter. "So, what are we wrestling over this time?"

"The Lost Soldiers, sir."

Caine scratched his ear. "Wasn't that what we were wrestling over *last* time?"

"Not exactly, sir. At least, not for the same reasons." She leaned forward; the light reflecting from the brass fixtures brought out red highlights in her hair. "Commodore, if the proconsul is forced to go public and reveal the existence and origin of the Lost Soldiers, it effectively admits that humans were kidnapped by aliens during the latter half of the Twentieth Century. That would spark widespread, if not universal, fear and outrage. And not just at the abductors, but at the governments that have been sitting on this information for two years."

Riordan nodded. "Sure, but I'll wager that what really keeps the politicos up at night is that any subsequent investigation will reveal that the abductors were the Ktor."

Phalon sighed. "There's no way it can be any of the other species."

Riordan nodded. "Which becomes public knowledge the moment the Lost Soldiers' public statements reveal that the Ktor aren't really aliens; they're just a modified branch of humanity."

Lorraine Phalon looked him in the eyes, paused, and then said in a tone so formal that it bordered on being brusque, "Sir, I cannot speak directly to that point."

Caine paused. Lorraine's reply was one of the many mantras of deniability learned by persons who handled confidential information. But Phalon was aware of the true identity of the Ktor and the ongoing campaign to suppress that information, and knew that Riordan had the same knowledge. Her steady gaze puzzled him until he realized what her stare and silence signified: she had new, relevant information that she could not officially share with him. So, in the best tradition of legally circumventing confidentiality, she was encouraging him to go fishing.

Which Riordan did. "I see. So, the Ktor genetic samples we brought back, are they proving to be, um, particularly interesting?"

"Geneticists always find genetic samples from new subspecies interesting, sir." Despite the brusque tone, Phalon's almost feline eyes were mischievous.

So, the Ktor are a subspecies; *they* do *have substantive genetic differences.* And, logically, if the CTR wanted to expand that research, they'd have to reveal the true identity of the Ktor to an increasing number of xenogeneticists. Which meant that the cover up was expanding. Which put the politicos at ever-increasing risk. Which meant Riordan now had the last thing the Procedural Compliance Directorate wanted him to have: extra leverage. At a particularly sensitive political moment.

Riordan nodded at Commander Phalon. "Thank you for the sitrep." He stood. "I'm ready to go."

She looked up at him. "I'm not sure you are, sir." Phalon gave in to a smile; it was slow and sly. She rose, straightened her lips, straightened her uniform. "Take your time." The right side of her mouth curved as she turned, hooked a finger at Caine's escorts, and walked briskly out of the Bosun's Chair.

The IRIS-bred he-bear and she-panther looked at each other, shrugged, and followed.

Before Riordan could resume his seat, another woman rose from one of the small tables cinched between the far end of the bar and the large picture window that faced out into the gathering dusk. Head inclined slightly, she approached without directly looking at Caine. She was Asian, slim, almost petite, probably about ten years his junior.

She stopped almost two meters away from him. "Commodore Riordan?" Her accent was faint, but distinctly Japanese.

"Yes?"

"I am Ayana Tagawa."

"I'm sorry; have we met?"

"No, Commodore. I doubt you would know of me. But I have come to know a bit about you."

Caine was about to extend his hand, but stopped. Her skirt went to her knees, her hair was impeccably but conservatively cut close and short, she was without jewelry, and her posture retained a slight forward lean. Riordan kept his smile faint and bowed from the waist.

She bowed even more slowly and deeply. "I am honored to meet you, Commodore." Her tone of voice—respectful but no longer quite so distant—said more: *I appreciate that you discern and respect my traditional choices.*

Riordan kept his tone quiet, almost inaudible given the noise coming from the diners in the next room. "I am honored to meet you, Ms. Tagawa. May I offer you a seat?" He gestured, not too emphatically, to the booth.

When they were seated, he waited. If he read Ms. Tagawa right, she had been brought up in the so-called neo-Edo fashion, and so a first meeting was an inherently formal matter. The best approach was simple, even minimalist, hospitality. "I will ask our server to bring us glasses of water. Would you care for anything else?"

"Thank you. Water would be most welcome."

They waited through an improbably long process of flagging down a waiter, asking for water, and then having two glasses delivered with a perfunctory smile.

Ayana took hers and sipped. "We share a secret, Commodore."

Well, that's a pretty frank opening statement. "Is it one we may talk about?"

Ayana nodded gravely. "But only because Commander Phalon has seen to the security of this establishment."

"You know Phalon?"

"Not well, but yes. From two years ago, when I was extensively debriefed on matters pertaining to your hearings."

Riordan nodded and reflected on her composure, the careful directness of her speech. Some of that demeanor was natural, but much of it was trained, groomed: professional. He played a hunch. "So were you active in the same places I was, after the Arat Kur were defeated?"

She nodded deeply this time. "Usually, I was in *exactly* the same places."

Riordan leaned back. So, two years ago, Ayana Tagawa had somehow followed his ambassadorial mission deep into Slaasriithi space. And then, somehow followed him to Turkh'saar, the world where he had found the Lost Soldiers. And then finally, back to Sigma Draconis Two and the near-fatal standoff with the Ktoran ships in that system. After which Caine had been removed from command and placed under "administrative protection" until his debriefings began. Therefore... "If you followed exactly the same path I did, then you were aboard the Ktor ship that tracked and attacked us. Three times."

Ayana sipped her water.

There was only one logical way that any Earth-born human could have come to be traveling as a prisoner of the Ktor. "So you were taken captive when the Ktor seized the megacorporate shift-carrier *Arbitrage* to pursue us."

She put down her water soundlessly. "I was the executive officer of *Arbitrage's* prize crew. We were put aboard after it was learned that her owners had collaborated with the enemy before the invasion of Earth."

Which meant that she was almost certainly Japanese intelligence. "I suspect you were more than just the XO."

Ayana bowed her head almost imperceptibly. "Your suspicions are probably correct, but it would be best not to speak of them. That way, neither you nor I shall ever find ourselves in a situation where we would have to lie about what we have learned of each other."

Riordan nodded back. "Very prudent. So, the secret we share is the Ktor."

"Yes. But they are also a puzzle, of which we seem to hold different pieces."

"What do you mean?"

"You have interacted with their cadre and highest officials. I was the prisoner of renegades, the survivors of an extirpated 'House.' I lived with them, learned how they thought, even heard their language on occasion. You saw their public face; I saw what was behind it."

Caine leaned back. "I'm surprised IRIS released you from 'administrative custody' at all."

"I gave my word to Director Sukhinin that I would remain silent. He understood that by doing so, I put the honor of my family at stake, as well." She looked down slightly. "However, the recent attack upon you proves that some powers do not trust individual oaths. And perhaps mine will be the next one they feel must be... revisited."

Riordan considered the bright rim of his water glass. Ayana Tagawa knew more about the Ktor than anyone else who was willing to admit to such familiarity with them. But she had no knowledge of the state-to-state exchanges with their highest leadership, and so was completely unaware that the Ktor had promised all-out war if their identity was revealed. Meaning that she was the political equivalent of a thermonuclear device without even knowing it.

Riordan folded his hands. "Tell me how I can help."

"I walk in darkness, Commodore. We know the Ktor are human, yet the information is suppressed. Those of us who have seen the truth are sworn to secrecy, and some, like you, are removed from the public eye. But when you emerged, you became the target of assassins. So I must wonder: might I be next? And if I am, how can I hope to survive? I have no powerful friends watching over me. Worse still, I do not understand why knowing this secret has become a death sentence."

So that's why Lorraine had aimed Tagawa at him: for the knowledge Riordan could impart obliquely, just by sharing a few of the low-clearance details of the witch hunt he'd endured two years ago. Ayana would then have a chance to read between the lines and deduce why such a highly classified campaign of information suppression was still in force and, consequently, why her life was in such grave danger. Riordan wasn't sure Phalon's plan would work, but he was willing to follow the commander's implicit lead. "Where would you like me to begin, Ms. Tagawa?"

"You are very kind, Commodore." She straightened. "Firstly, why is there no mention of the specific charges brought against you during the hearings?"

Riordan shook his head, still smiling. "There's no mention of the charges brought against me because none ever were. Despite the accusers' attempts to compel my bloc and national government to do so."

"For what charges were they pressing?"

"They started with treason."

Ayana's eyes widened. "On what grounds?"

Riordan took a sip of water. *Keep the details vague, for* her *sake.* "After returning from Turkh'saar, I refused to relinquish control over certain individuals until I received official guarantees for their safety."

She nodded. "I heard many Ktor conversations about the Lost Soldiers while we were in the Turkh'saar system."

Okay, so she *did* know about the Lost Soldiers. That allowed Riordan to be a bit less oblique. "After it was determined that there weren't any grounds for treason, my accusers wanted me charged with mutiny."

"I presume you disobeyed a direct order to turn over the Lost Soldiers?"

"Correct. And since I never did comply with that order unconditionally, the chair of the board allowed the opposition—in the interests of interbloc amity—to lay out its argument and supporting evidence. Which took almost three weeks."

"And how long did it take for your side to present its case?"

Caine felt his smile become wolfish. "Five hours and thirty-six minutes. Including the recess for lunch. After which the accusations were dismissed as groundless."

"So your accusers spent all that time and achieved nothing?"

Riordan held up a finger. "Not quite. During their three weeks in the spotlight, the opposition sensationalized IRIS's procedural and jurisdictional 'inadequacies.' As a result, they gathered enough support to compel the Institute to establish an in-house watchdog division: the Procedural Compliance Directorate. Which then launched an 'objective assessment' of the conformity between IRIS's mandate and its wartime operating procedures."

Ayana nodded, understanding. "And is that how Director Downing was demoted to IRIS's 'Advisory' Director?"

Riordan sighed. "For the most part, he was just a scapegoat."

"So who was actually responsible? His former superior, Nolan Corcoran?"

Carefully, now. "Let me put it this way, Ms. Tagawa. The truly culpable parties, those who created IRIS and approved everything that Nolan Corcoran ever did, cannot answer questions on these matters."

Ayana's eyes opened slightly wider. "Why? To protect them politically?"

"No. Because they cannot be put in a position where their oaths of office would necessitate that they perjure themselves." *Because, even if asked directly, they cannot reveal what the Ktor have done and who the Ktor really are. Not without violating their own secrecy orders. C'mon, Ayana, connect the dots...*

Ayana's eyes opened even wider. Then she nodded slowly. "I thank you, Commodore Riordan. Very much."

Riordan swallowed the last of the water in his glass. Ayana Tagawa had proven to be a fast study, and as her eyes faded off into a hundred-meter stare, he could imagine them looking inward, seeing how the dominoes he'd just unveiled could fall. And crush her. The parties responsible for withholding and twisting information had put their careers on the line to avert a war that humanity could not survive, let alone win. And the assassination attempt against Riordan signified that some of them were willing to kill to protect those secrets.

Caine suppressed a shiver. What Ayana still didn't know was that, from the start, the DWC had militated for a "total" solution: the outright elimination of the Lost Soldiers and any other potential intelligence leaks. They had never relented on that point and, as their presence in IRIS grew, so too did their ability to identify and preemptively eliminate such threats. Threats such as Ayana Tagawa.

As Ayana's gaze faded back into the here and now, Caine saw the weight of realization settle in her eyes. She still didn't—couldn't—realize that in actuality, she was as good as dead. But Caine wouldn't allow that outcome: something else that Phalon had probably anticipated.

"Go to my people," Riordan said, surprised as the unplanned words came out of his mouth.

She blinked. "Your... people?"

"Not the ones here." After a pause, he glanced at the ceiling. "The ones out there."

"But how will they know that I—?"

"They no longer have the ability to reach me, but I can tell you how to reach them. No promises, though. It was arranged as a dead-drop. They may have abandoned it."

Ayana's attention was absolute, tense. "I saw reports that Colonel Bannor Rulaine, your former executive officer, was working as a military contractor on Epsilon Indi. I presume I must go—"

Riordan shook his head. "The only way he'd still be in that system is if someone there put him in a cell. Or a coffin. You go to Zeta Tucanae."

"But how—?"

"Zeta Tucanae, Ms. Tagawa. And you can't share that destination with anyone. That secret is also on both your own and your family's honor."

She nodded sharply, breathed out a hoarse, "*Hai.*"

Riordan nodded back. "Zeta Tucanae used to be a year and a half by shift-carrier. It's a lot less now if you get a ride on one of the upgraded ones."

"That—that would require all my funds," she stammered.

Riordan stared at her. "Ms. Tagawa, you're the intelligence professional, not me. But if you're not sure what's at stake, let me make it clearer: if you stay here, whatever money you've saved is going to be your burial fund. If you don't have enough money, then take out a loan and run. Default."

She stiffened at that suggestion. Two resolves—honor and survival—vied in her eyes.

"Look," Caine added, "you don't have a lot of time. Now that these assassins are acting openly, their operational timeline *has* to be accelerated. So whatever time bomb you are already sitting on has just had its fuse shortened. Drastically."

She nodded, her lips an unflinching line. "So," she almost whispered, "Zeta Tucanae."

He nodded back. "Once there, go to a place called Theresa King's Outfitting and Overnight. Post an ad—just a handbill—looking for work as a combination translator and assistant office manager. The second Tuesday after you put it up, go to a bar about a block away called Charny's, just after local sundown. Go there again the following Tuesday, same time. If no one shows on your second visit, it means my people have been compromised, are gone, or were never there. Or you've got a tail, so they're not going to show." He met and held her gaze. "That's all the information I have."

Her smile was small but genuine. "I quite understand, Commodore. Basic operational security. We cannot reveal what we do not know."

He nodded. "You know the drill better than I do. I just hope this helps."

She stood. "It is a destination and a chance to preserve both my honor and my life." She bowed slightly and held it. "Thank you, Commodore Riordan."

He rose and returned her bow. She dipped slightly lower, then turned and headed for the exit. She didn't seem to be rushing— her individual motions appeared almost casual—but she was gone with remarkable speed.

Riordan waited thirty seconds and then strolled toward the darkened windows and the vehicle that Phalon surely had waiting just outside.

Chapter Eight

JULY 2123
WASHINGTON D.C., EARTH

"If you would please take your seat, Commodore Riordan." The Marine held it out for him.

Before Caine could sit, the Asian woman behind the table on the other side of the room uttered a sharp correction. "Our visitor is to be addressed as 'Mister' Riordan. He is here as a private citizen."

Lorraine Phalon strode in at the end of her admonishment, a tall, lean man in USSF blue following her. "Ms. Yan, Commodore Riordan is still a reserve officer of the USSF. It is proper and fitting that service persons, as well as any others who wish to do so, address him by his rank." She sat. The man in the service dress blues, by far the youngest in the room, sat beside her.

Riordan glanced past Lorraine at the young fellow and whispered, "Who's the new guy?"

"Lieutenant Kyle Seaver. Intelligence liaison. Between JAG and IRIS."

"And the woman who gave me such a warm welcome?"

"That's Yan Xiayou, Director of the Procedural Compliance Directorate. The older man next to her is Dalir Sadozai, currently the Associate Director. But he's had a lot of different positions."

"Where?"

"Any place the DWC needs a hard-liner."

The youngest person at the opposing table adjusted his collar-mic. "Good morning, Commod—Mister Riordan. I am Enis Turan of the Procedural Compliance Directorate. I am responsible for assessing possible security risks posed by your possible travel to the Dornaani Collective. Specifically, we are concerned that information regarding the existence and disposition of the expatriate group known colloquially as the Lost Soldiers could be shared with Dornaani individuals, thereby compromising the strategic interests of the Consolidated Terran Republic."

Riordan frowned. "Compromise how?"

"Two years ago, the Ktor ambassador Tlerek Srin Shethkador asserted that if it was revealed that the Ktoran Sphere had kidnapped the Lost Soldiers from Earth, the political fallout would result in the Ktor being ejected from the Accord. If that occurred, they were resolved to immediately declare war on us."

Riordan leaned forward. "Mr. Turan, since you have obviously read my testimony about that confidential meeting, you know that one of the five people there was the ranking Dornaani on site: Alnduul, a Senior Mentor of the Custodians. So you can be sure the Dornaani Collective is already fully informed about the Lost Soldiers and what is at stake if their true identity becomes common knowledge."

Sadozai brushed gently at his mustache. "Yes, but Mr. Turan's statement includes the possibility of your revealing something the Dornaani would not already know: the *current disposition* of the Lost Soldiers. Which is to say, their present location."

Phalon's tone was measured. "Which the Lost Soldiers did not share with Commodore Riordan. As per the commodore's testimony the last time he was being grilled in this room."

Yan nodded. "Be that as it may, Commander, Mr. Riordan's changed circumstances require that we revisit the existing agreement with him. Specifically: when Mr. Riordan emerged from hiding, his knowledge of the Lost Soldiers emerged with him. This is too great a risk to go unaddressed."

"Okay," Riordan said with a shrug, "what do you need me to do?"

Sadozai shrugged. "To reveal the location of the Lost Soldiers. Of course."

"Even if I had that information, why would I share it now?" Riordan glared at the three faces across from him. "Both at Turkh'saar, and then later in this very room, your own representatives *refused* to guarantee the Lost Soldiers' safety." Caine paused, considered. "So, let's try this again. Will you *now* agree, on the record, to guarantee the safety and fair treatment of the Lost Soldiers, and all the other personnel who were under my command on Turkh'saar? And, if they must be remanded to administrative custody, do you promise that their condition shall be independently monitored to ensure that those guarantees are being met?" Riordan stared at them and waited.

But instead of their eyes, he saw Elena's. Becoming more and more distant.

Sadozai waved away Riordan's questions with a lazy backhand. "Since you evidently perceive us as your adversaries, how can we trust *you*, Mr. Riordan? How can we approve your travel to the Collective? You might leave timed press releases behind, revealing the existence of the Lost Soldiers and so, single-handedly initiate the cascade leading to war."

Kyle Seaver leaned forward. "It is strange that you are the one talking about trust, Mr. Sadozai. After all, whoever attempted to ensure that Commodore Riordan never left Nevis has the same objective you do: to make sure he cannot leak the location of the Lost Soldiers."

Seaver ignored Sadozai's suddenly bristling mustache. "Of course, even though the assassination attempt failed, it's still likely to achieve the intended result: to keep the commodore from reaching the Dornaani. Because his required presence at inevitable and innumerable hearings—like this one—is very likely to make him miss the rendezvous."

Caine worked very hard not to smile while everyone else sat in stunned silence. *Thank God Seaver's on* my *side.*

Phalon folded her hands and spoke to a spot on the wall behind the three representatives of the Procedural Compliance Directorate. "Lieutenant Seaver's analysis obligates me to initiate an investigation of every agency and organization which had advance knowledge of Commodore Riordan's departure from Nevis and his pending travel to the Collective."

Yan's riposte was heated. "A breach of security within IRIS is an IRIS matter."

Phalon nodded calmly. "Normally, yes, but in this case, the part of IRIS that handles internal affairs is under suspicion itself: namely, your own Directorate, Ms. Yan. Consequently, I'll be reporting directly to Director Vassily Sukhinin of IRIS, whose regard for the commodore is, I presume, well known to you."

Yan reddened. Sadozai went pale. Turan, nervously noting the uncertain silence of the other two, asked, "Could this investigation be...avoided, somehow?"

Phalon shook her head. "No. Attempted murder requires an investigation. However, it can be mounted in a less immediate, and less aggressive, manner. Indeed, if the primary witness—the commodore himself—should happen to be traveling in the Dornaani Collective, the investigation would be severely delayed."

Riordan watched the combative look on Yan's face transmogrify to resignation. *And checkmate.*

Yan ordered her notes, folded her hands, and stated, "This board can find no immediate reason to deny Mr. Riordan the opportunity to travel to the Dornaani Collective as a private individual. However, since he has remained uncooperative in addressing the security and intelligence concerns of this board, and that of various political entities—"

—translation: "the Developing World Coalition"—

"—it will also be necessary for him to be interviewed and approved by the Interbloc Working Group on Exosapient Interaction."

Phalon's jaw stiffened. "And how long will that process take?"

Yan's smile was wan. "Who can say?"

Riordan leaned forward. "I think I can. Specifically, if I reveal the location of the Lost Soldiers now, the process will take less than a day. However, if I don't give you what you want, the process will drag on for as long as it takes to keep me from reaching the Dornaani in time."

Yan looked uncomfortable. "It would certainly streamline the process were you to agree to our one request."

Seaver tapped his dataslate meditatively. "So because Commodore Riordan does not give you information that he doesn't even possess, you are going to procedurally stymie his ability to travel?"

"If he will not cooperate, the Interbloc Working Group is likely to do that, yes," she replied.

Riordan leaned forward. "Director Yan, which scenario do you like less: me being the first human to visit the Dornaani, or getting absolutely no useful intel on them? Intel which might finally provide us with an adequate strategic snapshot of this area of space, since Dornaani are the only ones who can tell us what was going on in this stellar cluster twenty thousand years ago. They are the only ones who might be able to explain the unfathomable preponderance of genetic compatibility and even conformity that we have encountered on the majority of green worlds. They are the ones whose technology shows us, and gives hints at the pathways to, the capabilities humanity might achieve in the years and centuries to come. And lastly, they are the only ones who could, and yet don't, autocratically lord it over all the species in known space—but why? And more importantly, what might cause them to change their minds?"

Riordan opened his hands in appeal. "This is not just about my going to the Collective to find Elena Corcoran. This is about getting answers and intelligence we desperately need. As a species. Don't you want that information, so that we can adequately prepare for our next contact with the Dornaani? Don't you want to respond to their first gesture since the war, pave the way for an exchange of envoys, then delegations, and finally, consulates and embassies?"

Turan looked inquiringly at Yan, who pointedly did not return his gaze; her eyes were locked with Caine's. After several seconds they faltered; he imagined he might have seen a hint of regret in them. She answered in a low voice. "What you and I want is not the only consideration, here, Mr. Riordan. But be assured: I will send the Interbloc Working Group your assessment regarding the consequences of blocking your travel."

Seaver smiled mirthlessly. "Which the Working Group will doubtless ignore until after the commodore has missed the window for contact."

Yan waved a listless hand. "There are no perfect answers. These are the only ones I am able to offer you." She rose. "The Interbloc Working Group will give Mr. Riordan's replies and perspectives due consideration and will notify you when they are ready to commence their hearings." She nodded briefly and led the other two out of the room.

Riordan smiled crookedly at Phalon and Seaver. "That seemed to go well."

Phalon's response was a faint frown. "Actually, it might have gone *too* well."

"Is that possible?" Riordan wondered.

Seaver nodded. "Dalir got nervous and pushed too hard on the Lost Soldiers."

Riordan nodded. "He knows that someone in his bloc is still looking for them. He may even be a part of the operation, himself."

Seaver smiled ruefully. "Either way, he tipped his hand and now *we* know that he knows. Which means that, before the end of the day, Sadozai is going to be on a plane to somewhere we can't subpoena him and threaten to pursue an embarrassing line of questions. Which has given us enough leverage to stare down the Working Group."

Phalon nodded, yanked the door open. "Now, they're likely to sequester you again, Commodore. As soon as they can set a date for the first hearing."

Riordan shrugged. "Any guess how *long* the Working Group can tie me up?"

Seaver's eyes and voice became grim. "Too long."

Chapter Nine

JULY 2123
WASHINGTON D.C., EARTH

Richard Downing closed the cover of the transcripts. The hardcopy-only distribution signified how highly classified it was: sharing electronic documents virtually guaranteed that they would eventually fall into the wrong hands.

He poured another glass of seltzer, longed to add a touch of gin. Just a touch—

He grabbed the still-effervescing drink, downed it in a swallow so long that his esophagus cramped. He slammed the glass down, resisted the urge to bat it across the room, just to see and hear it smash. Two months now, and it still wasn't any easier to stay sober. He wondered if it ever would be.

Downing pushed the transcripts away. Pretty much what he'd expected. IRIS's new, externally imposed Inquisitors had thought to cow Caine and Phalon. But, aided by Seaver, they had turned the tables. Unfortunately, according to the scuttlebutt, the Interbloc Working Group on Exosapient Interaction wasn't going to risk more of the same. They were going to stall, not engage.

There would be days, even weeks, between each meeting. And every one would seem to bring Riordan a little closer to reaching the Dornaani and Elena. But then new wrinkles would emerge to erode the progress: a carefully timed dance of one step forward, one step back. Which Caine probably expected, being the smart chap he was.

Downing almost shook his head. *Caine, Caine. If you'd been just a little smarter, you'd have prevented others from learning just how smart you really are. Or unlearned your reflex to put yourself at risk for a friend, or a comrade. Damn it, Riordan, when will you learn to think of yourself first?*

Richard's mind rounded on him: *And when will you* not, *Downing?* The guilty thought lingered like the aftertaste of bile. The old counterarguments and rationalizations rose up: his job necessitated what he did, necessitated putting the welfare of humanity ahead of every other consideration. Once again, he felt the terrible power, and the terrible truth, of those reasons.

But in the course of his doing that duty, Richard Downing had fallen from the high ground of necessary action into the gutter of simple expedience, had tumbled from principled prudence into a blind mania for risk avoidance. Because someplace on that slippery slope, a place well behind him now, he had failed to notice when the exigencies and reasons for his work devolved into mere validations.

Downing discovered he was staring at the cover of the transcripts again, or rather, at its simple label: "Caine Riordan." And for the fifth time that day, he thought: *If I'm willing to break rules, I can probably turn this around.* Despite being stripped of all day-to-day operational authority within IRIS, Richard still had his clearance, his rank, his access. If he played all those cards in the correct sequence, and quickly enough, there was a reasonable chance he could lower the official hurdles long enough for Riordan to jump over them all.

And don't I have to do that, with Elena's life at stake? Don't I owe that much to Connor, and to the memory of her father, my best friend?

He looked at the folder. *Of course, if I do this, I will burn. Literally, perhaps. But I owe this to them. And to Caine.*

He angrily rebutted the morally bankrupt mantras that he'd memorized, that rose up now like wizened misers intent on decrying personal feelings for an intelligence asset. *So what if I never explicitly guaranteed Riordan my loyalty? Does that really matter? After all, when does a person really become our friend: the first time we say it openly, or the day we realize and acknowledge it in our heart?*

The day he met Caine, back in September 2105, was one of those days. Downing had known—immediately, illogically, unreasonably—that here was a person with whom he fit. Riordan was the kind of bloke you could rely on, who'd forgive you your failings as you'd forgive his, and who you hoped you'd be sharing a pint with when you weren't good for anything more than doddering up to the pub and back again...

The rapid tone of the commplex startled Downing out of his memory. Cautious, he accepted only the audio component of the secure call.

"Mr. Downing?"

"Yes. Who is this?"

"Kyle Seaver, intel liaison to Commander Phalon."

"Ah, yes. I've just been reading the transcripts. Thank you for, er, 'facilitating' their delivery."

"Happy to oblige, sir. I'm calling to tell you that Director Sukhinin has greenlighted your request to meet with The Patch."

"Thank you, and please thank Vassily. And, Lieutenant Seaver?"

"Yes, sir?"

"I have another favor to ask of you."

"On behalf of Commodore Riordan, sir?"

"I suppose one could put it that way. I have need of some special transportation..."

Caine Riordan pulled his shirt back down, resealed the tabless smart collar. As the doctor watched her commplex chew through the results of his physical, Riordan glanced at the faded walls. "Looks like it's time for a new coat of paint, Dr. Brolley," he observed.

She laughed. "At Walter Reed, that's always true someplace. At least it's not as bad as it was when they tore down half the facility in the 2050s. And if you don't start calling me Christa, I'm going start calling you Commodore again."

Riordan raised his hands in surrender. "You win, Christa."

"That's better," she said agreeably, and then frowned at her screen. "This can't be right."

Caine raised an eyebrow. "What can't be right?"

Although her words were addressed to Riordan, the majority of her attention remained on her commplex's display. "Glitch in the system, I guess. The data is formatted correctly, but definitely off. Hmmm...no system warning, either." She aimed her voice at the pickup. "Q-command, reboot."

The screen went black as she turned back toward Caine. "So what's the rush with this physical?"

"Might be traveling in a few weeks. Beyond quarantine control."

Her smile became knowing. "Given what I've read about you, I've got to ask: *how far* beyond quarantine control?"

"I wish I knew," Riordan answered honestly. "But if and when I get the green light, I need to be ready to go at a moment's notice."

"Well, you will be, although given your exam request's priority code, you were never going to be waiting in a line."

"I'm very fortunate in my friends," Caine said with what he hoped was a winning yet modest smile.

"I'll say. If I had friends like that, I'd—" The commplex toned its readiness. "About time," Brolley groused, and turned back to inspect it.

And frowned more deeply than she had before.

Riordan felt cool currents of concern creeping up his neck. "What is it?"

Brolley didn't answer. Instead she strode toward him and said, "Lift your left pant leg, please."

Caine complied.

She kneeled down, examined his tibia and calf. Her frown deepened. "Other leg, please."

Caine obeyed and reflected that the last time he'd had both pants legs up this high, he had been fourteen, preparing to wade through his parents' flooded basement.

Brolley leaned back, looked up. Her eyes were as focused and sharp as the scalpels on one of the nearby trays. "Which is the leg injured late in 2120? You know, during the incident you can't discuss, on the planet you can't reveal?"

He wiggled the left one. "If you know that much, don't you have enough clearance for me to talk about the 'incident'?"

"Unfortunately, no." She examined his leg even more closely, as if she was hunting for microorganisms. "I have your complete medical history, but a lot of the situational details are redacted. All those records tell me is that you sustained a very severe fracture of the left tibia just under three years ago." She looked up. "There is no sign of it. And I mean *no* sign. I could run the scan again, but it's going to show the same thing."

The hairs on the back of his neck rose in response to the certainty of her tone. "Why?"

"Because none of the things that *should* be in your scans are showing up."

"Such as?"

Brolley sighed, stood, and stepped back to look him over. "Such as the lung damage from the spores on that same world. When you got home and cleared the quarantine exit exam, the med-techs were already surprised at how little scarring remained on your lung tissue. Now it's gone.

"Same is true with your older, even more serious wounds, the ones you sustained during the liberation of Jakarta." She glanced at her palmtop. "Let's see: 'Lacerations of the right latissimus dorsi, the right lung, and the liver. Splintering fracture of T5 vertebra.' Which, thanks to the Dornaani who were with you, all healed. A miracle, our doctors said." She leaned closer. "They were wrong. The real miracle is that now, there's no indication you were ever wounded. No place where the bones reknitted, no scar tissue in the muscle or at the wound site on your back. Your T5 looks showroom new. Your liver is fully regrown, no sign of damage."

A chill moved up his torso. "But how—?"

"I'm not done. The wound to your arm from the assassination attempt on Mars? Like it was never there. Same with two minor bone breaks from playing sports as a kid."

The cold front that had moved up Riordan's torso now penetrated his bones, but not due to the unnerving exam results. It was because he knew what had caused them.

"And those are only the gross deviations from what we should see," Brolley continued. "There's also freakishly low dental wear. Your age-normal gum recession has disappeared. Even the bone and muscle wear that starts changing your shape after a few decades in a gravity well are absent. Your endocrinology looks like that of a twenty-year-old: adrenaline, endorphins, entire lymphatic system is textbook for a young adult male.

"But here's the weirdest of all—and we would never have detected it without the baseline we took after you picked up some rads while you were stranded off Barney Deucy. Today's telomere test came back abnormal, but not the way we'd expect. The chains are *longer* than they were. By four sigma shifts." She sat and shook her head. "These results—there's no way to explain them."

"There is," Caine corrected quietly.

Brolley's surprise doubled. "How?"

Caine nodded toward her palmtop. "Look at the entries for the respiratory trauma caused by the exobiotic spores on the planet I can't mention."

Brolley frowned, scanned. "Yes? What am I looking for?"

"Does it say how I was treated?"

"Er, just that the Slaasriithi used a therapy they translated as a 'theriac.'"

Riordan nodded, felt like he was outside himself. "I presume you are familiar with that word?"

Brolley had to think. "That's from classical references. Not scientific. Some honey-based mixture that was supposedly a poison antidote."

Riordan shook his head, felt like he was looking out of someone else's eyes. "There's another definition."

"There is?" Brolley entered the word into her commplex, waited a moment, then looked up, her eyes wide. "A cure-all? You think—?"

"I think that when the Slaasriithi used the term 'theriac,' they were not using it incorrectly or fancifully."

Brolley leaned back on her exam stool. "Commodore—Caine, this has to be repor—"

"Suppressed." Riordan could barely believe the word had come out of his mouth. Just a day ago, he'd damned IRIS, and then Yan and her ilk, for doing what he was now suggesting. "Sit on it for a few weeks. After that, it's in your hands."

"*My* hands?" Brolley's laugh was ironic but genuine. "You of all people know that the powers-that-be are not going to allow *me* to decide what to do with this information. And if they did, suppressing it is the last thing I'd do."

"Then you'd better get ready for everyone with a terminal disease, or a crippling injury, or encroaching dementia, to come lining up at your doors like it's the new Lourdes."

Brolley bit her lip. The healer in her was clearly at war with the pragmatist. "Yeah. You have a point. A whole mess of points, actually. But even so, it's not up to me to hold back this information. This has to be—"

Caine leaned toward her. "If you share this, they won't let me leave Earth. Ever again."

Brolley's eyes searched his, probably looking for any hint of deceit or exaggeration. After two long seconds, she sighed, looked away. "All right. What's so important about this next trip of yours?"

Caine told her. With admirable brevity, he thought.

Brolley's frown was back, deeper and more frustrated than

ever. "Well, that's just great. So now I've got to choose between preventing you from retrieving the love of your life—"

"—*and* mother of my son—"

Brolley closed her eyes. "—or withholding information on what may prove to be a ground-breaking panacea."

Riordan nodded. "But only until I'm out-system."

"Yes," she agreed, eyeing him. "Out-system and away from our labs, our ability to use you to help replicate—"

"Christa, did you hear how you just phrased that: 'our ability to use you'? That's the other thing I'm worried about: becoming a lab animal."

"Caine, I'm sorry, but whatever is in you—if it can be isolated—could change everything."

"You have no idea how many times before and after the war I heard some variation of the phrase 'if you do this, it could change everything.'" Riordan closed his eyes. "You already have a pint of my blood and plenty of other samples. That should get you started."

"And then? Caine, I hate to be blunt, but what if you get killed on this mission? Should Earth lose this unique opportunity just because you die in some accident?"

Riordan met her stare. He saw Elena's eyes. He looked away, toward the window: it was Elena's eyes, not his, that he saw reflected there. Even after shutting his eyes, he still saw Elena's. "Christa, the Slaasriithi had a major debate over using the theriac. They had lots of restrictions against doing so." He opened his eyes. "Now I understand why."

"You mean, because we're not ready for it?" She was frowning again.

"Well, are we? And more to the point, who's to decide that? And how hastily? For instance, what if your research shows that it will cost a billion credits a dose. Who gets it? Based on what criteria?"

"I don't know. That's not my decision. That's why I have to send it up the tree."

"And you will. I am just asking you to keep it under wraps for a few weeks. At most."

"Yes—until you're out of our reach."

"And isn't that my right?"

Brolley shook her head. "Caine, I don't know if I can agree. What this could mean—"

"May be wonderful. May be a disaster. May be something we

won't be able to replicate, no matter how hard we try and how much we spend. But you can be sure of this: when you submit this report, the powers-that-be are going to put this under wraps and sit on it for months. Because they're not going to act until they learn if the theriac can be extracted from my samples and until they have some idea about how it works."

"And if there's none in your blood, or if we can't figure it out from what we find there, we'd need you here. For research."

Riordan leaned back. "Listen to yourself, Christa. You may mean that in a humane context, but tell me: how many of your colleagues would be tempted to suggest vivisection if all other experimental avenues prove fruitless?"

The color drained out of Brolley's face. "Shit."

Caine held in a sigh of relief. "You know I'm right. You know they'd recommend that, given what's at stake."

She was motionless, her face pinched, for several long seconds. Then she nodded. "I can't deny it. Most wouldn't, but some would. And a lot of those are the power players. That's how it is in research. Ruthlessness and monomania tend to get promoted fastest. And then run roughshod over human rights and social wisdom almost every time. Okay. I agree. But I'm not sure I can give you the blackout period you need."

A new wave of cold passed through Riordan. "Why not?"

"Because your exam results are already in the system. They get centralized *before* they are sent to me, not the other way around."

"And you can't get to the central records and delete or hide them for a while?"

"I'm a doctor, not a hacker. Sorry."

Riordan thought. "When you get unusual results like this, and you want to confirm them before they get passed on to other doctors or institutions, what happens?"

Brolley frowned. "I delay authorization of release if the results are incomplete or need further review by a specialist. Which I could easily justify, given how whacky these results are. I could claim that I was researching precedents and trying to schedule you for a second set of comparative tests. That would keep the results under the rug for a while, but would create another problem."

"What's that?"

"How do I clear you for your trip if I can't release the results of your physical?"

Riordan thought back to the various examinations he'd been subjected to over the years. "Except for when I've returned from beyond the CTR quarantine line, all I ever see is a report that my physical was passed."

Brolley shook her head. "That's a general physical, like the kind you are given before participating in a sport or entering service. You got the works, today. There's no way to hide that."

"Okay, but can we change the order in which you conducted the two levels of physical?"

Brolley folded her arms. "'Conducted the *two* levels of physical?' I only conducted one, and you know it."

Caine shoved off the exam table. "Let's say I came in here to simply get a general physical. Which I could have chosen. In the course of that, you would have noticed the absence of my scars. That would then have prompted the complete physical. But it would have occurred *after* you had given me a clean bill of health on the general physical."

Brolley raised an eyebrow. "So now you're asking me to lie about performing two physicals?"

Caine started removing his shirt. "You can perform the general physical now, if you like."

She waved for him to stop. "No, no. I already know you are in very—well, impossibly—good health." She nodded. "I'll report that you passed a general physical. That will clear you for travel."

"Great. And thank you. This means a lot to me." Caine shook her hand, headed for the door.

Brolley called after him. "I can't guarantee how long I can keep the full results under wraps, though. So don't waste any time."

"I won't. You can count on that."

Brolley smiled, waved. "Well then, nice meeting you. And bon voyage."

Caine returned the smile and the wave, and exited at a brisk pace. Now more than ever, he had to leave as quickly as possible.

Or he was never going to get off Earth at all.

As soon as the door closed and Riordan's footsteps faded from hearing, Christa Brolley went to her desk, tapped the screen.

The commplex brightened. "Ready," it affirmed.

"Voice grade only. Encrypt and scramble. Connect to secure contact number fourteen."

"Connecting." A pause. "Secure contact number fourteen requires authorization code."

"Submit code."

"Submitting. Contact established."

A new voice answered: the audio filtering made it sound like a drunk talkbot. "Sign is ginger blossom."

"Countersign is cherry ale. Subject examination is complete. Am forwarding results by live courier. Require temporary removal of report from central records. Can you comply?"

"We can comply. When did the subject depart?"

"One minute ago." She couldn't keep from asking, "Am I done now?"

"Negative. Further instructions may follow. Disconnect so we can purge record of this contact."

"Disconnecting," confirmed Christa Brolley, who severed the link, powered down the commplex, and, elbows propped on her desk, leaned her head forward into her trembling hands.

Chapter Ten

JULY 2123
WASHINGTON D.C., EARTH

The approaching aircar's body was coated with smartpixel laminate; it was a restless canvas of ever-changing and eye-gouging ads. Downing's two new guards stared at the clearance code the vehicle was sending to the taller one's dataslate, watched as it was checked against and matched the travel permit code they'd received twenty minutes earlier. She turned toward Richard. "That's your ride, Director Downing." Although it was a statement, the rising tone at the end made it sound like a question.

Downing affected to stare at the aircar in surprise. "It's not what I was expecting either, Ms. Oruna. I just hope it flies better than it looks."

She smiled. "Enjoy your time out of the box, sir."

"I shall indeed," he answered cheerily, presenting his wristlink to the other security officer. The man swept a control wand over the government-issued wearable as the vehicle landed, kicking up dust and grit. "Your perimeter constraint is deactivated, Director Downing. It reactivates in three hours. Don't be late, sir."

"I don't dare," Richard answered as he walked toward the vehicle, one of its gull-wing doors rising. "I'm told this carriage turns into a pumpkin after that."

The male guard stared, either unfamiliar with the reference or too glum to care. Agent Oruna grinned with one side of her mouth.

Downing made his way around the far side of the dark-windowed aircar, waved as he slipped into it.

As the door closed, he turned to the solitary passenger. "I take it this is one of your cars, Captain Weber?"

David Weber—who, in a room full of big men would still have stood out as an especially big man—shrugged with what Downing presumed to be his good shoulder. "In a manner of speaking, Director." He aimed his voice at the audio pickup. "Q-command, commence route."

The air car's reply was closer to normal speech than most airtaxis, one of the telltale signs that it only looked like a public conveyance. "Commencing trip to Capitol Mall. ETA: four minutes."

Downing watched as the office building that was actually a safe house dropped away, shrank, and became just another glimmering tile in the mirror-windowed architectural collage that was Chantilly, Virginia. "Thank you for agreeing to see me on such short notice."

"Well, Mr. Downing, you *are* still a director."

Downing exhaled a weak laugh. "In name only, Captain, in name only."

Weber shook his head. "Not to all of us, sir." The gray-green eye on the right side of his face was hardly more expressive than the patch where the left one should have been. That cyclopean gaze softened a moment later. "Besides, sir, we have a mutual friend."

"Which one, Captain? Rinehart? Sukhinin? Phalon? Seaver, even?"

"I suppose I should correct my statement, Director Downing. We have quite a few mutual friends. Better you don't know which one made today's ride possible. Now, what can I do for you?"

That was Weber—a.k.a. The Patch—to a tee: discreet, formal, businesslike, and more heart than he was usually willing to show. Bloody hell, he could have been English. "I need some requests—which are in fact requirements—processed quickly."

"I can help with that, Director. Do they concern Commodore Riordan?"

Downing could not keep from smiling. "In fact, they do. Shall I transmit them to your wristlink?"

Weber nodded, watched as Downing started the transfer. "Sir, because of the channels I monitor, I think I have an idea of what those requests might be."

Downing looked up, raised an eyebrow. "Then I'm sure you are also aware that any request that involves another organization—let us say, the State Department—should be allowed to move at a normal pace. To avoid detection."

Weber nodded. "Yes. But if my latest reports are accurate, that may not be a luxury that we—or Commodore Riordan—can afford."

Downing forgot about his datalink, looked full into Weber's face. *What have you heard, David? And why won't you say it straight out?* He spent an extra second waiting, hoping that continued scrutiny might wring another useful fact or two out of the big man.

But Weber's was a good face for playing poker, for keeping secrets. Many of which pertained to the mysterious combination of good fortune and sheer will he had used to rebuild his life after having a control frigate blasted out from under him at the Battle of Barnard's Star in 2119. One of the most seasoned officers on station, he had been the deputy commander of the contingent of manned hulls that had remained behind to control the decoy ships.

Not much more than armed frameworks, the decoys had engaged the Arat Kur fleet, ultimately convincing them that they had destroyed most of Earth's force in being. However, because the decoys were uncrewed, they had required direction from control frigates. And since authentically swift reaction times required that the range between them remained under 150,000 kilometers, the much smaller frigates had come under fire from the Arat Kur equivalent of capital ships. They had been ruthlessly savaged.

That Weber survived at all was a near miracle; he was one of only six from his own ship. That he was walking straight and tall and not merely performing but excelling at his tasks as leader of the Oversight Directorate of Interbloc Network Systems was in full defiance of the most optimistic clinical projections of his recovery.

And yet, some part of him had not come back from beyond the farther orbits of Barnard's Star: that part which used to laugh long and deep and was fond of puns that left entire wardrooms groaning. That part of David Weber was still MIA, out beyond the wreckage of his ship and the monomolecular remains of his crew.

Weber's return stare showed no sign of relenting. "Sir, any actions on Riordan's behalf must be completed swiftly. And they will be impossible to conceal entirely."

Downing nodded. "I presumed that, Captain." He glanced at Weber's datalink. "Tell me, can it be done?"

Weber was scanning the requests. "It has to be, sir. So, yes. Failure is not an option."

Those had been Weber's last words before he went off-line at Barnard's Star. "That's something of a motto of yours, isn't it, David?"

Weber touched his eyepatch distractedly. He answered in a lower, slower voice. "There have been times I wish it wasn't." Then, as an afterthought: "Sir."

Downing would have liked to pat the poor fellow on what was said to be an entirely artificial knee, envisioned himself doing it: a wiry scarecrow tapping a gigantic partial-tin-man in a feeble gesture of solace. He decided against it. "That motto has come with a heavy cost," Downing observed soberly.

"Honor demanded no less, sir," Weber replied. "We'll get it done."

Downing nodded, looked out the window. The Reflecting Pool loomed up at them as they dropped toward the vertipad just behind the Lincoln Memorial. "I say, Weber, I'm wondering if you could by any chance initiate a scan for—"

Weber was already looking up from his palmtop. "Riordan's right there, sir. Near the Vietnam War Memorial." As the door started to rise, he added, "Watch your step, Director."

Downing had the impression that Weber was not just referring to exiting the aircar.

Caine detected Downing's approach more out of reflex and instinct than a conscious application of training. Riordan turned to face away from him, began walking slowly through the crowds lining the south side of the Reflecting Pool.

Within half a minute, strolling slightly faster, Downing had caught up to him. They slowed in sync with each other, keeping two loud groups of tourists on either side of them.

"I thought you were sequestered," Caine said softly, not turning to look at Richard.

"I am. But it's the kinder variety. You can get out for a stroll now and again, enjoy the occasional conjugal visit." Downing's weak sputter of sardonic laughter sounded more weary than bitter.

"I see. Well then, since meeting here isn't wild coincidence, I don't know whether I should be honored or worried."

Downing stared up at the sun, said casually, "You have to leave."

"I know. Just as soon as I'm able to—"

"No, Caine. You can't wait until you're 'able to.'"

Riordan almost missed a step. "I'm not sure what that means."

"It means that if you hang about to dot all the i's and cross all the t's, you will be too late. You have to go now. Before the Interbloc Working Group can announce new hearings and slap a new sequestration order on you."

Riordan glanced briefly at Downing. *Is this timing chance, or does he still have enough connections to—?* "Have you heard?"

Now it was Downing who looked surprised. "Heard what?"

"The results of my physical. At Walter Reed."

Downing shook his head. "No. Tell me."

Caine did.

Toward the end of Caine's one-minute synopsis, Downing appeared so stunned that he almost veered off the promenade. "So that's why The Patch was pushing," he murmured.

"Who or what is 'The Patch'?"

"Doesn't matter." Downing was already refocused. In fact, he seemed more focused than Caine had seen him since the war. "It so happens I can get you out."

"So you've said."

"No, Caine, I'm talking about a radically accelerated timeline. Even more accelerated than I was assuming five minutes ago. That Slaasriithi treatment might be much more than an elixir; it could be the bloody fountain of youth. And they will not allow you to leave when they realize that you are the only known source."

"Yep. That's why I'm trying to leave. But it takes time to get the State Department to—"

Downing turned and took Riordan by the shoulders. "Caine, this is no longer about how fast you can act. The only question is how fast *I* can act. And, with the help of some friends, the answer is, 'very fast indeed.'"

Caine frowned. "Just *how* fast is 'very fast indeed'?"

Downing checked his wristlink, nodded at what he saw there. "We'll have you on your way tonight."

PART TWO

Collective Space and Earth
September 2123–July 2124

CUSTODES

Quis custodiet ipsos custodes?
(Who shall guard the guards themselves?)

Chapter Eleven

Caine flinched awake. The alternating tone of the "all-clear" wasn't deafening, but neither was it a sound one could sleep through. But that was just fine with Riordan: it meant that the shift-carrier *Down-Under* had completed its transit from Wolf 359 and was safely beyond CTR space.

Riordan propped himself up in his combination acceleration couch and bunk, felt a subtle sideways tug; the ship's rotational habitat, or rohab, was slowly resuming spin. He resisted the urge to lie back down. Drowsiness was exerting an even greater force than the slowly increasing gravity equivalent. By scheduling shifts toward the end of passenger sleep cycles, commercial carriers minimized tumbles and injuries from post-transit vertigo.

However, *Down-Under* was currently a commercial hull in name only. She had been leased by the Commonwealth government for a logistical run to Wolf 359 and then the naval depot at Lalande 21185. Most of the eighty conscious passengers were civilian contractors who disembarked at the first stop, hired to update the automated facilities there. The remainder were naval personnel who were subsequently briefed that there would be a previously undisclosed stop before they reached the naval depot: Wolf 424. What they did not know was that a Dornaani ship would be waiting there for Caine. Hopefully.

Riordan unstrapped, rose into a sitting position. The gravity

77

equivalent was already close to point two gee. If Captain Kim Schoeffel ran the ship according to civilian norms, she'd stop the steady increase when it reached point three, then push it up another tenth of a gee every half hour or so.

Caine stood, moved carefully to his stateroom's locker, pulled out a civilian duty suit fitted with an EVA hood and liner: his invariable daywear. The civilian contractors had joked about it amiably, alternately ensuring him that the hull was leakproof and that the war was over. Riordan had just nodded, smiled, and silently hoped they'd have no reason to regret their jibes.

He attached a drinking bulb to the tap, filled it to half. As he sipped the water and swirled it around in his mouth, the door's courtesy pager emitted a single tone. "It's open."

The pressure door slid aside and Ed Peña entered. Slowly. Which was how he did most everything, unless the tempo of events demanded otherwise.

Riordan had seen that occur only once. Ed had been at the helm of the cutter Downing requisitioned to get Caine to *Down-Under* before she began her preacceleration burn to Wolf 359. When DWC drones began threatening to obstruct their rendezvous vector, Peña had gone into piloting overdrive, then alternately flummoxed and fooled the Jovian traffic controllers until the cutter was docked. As soon as the unwelcome excitement was over, Ed had slunk back into contented lassitude: evidently, his preferred state of being.

Ed waited patiently just inside the hatchway. "You're wanted in the captain's ready room."

Riordan made for the door. "Why didn't the comms adjutant just call me on the intraship?"

"Same reason you're being asked to the ready room instead of the bridge. To keep you from being seen in places or doing things that would suggest you're an important passenger." He hadn't appended his sentences with "commodore" since they'd stepped aboard *Down-Under*. If at all possible, Riordan's journey was to be incognito. But Caine could still hear Ed's unvoiced addition of the military title, could sense it in the small nod with which he ended almost every sentence.

Riordan nodded back and led the way.

Walking a few dozen meters keelward put them in the rotranzo, or rotational transfer zone: the juncture where the parts of the ship that were rotating interfaced with those that were not. They stepped quickly from one slideway to the next, each slowing them until they were within the main, keel-following hull, motionless and in zero gee. Once there, Caine and Ed relied upon magboots and handholds to stay in contact with the deck.

As they approached the ready room, the bulkhead-rated door slid open before Caine could touch the courtesy pager. Captain Schoeffel waved them in. "Good shift?" she inquired.

Riordan smiled. "Can't say. I slept through it."

Peña shrugged.

Schoeffel returned Caine's smile after shooting an annoyed glance at Peña. "We've finished our first set of scans. No sign of your ride, Commodore."

Caine raised an eyebrow. "'Commodore?' I thought I was 'Mister' Riordan."

She nodded at the closed door. "Benefit of privacy. I figure if we're going to speak openly about your mission, we can dispense with the civilian labels they wanted to stick on you."

"That's very kind, Captain. How can I help you?"

"Well, you can start by telling me what we should be looking for. We've already swept the EM spectrum for any sign of a beacon or buoy. Nothing. So either your friends aren't here yet or they are waiting and watching. Any idea which it is?"

Caine shook his head. "Sorry, not a clue. The invitation was pretty short on details. It wasn't even clear that they would wait here throughout the entire date range they gave us. And there was nothing about methods of signaling or their likely coordinates."

Schoeffel frowned. "For a supposed super-race, they don't seem very organized."

Riordan shrugged one shoulder. "The Dornaani have their own ways of doing things. And they don't always clue us in ahead of time."

Schoeffel waved Caine toward a chair, included Peña in a second gesture that looked a lot like an afterthought. "So when they do show up, what should I expect?"

"Expect the Dornaani ship to be small, tiny by our standards. The one we've seen most frequently is one hundred eighty meters from bow to stern. Widest beam is at the rear: about eighty meters. Best estimates put it at about one hundred thirty thousand cubic meters."

"Okay, but how big are their shift-capable hulls?"

Riordan smiled. "Captain, that *is* a shift hull."

"So they're about fifteen percent as long as we are and ten percent of our volume. And they have longer shift range."

"I can personally confirm a sixteen-light-year range. I don't know if that's at the top, middle, or bottom of their performance spectrum."

Schoeffel's features moved past incredulity, approached something akin to terror. "That exceeds the theoretical maximum of any shift drive built according to Wasserman's paradigms."

Riordan nodded. "It's pretty clear they use something else. Transition on them is not like on our ships. Or Arat Kur or Slaasriithi. You don't feel that dip in your consciousness and then the wave of vertigo as you come back up. It's as if your awareness is shuddering, like it's a stone skipping across a pond."

Schoeffel leaned forward. "Any idea why that is?"

Riordan nodded slowly, using that moment to consider. Schoeffel's questions were nearing the limit of what she needed to know for the mission. Additionally, Caine had to be careful that his remarks did not raise suspicions that Alnduul and his fellow Custodians had allowed Earth's experts to discover the secrets behind making deep space shifts. "I heard some of our researchers speculating that if the Dornaani drive doesn't use stellar gravity wells to navigate, then its extreme precision could enable a rapid series of microshifts, rather than one big jump."

Schoeffel exhaled. "That could be what causes the shuddering of consciousness: a string of split-second blips in and out of space normal. Damn." She seemed to stir from a daze. "So, do they even need to preaccelerate?"

"No, but a 'standing shift' seems to put lots more wear on their drive. So they don't use it much."

Schoeffel shook her head. "Do the Dornaani have any more magic tricks I should be aware of?"

"Your sensors could have a hard time picking them up. Their hulls are unipiece, streamlined, and evince properties of both thermoflage and chromaflage. Our analysts call it comboflage."

Schoeffel's face was stony. "So, the short version is that if they don't want us to see them, we won't."

Caine shrugged. "Anything else, Captain?"

"Not at the moment, Commodore. Except, that I want you on hand when they finally show up, to make sure that everything goes smoothly."

Anything to keep me heading toward Elena. But what he said was, "I'll be there, Captain."

Chapter Twelve

DECEMBER 2123
REFUELING ORBIT AROUND PLANET IV, WOLF 424 A

For the thirty-second time, Riordan started his day at Wolf 424 A by turning on the commplex. Nine hours ago, just before rolling into his bunk, he'd finished his fourth complete read-through of all the available material on the Dornaani, taking notes as he went. Today, he'd start—

The walls emitted the distinctive double yowl of the emergency klaxon: unidentified contact.

Riordan was on his feet, moving toward his rack. "Q-command, hi-gee configuration." His bunk began converting into an acceleration couch, a pressure-rated cover rotating up into seal-ready position.

Just as he reached it, his intercom chirped through a flurry of tones: message from the bridge.

"Riordan here."

"Commodore, the captain asks you join her. All possible haste, sir."

Riordan smiled. "About time the Dornaani got here."

"No, sir. It's not the Dornaani. It's the Arat Kur."

Peña was already on the bridge when Riordan arrived, half drifting, half glide-walking into the tiered chamber. Ed reached out an arm to ensure that Caine stopped where he intended.

Riordan waved it off as he got a grip on the intended handhold, smiled crookedly. "Not a *total* newb."

Peña shrugged, didn't say anything. It was unclear if that was simply his natural taciturnity or because he decided not to contradict his superior.

Schoeffel came swim-dancing in from the other side, hooked a finger at Caine. "Come take a look." She adjusted her drift with a slight deck-kick and bulkhead push; that angled her down toward the sensor station. She jabbed a finger at a cluster of five red motes. "Those bogeys are Arat Kur, or I'm a shave tail."

Riordan took hold of the back of the sensor officer's seat, pulled himself closer. "Bring up whatever data you have on their thruster emissions."

"Mister—eh, Commodore Riordan, like I told the captain, they're still two light-minutes out. We don't have enough—"

Schoeffel nodded at the officer. "Do it." Face suddenly devoid of expression, he complied.

Riordan glanced at the density of the particle trail, the heat of the exhaust, and its approximate shape. Nodding, he checked the acceleration of the oncoming craft. "Definitely not one of ours. Anything we have with that kind of performance leaves a much bigger exhaust smudge and lots more particles." He looked up at Schoeffel's face, saw eagerness and concern in equal measures. "How'd *you* identify them at this range, Captain?"

"Same way you did: saw roach combat drones up close and personal, four years ago."

Riordan glanced at the navplot near the center of the bridge. "So where the hell did they come from?"

Schoeffel drifted toward the faux 3-D chart table, shrank the scale. Both of Wolf 424's red dwarfs came into view. The guidon indicating *Down-Under*'s position was tucked behind what appeared to be a blue marble orbiting the closer star. She pointed to it. "That's us, snugged in on the dark side of the only gas giant, not quite as big as Neptune." She pointed to the five red motes. The computer projection traced their known vectors and then extrapolated backward, showed them as emerging from around the far side of Wolf 424 A. "Didn't see them coming, given the angle."

"The angle?" asked Ed, who had drifted closer.

Schoeffel pointed impatiently at distant Wolf 424 B, which was mostly eclipsed by the primary star. "The planet and two stars are almost in syzygy. From our position at the gas giant, Wolf

424 B is almost in perfect opposition and only a few degrees off the ecliptic."

Ed nodded. "So, when they came from the far side of 424 A, probably a week or so ago, they had the other star—424 B—at their back. Sensors couldn't pick them out."

Schoeffel nodded. Her expression suggested that Peña had risen slightly in her opinion. "Even if they were under thrust, our sensors would have had to stay fixed on exactly the right spot to have any chance of noticing any spectral wiggle their exhausts would have caused." She glanced at Riordan. "Sorry, sir. This tub's arrays are nothing like milspec."

Caine nodded. "Which they were counting on. Just as they were counting on our main hull—and therefore, the main array—being behind the gas giant, shielding ourselves from flares while we refueled. Textbook. What do you think they are, Captain?"

"Drones. No doubt about it. Ratio of acceleration to approximate mass says those platforms are extremely compact. No room for life support systems."

Riordan looked at the navplot again. "I agree. Which is why there's probably another piece on the game board that we haven't seen yet."

"Their shift-carrier, sir?" The sensor officer pointed behind Wolf 424 A. "Almost still on the far side, where we can't see her."

Riordan shook his head. "I'm thinking there's something a lot closer to us."

The captain frowned at the navplot, then raised an eyebrow. "A control craft."

Riordan nodded. "We are almost two AU from 424 A: sixteen light-minutes, more or less. If these are unpiloted vehicles, then their actions are being controlled in one of three ways. One: from their probable point of origin, which means a thirty-two-minute command cycle. Two: they are in a fully autonomous attack mode. Or, three: there's a control ship that's probably within a few light-seconds."

Schoeffel nodded. "The last option is the only one that makes sense. Those drones will be dead twenty times over if they have to wait half an hour for orders. On the other hand, autonomous controls might fail to engage the priority target." She looked meaningfully at Riordan. "But if they've got a control ship out there, it must be lying doggo."

Riordan scanned the plot. "Does this gas giant have any satellites?"

"None. And only one other starward planet within an AU."

"Then it's probably a very small craft maintaining a position on the opposite side of this gas giant."

Schoeffel shook her head. "I doubt it. We've had automated fuel skimmers making runs around the bright side. Never got a sensor return."

Riordan raised an eyebrow. "Were the skimmers running autonomously?"

Schoeffel nodded, then grinned ruefully. "Yeah. Rudimentary sensor package slaved to even more rudimentary auton." She maneuvered closer to him. "That means they could have doggo drones back there with the control ship."

Riordan nodded. "Expect these bogeys to make a pass at such high relative velocity that you have damn little chance to hit them. The doggo drones could then swing around from the blind side of the gas giant and clean up whatever the first group didn't get."

Schoeffel glanced at the plot. "Judging from the bogeys' rate of approach, they'll cover those two light-seconds in about ten minutes. At most."

Riordan nodded. "Right. So how can I—?"

"You can go with Mr. Peña, Commodore," Schoeffel interrupted. She nodded to Peña, who drifted unusually close to Riordan. "We have a contingency for this, but we don't have a lot of time." She nodded aft. "So, smartly now."

"Captain—" Riordan stopped, momentarily caught between his resolve to survive and save Elena, and his reflex to never leave comrades to fight in his stead.

Apparently sensing that, Schoeffel pushed closer, her breath soured by anxiety. "Commodore, you've got to go *now*."

"But the mission—"

"You *are* the mission," Ed added from behind. It was the first time Caine had heard any emphasis in his otherwise monotone voice. "C'mon, sir. We've got to go."

Riordan felt rage, gratitude, shame, looked to find words, couldn't, knew every passing second was an unacceptable risk.

He turned and launched himself into a long glide back toward the entry.

✧　　✧　　✧

Once they were inside the keel-following shuttle-car, Peña nodded for Caine to strap in. Caine did, just as the car's sudden acceleration almost threw him out of his seat. They were pulling more than a gee.

Peña smiled slightly. "The Old Lady has overridden the safety parameters. We'll be there in about ninety seconds."

"Where?"

"Aft cargo moorings."

Riordan frowned, then realized. "Not all of those bulk cargo containers are filled with routine stores, are they?"

Peña shook his head, watched the overhead transit monitor plot their progress down the keel.

Riordan tapped his collarcom. "Access command channel. Authorization: Riordan One." Bridge chatter abruptly emerged from his tiny communicator, as well as one-sided conversations with engineering, flight operations, and gunnery. The latter was a woefully short exchange. As a commercial shift-carrier, *Down-Under* had no offensive systems, just point-defense fire lasers for splashing inbound warheads.

Peña seemed distracted by the chatter, as if he didn't want to listen to it but couldn't keep from doing so. When he saw Caine studying him, he looked away. Quickly.

Suddenly, Caine understood. "You and Schoeffel sure did have me fooled. Are you two still an item, or is that long past?"

Peña sighed. "Past. Had to be. Happened when we were serving."

"And you were enlisted and she was an officer?"

He shrugged. "You know how it is. Even if people are willing to look the other way, the stable boy still can't date the princess."

Riordan nodded. "You two make a pretty good team."

"We did. I guess we still do." The car braked hard, pushing them sideways against their straps. "Here we are. Move out. Sir."

Riordan threw off the restraints, took a long step to the opening door, and stopped in surprise. There, clearly visible beyond a double docking collar, was a short passageway he knew very well: the entry to his old ship, the *Puller*. But, even as Ed's hand locked firmly on his bicep and began propelling him forward into the boarding tube, Caine realized that although this was indeed a Wolfe-class corvette, it was not *Puller*. She had none of the same dings and dents. Or Slaasriithi modifications.

Ed explained. "There are three corvettes inside this cargo

container: *Mercer*, *Cradock*, and *Bridges*." They crossed over the coaming as the tempo of the clipped bridge chatter and preflight checks accelerated. "This corvette, *Mercer*, has extra fuel: she can sprint a long time." They headed aft. "The other two Wolfes are carrying double ordnance loads. We run, they fight."

"Then why are you leading me away from the bridge?"

"Because *Mercer* has also been retrofitted with an escape system."

Caine rounded the corner into what would have been, on any other Wolfe-class corvette, the last bunkroom—and saw a nightmare, instead. An escape pod. The kind that not only powered you swiftly away from a stricken ship, but automatically strapped you down and forced you into cryogenic suspension. "This isn't neces—"

Ed pushed him hard from behind. "I know you hate this, Commodore. If I'd been in an icebox as often as you have, I'd feel the same way." There was a loud *kra-thrunk*, a sudden sideways motion, and a shift in balance. "*Mercer*'s away, sir. You've got to get in. Now."

Riordan nodded, started stripping off his duty suit, hung on to the collarcom.

Schoeffel's voice was snapping rapid orders. "PDF batteries three and four, keep an eye on planet horizon to aft. Slower drones could come from that direction. *Cradock*, you have the ball when we go active with the remote arrays. Comms, I need redundant lascom links to all ships and platforms. Yolanda?"

"Flight here. What you need, Skipper?"

"Push those skimmers out further; make them look like patrolling hunter-drones."

"Yeah, well, I'll try."

"You do that. And stay in our shadow as long as you can."

"No argument there, *Down-Under*."

Then a voice that was more surprised than worried, more perplexed than urgent. "Captain, Sensor Ops here."

"I can see your code, Mister Guzman. What have you got?"

"I'm not sure, Captain. I—"

"Holy shit!" shouted another voice; the tone froze Riordan in place. "What the hell is *that*?"

"Energy spike. Range seven light-minutes. No! Range one light-min— Wait. This can't be—"

"It's the Dornaani!" yelled the XO, Malatesta.

"Or Ktor, or something else," Schoeffel said in a loud, grim voice. "Settle down. This could be a trick." The channel changed. Peña's own collarcom toned. "Eddie: is the package secure?"

"He's just about to—"

"Eddie, secure the damn package! *Now!*"

Peña put a hand on his holster. "I don't want to use the tranq gels, Commodore."

Riordan nodded, felt *Mercer* buck and rock: evasive action. He jumped into the cryopod, flopping facedown on the belly couch. Orders and counterorders screamed out of his collarcom. One of the shuttle pilots yelled about a new bogey—then static.

Peña slapped the pod actuator, shouted, "Package secure!"

Restraints went over Caine's arms, shoulders, waist, legs, and snapped tight. The belly couch slammed forward, locked in place as the cover descended and sealed overhead: an egg bounded within an egg.

The collarcom was still emitting commands and curses and shouts about the Arat Kur and the Dornaani and the new bogeys when Riordan felt the first needle go into his arm: just as brisk, efficient, and icy as the first time, five years ago.

The synthetic morphine rushed into him and then flowed rapidly outward into his extremities, a sensation at once warm and treacherous as he tried to hold on to thoughts that might very well be his last.

Connor's sun-brightened smile. Elena's high cheekbones and fine nose. Then Caine was there with her, their eyes and their lips moving closer, closer—but instead of a kiss, their faces flowed together, merged. And became Connor's.

Just before darkness washed in from everywhere, drowning everything.

Chapter Thirteen

Consciousness.

More accurately, just a vague awareness that he existed. True consciousness—the immense web of associations that create selfhood—followed an instant later, but was still indistinct. Then, with a rush, he was inside that web, inhabiting it—

He awoke with a gasp, tearing himself out of an ink-black dream of blind drowning—

"You are safe, Caine Riordan."

Caine realized his eyes were already open. The light was soft and diffuse, and the ceiling—if that's what it was—curved gently over him, a muted white. Memory summoned the face that went along with the voice: "Alnduul?"

"Yes. Be at your ease. Allow the restoratives to hasten your recovery. Distress impedes their function."

Riordan discovered he was lying upon a slightly yielding surface, his body covered by a thin, but surprisingly warm, sheet. Alnduul's large eyes were visible over the twin crests of his draped feet.

Memory rushed back in. "The ship, the *Down-Under*, is it—?"

Alnduul rose. "Captain Schoeffel sends her regards and wishes you 'god speed.'" Centered beneath his large eyes, the Dornaani's single nostril flared slightly. "The shift-carrier and all but one of its subcraft survived the encounter."

"I suspect we have you to thank for that."

The Dornaani's head bowed stiffly. Seen from that top-down angle, it was reminiscent of a teardrop, the narrow end a tapering, postcranial ridge. "We did intercede. But it should never have occurred."

"What do you mean?"

Alnduul's mouth, a flexible and unsightly lamprey sucker, pulled back from its extruded position, became a brittle rictus. "We arrived at the star you catalogue as Wolf 424 A two weeks before the arrival window. However, our antimatter stocks were lower than planned and it was necessary to return to the Collective and refuel, which took far longer than it should have. The ship that deposited the attack drones arrived and hid during our absence. The fault was ours."

Caine raised himself up on his elbows. As he did, the bed—if that's what it was—rose up to support him. "You could hardly have expected an Arat Kur attack."

"That does not absolve us of failing to be present. Besides, it was not the Arat Kur who attacked you."

Riordan frowned. "Alnduul, those drones were Arat Kur. No doubt about it."

"They were Arat Kur craft, but they were neither provided nor controlled by the Arat Kur themselves." One of the four reedlike fingers of Alnduul's left hand gestured toward the deck: a negation. "Both the Arat Kur and your own postwar monitors indicate that all their interstellar craft were accounted for during the two months preceding the attack. This is confirmed by our own intelligence.

"However, hundreds of their drones were arrogated by your government for technical study. They are held in various secret locations. One of those was doubtless the source of the attack drones."

Riordan's stomach knotted. "But that means it had to be one of our shift-carriers that ferried them to Wolf 424 A. So it must still be there. It would take at least thirty days to preaccelerate."

"It is presumed to be hiding. Wolf 424 A and B both boast numerous airless worlds and satellites, as well as asteroids large enough to conceal a dozen human shift-carriers." Alnduul considered Riordan gravely. "It is distressing to see that members of your own species remain determined to end your life, Caine Riordan. Do you require further rest, or are you ready to move about?"

"I'm ready, but I'm surprised Schoeffel didn't request your help in trying to find the shift-carrier."

"She was unwilling to incur either the delay or risk to do so," Alnduul answered as he led them through the opening iris valve into the curved corridor beyond. "Besides, I could not have complied."

Riordan stared. "You would have refused?"

The Dornaani's outer eyelids nictated twice, so forcefully and rapidly that they made an audible *snik-snik!* "I would have been glad to render aid, but it is beyond my mandate to interfere in what is a purely human matter."

Riordan glanced over at his host. "But the attackers were in neutral space and you're a Custodian. A Senior Mentor."

"I am," the Dornaani confirmed. "At least for now."

Caine slowed. "What's happened?"

Alnduul did not reduce his pace. "Consequences of the failed Convocation, and the invasion of your homeworld, continue to unfold. Even in the Collective."

"And continue to impact your fortunes, it seems."

"That was inevitable." Alnduul waved two casual fingers in the wake of that assertion. "As we move deeper into the Collective, you will attain a deeper understanding of the situation."

Riordan hoped his friend was correct. "So when do we start?"

"Start?" Alnduul halted before an iris valve so finely crafted that its scalloped sections seemed to be one seamless surface.

"I mean, start our journey."

The Dornaani's eyes cycled slowly. "We already have." He waved a hand at the portal.

The valve dilated and Alnduul advanced into the compartment beyond, gesturing toward what looked like a cross between a couch and a cocoon. "Be seated, if you wish."

But Riordan was rooted in the doorway, flat-footed, staring.

This larger compartment and its machinery were also streamlined. However, the words "compartment" and "machinery" didn't really seem to fit. Caine had the sensation of standing inside a slightly recontoured egg, and the machinery was wholly unlike the tightly fitted utilitarian controls that typified a human bridge. It resembled the appointments of a trendy entertainment room: multipurpose furniture; sleek surfaces made of smart materials that adjusted to the posture and position of the crew; dynamically reconfigurable controls and readouts that, when inactive, vanished, leaving the surface featureless.

Only the four startlingly detailed holograms suggested that it was a working bridge. Three were straightforward: a comprehensive display of the current stellar system, the neighborhood of nearby stars, and a constantly rotating view of the hull. The fourth appeared to be a geometric mobile made of bright, shifting geometric shapes.

Alnduul wandered over to that floating collection of interfaced spheres and disks and touched two lightly. The mobile morphed; the spheres transformed into tetrahedrons that spun, bulged, narrowed in response to changes in a slightly tilted disk and a few dancing motes that intermittently linked them. Caine stared at the display, felt like a toddler facing an unfathomable device that adults operated with ease.

Alnduul moved to one of the hybrid couch cocoons. It reconfigured into a saddle-shaped command chair. A tray of controls and readouts emerged from its seamless side. "You look concerned, Caine Riordan."

"How do you control the ship if its smart materials are damaged?"

By way of answer, Alnduul touched one of the few non-dynamic controls on the side of his chair. The section of the deck closest to the bow rose up, revealing a dense cluster of more familiar interfaces, and two Dornaani chairs. "This more conventional control station can also be raised and activated manually. There is another in the auxiliary bridge. And in the event that we lose remote sensing..." The room's forward-sloping bulkhead seemed to ripple, then peeled back in reticulated segments. Like a lobster impossibly hitching up its skirts, it revealed the stars.

Caine smiled out through the oversized cockpit blister, then pushed himself over to the astrographic position hologram, the largest of the four. He pointed into the slowly rotating blizzard of multihued chips of light. "So, are we at the central star?"

Alnduul's couch finished transmogrifying itself by adding a high backrest. "We are. In your catalogs, it is listed as GJ 1119."

Caine frowned, examined the stars more closely. He had seen the center of this configuration many times before on the bridge of the *Down-Under*. "This system, it's only a few shifts beyond where you picked me up."

"That is correct."

For a moment, Riordan wasn't sure why this alarmed him.

Then his body provided the answer: subtle signs that he'd been in long-duration cryogenic suspension. Although the pervasive fishy-glycerin taste and smell of the blood substitute was not strong, his swollen eyes painted faint halos around bright lights, and there was a persistent, tingling itch in his extremities and mucosa. "How much time has passed since the ambush at Wolf 424, Alnduul?"

The Dornaani may have paused a moment. "Thirteen weeks."

Riordan turned to stare. "During which you've made—what— five shifts?" Riordan sat. The couch tried to turn into a chair; he pushed the smart fabric away. Like a spurned pet, it recoiled and lay quiet. "Alnduul, your ships can make a shift every week. What's been happening?"

The Dornaani's outer lids cycled very slowly. "The Collective remains divided over your visit. Upon returning to refuel, we were informed that clearance for unrestricted travel had not yet been granted."

"Wait, are you telling me that you don't have freedom of movement in your own systems?"

"I do, Caine Riordan. But not while carrying a human from the Consolidated Terran Republic. When your invitation was approved, I presumed freedom of movement was included. Shortly after our rendezvous, I was informed that this was not the case." Alnduul burbled fitfully. "The events surrounding your arrival stimulated considerable debate. The Senior Arbiters of the Collective have gathered at the regional capital to deliberate upon how they wish to interact with you."

"They're only doing that *after* I've arrived?"

Alnduul's mouth twisted unevenly. "I understand your frustration, and your desire to return home with Elena Corcoran as soon as possible. I can only assure you that we shall not waste a single hour in idleness."

Riordan nodded his thanks, smiled, felt rue bend his lips. "Actually, you don't need to accelerate *my* return. Hell, I'm not even sure I can go back."

"You refer to the risk of assassination?"

"Well . . . that, too."

Alnduul's inner eyelids nictated so rapidly that they seemed to flutter. "There is a further threat to you?"

Caine looked away. "When I was on Disparity, one of the

Slaasriithi worlds, my respirator was sabotaged and my lungs were infected with spores gengineered to incapacitate humans. I was as good as dead. Even the Slaasriithi physicians couldn't help me."

Alnduul sat in a very erect position. The focus of his large eyes was unnerving.

"They had a treatment, but it required special permission." Riordan shrugged. "None of us thought much of it at the time."

Alnduul's mouth had puckered into a rigid asterisk. "They administered the theriac."

Riordan nodded slowly. "That's what they called it, yes."

"And you have discovered that it has...other properties."

Caine nodded again, shared Brolley's findings. Alnduul sat unmoving during the silence that followed.

"Well?" Caine prompted.

Alnduul shut his eyes and left them that way, a reaction Riordan had never witnessed in a Dornaani. When Alnduul finally spoke, he did so slowly and quietly. "Since you arrived at Convocation, much of humanity's path has been generally foreseeable. But this could not be anticipated."

"So is the theriac a positive or a negative variable in your calculus?"

Alnduul kept his eyes closed. "It is too early to tell. The ultimate context of this event will be determined by what follows, not what came before." He opened his eyes. "You were wise to foresee that the theriac problematizes your return to the Consolidated Terran Republic. If your leaders are prudent, they will suppress news of its existence."

Riordan discovered a perverse impulse to become the devil's advocate. "Don't you think Earth has had just about enough information control for one century, Alndu—?"

"No!" It was the first time Riordan had ever heard a Dornaani raise his or her voice. "Do not be blinded by the debates over your government's control of information about exosapients, about IRIS, about your attending Convocation, about what came before the Accord, about the impossible plenitude of green worlds. Even the question of whether or not the Ktor should be revealed as humans pales in comparison.

"This, the theriac, has the power to change everything—unpredictably, cataclysmically—in the space of a single decade. No one can 'manage' such news; the theriac is the social equivalent of a force majeure. Once revealed, you cannot control the effects. The most your leaders can do is to ready your species for the changes that will follow as surely as thunder follows lightning."

During the war, Riordan had been marooned in space, but even then, he had not felt so gnawingly, chillingly isolated as he did now. "So, the theriac is not just a retroactive cure-all."

All of Alnduul's fingers jabbed downward. "No. It is much more than that. It confers a variety of unusual immunities. It resets and replenishes the rejuvenatory systems of your body." The Dornaani studied the look on Riordan's face. "No, it does not confer immortality, Caine Riordan, but you will not age as swiftly and, in time, there will be no way to conceal that discrepancy." He looked away. "We must put this topic aside for now. Let us turn to something practical: familiarizing you with my ship and its crew."

Caine rose, mentally readying himself for an extended meet and greet with scores of socially reserved Dornaani. "Okay, let's start with your crew." *While I still have enough energy to do so.*

"Very well. Because this is an unusual mission, my current crew is somewhat larger than usual."

Just great. "Well then, let's get going. We don't want to be at it for hours."

Alnduul stared at him. "Caine Riordan, counting myself, there are seven on the *Olsloov*. Afterward, I will familiarize you with our basic emergency systems, should there be a mishap during our shift to LP 60-179. Please follow me."

Chapter Fourteen

Ironically, the shift to LP 60-179 marked the end of the most uneventful period that Riordan had ever spent traveling between the stars.

The transit itself was so subtle that it didn't even wake him. The star, an unremarkable red dwarf, had no features or planets of interest, just a collection of small, sunbaked planetesimals and a single distant gas giant. The only redeeming aspect of their visit was that it lasted less than a week.

Riordan was happy to learn that the next system, BD +71 482 A, had a few elements of interest, including a marginally habitable moon orbiting a massive, tidally locked planet with a molten core. He had considered remaining awake for the shift, but a slightly larger than average meal of terrestrial foodstuffs—mashed potatoes, brussels sprouts, even a passably prepared brisket—put paid to that idea; postprandial grogginess triumphed over curiosity. Caine collapsed into his couch bunk with a sated sigh several hours before transit.

Riordan awoke to a steady, insistent moan: the *Olsloov*'s emergency klaxon. Fighting up through both a cognitive and visual haze, he discovered he was not alone in his compartment. The most unusual of the Dornaani crew, Irzhresht, was there in a posture of readiness. Almost as tall as Caine, she was extremely thin: a byproduct of hundreds of generations of ancestors who had been born in zero gee. Her longer arms and elongated head hovered urgently over Riordan. "May I assist?" she asked.

Riordan pushed through the mental murk. "I'm . . . I'll be fine."

The Dornaani stepped back, the irregular patterns on her cream-colored skin rippling as she moved. It was simply an optical illusion—her long torso was already subtly striped and mottled—but disconcerting nonetheless. Caine rubbed hard at his eyes. "Why the alarm?"

"Difficulties with landing." Irzhresht handed Riordan one of the flat, shining circlets that the Dornaani themselves wore when working around the ship. "Put this on. It is calibrated for you."

Riordan placed the silvery hemicircle on the crown of his head. When he removed his hand, the minimalist victor's laurels self-adjusted, snugging to the contours of his skull. "And what should I do with—?"

"Await instructions. Follow me." Irzhresht exited the compartment's already opening iris valve. Only two steps behind, Riordan noticed that her skin was becoming darker and that additional markings were becoming visible. Standing out in high relief against the ghostly slate-and-cream camo pattern was a constellation of circles (or planets? or spheres?) arrayed in a shifting dance of fractal variation. The enigmatic semiology had been orchestrated to invoke a common theme, but Riordan could not discern what that might be.

Irzhresht was hurrying aft along the curved passageway. Riordan glanced sideways as they passed a small orange hatch that led to a cluster of escape pods. "Irzhresht, where are we—?"

Alnduul's voice interrupted, from inside Caine's head. "Do not disturb Irzhresht unless it is absolutely necessary. She is coordinating a variety of tasks, even as you move. She is bringing you to the ventral interface bay."

"Why? And how the hell am I hearing your voice *inside* my head?"

"The control circlet you are wearing stimulates your mastoid process, thereby inducing sound that emerges in your middle ear. This ensures clarity in chaotic audial environments. You are wanted in the bay to provide assistance. There is a problem with our landing."

"Landing? We're at the planet already? I never even felt us shift."

"I am not surprised. You ate a considerable meal. Also, we arrived within twenty planetary diameters of our destination."

"You mean the moon with the breathable atmosphere?"

"Yes. As per our standard operating procedure, the local port authority was given control for *Olsloov*'s final approach. That is the problem."

Irzhresht turned, gestured that Riordan should proceed through a large bulkhead door. She continued on. Riordan nodded his thanks, but the spindly Dornaani was already stalking out of sight. Shrugging, Caine approached the door, and almost banged his forehead into it. Unlike the others on *Olsloov*, it had not opened automatically.

Alnduul sounded like he was situated between Caine's ears. "Tell it to open."

"Uh...'open,'" Riordan ordered the door.

"Not with words," Alnduul corrected. "Visualize what you wish it to do. A gesture may help focus your will."

Riordan pushed past the implausibility of a machine capable of reading his mind, waved the door aside as he imagined it complying.

The door opened. Not far beyond, Alnduul was strapping himself into a unipiece belt-and-backpack unit. Narrow control arms sprouted from its sides, each one ending in a joystick. "Your unit is to the right of the door. Don it."

Caine removed the device from its rack, wondered if he had ever heard anyone use the word "don" as a verb before, and fought against becoming mesmerized by the other contents of the bay. Sleek shuttle-sized craft lined the bulkhead walls, each moored in a hexagonal framework that resembled a reconfigurable geodesic grid. Impossibly small aircars fitted with clear canopies were snugged in smaller but similarly angular webworks. A wide variety of what appeared to be storage units were fixed to the deck, but Riordan could not bring himself to think of them as "crates." Smooth-surfaced orthogonal solids, they looked more like cubist evocations of basic geometric shapes.

"Caine Riordan, greater alacrity, please. Time is short."

Riordan finished wrestling his way into the strange backpack-belt device, felt the smart straps of the five-point harness cinch tight against his body. Now that he was actually wearing it, the device reminded him of an MMU, or manned maneuver unit.

But if this was for propelling oneself in space, then—"Alnduul, if we're about to go EVA, shouldn't we put on spacesuits first?"

Alnduul's extruded mouth seemed to shimmy around its axis; it was like watching a dancing lamprey, head-on. "Your conjecture is reasonable but inaccurate. We will not be operating in vacuum. We are already entering the atmosphere of the moon." He grasped the hand controls of his unit and floated off the deck. "These are the only means of reaching the planet's surface."

Riordan walked behind Alnduul, frowned. "Where's the thruster, the exhaust? I can't even feel any heat coming off the unit."

"That is because there is no exhaust. Hence, no heat."

Riordan squinted. "Then how does it work?"

"It leverages gravitic forces against themselves."

Riordan had to tell himself to resume breathing. "Are you saying this is . . . is some kind of antigravity device?"

Alnduul's inner eyelids nictated once. "I am."

Riordan shook his head at Alnduul's affirmation, at the device that was keeping the Dornaani half a meter above the deck, at any universe in which physics could be so effortlessly and economically violated. "That's impossible. You can't—"

"Caine Riordan, I understand your surprise and your skepticism. Unfortunately, we do not have the time to alleviate either. This moon, Zhal Prime Second-Five, is no longer inhabited, so its port authority systems are automated. They are also malfunctioning. They have failed to recognize *Olsloov*'s authorization codes. Consequently, the port authority auton will not relinquish control of the helm."

"And if we don't correct that?"

"The port authority will either land the ship and impound it, or it will divert us into a fatal crash."

Riordan grabbed the hand controls. "So let me guess. This, uh . . . this antigravity unit"—*I did* not *just say that*—"works the same way as the door: mental instructions."

"Correct. The control grips and their arms are flexible. Physical feedback can be combined with mental instructions for greater surety and speed of operation. Activate the sensor interface."

"How?"

"Command it into operation."

Riordan visualized the interactive holographs he'd seen on *Olsloov*'s bridge. He felt faint movement near his temples. A wire-thin filament extended from either end of the control circlet. The wires illuminated, lowered a glowing curtain of light in front of his eyes that, when fully descended, became a heads-up display. He discovered that, depending upon how he focused his eyes, he could either read it in great detail, or see straight through it, much like the surface of polarized glass. "Okay," Riordan exhaled. "I guess you'll talk me through the rest. What's our job?"

"To either terminate the port authority's override of our helm controls or to update its registry database. Both of which require physical access."

"How do we achieve that before the port authority rams us nose-first into a mountain?"

Alnduul stepped closer to the uncluttered deck space at the center of the bay. "The bridge crew has created a cascade of code errors. Once released into *Olsloov*'s computer, they will trigger a default to manual control, at least until the port authority auton determines that the error warnings are spurious. Those few seconds are the crew's only opportunity to land *Olsloov* atop the most suitable planetary feature in range."

"So instead of letting the port authority robot crash this ship, your bridge crew is going to crash it themselves?"

Alnduul's mouth rotated slightly. "Your optimism is inspiring. Once the ship is down, the crew will disable *Olsloov*'s computer. You and I will then descend and correct the flaw in the port authority's automation."

"How long will it take to reinitiate *Olsloov*'s computer?"

Alnduul's stare became somber. "I failed to explain adequately. To ensure that *Olsloov*'s computer cannot be reaccessed by the port authority auton, the crew must render it *physically* incapable of restarting. Repairs will require several weeks. Perhaps more. I am sorry, Caine Riordan. There is no other way."

Caine mentally adjusted the probable duration of his stay in the Collective by adding a few months. He suppressed a sigh, nodded at Alnduul. "Then let's get going."

Alnduul walked further out onto the expanse of empty deck. "Command the unit to activate, just enough to suspend you."

Riordan visualized rising slowly, moved the hand controls slightly upward. His feet lifted off the deck, stopped when they were dangling a third of a meter in midair. The only sensation from the antigravity unit was a fast, smooth vibration against his back.

Irzhresht's voice was now inside his head, also. "Alnduul, we are approaching the drift-butte. You must be away from the hull before *Olsloov* loses power and we begin banking."

"Acknowledged," Alnduul answered. "Open the bay for personnel exit."

A seam appeared in the center of the deck. It widened swiftly, wind howling steadily louder until the aperture was three meters wide and five long. Riordan looked for doors, hinges, retracting panels: there were none. *Okay, more magic tech.*

Down below, Riordan saw a lone, strangely flat mountaintop rising into view. "Is that where *Olsloov* is heading?"

"Yes," Alnduul answered, walking to the forward edge of the aperture. "We must not be on board when *Olsloov* attempts to land. My crew's attempt to terminate the port authority override could easily fail."

"Wait, if they're at such high risk, then we can't just abandon—"

"Caine Riordan." Alnduul had turned his wide eyes upon Riordan. "Your courage and loyalty is appreciated, but I cannot risk your demise. Not only are you my friend, you are my official responsibility. The Senior Arbiters have ordered me to prevent any and all hazards to your person." He turned toward the hurricane-howling slot in the deck. "Stand by me. Jump after I do. Do not reascend, even if you have tumbled and are falling. You must dive swiftly until you are clear of the *Olsloov*. Then follow where I fly."

"But the wind velocity will—"

Alnduul stepped beyond the leading edge of the aperture, disappeared down and to the rear in a sickening rush. He was either too far behind, or too distant to see, within the space of a single second.

"You must jump, Caine Riordan. Not step. *Jump*." Because of the mastoid transducer, Alnduul's voice was clear over the shrieking wind.

Riordan made himself stop thinking; he leaped forward.

The wind snared his legs, yanked him backward into an abrupt, bone-jarring tumble. The underside of *Olsloov*'s stern jumped toward his face. He ducked, pushed down hard with the hand controls, his arms extending in a desperate stretch toward the ground.

Olsloov shrieked over and past. Caine straightened into a nose dive toward lake-mottled flatlands. Despite his speed, the wind that pinned the rippling duty suit against him was mild upon his face: the virtual heads-up display was not merely made of light, but some kind of resistive plasma field. Magic layered upon magic.

Time to reorient and find Alnduul. Riordan pushed the up-rushing ground away from him. But too hastily: he snapped into a hover, intestines ramming up against his stomach. He clenched his esophagus against a rush of vomit.

"Be careful," Alnduul's voice urged. "The unit's hazard overrides are suspended. It will obey your commands without regard to your ability to survive them."

"Isn't that kind of dangerous?"

"It is, but we must have complete control. We do not know what threats we might face, or how fast they might arise."

"So I learn on the job or die."

"Those are the circumstances the crisis has forced upon us. Despite the orders of the Arbiters."

Riordan started scanning the wide sky for Alnduul. Quick as the desire to locate him arose, a small violet dot appeared on his virtual HUD, pulsing softly.

Hmm . . . let's see what else it can do. "Set tracking guidon on Alnduul." Again, as quick as thought, the dot turned into a small red reticle. "Designate as friend." The reticle turned aqua.

Well, okay then . . . "Locate and track *Olsloov.*" Another, slightly larger reticle appeared at the lower edge of Riordan's HUD. "*Plot and execute rendezvous with Alnduul.*" The hum of the grav unit increased, sent him zipping briskly toward a point slightly ahead of the smaller aqua reticle. Caine considered, then added: "*Incorporate randomized evasion.*" His vector became a stomach-knotting cascade of dips, jumps, veers.

Alnduul's voice sounded both approving and worried. "You are adapting well to the control circlet, but be selective in your commands. New users can endanger themselves by attempting to manage too much."

"Just like our systems," Riordan answered. "So, are you heading for that mountaintop?"

"I am. But it is not a mountaintop."

Riordan frowned, studied it more closely as his vantage point changed and discovered that the strange, column-shaped peak was not part of a mountain.

It was suspended in midair. Unable to speak, Caine stared in disbelief.

Yet there it was: a floating spike of stone, more than a kilometer long, capped by vegetation and small pools of greenish water that reflected the hazy vermillion sun. "Alnduul, what the hell is—?"

"It is a protected artifact of the prior epoch. I will share more later. Right now, we must accelerate our approach; *Olsloov* is about to trigger the system failure."

Riordan demanded greater speed. The gravitic thrust unit complied, but without discontinuing the evasive maneuvers. Now, each dodge and jink pulled painfully at his organs, joints, tendons. *"End evasive maneuvers."*

The unit's vector became as steady and smooth as its sharply diminished hum. Caine tilted over into a steep dive toward the top of the floating butte. For the first time since leaping out of the *Olsloov*'s belly, he had a moment to think. *If the Dornaani have this kind of technology at their disposal, then—*

Irzhresht's voice was not merely calm; she sounded bored. "Engaging failure codes."

Far below, *Olsloov*'s orange-glinting delta shape seemed to shake, then skitter sideways into an imminent tumble from which it immediately righted itself.

"Computer disabled," Irzhresht continued. "Commencing landing sequence."

Olsloov heeled hard to port, rolling through forty-five degrees. The hull shuddered beneath the high-speed buffeting as its leading edges and lifting surfaces bit hard against the air. It banked sharply toward the stone spike's largest lake.

Riordan's intercept vector changed to match Alnduul's. "How is *Olsloov* maneuvering without power?"

"It has standard flaps, but drag management is mostly handled by smart-hull recontouring."

Riordan watched the ship continue to shudder. One significant downdraft could drive it into the stony flanks of the "drift-butte"—

The top margin of Caine's HUD pulsed a bright orange: the color that Dornaani used to signify danger.

"Identify threat," Riordan thought at the circlet. It painted a throbbing orange vector that rose up from the ground and pointed at *Olsloov* like an accusing finger. "Ground emissions detected. Active sensors consistent with targeting array," the circlet explained.

Damn it. A dirtside defense site. If Olsloov evades, it can't land. But if it doesn't evade, it's a sitting duck. Unless...

Riordan jammed his arms outward, toward the source of the narrowing sensor emanations. *"Wave ride to source, no evasion,"* he ordered the circlet. *"Engage active sensors. Acquire reciprocal lock on point of emanation."*

As Caine's steep, accelerating dive turned the thready thunder of the wind into a ululating howl, Alnduul's panicked voice was loud in his head. "Caine Riordan, terminate your active sensors at once! The ground array will detect you and aim along your own emissions—"

"That's the idea, Alnduul. Is *Olsloov* still in enemy target lock?"

A pause. "No. Enemy sensors are shifting to you."

"And if you joined me, there'd be *two* targets behaving more aggressively than *Olsloov*."

"Understood."

In Riordan's HUD, the orange targeting beam swiveling around to spear him split in two. The new one roved after the aqua reticle that signified Alnduul. The flanks of the floating butte sped past, several kilometers to Riordan's left.

"Caine Riordan, if we wait too long—"

"Are the air defenses projectile or beam?"

"At this altitude, projectile. Atmospheric diffusion erodes laser effec—"

Ignoring the rest, Riordan widened his HUD's focus but kept the display centered on the targeting beam's origin point. *"Activate weapons,"* he ordered.

"Onboard lasers ineffective at this range," the circlet informed him.

"Understood. Activate weapons. Target sensor source. Fire when lock is acquired. Maintain target lock. Scan for energy spike within larger footprint."

From either shoulder of the backpack, a broken sputter of crackling flashes reached down toward the ground. They died out within three hundred meters. Riordan kept his groundward plunge between his two beams' vectors, caught a fleeting whiff of ozone: the remains of the air vaporized by his lasers. Caine wrapped his hands more tightly around the handgrips, forced himself to watch the whole HUD at once.

Three kilometers to the right of the targeting sensors, a painfully bright orange glare flashed at him like a malevolent eye opening. "Power spike..." began the command circlet.

"Terminate active sensors!" Riordan yanked the grav unit's handgrips to the left, felt his organs crush sideways as both the HUD and the circlet's voice finished telling him what he already knew: the energy spike was consistent with a railgun discharge. "Incoming!" he shouted at Alnduul. The Dornaani was already arcing away in the opposite direction.

Riordan's own tight turn reached ninety degrees. The tapering base of the floating butte loomed in front of him, less than six kilometers away. He aimed his outstretched arms at it, pulling out of the turn as he called for maximum acceleration...

Two bolts of fire ripped through the air less than a hundred meters behind, double thunder crashes and shock waves tumbling him. "Straighten and resume course," Riordan ordered both mentally and aloud, even as the grav thrusters whined and rattled in an automated attempt to do just that. The unit lurched, spun, adjusted, shot further away from the ground. Riordan vomited as he soared upward into the shadow of the floating butte.

Down below, two more jets of fire—the atmospheric combustion tracks left behind by railgun's hypersonic warheads—reached up toward him...and then ended in twin explosions, a kilometer beneath his feet.

Alnduul had moved so that, like Caine, the floating pylon of rock was now between him and the ground battery. "Caine Riordan, are you injured?"

Caine's guts felt as if they had been spun in a centrifuge. "Don't know. Don't think so." To the unit: *"Climb, remaining behind shielding face of floating rock. Move to position two hundred meters above center of the rock and hold relative position."*

As the grav pack carried him to the designated spot, Alnduul's voice reproved, "That maneuver was foolish, Caine Riordan. Brave, but foolish."

"Was it?" Riordan grunted, a dull ache persisting in the vicinity of his liver. "You said this, uh, drift-butte was a protected object.

Seemed unlikely that your ground batteries would be authorized to conduct fire missions which might strike it."

"Logical. Yet still, only a guess."

Riordan rose up beyond the sharply cleaved sides of the floating spike, scanned its top; thorny black bushes and swards of red lichen rolled away toward sky-blue fronds waving in the high-altitude winds. "Sometimes, guesses are all we humans have to act upon," he muttered.

To his right, *Olsloov*, half flying and half falling, eked its way over the stony lip of the topland, wobbled down toward the largest of the mirror-green ponds. On his left, Alnduul rose into view, accelerating after his stricken ship. "As your saying has it," the Dornaani conceded, "there are the quick and the dead. But in the future, I exhort you to temper your devotion to that axiom."

"How?"

"By obeying another human axiom: 'make haste slowly.'"

Ironically, that was the moment Alnduul doubled his speed to get ahead of the belly-falling *Olsloov*.

Chapter Fifteen

MARCH 2124
SECOND-FIVE, ZHAL PRIME (BD +71 482 A)

The Dornaani ship faltered at the last moment, its nose tilting down to port as it kissed the surface of the lake. Steam roiled up from that area as the attitude control thrusters detected the imbalance, fired at maximum, vaporizing the water.

The bow didn't come up fully, but the angle of impact became shallower. Instead of flipping into a massively destructive ass-over-nose cartwheel, *Olsloov* simply dug into the water. A wall of spray and hot mist fumed outward as she ploughed forward.

Ugly sounds—as if a trash compactor was brawling with a quarry saw—ripped the air as *Olsloov* bottomed out, dragging its belly across the shallow, rocky bottom. The drooping delta shape shuddered, bucked, and then stopped just fifteen meters from the far end of the lake.

Alnduul swung closer to examine the underside of the ship. Caine followed. *Olsloov*'s once smooth belly was now a battered curve of crumpled metal composites punctuated by several jagged rents.

"Doesn't look like we'll be flying anywhere soon," Riordan commented.

Alnduul made an impatient *tch*-ing noise. "Once main power is restored, the smart materials in the hull will reform and seal the worst of the breaches. We shall be able to lift to orbit, albeit slowly and with great care. But complete restoration will require longer repairs, perhaps during our stopover at BD +66 582. Assuming they still have sufficient facilities."

Riordan nodded, willed the grav unit to lower him to the ground. The wind was cool and brisk, but his duty suit's smart fabric and EVA insert combined to keep him comfortable. He looked up at the sun. "I thought this star, BD +71 482 A, was a red dwarf."

"It has been listed as such in your catalogs." Alnduul was silent for a moment, seemed to be inspecting a particularly ragged tear in *Olsloov*'s hull. "Now that you are here observing it, what would you presume it to be?"

Riordan thought, *"Adjust HUD screening to enable safe observation of local star."* The plasma curtain in front of his eyes darkened to a ghostly slate color. "Looks more like a K9 V to me. Still enough to keep Zhal Prime Second tidally locked, even with multiple moons tugging on it."

Alnduul boosted higher, searching for damage to the hull's dorsal surface. "Indeed." He gestured to the left. The large gray and brown planet in question was strangely diaphanous, a ghostly sphere that barely managed to superimpose itself upon the teal sky of this, its fifth and most distant moon. "Fortunately, Second-Five has enough distance and mass to ensure that it is not face-locked to its parent, but rotation is slowed. This moon only revolves six times in the course of its twenty-four-day orbit."

Riordan tried to do the math, then tried to visualize a model, then gave up. "And what does that mean in terms of day and night cycles?"

"A complex pattern, with libration effects creating extended dawns and dusks."

Riordan looked at the deep orange sun. "So how much daylight do we have?"

"Approximately thirty hours, the last twenty of which will be dangerously dim."

"Dangerously?"

Alnduul floated down beside Riordan. "The surface has not been visited for almost two centuries. Hazardous biota may have returned to this region. We will find out when we descend."

Riordan watched the last wisps of steam rise up from under *Olsloov*. They evaporated almost instantly. "Alnduul, I'm happy to help out, but if I'm too important to risk, then why am I the one going with you?"

Alnduul's mouth rotated slightly, tightly: wry amusement.

"Because there are only two gravitic thruster units on *Olsloov*. One is part of its allotted equipment. The other is a human model, on loan for your use." He began walking back to the edge of the drift-butte's topland. "So it was either attempt these missions alone, or with your help."

Riordan nodded. "I take it that Irzhresht is too slender for mine to fit, despite her height?"

"That is only part of what precludes her participation. Extended exertion in a gravity well would gravely damage her health. Her people are a subspecies of the main Dornaani genotype: she is a 'low-gee.'" Alnduul slurred it into a single world: "loji."

Once at the lip of the drift-butte, Riordan surveyed the terrain five kilometers below: mostly flat, speckled by lakes. "So where is the port authority complex?"

Alnduul pointed far to the left. "There."

Riordan squinted, looked for buildings but didn't see any. However, near a great confluence of lakes and rivers, there seemed to be a distortion which blurred the outlines of the waterways beneath and beyond it, as if they were being seen through an unfocused lens of impossibly strange shape.

The clouds moved. Dark amber light fell across that stretch of land, and then glinted on an impossible midair arc.

"What the—?" Riordan murmured before thinking to use the circlet. *"Twenty times magnification on central object."* The curve of light enlarged, limning a ghostly arch that grew until it loomed titanic and graceful. "It that a structure?"

"It is," Alnduul replied.

"And it's transparent? Like glass?"

"More perfectly transparent than glass, but yes. It is a marker and also a piezo-electric receiver, when need be."

Riordan measured the gold-gleaming hemicircle with the magnifying center of his plasma-HUD. "That must be—what? Three kilometers high?"

"Slightly more."

"And is it part of the port?"

"No. It is an outlying facility and navigation landmark. We shall go there first. It is a comparatively safe point from which we may observe the port authority complex and assess its conditions."

Riordan saw white, sinuous aviforms wheeling closely around the arch, possibly attracted by its glow. Although the peak of its rim was barely half as high as their current perch, the idea of standing on that smooth, probably frictionless curve sent a pulse of height-panic up Riordan's calves. He made sure his question sounded casual: "So, we're just going to fly over there and take a look?"

Alnduul's voice may have been somewhat amused. "Whenever you are ready."

Riordan found it difficult to trust his eyes during what felt like the slow-motion fall toward the arch of glass. As reflections of sky and sun vied with the view through to the terrain below, his eyes kept shifting between different depths of focus. To compensate, he instructed his HUD to outline and graph the arch. Faint, glowing lime-green lines transmogrified the ghostly structure into a grid work—much easier to keep track of its dimensions and shape that way.

Slowing as he drifted toward the peak of the arch, the cream-white aviforms rose up higher along its arms. Each snakelike body had a pair of large, membranous wings, with smaller auxiliary flaps near its pointed nose (canards?) and a bifurcated tail (horizontal stabilizers?). They were predominantly gliders, catching updrafts rather than working their wings.

However, Riordan could not detect any sense organs or orifices. As his feet settled carefully on what now felt and looked like a perfectly flat plane of glass, he asked Alnduul, "Those snake-gliders: how do they see? Or eat?"

The Dornaani landed beside him with a nonchalance that suggested long years of familiarity with the grav unit. "The datafile I perused indicates that their alimentary orifices are all located on the anterior surface. Much akin to the design of your home planet's ocean rays, if I recall correctly. Their complex eyes are located to either side of their mouth, as are their audial receptors."

Riordan watched one of the serpentine avians circle the arms of the arch in a nimble, twisting arabesque. A row of tan spots ran in twin tracks from its nose to the area just behind its rearmost canards. He commanded the HUD to capture the image and send it to Alnduul. "Primitive eyes, do you think? Defensive light sensors?"

Alnduul studied it for a moment. "Quite likely. However, the datafile defines these as the largest aviforms on the planet, without predators. In the air, that is."

"And on the ground?"

"They are at the mercy of many creatures, including the adult forms of their own species."

"They ultimately become ground-dwellers?"

Alnduul raised an affirming finger. "When they attain breeding age, they build a cocoon. They emerge with fully developed sex organs and with legs rather than wings."

Riordan studied the snake-gliders. Their wings were too flexible to have a rigid bone structure. Something more akin to cartilage, probably. "It doesn't look as though those wings could ever develop into limbs."

"They do not. They wither and are absorbed by the organism during its quasi-chrysalis stage. Note, however, the two pairs of prehensile manipulators they keep against their bodies as they fly. Those are the appendages that evolve into limbs."

Riordan waited for one of the snake-gliders to roll over and was rewarded with a glimpse of the manipulators. They were reminiscent of a shark's claspers, except they were longer and stronger. That was also when he saw one of their mouths: a constantly active maw in which heavy shearing teeth gnawed at the air. Caine reconsidered the creatures: no longer just intriguing and beautiful, they were now a swarm of potential killers, as well. "I take it they are carnivorous."

"They are said to be indiscriminate hunters," Alnduul confirmed. "If a ground animal is no larger than they are, they will attack it."

Okay, so not potential *killers;* proven *killers.* "And if they come after us?"

"You employ the lasers with which you drew the ground batteries' fire. It is unlikely the beams will kill the creatures, but the resulting wound should chase them off."

"*Should* chase them off?"

Alnduul's inner lid nictated lazily. "There are no certainties when it comes to the behavior of fauna, Caine Riordan."

Caine looked down, discerned a paved square about two kilometers to the left of their position. "Is that the port authority complex?"

"Yes."

"It looks pretty overgrown."

"Evidently the automated tenders have failed."

Riordan zoomed in on the square. A low-set building dominated its far end, overgrown with vines half a meter thick. "So
what's the plan?"

"The vegetation on the roof obstructs any possible means of
ingress there. So we must use the entrance that faces the paved
area. We shall descend to the far edge of the square, inspect it
for automated defenses, disarm or disable them, breach the doors,
and make our way to the computing core. At that point, it will
either accept an update or we will have to disable the facility."

Riordan studied the square more carefully. "Is the square
protected by an aerial defense envelope?"

"Yes, out to its far end. However, if we are not airborne above
it, we will not be attacked."

"And the ground defenses?"

Alnduul's mouth twisted slightly further. "The air and ground
defenses are provided by the same units. We will not be able to
avoid engaging them. Are you prepared?"

Riordan took in the strange landscape of scattered lakes and
the rust and bright green vegetation that wound among them, all
of which faded into a hazy horizon. The unearthly vista was not
just compelling, it might also be the last he'd ever see. If it wasn't
for alternating memories of Elena's sleeping face, and Connor's
eager, hopeful one, he might just have told Alnduul to put him
back in cold sleep until some other ship came along and used
its weapons to flatten the port authority. Flying into unscouted
terrain to enter an unknown structure, both of which might be
populated by hostile biota and automata, was not Caine's idea of
a tactically prudent solution. But unless he wanted to lengthen
an already overlong journey...

Caine brought his chin up. "I'm ready. Let's go."

Chapter Sixteen

The descent to the square was uneventful. However, when Riordan ordered the HUD to display nearby biosignatures, the result was an unreadable litter of data. He restricted the scan to a footprint centered on the square and two times its dimensions, filtering out everything with a signature smaller than a child.

It was still a mess. Evidently a lot of creatures dwelt in, or lurked near, the port authority. Some contacts disappeared and reappeared without warning: creatures moving through dense brush or into and out of burrows. It wasn't quite as bad as going in blind, but it wasn't a whole lot better.

As Caine and Alnduul floated down through five hundred meters altitude, perimeter markers became visible. They were stelae of some kind, sigils scored into their angled surfaces. And still, despite the churning biosigns on his sensors, Riordan could not see any movement.

That was totally unacceptable. *"Orange tag life-signs moving to intercept Riordan or Alnduul. Double tag any that doubles its movement rate within any three second sampling interval."* Riordan hoped that would give them enough warning. And, while on the topic of warnings: *"Show remaining power. Show average power consumption. Show power consumption per single laser discharge."*

The resulting data was not promising. Riordan called Alnduul's attention to the speed with which the lasers would drain their remaining power.

113

Several seconds passed before the Dornaani replied. "I can fire ten times and retain a sufficient power margin to reascend to the drift-butte. Your more aggressive maneuvers have reduced you to eight safe discharges. Logically, then—"

"—I should land first and lead the way." Riordan grimaced, mostly because it made inarguable sense. Alnduul had more firepower left, was accomplished using weapons via the control circlet, and so could better maintain a base of fire to cover Riordan. Obversely, Riordan was the logical point man for a quick charge to the control building. Human legs were longer and cycled faster than Dornaani's.

Details of the square's seamed gray surface became visible. Weathering had cracked it with crevices, most exploited by smaller versions of the vines that sat atop the port authority complex like a knotted wig. Caine pushed his hands out, slowing his approach until his feet came to rest softly on the bordering lichen. "I'm down," he muttered.

Alnduul was hovering five meters behind him. "I will overwatch as you cross to the facility. I have a clear field of fire and am too high to be engaged by any adversaries on the ground."

That sounded entirely too confident to Riordan. "Even so, keep an eye on your flanks." He made sure his backpack's lasers were set to fire alternately rather than together, and stepped onto the square.

Nothing happened.

So, instead of sprinting and calling attention to myself, I think I'll take a nice, leisurely walk. Trusting that this planet's creatures would lack the olfactory context to correctly interpret the fight/flight scents he was emitting, Caine began strolling to the port authority building.

The scrub on the left edge of the square rustled briefly. Riordan swiveled his left laser in that direction and discovered that the associated biosign was not charging him, but moving rapidly away. A droplet of sweat crept out of his right armpit, then sped down along his ribs, trailing cold wetness.

Ten meters further on, his HUD's motion detector flagged something approaching from above, and behind. "Alnduul—"

"I have seen it. Avians. Do not stop. I shall interdict them."

Riordan continued to walk, heard the faint hum of Alnduul's laser. Caine's HUD showed two of the aviforms falling, tumbling, trying to pull up. One was able to straighten out just before it collapsed; senseless, it slammed down into the square twenty meters ahead of Caine.

Who stopped. Checked his HUD again. All the movement at the edges of the square had come to a complete halt.

And then went wild.

Two creatures, about the size of mastiffs but built like small boars, lunged out of the drooping ferns closest to the stricken snake-glider and pounced on it. Discovering themselves to be competing for the same meal, their hides rose up into masses of writhing polyps just before they fell upon each other with warbling shrieks: incongruously high-pitched, given how heavily muscled they were.

A mature snake-glider—now a wingless, eyeless cross between a torpedo and a Komodo dragon—burst out of a heavy tangle of vines and slither-scrambled across the plaza toward the melee. It stopped abruptly, its "head" swiveling toward Riordan. From every other point of the compass, smaller signatures were emerging as well, some fleeing, some chasing, all agitated.

Riordan managed not to move. "Alnduul..."

"Caine Riordan, I know that on Earth, becoming motionless often stops the attack of territorial creatures—"

"That's why I froze."

"I know. But no such behavior exists on this planet."

Shit. The slate and cream Komodo torpedo was starting to move again—straight at Caine. Its nose rolled up and back—*how does it do that?*—revealing two rows of impressive teeth in its almost round mouth. Its overground speed was even more impressive.

Since his lasers were too weak to kill it, Riordan pushed up and forward with his arms. The grav thruster shot him over the Komodo torpedo, which coiled into an upward leap with surprising speed and agility.

The jaws snapped behind Riordan as he stretched his legs out to land, ordering, *"Target proximal creature to rear. Fire twice at the mouth"*—an orange flicker warned him that the system was uncertain of success—*"or closest ventral area."* Just as Caine began leaning away from the forward momentum at the end of his grav hop, he heard two-tap hums: one from the right laser, the other from the left.

Riordan landed into the first long stride of his sprint toward the complex. Creatures approached from either side. Alnduul hit the leaders. Most of the others skittered to a halt, fighting over the soon-to-be-carcasses of the ones felled by the covering laser fire. But others swerved after Riordan.

Too many to shoot. No time to stop, turn, and give his lasers a stable firing platform. The only alternative was... *"Twenty-meter leap. Decelerate before landing."*

He left the ground, three mastiff-boars gaping upward as he passed over them. He turned in midair, mentally tagged his three closest pursuers: *"One discharge each. Target closest leg."*

Alnduul's uncharacteristically urgent exclamation, almost a shout, was loud in his head. "Caine, you *must not* leave the ground!"

Oh, shit.

His backpack-mounted lasers hummed. Two of the three creatures went down and were swarmed. The third persisted with a broken stride.

If I've triggered the perimeter defenses...

As Riordan rotated back around to land, the HUD painted five bright orange icons on the square: two behind him, three in front. Those parts of the plaza seemed to be unscrewing themselves upward. Each became a low, round protrusion that then unfolded into a hexapedal robot. They began turning toward him, the HUD painting them with the orange symbol that warned of an energy spike.

Building, but not quite ready to unleash... whatever. Which meant that Riordan, for the first and probably last time in this chaotic melee, had about half a second to get a glimpse of the bigger tactical picture.

Alnduul had landed and was making good progress. Instead of running, he was almost skating forward, fine-tuning the grav unit so that he flew mere centimeters above the ground, using his feet to change his vector and slalom around the creatures swarming toward him. Plummeting down to attack from the rear were a flock of the snake-gliders: five of them, diving fast. Some of the earthbound creatures were still fixated on Caine, but many were reacting to the crablike bots that had risen up from the plaza. For every animal that now hissed, spat, or leaped at the machines, two fled the strange smells and sounds.

In short, the tactical picture was a tableau of utter chaos. With the exception of Alnduul and him, almost every creature was poised to happily kill any other. There was no predicting the actions of any of them. Except...

Riordan estimated the range and speed of the diving snake-gliders, queried the circlet, *"Are the defense bots known models?"*

The circlet pulsed in the affirmative.

"Is bot targeting prioritized to engage the most dangerous or the most proximal threats?"

Another of the Komodo torpedoes erupted from the nearest brush line. It stomped one of the polyp-covered mastiff-boars and bit a deep chunk out of its notochord before flowing like a belly-greased snake toward Riordan. Two more of mastiff-boars, pelts writhing in agitation, were bearing down on him from the other direction, fang-lined mouths agape.

The circlet answered in his head and on the HUD. "Threat robot prioritizes proximity targets—"

Riordan shouted as well as thought: "Vertical! Maximum speed!"

Riordan shot upward like a rocket, felt his liver and stomach mash down into his intestines, heard jaws snap shut where his body had been a fraction of a second before, waited until he reached two hundred meters, then thought, *"Gradual stop."*

Alnduul, who continued to skate around threats, shooting only when necessary, sounded dismayed. "Caine Riordan! At that altitude—"

"I'm safe. For the moment. Get up here. Now."

"But—"

"Just do it!"

Alnduul complied, expertly accelerating into a smooth, steepening parabola. The snake-gliders screamed frustration as he went up through their formation, swooped around, tried to gain altitude for pursuit, flapped their wings strenuously.

One of them exploded in midair.

"What—?" started Alnduul.

"The bots identify them as airborne threats. And now that we're above them, they're more proximal than we are," Caine explained. Another of the avians blew apart, raining chunks down upon the plaza. The rearmost of them was taken through the wing by a rocket, which exploded just a meter further on. Whether by virtue of concussion or fragments, the snake-glider flapped backward, went limp, tumbled down, and was immediately set upon.

As the defense bots continued to demonstrate their lethality, the various creatures that had streamed on to the plaza—either to scavenge from bodies or bring down new ones—fled back into the bush with even greater alacrity. Oblivious, the bots targeted the last of the avians.

Alnduul dove straight down. "Do as I do," he instructed, sending the feed from his HUD to Riordan's. "We can degrade the robots while they are focused on the remaining avians."

Alnduul pulled out of his dive at only two meters altitude, rushing straight at the rearmost bot. Staying just ahead of its attempt to switch targeting to him, Alnduul swept around the machine on a flat but low course. Too predictable, so far as Caine was concerned.

But in a moment, the reason for Alnduul's maneuver became apparent. Just before he swept all the way around to the front of the bot, one of his lasers pulsed. Sparks showered from a top-mounted cluster nestled under an armored disk: the bot's sensors. The machine moved erratically, then steadied, but its new movements were less fluid.

Riordan dove to follow Alnduul's example, deciphered what he'd seen as the ground rushed up at him. The bot had been blinded by the laser, but had quickly patched into its mates' sensor feed in order to keep moving and attacking. As Caine reached the end of his own dive, he leveled off, shot low and fast toward a new bot, instructing his circlet, *"Target sensor cluster."* A yellow warning light signaled the circlet's inability to comply. It went out the moment Riordan ordered: *"Execute autonomous approach and attack."*

The circlet took over. Suddenly, Riordan was being steered around the bot in a tight, hard loop. His laser pulsed. The bot staggered as if drunk.

The other bots still categorized the flying predators as priority targets and fired rockets as the last two dove after Riordan and Alnduul. The warheads exploded in a long, rippling volley; Caine's HUD was suddenly free of flying threats. But now he and Alnduul were the only objects not rooted to the ground, and that, along with their proximity, made them the new primary targets.

Riordan and Alnduul stayed low and sped for the port authority complex. They swept around the corner of the squat building just before the bots fired again. With the predictable determination of automatons operating without the guidance of a more sophisticated computer, they stolidly followed the path of their prey's retreat At the edge of the square, they began picking and stumbling their way into the tangle of vines, creepers, brush, and ferns separating them from their two targets.

By that time, Alnduul had ordered Irzhresht to fetch, properly position, and activate *Olsloov*'s largest portable sensor. Although individual biosigns had proven too faint to detect at that range, the Dornaani array easily locked on to the remaining bots' emissions and tracked their stiff movements. Increasingly isolated from each other and unable to anticipate the dead ends ahead of them, they proved particularly susceptible to two time-honored military axioms. First, divide to conquer. Then, defeat in detail.

Putting these axioms into practice, Caine cruised close enough to get the most distant bot's attention. When Irzhresht's sensor array confirmed that the bot was pursuing and so, was drawing away from the others, Alnduul swept into its blind spot and took out its sensor cluster.

Ten minutes after the human and Dornaani had taken cover behind the overgrown port authority complex, they stood before it, the plaza behind littered with casualties both biological and mechanical. Riordan breathed deeply, smelled a rank sourness, recognized it as the product of multiple tides of fear-sweat that had soaked him since he had bailed out of *Olsloov* less than two hours ago. He looked over at Alnduul. "Tell me that whatever comes next is the easy part. Please."

Alnduul's outer eyelids closed and then opened very slowly, usually a sign of sympathy or sorrow. "Yes. What comes next is easier. But arguably, less pleasant."

Caine frowned. "What? Why?"

Alnduul might have sighed... right before the world faded into gray nothingness.

Chapter Seventeen

MARCH 2124
SECOND-FIVE, ZHAL PRIME (BD +71 482 A)

Riordan awoke with a start. He was in his quarters. Alnduul was standing close to the room's iris valve, his eyes as somber as they had been in the dream...

No, not a dream. It had been too complete, too much like life itself in every detail...

Irzhresht appeared from behind Caine, skirting his cocoon couch on her way to the exit, a control circlet in her hands. Except this circlet was more like the lower half of a helmet, much wider and thicker than the one he had used on Zhal Prime Second-Five. *Or, what I* thought *was Second-Five.*

The iris valve dilated at Irzhresht's approach, contracted into a seamless disk behind her.

Riordan glanced at Alnduul. "That wasn't a dream."

Alnduul's outer eyelids cycled in slow motion. "That is correct."

"Then what the hell was it?"

"A simulation."

Riordan shook his head. "I've trained in sim chambers. You always know it's not real. You can feel the sense suit and the 3-D helmet, feel how the sensagel changes temperature, increases or decreases pressure on your body. It's all external. That"—he pointed at the featureless portal through which Irzhresht had carried the heavy half-helmet—"was internal. Direct manipulation of my mind."

"Yes."

Riordan waited, but the Dornaani did not expand upon his reply. "That's all you have to say? 'Yes'?"

The Dornaani looked as though he'd rather be on another planet.

"Alnduul, if I wasn't here to retrieve Elena, I'd demand you take me back to human space immediately. I'd rather face assassins than the possibility of having my mind hijacked every time I go to sleep. But since leaving isn't an option, you're going to tell me how and why you did this. If you don't, our friendship—and my support of the Dornaani and Custodians—is over."

Alnduul did something he had never done before: he looked away. "Threats are not necessary, Caine Riordan. I had hoped to express my deepest apologies before we began this conversation in earnest. But for you to truly understand the power of virtuality, it was essential that you experienced it without warning."

"Wrong. Nothing is more essential than freedom of choice. Or don't the Dornaani believe that individuals have the right to self-determination?"

"We do, Caine Riordan. But even in the most enlightened of your states, there are circumstances under which those rights may be abridged, albeit as briefly and mildly as possible."

Caine rolled up out of the couch. "Cut the excuses, Alnduul. You didn't even bother to seek my consent."

"It was a violation. I have apologized. I shall do so again, if that will help."

Riordan considered the exosapient's tone. "But if you had the chance to do it again, you'd do the same thing."

The Dornaani closed his eyes. "Yes. Because your safety is paramount."

Caine studied Alnduul's posture. One of the few nearly universal constants among the body language of the five known species was that a forward slouch like Alnduul's signaled dejection. *Maybe he really* was *trying to help me.* "So how does surprising me with this sim ensure my safety?" *And Alnduul, you'd better have a damn convincing reason.*

The Dornaani's reply was slow, the way one sibling would reveal something damning about another. "In the last five centuries, virtuality has become widespread within the Collective." Alnduul swiveled his large eyes back to meet Caine's. "As a result, many of my species are no longer reliable. Or forthright."

"Because they spend time in some virtual playground? How does that—?"

"Beware of drawing hasty parallels, Caine Riordan." Alnduul's mouth quavered. "The social effects of your interactive entertainments are not analogous to those of virtuality. Think back upon your experience of it and you will implicitly understand the distinction."

Riordan didn't even get as far as a single reflective thought. The obvious answer pushed it aside: *I never suspected it was an illusion. And it was exciting. There was always either a danger to overcome or a novelty to explore. If I hadn't been shit-scared half of the time, it would have been one hell of a ride.* Caine nodded. "So the Dornaani are spending *way* too much time in virtuality." He saw where that could lead. "Detachment? Diminished empathy? Decreased social skills and instincts?"

Alnduul stiffly imitated a human shake of his head. "It goes much further than that. But at least you now have the necessary context to understand what causes much of the disaffection you may encounter in the Collective: the seduction of constant sensory gratification." His fingers drooped. "Ironically, the version you experienced has the least fidelity of any form of virtuality."

Riordan blinked. "But... it was seamless."

"Was it? Think back carefully. Initially, you probably felt that your vision was blurred. You may also recall that olfactory sensations were less acute than normal. Taste is even more affected."

Riordan nodded slowly. "But you chose a scenario in which I didn't have much reason to focus on smell or taste, and which left me no time to notice that they weren't as keen as usual."

Alnduul raised both index fingers slowly. "All so that I might now ask this one question: would you enjoy entering virtuality again?" His two fingers became rigid. "Do not answer according to what you think, but what you feel."

Riordan shrugged. "If going back was my own choice? Then, yes."

"Despite the dangers?"

Riordan shrugged. "There are no dangers if you know it isn't real." Even as he said it, Caine felt the deeper implications of Alnduul's warning rising around him.

The Dornaani's inner eyelids nictated once. "Perpetual excitement without risk is a powerful stimulant. An opiate, even." He looked away again. "Only by feeling the seductive appeal of virtuality yourself could I be certain that you would then understand and heed this warning: the Collective's high ideals are not always manifested in deed. Accordingly, be prepared to act as your own advocate in all matters."

Riordan realized that his shoulders had slumped almost as much as Alnduul's. Although Dornaani motivations were enigmatic and their engagement uncertain, humanity had reposed a basic sense of security in the support of the Collective. But now, Caine realized, he had the dubious honor of being the first to discover just how mistaken and misplaced that confidence might be.

Still, before the topic slipped away, there were important questions to be asked. "So, the technologies we used on Zhal Prime Second-Five: are they real or not?"

"Many are." Alnduul gestured for Riordan to follow him through the iris valve. "Others were probably real at one time, but have been lost to us. However, the most extraordinary accomplishments—such as the drift-butte and the gravity thrusters—are objects of legend, myths arising from misperception or whimsy."

Riordan felt a shade of disappointment flit past. The real world seemed a shabbier, less exciting place if there weren't floating mountains or antigravity backpacks to be found somewhere. "And Second-Five itself? Was that real?"

Alnduul led them toward the bridge. "The satellite's actual environment is less congenial to both our biologies. To correct that, its density in the simulation was doubled, thereby increasing its gravity to sixty percent of Earth's. In consequence, it retained most of its free oxygen. We also adjusted the star so that it experienced fewer flares, resulting in less atmospheric erosion."

As they entered the bridge, Alnduul gestured toward the largest hologram. The actual planet-moon system was displayed there in arresting detail. "In actuality, Second-Five has little more than point four gravity. The crucially thinner atmosphere requires a compressor mask. The fauna are significantly smaller and less energetic. Your own catalogues correctly identify the star's spectral type and magnitude as M1.5 V. The ambient light tends to be dull and reddish, and the vegetation is neither so colorful nor so pervasive."

Riordan watched the small satellite make its way around the large central planet, experienced a sense of cognitive dissonance so strong that it felt like vertigo. Looking closely, he saw every disappointing detail that Alnduul had described—and yet, he could still see the Komodo torpedoes charging him, could still hear the swoop of the snake-gliders...

Alnduul spoke from his elbow. "Virtuality claims the authority of our senses. For any species that still depends upon those senses for survival, nothing can leave a deeper imprint."

Riordan nodded, tore his eyes away from the sad little holographic world, resolved to mentally bury the pseudo-experiences beneath its forlorn surface. In the same instant, he wondered how long it would take before even a highly sophisticated and orderly mind began to confuse actual and virtual events, sensations, experiences.

Alnduul's voice was no longer at his shoulder. "We have just now completed refueling at the orbital tankage facility." Riordan turned, discovered the Dornaani considering the slowly rotating stellar holosphere. He pointed into it; a glowing reproduction of his fingertip began tracing a path from the bottom of the three-dee plot to the center. "From here, we shall shift through Pi Ursa Majoris, then lay over briefly at BD +66 582. After that, we have but one more system, LP 38-98, between us and the regional capital at BD +80 238."

"And that's where I'll find Elena?"

"I believe so."

Riordan didn't even try to keep his voice level: "You *believe* so? What the hell kind of answer is that?"

Alnduul's fingers spread until they pointed away from his body in all directions. "We Custodians were compelled to relinquish her care to the Collective's experts. They were deemed more likely to restore her to a condition that would permit surgery. They declined to send updates."

Caine closed his eyes. "Every time I ask you a question about Elena, it seems I get further away from her."

Alnduul's head lowered slightly. "I am sorry, Caine Riordan. I wish it was not so." He sat, raised a finger toward the only other crewmember on the bridge. "Lock in our vector for outshift. Commence preacceleration. Full thrust."

Chapter Eighteen

The second planet out from BD +66 582, a K5 main sequence star, actually had a name: Rooaioo'q. Somewhat larger than Earth, but not quite as dense, it had both slightly lower gravity and a slightly thicker atmosphere. Located toward the outer edge of the star's habitable zone, the increased greenhouse effect nicely balanced the somewhat weaker insolation. At least that's how Alnduul translated the data streams scrolling next to the holographic representation of the world.

Riordan squinted at it. "The image looks kind of, well, smudged."

Alnduul's mouth twisted slightly. "You may soon judge for yourself if the holographic representation is inaccurate. We shall make planetfall within the hour."

Shortly after boarding an almost featureless shuttle, Riordan voiced disappointment at the lack of cockpit windows. Irzhresht turned her attention away from the helm long enough to wave a hand at the nose of the craft. Two previously undetectable panels slid aside, revealing a commanding view of the planet.

Rooaioo'q was a patternless, crowded collage of green landmasses and blue seas, the details of which, even in this view, were slightly blurred by the dense atmosphere and constantly forming, dissipating, and regathering clouds. Beyond the ink-black terminator line, two moons, one about the size of Luna, one about half as large, kept orbital pace with the world.

Riordan studied the tangled white whorls of storms strewn

across its surface. "With two moons and so much coastline, there must be a lot of flooding. Bizarre tidal patterns, too."

The third Dornaani aboard, Ssaodralth—a mere apprentice at thirty-five years—pointed to the satellites. "You are correct. However, without those moons, Rooaioo'q would barely support life. If at all." Seeing that Riordan's comprehension was not immediate, he added, "The satellites' combined gravity is a counterforce to the pull of the star, which is closer than your sun is to Earth. Otherwise, Rooaioo'q would almost certainly be tidally locked."

Riordan nodded, watched the outline of the planet become larger and less curved as they descended toward it.

As soon as the shuttle's engines shut down, Riordan undid the seat's straps, scanned the interior for a filter mask.

Alnduul shook his head. "You will not need it."

Riordan stared. "Another world where humans can just walk around in shirtsleeves?"

Alnduul shrugged. "Perhaps that is not so surprising as the fact that all five known races breathe the same air." As if to underscore his point, Alnduul waved at the iris valve. As it opened, a musky scent entered along with a warm, moist breeze. Riordan's brain chased after subtle olfactory hints of ginger, lilies, and wet moss, but none of them were exact matches.

Irzhresht touched her control circlet lightly. "You may debark, Alnduul. The area has been cleared."

"Cleared?" Riordan looked from Irzhresht to Alnduul. "Cleared of what?"

"Cleared of younglings," Alnduul explained as he rose to exit the shuttle.

"Why?"

"So they will not see you."

Riordan waited until the iris valve was contracting behind them. "Is there some particular reason why Dornaani chil—uh, 'younglings' shouldn't encounter humans?"

"It is not a general prohibition. It only applies to this planet."

"And what's different about this planet?"

A new voice answered from the thicket they were approaching. "That is a brief question with a lengthy answer, human."

Caine started, but Alnduul padded forward rapidly, his mouth so twisted that it was almost upside down. A broad smile? Beaming?

"Thlunroolt," Alnduul said in an unusually loud tone. He put his elbows against his waist, rotated his arms outward, spread his fingers so that his hands looked like four-rayed stars. "Enlightenment unto you."

A much older Dornaani emerged from the underbrush, returning the gesture. Although not presenting the shriveled grape appearance of the only venerable Dornaani Riordan had ever met—Third Arbiter Glayaazh at Convocation—this male's body was more worn, more bowed. Wearing a control circlet and leaning upon a walking stick, his face was no longer smooth, and his arms and torso were festooned with patches and adorned by a fading fractal pattern of tattoos.

Riordan realized that the elderly Dornaani was staring back at him, eyes wide. Both hands atop his walking stick, he leaned toward Alnduul. "Does the human speak?"

Riordan tucked his elbows against his ribs, pushed his hands and forearms to either side, splayed his fingers as wide as he could. "Enlightenment unto you, honored Thlunroolt."

The older Dornaani's gills popped open with a faint hiss; both inner and outer eyelids nictated sharply. He returned the gesture, still leaning toward Alnduul. "So, it *does* speak. But how did it learn that archaic honorific? Tell me it was not you, Alnduul." He made a slight burbling noise. "I presume it also has a name?"

Alnduul's eyelids cycled sluggishly. Caine struggled to remember the human equivalent. A shrug? No, more like rolling one's eyes. "Yes, Thlunroolt. The human has a name. Caine Riordan. He is my friend."

Thlunroolt's gills puffed silently out from both sides of his thin neck. "You name him so?" He stared at Riordan. "You are one of the humans who attended Convocation."

"I am, hono—Thlunroolt."

The old Dornaani's eyes remained fixed upon his own. "This human is a friend, you say? Well, it, er, *he* seems to learn quickly. At least when it comes to abandoning recidivistic titles such as 'honored.' I suppose that is promising. I also suppose it is incumbent upon me to offer you refreshment. Come along." He turned, indicated an almost invisible trail that led into a copse of what looked like tree-sized goldenrod, except that their flowers were purple and crimson.

Alnduul made to follow, halted when he noticed that Riordan was not moving. "A question?"

"Many, actually. But for now, just one."

"Yes?"

"Thlunroolt *was* expecting us, or at least you, wasn't he?"

"He was."

"Then why is his behavior so...eccentric?"

Alnduul's eyes half closed. "Thlunroolt is unique. Let us follow him."

Thlunroolt ushered them into what looked like a cottager's house built around a sweat lodge. Except instead of a central fire pit, there was a large pool from which vapor rose lazily. Alnduul sat on its edge. Riordan followed his example, crouching in order to do so; the ceiling was only a meter and a half high. "I see your dedication to the old ways is complete," Alnduul murmured.

"Don't judge from a single example," the older Dornaani almost snapped. "You should see my rooms. The latest in environmental controls and medical monitors. Speaking of which, the human's dermis is emitting droplets. Is he ill?"

Riordan shook his head and tugged open his duty suit's smart collar. "Not ill, Thlunroolt. Just hot."

"But the droplets?"

"Perspiration. It's our primary way of shedding heat, cooling our skin."

"Ah. Yes. Now I remember. It has been a long time since I observed humans."

You observed humans? Riordan's interest in the conversation increased sharply, although not as fast as the room's humidity.

The older Dornaani sat and, in one smooth motion, laid aside his stick, rolled on to his belly, and slid into the pool. He emerged on the far side, where he removed lids from two earthenware containers. He did not exactly wade back to his guests; his progress was more akin to a swimming walk.

Thlunroolt laid the containers down between Riordan and Alnduul. "I chose juices that will suit a human palate and biochemistry." The lower margin of his eyelids wrinkled. "Or so I believe."

Riordan hoped his concluding tone was mischievous, but was not entirely sure.

"You looked alarmed, human. Do not be so. If the juices do not agree with you, my medical resources are as excellent as I have claimed, even for an exosapient such as yourself." Thlunroolt's mouth may have twisted slightly. "You may rest assured that the technological pedigree of our local services is well above those you might associate with your current surroundings."

He noted Riordan's renewed attention to the patches and tattoos on his body, tapped the meandering path of circular and oval objects that began on his arms and wandered down his lean, seamed flanks. "These are dosing appliques for life-prolongation. The modalities vary: retroviruses that induce gradual modifications of key organs for greater durability and vigor, stimulation of hunter-killer phages that detect and consume cells poised for faulty replication, and rejuvenatory stimulants for the immune and cellular replacement systems."

Riordan leaned forward. "How long do Dornaani live?"

Thlunroolt's gills flittered shut. "How long do *humans* live? The answer to any such question depends upon many variables. Modern Dornaani that are reasonably healthy and prudent have natural lifespans of one hundred fifty to one hundred seventy Terran years. This is the unaided maximum for our species, achieved after millennia of grooming our genes both to remove weaknesses and amplify our body's capacity for self-rejuvenation. With gene therapy such as mine and, at need, cloned replacement organs, we can live as long as three hundred fifty to four hundred fifty years."

He moved a finger so it rested upon one of his tattoos. "I see you have also noticed these permanent markings. They are not what you call 'body art.' For those of us who elect to wear such markings, they declare our ideology-affinity matrix. I am familiar enough with human facial expressions to see that you have misunderstood. These are not analogous to your race's ritual markings of group or tribal allegiance. These"—he ran his long fingers from armpit to waist—"record my heritage, deeds, and choices, including matrices that signify my preferred epistemological and ontological methodologies and the philosophical and cosmological postures they have led me to adopt." He paused, burbled through the crooked line of his mouth. "Be at ease, human; I do not expect you to understand."

Riordan smiled. "But I think I do. They are a public statement of the biographical and intellectual factors that have given rise to both your concrete world view and metaphysical outlook." Riordan took a breath. "More or less."

Thlunroolt's mouth straightened into a rigid line; his eyelids nictated so quickly that Riordan barely saw it. "That is an adequate perception. If crude."

Alnduul lowered his head, possibly in an attempt to conceal a wry twist of his mouth.

Thlunroolt was still staring at Caine. Without warning, he exited the pool in a single bound. "Have you had sufficient refreshment?"

"I, um—"

"Excellent. Follow me. There is much to see." Winding himself into a modern environmental wrap that he snatched from a gnarled, fibrous hook beside the door, he exited without looking back.

Riordan looked after him, then at Alnduul. "Eccentric," he muttered.

"Unique," Alnduul corrected.

Chapter Nineteen

After three hundred meters, the dense cover—mostly goldenrod trees and five-meter tall clusters of Day-Glo green tubules—began thinning.

"Silence, now," Thlunroolt murmured, even though none of them had uttered a single word during their walk.

They emerged into a glade dominated by an almost perfectly oval pond, hemmed in on three sides by trees. The fourth side was a sand-and-scree shore, beyond which the roofs of primitive structures were visible. Several Dornaani were standing near the water, two of adult height, the remainder considerably shorter and thinner in build. The young had vestigial fins along their spines, their arms, and the top of their heads. They were staring fixedly toward what was, from Riordan's perspective, the right-hand bank.

Thlunroolt gestured to the general scene. "A breeding pool. There are shallows on both the right- and left-hand shores. The direction in which the younglings are looking is the bank where the spawn shall begin their crossing. The opposite bank is where they shall complete it."

Riordan looked at the latter side more closely. "It's higher, and there's more overhanging vegetation. Is that chance?" He peripherally spied Thlunroolt glance at Alnduul once again, whose only reaction was another wry look.

Thlunroolt rested on his walking stick. "You have keen eyes, human. The bank along the shallows to the left is notched by small inlets. Those are the First Calling grottos."

131

"First Calling?"

"Mature Dornaani quickeners—you would inaccurately call them 'males'—shall be in those shallows when the newly hatched young swim across. The quickeners' aquatic movements reprise the basic kinesthetics of their respective Callings. The younglings who complete the crossing gravitate to one of those grottos based on the pattern of motion they find most pleasing or congenial to their sensibilities. That determines much of their initial mentorship." He stared out at the pond. "At least, it does here."

Riordan waited before asking, "And elsewhere?"

Thlunroolt stared up into the sky. "Elsewhere, these ways have been forgotten. They are too troublesome to preserve, or even replicate. New fertilizations are now so rare that they must be arranged in advance."

Riordan frowned. "But there must still be some need for them. Otherwise, your race would have died out. Wouldn't it?"

Thlunroolt met his eyes. "Over eighty percent of all Dornaani reproduction is now fully artificial. Reasons vary, but since we do not have families such as you conceive them, natural reproduction has become either a distinctive choice or merely a curiosity for primitivists. Our species' replacement rate dropped into negative integers several thousand years ago." He stirred the water slowly with his walking stick. "Very few of us remain truly active. This diminishes the personal affiliations and social networks that sustain a species, keep it evolving, growing."

Caine hardly knew what to say after such a melancholy summation. He leaned back, inhaled deeply. The lily scent was particularly strong here. The glade was calm, but not completely silent; the sound of animals, of wind, of water created a natural soundtrack to go along with the serenity of the place. Riordan sighed. "I certainly didn't expect to find *this* on my first visit to a Dornaani world."

"Oh?" Thlunroolt's stick trailed agitated bubbles. "And what *did* you expect?"

"I suppose I envisioned sleek machines, busy cities."

The stick stopped making slow circles in the water. "You are disappointed?"

Caine shook his head. "No, just surprised. I didn't expect visits to sites of natural beauty." He paused. "It's reassuring."

"Reassuring? In what way?"

Riordan drew another deep breath. "It's easy to imagine that when a race achieves the level of technology, of mastery, that you have, that it might forget the importance of"—he waved his hand at the pastoral scene—"all this. It's nice to discover that Dornaani still appreciate it."

Thlunroolt's stick started tracing slow, watery circles again. "I must disabuse you of your optimistic impressions, human. Do not expect to find such a place on our other worlds. Those of us on Rooaioo'q have made a very conscious and costly decision to live this part of our lives, the propagation of our species, in keeping with our biological origins and cultural roots." He withdrew his stick from the pond. "Rooaioo'q is not known for serenity, human. We are known for being intentionally simple. In all the least flattering intimations of that term."

"As in simple-witted?"

Thlunroolt moved away from the water's edge. "We have been called far worse. But enough of that. Alnduul, you and this human will be housed near here so that we may—" He stopped as if struck. The old Dornaani's eyes narrowed, focused on something over Riordan's shoulder.

Caine turned.

Irzhresht had appeared where the narrow trail widened into the glade. Her limbs sagged; her breathing was labored. "Alnduul, if you mean to return to the *Olsloov*, we must—"

"*You* should not be down here at all," Thlunroolt articulated with great formality. "It is unhealthy for you. And very possibly, for us."

Irzhresht's eyes opened very wide, rims quivering. Her markings and mottled stripes darkened, became maroon-mauve.

Alnduul walked to her quickly. "I thank you for bringing this message to me personally, Irzhresht."

"I had no choice. Someone on the planet has blocked communications."

Alnduul met her gaze steadily. "I understand. Return. Wait for me."

"I shall." Irzhresht backed out of the glade. Riordan had the strong impression that she kept her face toward Thlunroolt out of caution, not respect.

Alnduul turned back to the older Dornaani after the sounds of Irzhresht's retreating footsteps faded. They stared at each other for at least ten seconds. If Riordan had any place else to be, he would have headed there in an instant.

"You cannot trust lojis." Thlunroolt's utterance was more raw than any Caine had heard emerge from a Dornaani. He was not sure whether it had been directed at Alnduul or at him.

Alnduul gestured toward Caine with one hand, spiked the fingers of the other down toward Thlunroolt's spatulate feet. "You would put a guest in so awkward a position? He has no—"

"No what? No need to know the truth, that our race is split down the middle? That any overture from a loji may be an invitation to treachery, to doom?" Thlunroolt turned toward Riordan. "Would you not say the same of the Ktor, even though they too are human?"

"I—I don't know." When Caine had begun his journey to the Collective, he thought he'd anticipated almost every path a conversation there might take. Now he was struggling to find any words at all. "We've only met a few Ktor. There might be others who are less predatory, less obsessed with conquest and dominion. And to presume that we know the entirety of their society from those few we've met would be—"

"Racism? And do you believe that is the basis of my reaction?"

Before Alnduul could intervene, Riordan answered. "Isn't it?"

Thlunroolt became very still. At first, Riordan suspected that, like Irzhresht, he had become *persona non grata*. But when the old Dornaani resumed speaking, his voice was calm. "No, my reaction does not arise from racism. Not as you mean it. I do not care about the shape of the loji. But I do care about what *causes* that shape."

He waved a warding hand as Alnduul stepped closer. "Do not interrupt. You will travel with Riordan for many months, so you will have many opportunities to make your many rebuttals."

The old Dornaani turned toward Caine, approached to within arm's reach. "The loji consider green worlds pestilential affectations, objects of senile nostalgia. They are born, live, and die on rotating space habitats they call rings. They have done so for thousands of generations and pride themselves on having no need of help, either from each other or the rest of our species.

"They are organized into guilds or associations that you would call gangs or tribes. But the aspirations of your world's criminal collectives are paltry in comparison to the near-universal desire of lojis: to live in a universe purged of all creatures that require green worlds in order to exist."

Thlunroolt held up a hand in response to Riordan's startled blink. "Do not take my word for this, human. Rather, when you return to *Olsloov*, ask Irzhresht what *her* tattoos mean. At the very least, you will discover that they are badges of allegiance, conferred only after blood oaths—or acts."

Caine found himself leaning away from the agitated old Dornaani. "Loji society: is that what the Dornaani were like, earlier in your evolution?"

Thlunroolt pounded the end of his stick into the ground. "No! The opposite! The loji have not slid backward. They have jumped forward into a devolution, a darkness, of their own conception and creation. In our primitive state, there was no room for, and no thought of, such internecine violence, such horrible rites of passage, of survival."

Riordan frowned. "What do you mean, rites of survival?"

Alnduul looked away.

Thlunroolt placed both hands firmly upon the top of his walking stick. "The loji rings are utterly sterile: artificial complexes with little gravity, no germs, no diseases, and no greenery, not even hydroponics. Is it any surprise, then, that they themselves have become almost completely sterile? And when they do breed, shall I tell you what they have in place of this?" He gestured toward the breeding pool and its bucolic surroundings, did not wait for Caine's encouragement to continue his tale.

"In the water behind me, there are small but ravenous pisciforms. They have, since time beyond reckoning, culled our spawn as they emerge from their eggs. However, these pisciforms cannot survive in a low gee environment. Furthermore, the loji consider them 'extraneous': unnecessary biota and thus, expendable."

Riordan was careful to bring Thlunroolt back to his original point slowly, calmly. "You mentioned a rite of survival?"

Thlunroolt kneaded the head of his walking stick. "The rite is an outgrowth of their inability to breed, to cull, naturally." Thlunroolt's lids nictated rapidly, quivered. "They use their own younglings, still half-feral, to hunt the spawn. To devour their own kind. They starve the younglings for days, just to ensure that they become kinslayers even before they can speak." He glared at Alnduul. "Am I exaggerating?"

Caine was horrified to witness his friend look away again. He turned back toward Thlunroolt. "But don't you—even the lojis—have laws against murder?"

"Spawn are not deemed persons until they exit the far side of the pool, so their death cannot be deemed murder. But that does not mean we cherish them any less. They are our future and so, during the culling, we must actively resist our ancient instinct to aid them. However, the loji, in their rings of spinning metal and rolling cylinders of rock, are relentlessly trained to acquire different instincts. Brutal instincts."

Alnduul's voice was gentle. "Not all loji who come to maturity in those places are endued with their ways."

Thlunroolt raised a single accepting finger. "True, but how can we ever be sure which loji those are? How may we reliably distinguish the hidden predators from those who come to the Collective to legitimately seek their way in our society?"

Alnduul backed away. "I have no answer to your queries. And now I must leave."

"You mean to depart with the loji?"

"I do. She sensed your rejection."

"Yes. And so?"

"And so, I would be a poor mentor if I took any action that she could construe to mean that I share your opinion of her. So to show solidarity, I must accompany her back to *Olsloov*." Alnduul glanced at Caine. "If you are not comfortable in this place, you should return with me now. I will make planetfall again tomorrow."

Riordan wanted to be back in his cabin on *Olsloov*, to get away from the ghastly nightmare images that the old Dornaani had painted. But he also sensed that there was much more to be learned from Thlunroolt, some of which might prove useful as Caine's journey toward Elena took him deeper into the Collective. "No. I'll stay."

Alnduul's eyelids cycled once. Then he slid into the spread-hands posture of both greeting and farewell. "Enlightenment unto you both."

Thlunroolt returned an abbreviated version of the gesture, muttered the same mantra. He watched Alnduul walk away, burbled fitfully.

Riordan watched along with him. "You do not agree with his reasons for leaving?"

The seamed old Dornaani's dental shearing plates grated together: an irritated sound. "In fact, I do agree with his reasons. Once one has accepted the role of mentor, one must be extraordinarily scrupulous in such matters. My disagreement is with his choice of postulant. But, as your colloquialism has it, that is spilt milk under the bridge."

It took Riordan a moment to decipher the perverse amalgam of human colloquialisms. It had evidently been a *very* long time since Thlunroolt observed humans. "You and Alnduul seem to know each other quite well."

Thlunroolt gestured for Riordan to follow him back up the trail. "We should. I was his mentor." Noticing Caine's surprise, he shook the fingers of one hand loosely, dismissing the topic. "Surely you guessed that. No? Well, you will understand us, and our ways, much better after tomorrow."

"What happens tomorrow?"

"You shall witness our reproduction."

Riordan suddenly wished he was on Alnduul's shuttle, which, thrusters glowing, was whispering up into the darkening teal sky. "Is that why Alnduul brought me here?"

"He has not told me. Although I suspect that he wishes you to see our breeding traditions so that you may contrast what we were with what we have become."

They arrived at what looked like a cross between a hut and a cottage. Its doorway was over two meters in height. Clearly not for Dornaani. Thlunroolt gestured toward it. "You shall stay here. It has all the necessary amenities for your species." He walked away without glancing back. "Do not be late rising tomorrow. We start at first light."

Chapter Twenty

APRIL 2124
ROOAIOO'Q, BD +66 582

Riordan discovered Thlunroolt standing just outside the cottage's door when he opened it in response to the first predawn glimmers.

"Acceptable," the old Dornaani mumbled and started down the path to the breeding pool. Once again, he set a surprisingly brisk pace, given his short stride and advanced years.

Mists wound around and disappeared between the tapering black daggers that marked dense, shadowed stands of goldenrod trees. Beyond them, Caine heard distant, distempered grunting. A low, rattling challenge—part snarl, part growl—answered.

Riordan turned toward Thlunroolt. "What was—?" Before he could complete his question, a sudden duel of furious hisses escalated into wild thrashing. A few roars that sounded like falsetto grizzlies, and then silence. Caine became acutely aware that he lacked anything that even vaguely resembled a weapon.

Thlunroolt resumed walking. "It begins."

"W-what begins?"

"They have caught the scent."

"Of us?"

Thlunroolt's slow, deliberate speech was that with which exasperated tutors address very young children. "The bearers entered the pool before first light. The first will have released their effusions by now."

"Effusions?"

"Each bearer triggers the hatching of her eggs with a secretion: the effusion."

"And these animals can smell that from over a kilometer?"

"It is but one of several distinctive breeding scents. The first hatching of the eggs releases wastes and unconsumed nutrients into the pool. That induces swarming and an imminent feeding frenzy in the pisciforms we call *geel*: the culling predators to which I referred yesterday. Collectively, these olfactory and auditory cues arouse the appetite of the carnivores we just heard."

"Appetite . . . for the spawn?"

"No. But I should not speak further of this."

"Because there are some things I may not be told?"

"No, because the carnivores might be close." He turned to stare at Riordan in the gray gloom. "They prefer large prey. Let us finish our walk in silence."

Riordan concurred with Thlunroolt. Silently.

Arriving just before dawn, they discovered the surface of the breeding pool already stippled by small, ferocious eruptions. The accompanying sounds—irregular splashes and flops—reminded Riordan of schools of small fish snatching insects from the surface of a lake.

Thlunroolt must have noticed the sideways tilt of Caine's head as he listened. "It is the *geel*. They are catching the spawn."

"How many survive?"

"Perhaps one in ten."

Riordan glanced in the direction of the old Dornaani's receding voice: he was leading them into an overgrown thicket of what looked like immense broccolini. "How is one in ten enough to maintain your population?"

"How is it enough for your terrestrial fish and frogs?" Thlunroolt tossed a desultory hand of loose fingers in Riordan's direction. "Like them, we are evolved to it. And your frown tells me you have yet to jettison the prejudices of your own species' evolutionary suppositions."

"And what would those be?"

"That intelligence can only develop when a species' pre-sapient reproductory rate decreases to allow proportional increases in the time available for the gestation and then nurturing of sapient offspring. This paradigm—that more time and complex socialization enables and accelerates the rise of intelligence—is a correct analysis of human evolution. But it is not especially applicable to the evolution of intelligence in other species.

"Unlike you, our evolution did not involve collective hunting or fighting off rival species. We trapped fish cooperatively and retreated to a wide array of safe havens when threatened. Equally important, the higher reproductory rate made it normative for us to absorb significant losses and allowed slower, less adept offspring to be culled. Therefore, a comparatively high rate of casualties among our young actually aided our social stability, whereas it would have been disastrous to yours." He seated himself. "You will see that evolutionary difference exemplified in what you witness today."

He pointed across the breeding pool, where there was growing motion in the brush lining those banks. "The bearers are leaving the water. Their part in reproduction is now over, after having been quickened six months ago."

Despite Thlunroolt's casual tone, Riordan kept his own carefully respectful. "By quickened, I presume you are referring to fertilization? Mating?"

Thlunroolt's answering burble was exasperated. "Fertilization does not require 'mating.' Reproduction begins when the quickeners—whom you misleadingly deem 'males'—release a scent indicating that they are nearing what you call estrus in females of various terrestrial species. This attracts bearers who are not already gravid. They signify their reciprocal interest by releasing a scent of their own. This stimulates the quickener to deposit a substance analogous to the milt released by your planet's salmon. The bearers absorb these deposits through special vesicles which communicate it to the anatomical homologue of a terrestrial infundibulum. The milt stimulates the ovaries to release four to six eggs for fertilization."

The Dornaani seemed far more alien than they had only a minute before. "So once the bearers are gravid, does their behavior change?"

"No. Unlike many of your vertebrates, gravid bearers have no nesting or hiding instincts, nor do they require that sustenance be delivered to them. If anything, they become slightly more aggressive, both in securing sustenance for, and protecting, themselves."

"And the males—I mean, quickeners—do not help them?"

"No more or less than usual. I reiterate: our reproductory and gender paradigms have little overlap with yours. Quickeners tend to be slightly smaller and less aggressive. Gravid bearers are markedly more combative and dangerous to predators.

"After four months, they make their way to a breeding pool and lay their eggs. They return two months later to secrete their effusion and so, start the hatching." He looked out over the pond. There was no longer any motion or noise along the opposite bank. However, the surface of the water, now dull orange with the first glimmers of dawn, was alive with the constant, fitful feeding of the *geel*.

Riordan suppressed an impulse to rush out into the water in an attempt to disrupt or chase off the tiny carnivores. It was a pointless reflex here, one that had been evolved for, as Thlunroolt put it, a different reproductory paradigm. But as unnecessary and inappropriate as it might be, it kept surging up whenever Caine was not consciously combatting it. At least conversation and questions were a distraction. "So how many eggs remain now?"

"Almost all. They are hard-shelled, laminate structures, not unlike your ballistic armors. Few predators can breach them. Once they hatch, though, the spawn are completely vulnerable. To survive, they must swim across the pond to where the quickeners wait in the grottos."

"Do they fight off the *geel*?"

"There is no need. The *geel* avoid the smell of mature Dornaani."

"Well, that's convenient."

"No, it is a matter of evolutionary balance." Thlunroolt's mouth—visible now—twisted slightly. "There is ironic reciprocity between the *geel* and my species. When we are but spawn, they eat us. But when we are mature, we eat them." The once-placid surface of the pool was now thoroughly hazed and flecked by their frenzied feeding.

"So, do the quickeners, um, just scoop up the spawn and—?"

"Our young must demonstrate their own capabilities and their own choices. As I explained yesterday, they will choose among the quickeners that line this side of the breeding pool. But they will have to follow that quickener out upon the bank when he leaves his grotto at the end of this day."

"The spawn are already able to walk?"

"Some. Most wiggle their way out and only then discover the use of their legs. But those which cannot are left behind for the waiting *geel*. This is our way."

"So even once they've reached the other shore, this is still a dangerous day for them."

Thlunroolt dangled a pair of noncommittal fingers. "Here among the First Calling grottos, it is more dangerous for the quickeners."

"Why?"

The old Dornaani gestured into the thick vegetation at their backs. "The predators you heard earlier." He raised his head, neck corded by long, wrinkled folds. "They lurk nearby."

Riordan shifted until his right flank faced the pool and his left, the tangled cluster of goldenrod trees and Day-Glo green tubules that screened them from the deeper forest. "In the early days, those predators must have taken a terrible toll on your quickeners."

"They still do."

Despite the warm air, Riordan felt a sudden chill. He examined his surroundings more closely. The breeding pool's long use had smoothed or displaced any hand-sized rocks that might have once been there, and no weapon-worthy deadfall presented itself. "No one guards the quickeners while they're dancing in the grottos?"

"It could be arranged, of course. But it is not traditional, so they choose not to."

"'They'?"

"Those who come to reproduce in Rooaioo'q's natural environment." Thlunroolt waved a hand at the banks around them. "The quickeners and bearers are all here of their own accord. Many come from distant systems. I do not oversee their actions. Nor do I function as their mentor. I merely maintain the facilities and ensure the continuity of the tradition. Some of those who breed here stay on. Most depart."

"Okay, but why risk being eaten by predators?"

"There are as many reasons for accepting this risk as there are those who come to experience it. Most have become so committed to the concept of this traditional experience that they are not willing to modify it in any way. Many others believe that lessening any of the risks in this process—to the spawn, the bearers, or the quickeners—changes the secretions released, and so, produces subtly altered younglings. They assert that making the process safer also makes the surviving spawn—and so, us—less resilient and vigorous than in ancient times."

So part of the reason they come here is to play some primal game of Russian Roulette? Riordan glanced into the brush: no sign of movement. But it was so thick that he probably wouldn't have detected a creature hiding within leaping distance. "Any idea how close those predators are?"

"I cannot say. They are patient, silent."

"But you still hear them?"

"No, I smell their musk."

Close enough to smell *them? Great.*

"They will not attack until the first of the spawn begin approaching the grottos and the quickeners begin their kines-thetic repetitions."

"And what about us?"

"We are not in the water making the sounds that attract the predators. They will not be interested in us. Of course, if one of the *qaiyaat* is particularly ravenous, it may take a second oppor-tunistic kill before starting to gorge. We would be a convenient second meal."

So the longer I sit here waiting like a respectful guest, the greater the chance that one of these qaiyaat *is going to grab me before I find a weapon.* Picking up a woefully inadequate rock in his right hand, Riordan parted the foliage with his left, gritting his teeth against the primal terror of pushing through a blind wall of dark, unfamiliar brush.

A few meters on, enough light filtered through the goldenrod trees and tube bushes to illuminate the forest floor in rough patches. He found a promising arm-length piece of deadfall. It crumbled in his grasp, rotted through by the pervasive mois-ture. Shouldering his way deeper, he noticed a more sizable rock underfoot. He wrestled an obstructing fern aside with both his strength and body weight, but discovered that the stone was a completely useless shape. He peered into the thickening brush, wondered if it was worth going any furth—

Behind him, there was a splash and then a keening wail that cut off as abruptly as it started.

Damn it! Riordan, already smashing back along the path he had made through the brush, had never heard a Dornaani cry out in desperation. He was chilled by its similarity to a human child. He burst through the last tangle of bushes in a spray of leaves and tubules, squinting into a sudden flare of daylight. He saw a shape rising out of a crouch at the edge of the water, hauled back the rock in his right hand as he prepared to block with, and probably lose, his left forearm—

The shape was Thlunroolt's.

Riordan's pulse was still loud in his ears. "You're okay?"

Thlunroolt stared at him. "If I were not, I would no longer be here." He shifted his stare to the rock in Riordan's hand. His mouth twisted slightly.

Riordan tossed it away angrily. *Damned useless piece of—* "What happened? I heard—"

"A predator struck three grottos over. I suspect we have lost Glinheem, may his final enlightenment be full." The old Dornaani looked after the discarded rock, then back at Riordan. "You are impetuous. But then again, you are human." He turned back to the water, watching and listening.

Listening for another of his own kind to be grabbed, like a wide-eyed frog plucked off a lily pad. Christ, how can he just sit *there?* Caine took a deep breath, reminded himself that this wasn't his planet, wasn't his species, and, most of all, wasn't his fight. Because fighting was not what the Dornaani did in this situation. But that silent recitation of the facts didn't still the urgent heartbeats straining against the back of his sternum, straining for release, for action—

Thlunroolt had turned back, was staring at him. "You are . . . distraught?"

Caine realized that his breathing had become faster, deeper, that he was leaning forward, toward the angular shapes of the huts and shacks that he had seen yesterday. He nodded toward them slowly. "Those buildings. Are there any . . . tools . . . in them?"

"Yes, but not many." Thlunroolt's eyelids edged down a bit. "And none that you would find useful."

"What do you mean?"

"I am familiar with your species. You wish to fashion weapons."

Screw the subtle approach. "I do. Can you blame me?"

"I do not blame you. I merely reiterate: those of my race who come to this place wish it to be as it was. This means eschewing any tools, and any actions, that separate them from that experience."

Riordan nodded. "And I will honor those constraints."

"The only constraint upon you is that you may not enter the breeding pool. Other than that, you may come and go as you please. There are no limits on your freedom of action."

Riordan's field of focus tightened until he was only aware of the old Dornaani's face. He carefully repeated the phrase. "There are no limits on my freedom of action?"

"That is what I said, human. You are free to do what you will." Thlunroolt turned away. Riordan looked back toward the huts. Their sides were fashioned from thick logs: useless. But where the thatched roofs protruded out past the doorways, they were propped up by sturdy, narrow shafts of wood set in the ground. Ready-made spears. Caine started to rise...

And then sat again, slowly. No. He could leap up, fashion weapons, go hunting the *qaiyaat* who, unopposed, would no doubt kill many quickeners this day. But in so doing, he would also destroy the experience for which these Dornaani had traveled dozens of light-years: to breed as their first ancestors had. To ensure that their spawn would possess a greater measure of the vitality that was slipping swiftly from their race. To live a real experience, not some virtual imitation of one.

Caine realized he was still sitting very erect, tense, poised for combat. He forced himself to exhale, to sink back into a sitting position and acknowledge that here, his instincts could only mislead him. He had been invited to observe, not intervene.

If Thlunroolt heard his restlessness, or noticed the stillness that followed, he gave no sign of it.

Leaving Riordan in silence as reason and reflex continued to struggle within him.

Chapter Twenty-One

After three hours, Thlunroolt finally moved again, tilting his head upward to study the sun overhead. He picked up his walking stick, turned to look out over the breeding pool. The only sounds were faint and close at hand: the rhythmic movements of the quickeners in their grottos, sending the primal waves and shapes of their calling washing over the spawn who were soon to exit the water and, in that moment, become younglings.

The old Dornaani tapped his stick lightly upon the ground. "It has been an unusually quiet day. The *qaiyaat* have taken only a few quickeners." His mouth twisted. "Your scent probably disinclined them more than any weapons would have." His gills popped lightly. "I suppose Alnduul has arrived by now. We should join him." He stood, finishing on a disgruntled tone, "He will no doubt wish to gloat."

Riordan rose to follow him. "Gloat? Over what?"

"Over my erroneous presumption that you would not be able to restrain yourself."

"You mean, control my instincts?"

"No, most of your species can learn to do that. The true challenge is whether you can control your predisposition to presume moral equivalencies where none exist." His gills fluttered. "For your species, this is a difficult test. Not only is your first reflex to fight back, to meet force with force, but your best moral education teaches you to defend the weak, the innocent. The predation by

146

both the *geel* and the *qaiyaat* were sure to trigger both responses. Yet you suppressed them. You evinced the behavioral and mental discipline necessary to distinguish this morning's events from superficially analogous situations on your own world, and to adjust your reactions accordingly."

Thumping his stick down harder than he had to as he walked, Thlunroolt was silent for several moments before murmuring, "Humans will be worthy Custodians one day. But if our flaw has been reluctance to act, yours will be excessive zeal to do so. Yet it is my hope that the younglings that crawled up onto the banks today will indeed reclaim some of our lost decisiveness. Or maybe a bit more."

Wait, so Thlunroolt hopes today's younglings will be... well, more like humans? Riordan slowed, reconsidered the deep forest, the rude huts, the absence of advanced tools, the ever-present risk from predators. Until now, he had conceived of Rooaioo'q as a reenactment preserve where a subculture of primitivists could turn their back on modern Dornaani society. But now...

He stopped, stared at Thlunroolt's receding, perversely exaggerated hourglass shape. "Rooaioo'q is where Custodians come from. This is how they're born, how they are raised."

The old Dornaani turned. "Not all. But younglings who are spawned here are five times more likely to become Custodians. Those who are also raised here are twenty times more likely. And all of them tend to be the most decisive of their cohort."

Riordan nodded. "So this is Alnduul's home?"

"No, but Alnduul's first mentor, a native of this planet, brought out his pupil's natural decisiveness."

Ah. "You."

Thlunroolt's inner eyelids snicked once, quickly. "Yes." He turned, resumed walking.

Riordan caught up. "So if you were his mentor, you were a highly placed Custodian. Yet you left to return here? Why?"

"Besides being my home, it is close to the place I worked."

Riordan frowned. "I don't understand."

Thlunroolt's mouth twisted slightly. He nodded toward the northeast corner of the sky. "Tonight, look there. You will see your stars. Sol, Alpha Centauri, Epsilon Indi."

The pieces fell together. "So you were a Senior Mentor of the Terran Oversight group, too."

"Yes. Another served in the time between my tenure and Alnduul's. You met her at Convocation: Third Arbiter Glayaazh."

"But you never had a seat on the Collective's Senior Assembly?"

"No. In addition to their reluctance to confer such power upon a native of Rooaioo'q, one of the most turbulent episodes in recent history occurred during my time as Senior Mentor."

"Which was?"

"Making the Ktor Assistant Custodians. I foresaw it would be disastrous but was 'overruled' by individuals who preferred pandering to the millions of Dornaani who crave a placid existence over a principled one."

Riordan started.

Thlunroolt glanced sideways at him. "This outcome shocks you?"

"Somewhat, but not as much as the difference between your opinion of your species and the way most of humanity perceives it."

"And how does your species perceive ours, human?"

"Ancient, enigmatic, and, when it comes to your abilities, a bit godlike."

Thlunroolt stopped, his head bowed, eyes closed. "We are grave robbers, not gods."

Riordan frowned. "I don't understand."

"Human, we accrued our power by scrounging among the leavings of the past. And in doing so, we lost the vigor to weave a new world out of the whole cloth of the future."

His eyes opened. "Human, it is *your* species that possesses the truly decisive power: the inner drive that pushes you outward, the uncritical confidence in your own immanence and will to create."

Caine heard a last-second caesura. "But?"

"But that confidence can also make a race dangerous. A race capable of limitless creation is also capable of the hubris that comes with it. We traded away that vigor and risk for a serene and longer life. Only later did we discover that without vigor and risk, we were no longer living; we were merely surviving. We became accustomed to food without taste, excitement without vulnerability, accomplishment without sacrifice."

He wrung the top of his stick in his hands. "Your species has made the opposite choice: aspirations and dreams over safety. That brings an opposite but equal set of dangers. You imbibe dreams like strong drink. They inspire, they embolden, they intoxicate you with possibilities. But there is a tipping point where they begin to inebriate, distort, delude. And if your avidity for those impossible visions becomes too great, they will ultimately lure you over the precipice of your own limits into a final fall."

Thlunroolt shook his shoulders—annoyance? rejection? a desire to be done with the topic?—and started forward again, more briskly than before. Within a minute, they emerged from the ferns that separated the quickeners' bank from the sandy shore.

Alnduul and Ssaodralth were walking down the slope toward them.

Alnduul's inner nictating lids cycled slowly: recognition, gladness. "So, you have returned to the breeding pool to see the conclusion of the process."

Puzzled, Riordan looked at Thlunroolt, then back to Alnduul. "Actually, we were here all day."

Alnduul stopped in mid step, turned wide eyes upon his old mentor. "You assured me you would protect him."

"The human was in no danger. Indeed, I suspect his scent kept me safe from the *qaiyaat*."

Alnduul's gills popped open and remained that way. "Levity is inappropriate, cannot lessen the severity of your violation. You know the Senior Arbiters gave express orders that Riordan was not to be exposed to risk. None whatsoever."

Thlunroolt planted his stick upon the ground and rested both hands upon the gnarled knob atop it. "So. Do you intend to report me?"

Alnduul's lids nictated rapidly. "I am a Custodian. You know I am required to give a full accounting of a visitor's activities."

"I also recall that not all your reports to the Custodians have been painstakingly complete."

Alnduul blinked hard, as if trying to clear his vision. "You would stoop to extorting my cooperation, my collusion? *You*, Thlunroolt?"

Thlunroolt leaned forward. "Is it extortion to simply ask that, just as I have promised you my silence, you promise me yours in this instance?" He glanced sideways at Caine. "Besides, unless I miss my guess, you mean to include the human in your project, which will necessitate *expanding* the scope of my silence."

Riordan looked from one Dornaani to the other. *Extortion? Silence? Project? What the hell are they talking about?*

The two glared at each other until Alnduul drifted two fingers through the air. "We are agreed, then."

Riordan shook his head. "Wait a minute—"

Thlunroolt wasn't listening, remained focused on Alnduul. "So, it is as I thought. You have not informed Caine Riordan of your project—"

Riordan raised his voice. "Stop. Both of you. What, exactly, is this project?"

Alnduul let his hands descend toward the ground: reassurance, de-escalation, calming. "Caine Riordan, I shall explain, to the extent that I may, when we are back aboard *Olsloov*." He turned to Ssaodralth. "Hasten back to the shuttle. Prepare it for immediate return."

"Are we not remaining here to—?"

"Our plans have changed." He glanced at Thlunroolt. "Significantly."

Ssaodralth made the gesture of farewell and headed back in the direction from whence they had come. Thlunroolt and Alnduul followed at a leisurely pace. The old mentor glanced over at the Caine when he drew abreast of them. "I regret that we shall not finish the spawning day together, human. You were an acceptable companion." His mouth twisted. "Albeit a restless one, at times." His expression grew more serious. "It is customary that a visitor such as yourself is given a token of our esteem and appreciation. However, I have no idea what gift might please a human these days."

The comment hung in the air: an oblique inquiry. Riordan only had to think a moment. "A book. Particularly one on Dornaani history."

Thlunroolt's mouth flattened against his face slightly. "That is an unusual request. Reasonable—praiseworthy, even—but unusual. Why do you desire such a book?"

Riordan shrugged. "Except for the synopsis in the self-reference your representatives gave us at Convocation, we don't know a thing about your past."

The old Dornaani's gills closed with a snuffling sound. "I suspect that was what the Collective intended. And the Custodians are not at liberty to reveal information about any race, not even their own."

Riordan nodded. "Well, if histories are off limits, any personal narrative would do. Anything that shows life as it's lived in your communities."

Thlunroolt uttered a wheezing grunt. "'Communities.' As if we still have any."

Riordan frowned. "But you've spoken of capitals, of cities—"

"Those," Thlunroolt interrupted, "are population centers. Other than this world and a few others, the Collective is an atomized society."

Caine's palms and soles chilled. "Then how do you function?"

Thlunroolt stopped, head drooping as he leaned back and pushed his walking stick into the ground. For a moment, he seemed almost human, like one of the antediluvian Chesapeake locals of Caine's youth, preparing to dispense a crotchety mixture of local lore and dubious advice. "I would be candid with you, Caine Riordan. If you are amenable to that."

"I welcome your candor." Caine meant it. Mostly.

"Then do not ask how we 'function.'"

"Is the question too intrusive?"

"No, it is pointless, compared to what you *should* be asking."

Riordan managed not to smile in gratitude. "Tell me."

Thlunroolt looked up. "How do five separate species all have 'homeworlds' within the boundaries of our tiny Accord, an astrographic sphere only one hundred and fifty light-years in diameter? How is it that those races evolved so as to exist at the same moment in time? Why do all of us breathe essentially the same atmosphere? Why do so many worlds happily have just that atmosphere?" He huffed. "These matters should incite more urgent investigation than the technology you arrogated from your attackers. But like most primitive cultures, your reflex is one of stimulus and response: to focus entirely on the issues and actions of the moment."

Riordan allowed himself to smile. "Whereas the Collective's reaction to the war was consistent with the decrepitude of its advanced age: inability to act due to crippling inertia."

Thlunroolt's eyelids cycled through three rapid nictations, followed by a twist of his mouth and a glance at Alnduul. "I see why you have taken a special interest in this one. Very well. Tomorrow should prove most interesting. Return before dawn. And remember: it would be best if both you and your shuttle remained unobserved."

Chapter Twenty-Two

APRIL 2124
ROOAIOO'Q, BD +66 582

The *Olsloov*'s small, sleek shuttle dropped beneath the buffeting of the upper atmosphere. Riordan turned to Alnduul, his sole companion in the vehicle. "How do I know this isn't another trip into virtuality?"

"Because I would have informed you in advance."

"You mean, the way you did at Zhal Prime Second-Five?"

Alnduul's mouth flattened closer to his face. "I once again ask your forgiveness, but as I explained, that was an experiential necessity."

"And the lack of details about what we're doing today... is that also an 'experiential necessity'?"

The Dornaani was silent for several seconds before answering. "You are familiar with the experimental principle of the observer effect?"

"Of course, the presence and knowledge of the experimenter can change the outcome of the experiment."

Alnduul's eyes closed and opened in slow affirmation. "What we will attempt today requires that you have no advance knowledge of the process or its objective." Alnduul peered into the holosphere, confirmed that the shuttle was following the green-highlighted path down toward the landing pad. "We shall be arriving soon."

Riordan glanced at the terrain in the plot. He saw the breeding pool scroll rapidly out of sight behind them. "Looks like we're heading away from civilization."

Alnduul's mouth twisted slightly. "If I understand the subtextual question underlying that statement, then yes, our destination is a secret facility."

Riordan nodded and leaned back in his acceleration couch. Most of what Alnduul had shared about today's "activity" concerned what it did *not* entail. It posed no physical danger. It did not require any physical effort. It did not violate any laws. It would not take more than an hour. It would not require that Riordan reveal anything about himself that he considered private.

The one feature that Alnduul did volunteer was that it would involve a very brief, and very limited, pseudo-virtuality scenario: nothing immersive, nothing that would trick Caine's brain or sense organs into believing he was having a genuine physical experience. Which hadn't sounded as reassuring as the Dornaani had probably intended it to.

In the holosphere, a margin of clear ground between the edge of a forest and a razor-back ridge of naked stone was rushing up at them. Either Alnduul was one hell of a hotshot pilot or the semiautonomous guidance system made him look like one: despite the precipitous plummet toward the ground, the last ten seconds of counterboosting were so perfectly executed that there was no discernible bump when they landed.

As Riordan followed Alnduul out the dilating hatchway, he saw that the piloting artistry had included a last-moment pulse of sideways thrust which deposited the shuttle beneath the overhanging canopy of the forest. Orbital detection was pretty much precluded.

Riordan followed the unusually taciturn Dornaani across a sward of sponge moss toward the gray, saw-toothed escarpment. Riordan glanced at the sky, then around at the horizon: no sign of habitation or that anyone else had ever set foot on this world. "So is this a black box operation?"

It took Alnduul a moment to recognize that term. "This is neither an official facility, nor is it clandestine or military in nature. So I do not think that the expression 'black box' applies."

"So, a *private* secret lab."

Alnduul had reached the craggy stone face. "That might be a closer analog," he agreed, just before he stepped forward and shifted quickly to the right. And disappeared.

"Do not be alarmed," his voice assured. "The surrounding

stone is cut to effect what you would call a *trompe-l-oeil*. What appears to be a dark vein of rock in the shadow of the closest outcropping is in fact a small, sideways passage."

Riordan followed the Dornaani's voice, almost thumped his head into the ceiling.

"Caution. And apologies, the passage was not designed with humans in mind. Step sideways."

Caine did and suddenly, as if he were stepping out of a magical zone of darkness, lights swam up out of nothingness. Alnduul was standing directly in front of him.

"What—how do you do that?"

"You may recall that your sensors have difficulty detecting our ships, even when they are only one quarter of a light-second distant."

Riordan nodded, saw a natural passage winding away, deeper into the rock. "We dubbed it comboflage, since whatever you've got evidently manipulates both infrared and visible light."

"Which you, personally, hypothesized as being related to our hulls' ability to absorb light, even from weaponized lasers."

Riordan frowned. "Yes, but I never told *you* about that."

Alnduul ignored Riordan's caveat. "Both your theories are correct. A grid of endophotic nanoparticles has been embedded in the surfaces behind you. Collectively, they absorb and convert it into infrared emissions."

"But that means—" Riordan stopped. There was no way to articulate all of what that really meant, and how much more it implied. "So you can convert energy from different parts of the electromagnetic spectrum back and forth pretty easily. And you put this here so that no light would leak out. But why not just put in a door?"

Alnduul's eyelids drooped slightly. "Our densitometers are far more sensitive than yours, even at orbital ranges. A door would be detected as a manufactured feature in what is otherwise a natural passage. Please follow me."

After winding through natural caves, they arrived at a chasm. A stony chin jutting out over the lightless abyss proved to be an open elevator platform that descended swiftly.

Alnduul's voice was ghostly in the rushing dark. "Soon, we will be at a depth where orbital densitometers cannot reliably penetrate. Beyond that, we shall be essentially undiscoverable."

"And you are showing me all this because...?"

"Because there is no other way to bring you to the facility. But also, I hope to illustrate that those of us Custodians who are more proactive have always seen parallels between the secrecy of our *modus operandi* and IRIS's. At least, IRIS as it existed under Nolan Corcoran, and then, briefly under Richard Downing."

"Yes, well, that epoch is well and truly over."

"And yet, you may be certain that a new star chamber shall emerge. It always does, among humans."

The ledge elevator started to decelerate. "Dornaani don't have the same problems?"

"We do, but not with the same intensity or frequency. We are far less driven by rank, status, or class."

Riordan cocked an eyebrow. "I'm not sure I see the connection between the two."

Alnduul joined the index fingers of either hand. "Unlike your pyramidal paradigm of class distinction, our social structure resembles a web. Leadership does not appeal so greatly nor so widely among us. Conversely, there is less tolerance for activities that are not sanctioned by cultural habit or explicitly approved by the Collective." The lift drifted to a halt. Alnduul walked forward into a long, smooth corridor that was illuminated, but had no visible lights.

Riordan followed at a distance. "So the Collective doesn't approve of secret organizations or activities. Sounds like I'm risking expulsion just by being here."

Alnduul stopped, folded his long, thin hands. "Today's activity is not prohibited. And I am not pursuing it in cooperation with any other Dornaani except Thlunroolt."

Riordan looked around at Alnduul's almost archetypal secret hideout. "Then why all this?"

"Just because today's activities are not prohibited does not mean that I welcome scrutiny. You have a saying: to 'fly under the radar'? That is what I am doing."

Riordan looked up into the soaring darkness. "You most certainly are."

After all the not-quite-skullduggery of their journey, Alnduul's hidden facility was distinctly anticlimactic: another smooth-cornered room with few appointments.

Thlunroolt was already there, sitting behind a ubiquitous crescent-shaped desk and control center. He raised a hand, let his fingers trail through the air like loosely jointed chopsticks. "Welcome, Caine Riordan. I am glad you sustained your resolve to participate."

Caine smiled. "Well, it's not like I really know what I've resolved to do."

But Thlunroolt's attention had—conveniently? pointedly?—returned to the controls before him.

Alnduul led Riordan to a human chair positioned in front of an equally human desk. There was a streamlined HUD unit on it, sized for a human head. Riordan picked it up, turned a questioning look at Alnduul.

"Yes. Please put it on."

Riordan ensured it fit snugly. "Now what?"

"Can you see the chair?"

Riordan looked down. "Yes. But nothing else. Not even my own feet."

"That is as it should be. The rest of the scene will fade in when we begin. For now, be seated and relax."

"It would be easier to relax if I know what I'm expected to do."

"I would like you to conduct an interview."

"Of you?"

"No. We are simply asking you to use the skills you acquired as a defense journalist, and to ask the questions that we have prepared for you."

"You know I only did this a few times, right? I mostly did field research, spoke to a few people off camera, read a lot of briefs, wrote up my analysis."

"I am aware. Your skills and natural aptitudes are more than adequate for today's activity."

Damn, I travel fifty light-years to reprise the gig I hated the most? That's fate for you. "When do we start?"

"Now."

The HUD functioned similarly to old-fashioned VR goggles. The cream-nothingness of the null-image became a little more grainy, then shapes started emerging from it: a tan leather recliner, a hazy window, white drapes rippling in a breeze too light to feel, a hint of clear blue sky beyond. It wasn't virtuality, not even close. It was a minimalist dreamscape, softened by a layer of gauze. But no interview subject.

"Alnduul, where's the—?"

"Please! Do not speak, except to the subject. That is imperative."

Yeah, but there's no subject. *So who do I—?*

And then there was a hazy figure in the recliner: a tall man, but his clothes were a bit baggy, as if he had lost weight since first wearing them. *So, old or possibly infirm.* The resolution of the image swam and then suddenly sharpened.

Caine gasped.

"Hello," said the face of Nolan Corcoran.

Chapter Twenty-Three

APRIL 2124
ROOAIOO'Q, BD +66 582

Riordan could hardly think through the surprise. Not until the image of Corcoran smiled one of his avuncular smiles—*my God, it's just like him!*—and urged, "You can start any time you like."

Riordan swallowed; his throat felt like old leather rubbing across older leather. He coughed, glanced down, discovered a virtual data slate on a virtual table. *Okay, I've got a script. That will help.* "It's quite an honor to interview you, Admiral Corcoran. Thanks for agreeing to meet with me."

Corcoran smiled, his salt-and-pepper eyebrows crinkling. "My pleasure. Where would you like to start?"

Riordan forced himself to take a deep breath. The voice, the face, the small gestures, the nuanced shift between facial expressions that were as unique to Nolan Corcoran as his fingerprints... *Christ, how do they do this?* "So, how... how about telling us something about yourself that we probably don't know?"

Corcoran rubbed his chin. "Well, to do that, I need to know what your readers are likely to know about my career."

Riordan realized that he would get through this interview if he followed two strategies. Firstly, not to look at the Corcoran-image for more than two or three seconds at a time. Second, redirect that focus to the script. "Our audience will surely be familiar with your roles in the Highground War, the Belt Wars, and particularly, the mission to intercept the Doomsday Rock. And almost as many will remember your name in conjunction with the subsequent military initiatives that made the UCAS the CTR's preeminent space power, and ultimately, transformed humanity into a starfaring race."

"Well, it's very kind of you to think so, but I doubt that my name is as closely associated with those activities as you presume."

"On the contrary, yours is the name *most* associated with them. But today we're hoping to get a different, more personal sense of who Nolan Corcoran really is. So, let's try this approach, instead: which of your activities, including those of which we are not aware, are you the most proud of?"

"You mean, aside from my children?"

Riordan didn't have to fake the script-cued laugh. "I wasn't aware they were part of your resume."

"They aren't. And frankly, they are not the outcomes of *my* efforts." The Corcoran simulacrum frowned, interlaced his creased fingers tightly. "After learning that the Doomsday Rock had been pushed at us by exosapients, my life was no longer my own. Which means I was not present for my children or wife anywhere near as much as I wanted—as I *needed*—to be. So when it comes to my greatest sources of pride—Elena and Trevor—all the credit goes to my wife Patrice, who somehow managed to be both an all-star physician and family locus. She was the glue that held us all together." His head sagged wearily. "So I'm not proud of what *I* did as a father and a husband. I'm proud that my family thrived in my absence."

Riordan scanned the next line, felt his heart sink further. *My God, do I really have to ask him this?* "It sounds as though you're ambivalent about your life's work."

Corcoran forced himself to look up, unfolded his hands. "I think we can safely call that an understatement."

"Then I wonder if you wouldn't mind telling us what aspect of your career you feel most ambivalent about?"

Corcoran's chin came up; his voice was sharp. "Circumventing due process."

Riordan would have asked the next question even if he hadn't been prompted. "I beg your pardon?"

"Circumventing due process," Corcoran repeated firmly. "I swore an oath to uphold the Constitution of the United States of America. But when you take that oath, you never envision that you might wind up not merely authorized, but mandated, to suppress facts, avoid ready accountability, create the illusion of transparency where none exists, and just plain lie. All at the behest of my Commander-in-Chief, mind you, with a unanimous sign-off from the Joint Chiefs. All approved by the relevant Senate subcommittees.

"But none of that removes the raw reality of looking in the mirror every day and asking, 'How is it that I am fulfilling my oath of service by doing all the things I swore *not* to do?'" Corcoran sighed deeply. "And of all the circumvention and clandestine misrepresentation I had to carry out, the case of Caine Riordan is right at the top of my list of regrets."

Riordan could barely keep reading ahead on the dataslate. *How can this be happening?*

There was sudden sound in the actual room behind him, as though Alnduul had raced over to Thlunroolt and was now whispering urgently.

In the HUD, the copy on the dataslate altered, then flashed red three times. Riordan choked back a rush of tangled emotions—surprise, confusion, indignation, but most of all, mourning—and refocused on following the script. "I can see that this is a sensitive topic for you. However, it's also a natural segue into a related question that I'm sure you were expecting.

"Specifically, your detractors charge that you not only used information control and influence peddling to manipulate organizations, corporations, and even governments, but also to maintain one of the longest conspiracies on record: concealing the existence of an extraterrestrial threat. How would you respond?"

Corcoran sat straighter; there was no longer anything casual in his expression or his voice. "Well, firstly, I was in charge of a 'covert operation,' not a 'conspiracy,' and there is a profound distinction between the two. I was not operating as a rogue agent nor against the orders or interests of the United States of America. In the wake of the evidence discovered on the surface of the Doomsday Rock, a top-secret collective was created to coordinate global intel containment and assessment: the Institute for Reconnaissance, Intelligence and Security. Its formation and mandates were expressly ordered by the Executive Branch, following unanimous recommendations by a blue-ribbon panel from the Senate Near Earth-approaching Asteroid Response subcommittee, chaired by Arvid Tarasenko. Within five years, IRIS had official buy-in and clandestine assistance from the European Union, the Russian Federation, and select elements of what later became the Trans-Oceanic Commercial and Industrial Organization."

Riordan discovered that his emotional discomfort was rapidly giving way to intense curiosity: he'd guessed at the origins of IRIS, but had never had them confirmed. *Although I'm presuming the simulacrum will be as accurate about that topic as it's been about the others.* "Let's go back a moment. Arvid Tarasenko was a friend from your days at the Naval Academy, correct?"

"Correct. And once our activities became a matter of public record a lot of people misconstrued my work with him as evidence of some kind of 'Bilderbergers in the Making' relationship."

"Which your critics have since done. Repeatedly."

Corcoran nodded. "Naturally. However, that's putting the cart in front of the horse. Arvid and I were not late-met schemers who fell upon an opportunity to power. We were old friends who could trust each other and were in the right places to support any initiatives that accelerated Earth's accrual of the advances it would need to survive."

Riordan frowned. *What the hell are the Dornaani after with these questions, or with having them answered by this simulacrum they've concocted?* "As I'm sure you are aware, your detractors prefer the first interpretation of your relationship with Tarasenko: that you were power-seeking illuminati."

Corcoran's smile was rueful. "I'm sure they do. It makes for better copy. But if they stopped to think through the details, they might find some contradictions that they'd be at pains to explain away." The simulacrum stopped, frowned, seemed puzzled. "I must admit, though, that I can't remember the specific accusations of those detractors. Or their identities. But, er, your report of their existence doesn't surprise me. It's just that I, I—"

The HUD blanked to white.

Riordan started, ripped off the headset, jumped up. "What just happened?" Then, flooding in behind the disappointment of having Nolan taken away all over again, was a wash of horror at the technology that had brought his simulated ghost to life. "Why the hell are you doing this?"

Chapter Twenty-Four

Alnduul approached Riordan, hands outstretched. "We simply terminated the simulation. There is no problem—"

"No problem?" Riordan stalked toward the Dornaani, who stopped, retreated a step. "This whole simulation is a problem! An atrocity! Where... how the hell did you—?"

Thlunroolt's voice was loud. "Calm yourself, human. I can—"

"You can shut the fuck up, you smug bastard," Caine shouted, then closed with Alnduul. "Downing let you bury Nolan in space. Because you said you revered him." Caine felt his hands balling up, didn't care. "This... this is *reverence*?"

Alnduul stood his ground. Thlunroolt was reaching for something under the table.

Without looking at the old Dornaani, Riordan snapped, "If you put your hand on a weapon, you'd better be ready to use it."

"You are overwrought," Thlunroolt said quietly, withdrawing his hand. "You are not thinking clearly."

"I'm thinking clearly enough to tell you this: I'm done nodding at your evasions and half-truths and I'm done smiling through your condescension. But you *are* right about one thing: as a human, I'm extremely—excessively—proactive. So if you want to be on the receiving end of that, just keep pushing me."

"I deserve that remonstrance," Thlunroolt said quietly. "But threatening and harming us will achieve nothing. Except that it will end Elena Corcoran's only foreseeable hope of going home."

"Screw that," Caine bluffed. "Assuming I can find her and wake her up, what do I tell her? That you're building an electronic freak show with her dad as the prime attraction? If I haven't turned this place into a crater, she'd come do it herself."

Alnduul swallowed. "Caine. I am sorry. There was no other way to expose you to the simulacrum."

Riordan leaned forward sharply. "You know, I'm also done accepting that same bullshit excuse. Of course there was another way: you could have warned me. Or didn't that occur to any of you superbeings?"

Alnduul folded his hands. "Informing participants in advance of a simulacrum's first exposure to them is catastrophically counterproductive. Every time."

Riordan wanted to stay angry, wanted to have someone to blame, but Alnduul's statement and tone were too earnest, even miserable, to ignore. "Explain that."

"The first activation of a simulacrum has to be with someone that it recognizes and who recognizes them in return. However, the participant must not expect the encounter. It is their surprise which compels the simulacrum to begin reintegrating its memories in order to sustain and clarify the interaction. And, in the process, it initiates the creation of new memories.

"On the other hand, if participants are informed about their 'meeting' with the simulacrum beforehand, they invariably treat it like a fragile patient that must not be disturbed, alarmed, or challenged. And for every minute that a freshly awakened simulacrum is coddled, it is at an increasing risk of deconstructing itself."

Riordan frowned. "So this is why you mentioned the observer effect."

Thlunroolt opened his hands widely. "Precisely. If the participant behaves in a normative fashion, the simulacrum is too busy reacting to the surprise and new stimuli to detect the initial gaps in its own data template, which will fill in soon enough. Conversely, if the simulacrum is protected from strong external stimuli and challenges, that allows it to turn inward, where it quickly discovers those gaps. That initiates a self-assessment cascade that destroys the nascent homeostatic matrix."

"Which is, in plain English...?"

Alnduul glanced at Thlunroolt before he replied. "It is the

interactive and self-learning core of the simulacrum's pseudo-consciousness."

"Pseudo-consciousness"? Either that's psychobabble or this is a lot more sophisticated and troubling than I thought. "If you want me to remain calm, you're going to give me a one sentence answer—in plain language—to each of the following questions. What is this simulacrum, really? How did you make it? And what is its purpose?"

Alnduul's inner nictating lids fluttered before he answered. "This simulacrum is a partial artificial mind. It was made by accessing Nolan Corcoran's own memories and cognitive template. And its purpose—*my* purpose—is to make amends for causing his death."

Wait: what? "You didn't have anything to do with Nolan's death. He was killed by a Ktoran agent. Probably Tlerek Srin Shethkador." *Although I sure wish we knew* how *he did it.*

Alnduul's fingers drooped. "The Ktoran assassination was merely an indirect symptom of a greater disease: our—*my*—inaction. You have seen and lamented it yourself, Caine Riordan: how late we Custodians were in intervening during the invasion of Earth, and how little we were allowed to do. Even Nolan Corcoran's photographs of the mass-driver mooring points on the Doomsday Rock were dismissed as 'inconclusive.'"

"Had we contacted Earth when we should have, and had we protected your species as was our Custodial duty, the Ktor would never have had a reason to silence Corcoran. Our arrival would have made obvious all that he was forced to conceal and which they hoped to silence, or at least derail, with his death."

Riordan felt his anger being eroded by Alnduul's bitter self-recriminations, of the obvious pain he felt over losing Corcoran, a man he had never even met. *But still, this damn simulacrum—* "You still haven't explained how you created such an accurate imitation of Nolan, right down to the way he talks and acts in private."

"There was no need to create an 'imitation,' Caine Riordan. We have a complete recording of all Nolan Corcoran's significant behaviors, habits of thought, memories, and knowledge."

Riordan wasn't sure he'd heard correctly. "A recording... from where?"

"From the organism we insinuated into his chest after the

coronary damage he sustained while intercepting the Doomsday Rock. As I told you after Convocation."

Riordan lowered himself back into the chair. "So, for over thirty years, you were—what? Recording all Nolan's thoughts?"

Alnduul glanced away. "Yes."

Riordan looked from one Dornaani to the other. "Jesus. What are we to you, lab rats? Don't you have any respect for our privacy, either individually or as a planet?"

"As a planet?" Thlunroolt echoed uncertainly.

"Don't insult my intelligence by playing dumb. Unless you can magically teleport a foreign organism into a human body, you had to have an agent of your own on Earth to do it. Probably did it when the surgeons put in Nolan's coronary support pack at Johns Hopkins. One of the team, probably a senior nurse responsible for closing the incision, slipped it in. Which—let me guess—didn't require surgery to attach. The organism did that all by itself, didn't it?"

"Once it is awakened, the biot is self-directed," Alnduul admitted. He looked up. "I assure you that we have never done such a thing to anyone on Earth before."

"Then why did you do it to Nolan?"

Thlunroolt turned away from Alnduul, a movement that suggested this was an old point of contention.

Alnduul folded his hands. "I chose to add the cognition tap to the organism because I feared for Nolan's life. Three years after his return from the intercept of the Doomsday Rock, it was clear that he was becoming pivotal in your world's move to readiness. That made it increasingly likely that he would become a target of Ktoran agents."

Riordan sighed, rested an elbow on the table. "So, you wanted to preserve him. Just in case."

This time it was Alnduul who stepped closer. "I wanted to honor him."

Riordan looked up. Had there been a buzzing quaver in Alnduul's voice?

"You do not fully understand us yet, Caine Riordan. Since we Dornaani do not inherit families and parents, we find our primary affiliations through personal affinities. Nolan Corcoran was a . . . a profound inspiration to me. And with every step of subtle strategic brilliance he took, he also came closer to the end that finally claimed him. I could not sit by and watch that happen."

Riordan frowned. "I didn't know you could conceive of that kind of, well, connection to a human. Particularly one you never met."

"It is not typical," Thlunroolt observed sardonically.

Riordan kept his focus on Alnduul. "So, why did you have to terminate the simulation?"

Alnduul held up two fingers of either hand. "The Corcoran template is more fragile than the ones we typically work with."

"Typically work with?" If this is the only time they've done this to someone on Earth, then who are their usual *subjects?* "What makes it so fragile?"

"The final update from the organism was abruptly interrupted by Nolan's demise."

"That would make a lot more sense to me if I understood how this 'cognitive tap' actually works."

Alnduul's inner lids nictated. "It uses a noninvasive transceiver, much like the one used for virtuality, to record sensory impressions, cognitive activity, and emotions. With those, we build a map of the subject's mental attributes and functions."

Riordan leaned back, unsure of whether to be amazed or horrified.

Alnduul raised a temporizing finger. "If the subject's demise is sudden, the organism will autonomously attempt a rapid relay, but these are often incomplete, compromised. This was the case with Nolan Corcoran. In addition to losing most of the weeks leading up to the Parthenon Dialogues, there was considerable corruption to many memories that he did not consider significant."

"Can you give me an example?"

"Yes. You mentioned 'his detractors.' Although he remembered that such persons existed, he could not recall any individually. That was what forced us to terminate the simulation."

"But how would Nolan remember the concept of having detractors without remembering their identities?"

Alnduul rippled the spread fingers of one hand as if it was a sea fan. "The ability to discriminate data into prioritized hierarchies is one of the few mental traits shared by every species of the Accord. Indeed, most memories you have 'forgotten' are simply stored in a deep archive. However, the cognitive tap only records those that pass through the subject's mind. Data that leave faint impressions are neither strongly imprinted nor later refreshed by recall. In Nolan's case, many details pertaining to these lower priority memories were lost."

Riordan forced himself not to be distracted by the horrific possibilities of such a technology. "So if these memories are so minor, why was it necessary to stop the simulation?"

Alnduul's inner eyelids cycled slowly: affirmation. "If the pseudo-consciousness's expanding interactive matrix encounters a blank space where it expects to find memories, it can collapse. One or two such events are within its tolerance limits. However, repeated failures trigger a cascade of random self-checking, such as you would perform if you woke up with complete amnesia. If, at that early stage, the simulacrum discovers that it is not a complete and conscious entity, its matrix collapses."

"So, my remark about detractors unwittingly pulled on a loose thread in the tapestry of its self-awareness, and you feared it might unravel."

"Yes. Now I must ask *you* a question, Caine Riordan."

"You mean, will I continue?"

"Yes."

Riordan sighed. "So, if you get this simulacrum to work, do you intend to make it available to the Collective or other Dornaani?"

Alnduul's gills popped in sharp negation. "Absolutely not. That is why we are doing the work here. Our only intent is to preserve as much of Nolan Corcoran as we can."

"And if I refuse to continue?"

"We have no other participants the simulacrum would recognize, and so could not complete it. And if a matrix does not become a fully functioning simulacrum, then, if we were . . . audited, it could be erased by representatives of the Collective."

"But if it's completed?"

"Then it becomes a protected creation. Akin to an artifact."

"But to what purpose?"

Alnduul trailed three languid fingers in the space between them. "Your headstones, your mausoleums, your many urns of cremated remains: they, too, have no use and are nonetheless preserved. Yet this is beyond all those examples. For a simulacrum does not just honor a person who has passed, it saves some aspect of them from oblivion."

Riordan thought of Elena, of Trevor, of Nolan's widow Patrice, even of Connor. What would they want him to do? Authorize a memorial that bordered on quasi-sentience? Condone the use of an illegal copy of Nolan's mostly intact consciousness? Riordan clasped his hands where they hung between his knees, fought to still the spinning compass of contending loyalties, impulses, ethics.

And suddenly, there was clarity. *It really doesn't matter what I think, because I don't have the right to decide. All I can do is make sure that he is preserved for now, so that, one day, his loved ones can make that choice themselves. Which I guess means—*

"Okay. I'll finish the job."

Chapter Twenty-Five

When Riordan reentered the lab, Thlunroolt was once again seated behind the crescent table. His tone was less jocular. "My regrets for the delay, Caine Riordan. It took us four days alone to calibrate where you may safely reenter the simulation."

Riordan nodded. *And one more for getting everything ready.* Although, according to Alnduul, who was reviewing a hologram of the amended script, they would not have been able to leave, anyway. Word had arrived from the regional capital to stay where they were, for now. Reason: unknown.

Riordan adjusted the HUD. "Okay, I'm ready." After an interval of two seconds, the same fragmentary room faded in from the cream background. A moment later, Nolan was back in the chair.

That was Caine's cue. "You've frequently been accused of using information control and influence peddling to manipulate organizations, corporations, governments, and to maintain one of the longest conspiracies on record: suppressing proof of extraterrestrial intelligence. What's your verdict upon yourself: guilty or not guilty?"

The Corcoran simulacrum seemed disoriented for a moment, but quickly became both more focused and more animated. "Although I'd contest the term 'conspiracy,' I'd have to say 'guilty as charged.' However, some misdeeds are not well understood, or judged, without context.

"Stark violations of basic laws and conscience, such as the murder sprees of sociopaths, can be judged summarily. But at the other end of the spectrum are actions that occur in the gray of a perpetual ethical and moral twilight." The simulacrum shook its head. "That's where almost all covert operations are conducted. Ultimately, it is history that sits in judgment. And perhaps that is best. Those who occupy a more distant vantage point upon the unspooling timeline often see the total context of a deed more clearly than those who witnessed it firsthand."

Had Riordan been conducting an actual interview, he might have remarked that Corcoran's response was, in fact, a wonderfully poetic and circuitous non-answer. Instead, his lines were: "Are you suggesting that your own deeds will be better understood, and perhaps more widely praised, with the passage of time?"

Corcoran shrugged. "I'd like to think so. But I'm not sure that the complete story of our preparation for first contact will ever—or should ever—be told."

"Because people can't handle the truth?"

"No, because some truths are so profoundly convoluted and byzantine that there's no way to present them both concisely and comprehensively. Too much simplification and the context is lost. But too much detail and people get weary of all the onion layers that have to be peeled away to show the core reasons for the decisions made, the actions taken."

All true. Also an unimpeachable rationalization. "How would you respond to critics who claim that kind of appeal to 'undisclosable contexts' is just a redirecting sophistry? Consider this an open platform, with posterity itself as your audience."

Corcoran—*damn, it's hard to remember it's not* really *him*—smiled. "Okay, then, let's drop the elevated rhetoric and get down to brass tacks.

"Try to put yourself in this scenario: it's the day you learn what the Doomsday Rock really is. Someone, or some force, is threatening everything that you know and love, all the history that led to it, and all the generations that will come after. Do you carry on as before, decide *not* to take extraordinary measures in response to that extraordinary threat? Some call that 'moral transcendence,' to choose not to contemplate responses of questionable morality and to just let the cosmos unfold as it will.

"But even the Buddhists maintain that there are limits to the pursuit of an unsullied moral existence. To paraphrase their perspective, to choose to do nothing is still a choice. And every choice is an action. Which confronts us with this quandary:

"The universe may be maddeningly indifferent, but we humans must still choose our moral posture within it. Do we choose to act in pure self-interest, like a voracious wolf? Do we choose not to act at all, like rabbits that go limp under the wolf's paws? Or do we choose to act both for ourselves and others, like a wolf-hound, ever ready to drive off the wolf?

"I'd like to say I chose the latter course because of some transcendent, enlightened world view. But that's not my reason, any more than it was the reason for creating IRIS. I—we—just wanted to give our flawed, wonderful planet a fighting chance. I had seen the imprint of the wolf's teeth sunk deep into the surface of the Doomsday Rock and, damn it, I was not going to go down without a fight.

"I believe most human beings feel the same way when they think about their family, their friends, their unborn grandchildren. You don't just lie down and give up. You take the fight to the wolves just as hard and as long as you can. And you do so in the belief that someone will carry on the fight when you fall." He locked his eyes on Caine's. "All enduring hope springs from that belief. Because without it, you lack the will to persevere. And if you do not persevere, you cannot prevail."

The simulacrum hung its head. "That said, we made mistakes. Almost daily, we found ourselves on the horns of a dilemma that illustrated why no fight, and certainly no killing, is ever an unalloyed moral good. The best you can say is that sometimes it's necessary, if it's the only way to drive off the wolf."

"That sounds like a heavy load of guilt to carry."

"It is. Every battlefield and bloodstained alley *should* leave us with memories and uncertainties that we can't just dismiss. That is the price moral culpability exacts, and we must not shirk it. Otherwise, we become wolves ourselves."

Suddenly, Caine missed the real Nolan very intensely. "It sounds like you've given this a lot of thought."

Corcoran smiled. "You should know; you wrote the book. So to speak." Without warning, the simulacrum started, looked around, confused but also surprised. For a moment, the virtual world became grainy, static-ridden.

The virtual dataslate at the bottom of Riordan's HUD blanked, then reilluminated in bold red letters: REDIRECT THE CONVERSATION.

What the hell—?

The simulacrum stared around as if it had blacked out momentarily. "I . . . I'm sorry, I seem to have lost the thread of our conversation. What were you asking?"

Riordan's palms had become clammy. "Actually, we were just wrapping up. Maybe you got a little distracted, had a memory lapse."

The simulacrum seemed unable to focus. "Yes, maybe I did have a lapse . . . but I also seem to remember things. Things that didn't happen. I seem to know you . . . but I don't. Well, I mean I recognize you, but . . . How did we meet, again? And where are we—?"

The room almost grayed out. The simulacrum started violently.

Riordan kept his reaction honest but muted. "Are you feeling well, Admiral Corcoran?"

The simulacrum squinted as the room returned to its normal appearance. "I'm feeling disoriented. Like I'm not quite myself. Literally." He laughed weakly, looked up and, wide-eyed, stared. "Caine?"

Riordan had no idea how to respond. There was no script for this. So he did the only thing he could do honestly: treat the simulacrum just as if it was the real Corcoran. "Yes, Nolan. It's me."

"It's good . . . good to see you. So good to . . ." Corcoran's eyes grew shiny. "I'm sorry, Caine. I'm so, so—"

"There's no reason for apologies." It was both touching and terrible seeing Nolan Corcoran on the verge of tears, but Riordan followed his instinct to keep the simulacrum talking, interacting. "It's good to have you back."

"It's good to be back . . . but where?" The simulacrum looked around. Initial surprise gave way to increasing focus and wariness. "Caine, your house. It's strange."

"It's not my house, Nolan."

"No? So you . . . do you see it, too?" He gestured at the hazy window, drapes, sky.

Riordan watched Nolan's eyes, understood. "The lack of detail? Yes."

"So what I'm seeing . . . isn't really there?"

"Not exactly."

"That's a pretty lousy answer, Caine." Corcoran grinned, but not very convincingly. Then, his brow straightened and his voice became relaxed, casual. Too casual. "So Caine, how did you find out that Elena's favorite flowers are orchids?"

"But"—Riordan shook his head—"they're not."

"Sure they are. You left one outside our door. Back on Luna."

Ah. A test. "No, Nolan. I left Elena a single red rose. With a bottle of Châteauneuf-du-Pape. I guess you found both in the paper bag?"

Corcoran's answering smile rapidly changed from relieved to cautious. "Are we alone here . . . wherever 'here' is?"

"No."

Nolan was too intelligent to believe that there was any advantage to remaining circumspect. "Who's eavesdropping on us, then?"

"Exosapients. The ones you conjectured were watching over us. The ones who made it necessary for hostile aliens to resort to the subterfuge of the Doomsday Rock."

Corcoran's eyes opened wide. "Are they, the aliens, here? Or are we on their world? Is there any way I can talk to—?"

The HUD blanked; Nolan was gone. A warning appeared, flashing in an entirely different typeface. The bold orange text read:

ALERT ALERT ALERT

re: source-originated simulacrum "Corcoran"

Memory and cognition parameters flash-relayed to Collective for extended analysis of possible data corruption

Event investigation delegated to Glayaazh, Third Arbiter

By order of Dornaani Collective, Glamqoozht

Riordan slipped off the helmet, discovered that Alnduul and Thlunroolt were staring at each other, eyes widened to the point of distention. "What the hell just happened? What does that warning mean?"

Thlunroolt seemed hoarse. "It means that the simulation had a hidden subroutine that would terminate it when certain parameters are exceeded or violated. It also means that the simulation is fitted with a backdoor access. For monitoring by the Collective. They have just been alerted to what we have done."

"But the Collective is two shifts away. How can that message reach them directly? It's imposs—"

"Caine Riordan," interrupted Thlunroolt somberly, "for now, is it not enough that such a message obviously *can* reach them directly?"

Riordan shrugged. "I guess so." *But if you can send messages instantly over distances of twenty light-years, then we've got to reassess all your capabilities.*

"We are done here," Thlunroolt muttered.

Alnduul let a single finger dangle. "I will assess our last capture of the simulacrum's real-time template. I shall meet both of you on the surface."

Thlunroolt and Riordan had ridden the ledge elevator halfway up before the old Dornaani commented, "You were surprised that Alnduul was so devoted to the memory of Corcoran."

It wasn't a question, but it certainly invited response. "I was. But I suppose it makes sense. They contended with many of the same official constraints, the same problems."

"True, but that is not the important lesson to be learned from it, Caine Riordan."

At least Thlunroolt's tone wasn't condescending any more. "Go on."

"As Alnduul observed, we Dornaani do not inherit families, we choose them. Consider what that might imply, if the current crisis continues to unfold."

Riordan stared. "What crisis?"

"The Accord is paralyzed. The Arat Kur and Hkh'Rkh are under probationary suspension for invading Earth. The Ktor have refused to participate further until the Accord is changed, and would be expelled if the Lost Soldiers and their other violations are brought forth. Your Consolidated Terran Republic has postponed joining in order to settle star systems that would otherwise be off limits." Thlunroolt stared up at the first-level ledge, which had appeared out of the darkness above. "These circumstances are inherently unstable. A reckoning is approaching."

Riordan frowned. *Well, when you put it that way . . .* "Okay, but how is Alnduul's cross-species affinity related to any of that?"

"It points toward an important variable in the times to come: that some of us Dornaani have a marked tendency to gravitate toward, and identify with, humans. And through that, to 'adopt' them."

Riordan glanced over at the wizened Dornaani as the ledge elevator began slowing. There had been no hint of irony or facetiousness in his tone or in his expression. "How early did Alnduul know that he wanted to work in Human Oversight?"

Thlunroolt folded his hands in front of him as the elevator snugged up against the rest of the ledge. They stepped off. "To adapt a human expression, he was spawned to be a Custodian. It was the greatest joy of my career to be his mentor." As they entered the narrowest part of the tunnels that would bring them back to the cave mouth, the old Dornaani's voice took on a hint of reverie. "He has been observing your race for one hundred and forty years, the last forty as Senior Overseer."

Riordan saw the significance. "So he took charge in 2083, the year Nolan intercepted the Doomsday Rock."

"The affinity he felt for Corcoran is not, in retrospect, difficult to understand. As you said, in some ways, their careers paralleled each other."

They entered the dark zone near the cave mouth, exited into the crisp shadows of early midday. "I would give you a gift, Caine Riordan." Thlunroolt parted the folds of the deceptively plain-looking saturation suit he wore whenever the temperature and humidity dropped below that which prevailed around the low-lying breeding pool. He held forth a book. The wider-than-longer shape indicated it was Dornaani.

Well, maybe the old coot really does like me after all. "Thank you, Thlunroolt. It looks new."

"It is, relatively speaking." The old Dornaani's mouth twisted congenially. "Just under six centuries. It is, for want of a more adequate label, a history book."

Riordan stared at it with greatly enlarged interest. "But isn't this illegal? You're not supposed to reveal information about any other races, even your own."

"I no longer represent the Custodians or the Collective in any capacity, so I am no longer subject to that restriction."

Caine opened the book. A cascade of curls, swirls, and squiggles flooded across the pages. "I have to confess, I can't read Dornaani."

"Evidently. You are holding it upside down. However, there are translation programs. Better still, perhaps the desire to read this book may encourage you to learn our language. Which might prove useful." He backed up a step, assumed the farewell posture slowly, as if signifying regret at parting. "Truly, enlightenment unto you, Caine Riordan." His arms drooped slightly. "And be careful in your travels."

They turned at the sound of movement back near the cave mouth. Alnduul had just emerged from the shadows. Thlunroolt took a step in the direction of the sheer escarpment. "And now, I must say farewell to my old friend and pupil."

Alnduul slowed as Thlunroolt approached and asked, "So, what of the simulacrum?"

"Its cognitive matrix is intact. It is more developed than we dared hope."

"Excellent. It is no less than what you wished for."

Alnduul cycled his outer eyelids emphatically. "It is what we *needed*. Desperately. But the alert sent to the Assembly requires that we accelerate the timetable."

Thlunroolt's mouth tilted. He put an affectionate hand on the side of Alnduul's arm. "After today, it is not just this plan that must adopt an accelerated timetable."

"I am sorry I ever approached you with this, my mentor, my old friend."

"You were ever my favorite student, Alnduul. But you were also my most willful. So if there was one thing I never expected from you, it was a slavish concern with protocols. Or consequences."

"So you anticipated that one day I might attract unwelcome official scrutiny?"

"It was always a possible outcome. But more recently, given the Accord's accelerating dissipation, it became inevitable."

Alnduul let his breath burble softly, sadly, out of his gills. "Is that not the supreme irony? That a Custodian can only meet his mandate by taking actions that conflict with the protocols that are the root of his duty and the source of his agency?"

Thlunroolt's mouth twisted slightly. "It is just as the Corcoran simulacrum described. When the stakes are high enough, our duties often place us in covert violation of the rules we swore to uphold. It has ever been thus. It is simply more so, now. Enlightenment unto you, Alnduul."

"And unto you, Thlunroolt."

Back on *Olsloov*'s bridge, Riordan perched on the edge of his excessively responsive cocoon couch, watching the recently arrived Dornaani courier commence preacceleration for its outshift back to the regional capital. "So the Assembly has extended the delay even further?"

Alnduul scanned the message the courier had carried to them. "Unfortunately, yes."

"Because of what happened with the simulacrum?"

"Only in part." Alnduul looked up. His eyelids cycled slowly, apologetically. "There continues to be considerable disagreement over how to interact with you."

Riordan nodded, glanced down at the utterly alien book in his hands, a mute reminder of the Dornaani's complicated past. *The Dornaani's past—?*

He glanced over at Alnduul. "Coming to Rooaioo'q was about more than meeting your mentor, or seeing how you reproduce, or even interacting with the simulacrum. Thlunroolt was right: you wanted me to see your race's origins, what it came from, before I see what you have become."

Alnduul said nothing for several long seconds. "It is sometimes awkward, but always gratifying, to be fellow travelers, Caine Riordan."

"It is. Despite all the delays."

Alnduul stared at Caine. "I was not speaking of our current journey. I was speaking of our longer paths." Then he turned to regard the holograph of the Collective's stars, which stretched upward in a helix of many-colored jewels of light.

Chapter Twenty-Six

Alnduul closed the comm link to Glamqoozht's port authority. "We have just received permission to travel planetside, Caine Riordan."

Riordan looked up from the equivalent of a "teach yourself Dornaani" program. It had been almost a month since they'd left Rooaioo'q, and his mastery of the language was still lagging behind that of an early youngling.

Olsloov had completed in-shift to the regional capital exactly ten months after Caine left Earth. Alnduul communicated their arrival and was promptly ordered to take up a tether at the highport's spindock. Glamqoozht's was one of the largest such facilities: a thirty-kilometer rotating cylinder where ships moored to tethers of different lengths, thereby imparting differing values of equivalent gravity. Sparsely inhabited systems had smaller equivalents: spinbuoys, which worked on a thrust-and-counterweight principle. Alnduul had explained that the ubiquity of the spin facilities was not merely to reduce the medical consequences of zero gee, but to eliminate the travel conditions which had given rise to the lojis. Alnduul had moored *Olsloov* to a tether with a rotational rate that produced half a gee, and there they continued to spin, ignored by Glamqoozht's authorities.

Now, nine days later, they were finally being officially recognized.

Riordan waved the language program away. "When do we head down?"

178

"Tomorrow. We must arrive early. Few of our planets have screening as rigorous as Glamqoozht's."

Riordan wondered if he might be able to translate any part of the planetary name, tried, gave up. "Is Glamqoozht just a place name or does it mean something?"

"It translates imperfectly as Council Hub."

Riordan was guardedly hopeful. "Sounds like it's a place to get questions answered and decisions made." Unless, of course, it was like human capitals.

"Glamqoozht is also the administrative center of the Collective," Ssaodralth commented from the navigation station. "Although it is not the meeting place of the eight Senior Arbiters of the Assembly, it is the site of the government's supporting infrastructure, research and oversight agencies, communications nexus, and most records. It is also where the Arbiters spend most of their time."

Riordan frowned. "Then why not simply move the capital here?"

Alnduul raised a didactic finger. "Because this is not our designated homeworld."

Fair enough. "So is this meeting formal, with prepared statements, or more free-form and conversational?"

Ssaodralth and Irzhresht were absorbed reading their instruments. Alnduul's outer lids cycled once. "It will not be formal, but nor will it be relaxed. In addition to a number of Regional Arbiters, we shall be speaking to four Arbiters of the Collective's Senior Assembly: Nlastanl, Glayaazh, Heethoo, and Suvtrush."

"Why only four Arbiters? Ssaodralth just said that most of them reside here on Glamqoozht."

"They do, but several are gone. And one indicates that she is . . . indisposed."

"So, a snub."

"Some do not wish to be associated with the prominent human who suggested and supported Earth's delay at joining the Accord and subsequent unilateral expansion."

Riordan nodded. "Because if they meet with me, they could be accused of tacitly condoning those policies."

One of Alnduul's fingers lowered; the other became an affirming streamer. "This is why I did not press for an earlier invitation to the Collective. Because if the Collective ever formally disapproves of humanity's present 'land-grab' activities, your government may honestly reply, 'You neither responded to our attempts at, nor initiated, communication.'"

Riordan forced himself to exhale slowly, patiently. "So Elena's fate has been held hostage by your Assembly and its infighting. I just hope the Custodians remain my friends."

"I hope that also, Caine Riordan, but bear this in mind: my presence no longer confers the implicit support of the Custodians. To use your expression, I have been 'placed on probation' for my actions in support of Earth. However, I am still allowed to act as your translator and chauffeur."

"And you can continue to work as my advisor, too. Right?"

Alnduul's inner eyelid cycled rapidly. "That is part of what we shall learn tomorrow."

The moment Caine stepped out of the interface terminal alongside Alnduul, he fleetingly wondered if he was in another virtuality simulation. The cerulean blue of the sky and the mani-cured green of the pygmy rushes—which were more like terrestrial grass than any other world's ground cover—seemed impossibly pristine and perfect. The city itself was a study in alabaster and silver. Hemispherical domes and low rectangular frustums clus-tered around the bases of towers. Most of those tapering spires were capped by disks, each ringed by windows that reflected the sky and the mirroring blue of the quiet bay. The water stretched away from the city in an improbably perfect arc, lapping gently at pink sands that lined a coast-following slideway. In the dis-tance, aviforms swirled around cliffs and buttes towering above dark green skirts of forest.

The olfactory sensations were less ideal: a carrion sourness blended with a musky-pine scent. Given the Dornaani penchant for slightly aged seafoods, it was no surprise to find that odor included in what they considered a blend of pleasing aromas.

Alnduul gestured toward the slideway. "Shall we continue?"

Riordan nodded, stepped on to the moving pedestrian thor-oughfare. "Sorry. I was just taking it all in. It almost looks unreal."

"From a purely natural standpoint, it is. The weather is largely controlled, pollutants are both regulated and reprocessed, and the flora and fauna have all been carefully managed. Anything undesirable was removed long ago. What remains has been genetically engineered, even the rushes. They are completely resistant to pests and blights, and grow to a precise length and shape."

Riordan surveyed the scene again. Knowing that it could not be other than perfect made it seem less remarkable, much in the way a constructed vista in a theme park could never quite compare with a less perfect one discovered in nature. This was merely a technological achievement, and the price of its perpetual perfection was its inability to inspire a sense of grandeur. He wondered if the Dornaani had not, unwittingly, revealed something of themselves in their shaping of this environment.

As the slideway carried them into the first urban microcluster, Riordan was struck by yet another unusual feature: the serenity and sparseness of its inhabitants. "Where is everyone?"

Alnduul surveyed the spaces between the buildings. "Our cities are not dwelling places so much as they are work centers. What you see is typical."

As the slideway carried them into the center of the urban cluster and closer to Dornaani pedestrians, Riordan noticed that they seemed more completely naked. It took him a few moments to discover why. "No control circlets or vantbrasses." He turned toward Alnduul. "And you left your wearables back on *Olsloov.*"

"It is unlawful to have them here."

Riordan frowned. "Why?"

"Security. Glamqoozht has very few computers and, except in extraordinary circumstances, none of them have any means of exchanging data. Simple recording devices are permitted, but they can only relay their content via prelinked lascom."

"Then how does this place function? The Collective seems to rely on expert systems, semiautonomous machines, remote controls. And what about virtuality?"

"Virtuality is illegal here. And yes, our bureaucracy moves much more slowly here than elsewhere." As they neared a broad concourse, Alnduul gestured toward a swarm of mobile disks moving parallel to the slideway, or, in the case of further ones, churning in a sluggish imitation of Brownian motion. "From here, we must walk."

As soon as Alnduul's outstretched foot touched one of the disks, it adjusted to his speed, allowing him to exit the slideway without a wobble. It carried him across the current of other waiting disks toward an immaculate concourse that led between two of the tallest towers.

Riordan followed his friend's example, marveled at the responsiveness of the disk. He had no sensation that he was transferring from one moving object to another. As soon as Caine had joined him, Alnduul headed directly toward the soaring tower on the left, cutting diagonally across the concourse.

As he did, a loose cluster of pedestrians crossed their path just long enough for Riordan to realize that these weren't ordinary residents. They weren't even Dornaani.

One of the creatures was a pony-sized hexaped. Its patchy hide was a mix of spines, exoskeletal flanges, and bristles. It had a neck, but instead of a head, it sprouted a cluster of organs that resembled translucent eggs.

Walking casually beside it was a quadruped, its forebody vaguely reminiscent of a terrestrial hominid. Its barrel-chested torso tapered back into hindquarters constantly rippling with the motion of its spiderlike legs and long, narrow tail. As its four eyes blankly assessed Riordan, he reflexively stepped away. The high-jointed legs, smoothly scaled and muscled, evoked a momentary impression: a giant tarantula wearing a lizard suit.

The other two creatures were somewhat similar to deer, but did not have hooves. Their legs ended in wide stumps that changed shape and consistency as they came into contact with the surface of the concourse. Bony, wing-shaped protrusions lined with spiracles emerged from behind their shoulders, where strong planes of muscle supported a structure that Caine supposed was a head: a sleeve of calloused hide housing a writhing, questing mass of tendrils. Or polyps. Or maybe tentacles.

All four creatures walked calmly toward the disks that jockeyed lazily, endlessly, along the margin between the concourse and the slideway.

Caine realized he'd been staring. "What . . . what are they?"

"I am unfamiliar with two of the species. The last pair of quadrupeds, however, are familiar to me from my perusal of—"

"No, no. I mean, are they intelligent? Are they protected species?"

Alnduul's narrow tongue made a buzzing sound against the inner surface of his lamprey-mouth. "They are not sapient. They are bioproxies. More than pets, but less than true servitors. They can perform simple tasks."

"But they are moving as if they understand how to navigate the city."

"That is now instinctual for them, imposed by genetic manipulation. Their behaviors can be further altered by chemical infusions or embedded controllers."

Riordan stared after the four creatures. The streaming disks were depositing them on the slideway. "I didn't think that Dornaani used creatures this way."

Alnduul gestured that they should resume walking. "Caine Riordan, it is profitless presuming that there are still 'common' traits amongst Dornaani. Amongst the Custodians, shared tasks lead to some shared behaviors and attitudes. But we are the exception."

Riordan studied the few Dornaani pedestrians. They seemed unaware that anyone else was on the planet, let alone the concourse. "When Thlunroolt said that your species was almost completely atomized, I thought that was hyperbole."

"No," Alnduul said slowly, "it was not. Nor am I being alarmist when I warn you that, above all else, you must not mention the theriac, Caine Riordan. Some of the Arbiters might use that as leverage. We must move quickly to the chamber reserved for our meeting. We are expected in five minutes."

Upon entering the elevator just beyond the entry, Riordan worked at remaining calm. Finally, he would meet the Dornaani who held Elena's fate in their hands. With any luck—

Caine looked around, frowning. "This elevator is going down."

Alnduul glanced sideways at him. "Yes. It is."

Riordan suppressed a sharp pulse of disappointment. He had imagined ending his long quest in a wide chamber populated by solemn Dornaani, the bay laid out before them in the sectional panorama of windows that lined the tower's shining crown of silver.

Instead, the elevator doors opened to reveal stolid walls of fine-grained concrete. The lighting was dim. It could have been a subterranean access passage between any two office buildings on Earth.

It's better this way, Riordan told himself as he followed Alnduul. *No distractions. Hell, if I could just be sure of bringing Elena home, I'd gladly meet them in a broom closet.*

But somehow, it was still a disappointment when the meeting room was revealed to be, for all intents and purposes, a broom closet.

Granted, it was a very large broom closet. It was adequately lit, and the furnishings, including the single human chair, appeared comfortable. But there were no windows, no podium, not even a water pitcher. Or whatever the Dornaani used in place of one.

Twelve Dornaani watched him enter, seven of whom were holographic images. Of the five that were present, the oldest was familiar. Riordan adopted the customary posture of greeting. "Enlightenment unto you, Glayaazh."

She seemed pleased. "And unto you, Caine Riordan. You look well. Particularly considering all that has transpired since last we met."

"The Third Arbiter's gift for understatement remains undiminished. I heard this gathering would be larger."

One of the holographic Dornaani began scratching himself. "Almost half of those who originally considered attending have been called away by other responsibilities." His tone of voice and public scratching made the subtext clear: like him, those absent had nothing but profound disdain for Riordan.

Glayaazh's eyes narrowed in response to her colleague's rudeness. "What Yaonhoyz has neglected to add is that, as planned, three other Senior Arbiters of the Collective are here. They signal the importance the Assembly puts upon this meeting." She gestured to the Dornaani on her left and the two to her immediate right.

The older of those two emphasized his physical presence by loudly hunching forward in his seat. "I am Nlastanl. I shall moderate our discussions. Do you have any questions before we begin, Caine Riordan?"

Riordan reflected that Nlastanl's graceless introduction made Thlunroolt seem like a silver-tongued diplomat. "I want to confirm that you are aware of the reason I asked for this meeting."

Another of the physically present Dornaani emitted a burbling grunt. "It is not your request that perplexes me, human, but that the Assembly agreed to it. Sedged gills, you have no reason to be here at all. You have no official standing with your species' government, which itself has no official standing with the Accord or with the Collective. To say nothing of the marginal sapience that your race evinces—"

Nlastanl's loud hiss halted the Dornaani in mid word. "Laynshooz, do not compel me to acquaint you with the consequences of another such outburst."

Laynshooz hissed back, though less sharply. "I would welcome expulsion, even censure."

"Those," Nlastanl said slowly, "are the least of the consequences to which I am referring."

Whatever meaning Laynshooz associated with that threat, it was decisive. He leaned back and was silent.

Nlastanl stared around the table. "Laynshooz's derogatory remarks compel me to affirm, for the record, that the human Caine Riordan, while not here on official business, is held in high regard among the Custodians and many within the Collective. He is also our most promising conduit for eventually reinitiating official contact with the Consolidated Terran Republic."

What?

One of the holographic Regional Arbiters objected. "But he no longer has access to the leaders and planners of his own species."

"That is to our advantage. If Caine Riordan was still in the service of the CTR, we could not have a purely unofficial, and therefore frank, conversation with him."

Riordan tapped the table. Every pair of Dornaani eyes swiveled toward him. "I reiterate: does anyone know why I've traveled here?"

"Your mate," murmured the image of Heethoo, one of the other Senior Arbiters.

Nlastanl's outer lids cycled sharply: impatient affirmation. "We are aware of your desires, Caine Riordan."

"Then why did it take so long to contact me?"

"Because the Senior Assembly foresaw that official communications would prove awkward. The presence of Nolan Corcoran's daughter is the result of what many consider an egregious overstepping of authority on the part of Senior Mentor Alnduul. Until we achieved consensus on that matter, we deemed it premature to initiate official communications of any kind. But now, other concerns have forced us to reverse that decision."

Nlastanl barely paused to breathe before continuing. "Our discussions shall proceed as follows. At each meeting, we shall not speak for more than five minutes." He held up a hand to keep Riordan silent. "It is the majority opinion that human cognition might be unduly taxed by any greater intake of new data."

Riordan waited until he was calm. "I have come to wonder something about Dornaani hosting traditions: is it required, or merely customary, that your first interaction with a guest is to insult them?"

Suvtrush, the fourth of the senior Arbiters, leaned forward.

"Our decision in this matter is sound. It would apply no less to the other races of the Accord."

Caine counted to five before replying. "Very well. Then here's today's five-minute topic: Elena Corcoran. What is her status?"

Nlastanl unfurled a single finger toward the ceiling. "She is secure. Her life functions are stable."

So she has to be out of cryogenic suspension. "When did you awaken her? Where is she?"

Almost half of the gathered Dornaani made sounds or gestures of disgruntlement or annoyance. Nlastanl gestured toward them. "Perhaps if you prove yourself willing to provide the information *we* seek, our reluctant discussants would prove more willing to provide the information *you* seek."

Well, no harm in finding out what they want. "And what information do you seek?"

Nlastanl trailed a finger through the air. "Two issues are of particular interest to us: the location of the humans you collectively label 'The Lost Soldiers' and the location of the Ktoran cryogenic suspension units that held them."

Riordan managed to conceal his surprise... and wariness. "Why do you want to know?"

Suvtrush kept his hands folded. "That does not concern you, human."

The hell it doesn't. "Excuse me, but that's the kind of information that a responsible person wouldn't share without knowing what the other party intends to do with it."

Suvtrush's eyes widened. "Neither preconditions nor ultimatums will influence us. They only reinforce our dismay at your adversarial demeanor."

"You are dismayed at *my* adversarial demeanor? Arbiter Suvtrush, I have traveled over a hundred light-years and waited months to appear before you, only to be greeted with sarcasm, arrogance, and bigotry." *And no great eagerness to share information about Elena. Which means I can't risk revealing that I don't have the answers they're looking for.* "So until you provide details or proof that convinces me that Elena is still alive, this conversation is over." Riordan folded his arms.

And waited.

Chapter Twenty-Seven

Nlastanl was the first to realize that Riordan really did intend to remain silent. The Senior Arbiter raised a finger to still disapproving murmurs. "Perhaps there is a middle course, Caine Riordan."

So, Nlastanl either has less disdain for humans or less resolve. "I'm listening."

"Let us formally agree to an exchange of information. We shall answer your concerns regarding Elena Corcoran. In return, you will share what you know regarding the two locations we requested."

Sure: I'll be happy to share the full measure of my ignorance. "If I can verify your claims regarding Elena, I agree."

Nlastanl looked around the table. Most of his colleagues responded with diffident gestures. His eyes returned to Caine's. "As you are aware, it was the Custodians' Earth Oversight Group that took Elena Corcoran into their care. However, they are trained for social and political interaction, and so, lacked the skill to address major medical complications in a human."

"Accordingly, Elena Corcoran was placed under the supervision of the Collective's most accomplished specialists. However, inasmuch as expertise in human medicine is an esoteric rarity, a year elapsed before they could be gathered and then arrive at a consensus regarding treatment: a phased therapy of reconstructive nanites. The objective was to repair enough of her bodily damage so that she would survive full reanimation, the necessary precursor to surgery."

"And did that work?"

Nlastanl seemed genuinely regretful. "Not entirely. Before her body temperature could be elevated to the surgical minimum, her damaged organs began to fail. Given that we are constrained to using our shortest-lived medical nanites, the speed of her decline was greater than the speed at which they were repairing her."

"Then why didn't you use, well, longer-duration nanites?"

Nlastanl glanced at Heethoo, who took up the explanation. "Long-duration nanites are contraindicated when the patient is receiving certain forms of brain stimulation."

Riordan felt his stomach harden, more because of Heethoo's evasive tone than her words. "What kind of brain stimulation?"

"Elena Corcoran's partial reanimation presented our experts with a conundrum. Once her organs began to function, it necessarily meant that her brain became active. This presented both a challenge and an opportunity.

"The challenge was that, left without mental stimulation, she could slip into a coma. Consequently, in order to protect her mental functions, her brain was stimulated through connection to virtuality. That had to continue, even though she never became a viable surgical candidate."

A chill began creeping along Riordan's limbs. "You mentioned that her connection to virtuality presented an opportunity, as well as a challenge?"

Heethoo's eyes were wide as she raised three affirming fingers. "Further research suggested that if her brain received even more intense stimulation, her body's own healing responses might increase. If that occurred, it was reasonable to hope that the short-duration nanites would begin to show net gains. Theoretically, virtuality itself could stimulate a self-amplifying recovery trend that would ultimately free her from requiring brain stimulation, and so, enable the application of long-duration nanites."

"And did that work?"

Heethoo glanced at Nlastanl and Glayaazh. "We have no way of knowing."

Riordan blinked. "I don't understand."

Glayaazh extended her fingers weakly in Caine's direction: supplication, sympathy, a request for patience? "We are still attempting to locate her."

"Locate her?" Caine discovered that he had shouted and was on his feet. "You mean, you *lost* her?"

Glayaazh kept her fingers stretched toward him. "When a more advanced and immersive form of virtuality was prescribed, her care had to be transferred yet again. However, the experts capable of applying virtuality to such an atypical situation were widely scattered. They are also highly individualistic, frequently uncooperative, and often reclusive."

Good God. Elena, hovering in the twilight between life and death, was being cared for by the Dornaani equivalent of cellar-dwelling computer addicts. Maybe hackers. Riordan pushed back against the tumult of horrors. *One nightmare at a time.* "So you *did* lose her. How?"

Nlastanl answered. "We cannot answer that because we have been unable to determine *who* lost her. As Senior Arbiter Heethoo intimated, the medical experts were no longer required on site. They left to attend to other responsibilities."

Riordan snapped forward. "Bullshit. They got bored. She was just an inert human, so they drifted off to more interesting pursuits. Is that about the size of it?"

Nlastanl's mouth became a retracted, brittle crease. Whether it signaled annoyance at Caine's profane bluntness, chagrin over the situation, or both, Riordan couldn't tell and didn't much care. "Your summary lacks nuance but is fundamentally correct. when Elena Corcoran was to be turned over to the virtuality experts, the medical specialists were no longer present, and the mind-machine interface specialists had not agreed upon a treatment protocol. Consequently, no one had formal responsibility for her case when it came time to process her transfer."

Riordan was so stunned it took him a moment to find words. "So you're telling me she just vanished from whatever facility she was in? Without a trace?" Riordan felt as though he was coming out of his own body, unsure what he might do or say next.

Caine felt Alnduul's thin, almost frail hand on his arm. He realized it might be the first time he had ever been touched by a Dornaani. Some part of his mind registered that as unusually significant, but right now the only thing that mattered was that these bastards had lost Elena. They hadn't cared enough about her to even—

Alnduul stood. "Answer Caine Riordan's questions. You owe him that. And a great deal more."

"Do not take that tone of remonstrance with us, Alnduul," Suvtrush replied in a dangerously calm voice.

"Then cease acting in a fashion that warrants it," Alnduul shot back waspishly. "Did you pick up the trail of Elena Corcoran's transfer or not?"

Nlastanl motioned for Suvtrush to remain silent. "A lengthy investigation discovered that her transfer was not effected by an official vessel, nor by a subsidized transport contracted for that purpose. Rather, she was relocated by an independent carrier."

Suddenly, all of the Dornaani were looking somewhere—anywhere—other than in Caine's direction. Riordan, who had fought back up through the haze of barely suppressed physical rage, glanced at Alnduul. "What does that mean?"

"It means," Alnduul said slowly, "that Elena Corcoran's transfer was entrusted to a loji ship that is not subsidized by the Collective. These vessels are independently operated, serving outlying systems and individuals who require extraordinary...discretion."

Riordan's mouth sagged open. "You mean they gave her to *smugglers*?"

Suvtrush swung a finger through the air. "Sadly, many loji independents have been convicted of far worse crimes than that. They are but one drop in a rising tide that threatens to flood our weir."

Nlastanl silenced his colleague with a sharp, sideways sweep of splayed fingers. "Our investigators eventually found the ship that effected the first leg of Elena Corcoran's transfer."

"The first leg?"

"Yes. Since independent carriers do not maintain regular routes, your mate's life support module was off-loaded as open contract freight at a high port. From there, another independent carried it part of the way to its ultimate destination."

"Which is?"

"We are still awaiting that information."

Alnduul's neck was quivering. "How much time has elapsed since the last known transfer of Elena Corcoran's medical module?"

Nlastanl did not meet his eyes. "Slightly over two years."

"And in which system did the transfer take place?"

Suvtrush struck downward with rigid fingers. "The human wished to ascertain the physical condition of his mate. This has been provided to the best of our knowledge. He needs no additional data, since he has no means to travel the Collective in search of her."

"No," agreed Alnduul, "but I do."

Riordan glanced at his friend, ready to wave him off. Supporting an "adversarial" human brought too much risk. But then Caine remembered Elena's eyes, and all he could do was nod his thanks.

The other Dornaani were staring at Alnduul. Nlastanl gestured toward the ceiling with one finger. "We have exceeded the time allotted. At our next meeting, Caine Riordan, I hope you will be willing to exchange the location of the Lost Soldiers and the Ktoran cryopods for the last known movements of Elena Corcoran's medical cryopod."

He stood. "We are finished. We shall resume in two days. Perhaps three. Enlightenment unto you."

Chapter Twenty-Eight

MAY 2124
GLAMQOOZHT, BD+80 238

Five days later, after Caine and Alnduul met the escort sent by Nlastanl, they emerged from the interface terminal into yet another perfect day on Glamqoozht.

But only briefly. The junior facilitator who had overseen their processing followed them out of the building. "Senior Mentor Alnduul. My apologies, but there is an inconsistency in the registry data for your shuttle. We require your assistance."

"And I am required to meet with twelve Senior and Regional Arbiters. Regrettably, I cannot comply at this time."

"With respect, we took the liberty of contacting your meeting's organizers to inquire when you could comply. He indicated that you may do so now."

Caine shrugged, turned to reenter the terminal with Alnduul.

The junior facilitator waved one hand to the side. "You may still accompany your escort to the meeting, Mister Riordan. The Senior Mentor will join you shortly."

The escort gestured toward the slideway. "We should depart."

Riordan glanced at Alnduul, watching for any sign of misgiving, but saw none, just resignation to the vagaries of bureaucracy. Caine followed his escort.

Riordan found his second ride on the slideway surprisingly dull. The sights and sounds were unchanged. Even a closer study of the local architecture did not reveal anything new. Every structure was a variation on one of three themes: disk-topped towers, hemispheres, or low mesas of alabaster and glass that resembled immense bunkers raised to an art form. The walkway was even less populated, and there was no sign of any more autonomous pets drawn from the Dornaani's genetic bestiary of both extant and extinct creatures. Caine's attempt to engage his escort in conversation met with polite monosyllabic responses.

Until, that is, they neared the concourse. Riordan's escort gestured to the right: the path that would bring him to the same broom closet. "I have been informed that you are quite familiar with the route from here. I must complete another errand for the Arbiters." He moved toward a smaller, central median of transfer disks that circulated between the two lanes of the slideway.

Riordan called after his escort. "So I can just go to the building and—?"

"You are expected," he interrupted. "Enlightenment unto you." And then he was on one of the disks, heading across to the other lane.

Riordan shook his head. *I'm just lucky they don't make me use the servant's entrance.* He moved to the other side of the slideway, stepped on to a waiting disk, and was rapidly conveyed to the right-hand concourse.

Stepping off, he set out for the tall tower to the left and was rewarded by the sight of one of the strange arachno-reptiles he had seen on his first visit. However, this one was alone and apparently in a hurry. Its legs did not cycle swiftly, but they were so long that each stride covered a startling amount of ground. Riordan slowed to watch, realized he was in the creature's path, stepped aside. The creature altered course slightly.

In his direction. And it accelerated.

Riordan began backing away. For an instant, he couldn't believe what he was seeing. The creature *couldn't* be charging him, not here in the epicenter of Dornaani bureaucracy and intellectual aloofness. A tame creature suddenly gone wild, no warders in sight, endangering everyone?

Except it isn't *after everyone,* Riordan noticed as he turned to run. A Dornaani exiting the tower had halted abruptly, shocked into motionlessness by the creature's onslaught, only to watch the reptilian tent-pole legs go around, over, and past her. *No,* Riordan realized, *this creature isn't on the loose. It's after me.*

Sprinting, Riordan didn't bother to sort the tactical observations that hit his consciousness as a single wave. *I'm alone. It's faster. It knows this city. I have no weapons or comm device.* The only advantage he might have over the pursuing creature was agility, particularly the ability to maneuver in tighter spaces and change directions rapidly.

He gauged his surroundings. His sprint would not bring him to the slideway ahead of the creature and, even if it did, that didn't guarantee his survival. Although the disks were made for bipeds, the creature would be able to run alongside the slideway. And judging from the length of its clawed arms...

Riordan swerved across the concourse, dodged into a narrow passage between two small domes. Behind, the creature's claws clacked and clicked as, skittering, it changed direction to follow.

Before it could enter that narrow passage, Riordan scanned for and found an even narrower alley. It was cluttered by low, boxlike protrusions rising up from the ground. Were they seats, environmental subsystems, maybe weird art forms? Caine couldn't tell and didn't care. He slipped sideways between the first two protrusions, hoped he'd be out of the alley before the creature reached it.

No such luck. Within moments, the alien animal was already speed-stilting into the alley. But in that constricted space, Riordan was able to widen the gap: he sprinted hard, leaping over the protrusions as he headed for its other end. He didn't take the time to look, but the awkward scratching and scraping sounds behind him seemed to confirm that these tight quarters were not congenial to the creature's spindly legs. Caine darted around the corner at the alley's other end...

...and almost split his head open, diving aside at the last moment to avoid—what? A dangling steel weather vane? Riordan caught himself on a post to keep from falling, discovered himself in a forest of metal tubes, glass ribbons, and fibrous arcs of—maybe—wood and coral. Disoriented, he pushed his way through the chaotic jungle, realizing that he was in the middle of a soaring synthesis of kinetic sculptures and primitive wind chimes. As he broke free of the last hanging obstacles, a still-rising cacophony marked his path for the creature that came skittering out of the alley.

Riordan's first impulse was to continue running along this smaller concourse, but he steeled himself against that panicked

reflex. *You can't make a plan if you don't have information.* So
he spared a fraction of a second to take a mental snapshot of
his surroundings.

Straight ahead, after fifty meters and two more kinetic sculpture
chimes, the concourse terminated in a dead-end square. It was
more trafficked than the larger concourse and had more buildings facing on it. Which meant multiple doors. And one of the
closest doors was conventional, manual: the entry to an almost
primitive hut. It was not too different from the ones he'd seen on
Rooaioo'q. A historical recreation, maybe? He sprinted toward it.

Still, he wouldn't have reached safety in time if a Dornaani
had not exited that door just as Riordan came within arm's reach
of it. Caine raced in past the startled pedestrian who unwittingly
obstructed the animal's pursuit.

Riordan spun, slammed the door shut, braced his back against
it, looked for a lock. It had two. One was a cleverly concealed
magnetic lock used to secure the building. The other was a simple,
ancient, and *functional* door bar.

Riordan reached over, tipped the bar; it fell into its bracket
with a solid *clunk*. Panting, he studied the room: it was a museum
display of prehistoric Dornaani life. The thatch-and-palisade walls
were lined with nets, gaff poles, earthenware containers, short
clubs for stunning or killing catch...

Silence. No hint of movement either inside or outside the
pseudo-hut. Was the creature lying in wait? Was it seeking another
point of ingress? Had it given up?

Riordan was beginning to debate whether he should risk taking a peek outside when there was a firm knock on the door.
"Caine Riordan?" It was the voice of his escort.

"Yes?" Riordan kept himself propped firmly against the door.

"Please come with me."

"Are you aware that one of your bioproxies just chased me
through the streets? Would have killed me?"

"I am aware of the chase. However, it would not have killed
you. Please, come with me or we shall be late."

"So it was a *unanimous* decision to send that monster after me?"

"It was," Nlastanl affirmed. "We determined to send the
creature—a *pess*kss*—to intercept you after learning that your
cognitive acuity would be enhanced if your body experienced

the biochemical cascade that your physicians call the 'fight-or-flight' response—"

"*What?!*"

"—which would enable slightly longer conversations."

Alnduul, who had arrived less than a minute after Riordan, surveyed the other Dornaani faces in the room. "So it seems that you are resolved to not only verbally attack my friend in this chamber, but to physically attack him before he reaches it." Riordan had never heard Alnduul adopt a sarcastic tone before.

"Not invariably," Suvtrush clarified with widened eyes. "In order to initiate and sustain the flight-fight cascade, the human must not know when and where such an incident might occur. And so, to deny him both assistance and advance warning, you are hereby instructed not to accompany him on his subsequent visits."

Alnduul's eyes seemed to quiver in their large sockets. "You cannot supersede my orders to accompany our guest, to ensure his safety."

"We have voted, as a body, to do just that. And with four Senior Arbiters in attendance, that confers the necessary authority to suspend your orders."

"Does it? Those orders were issued unanimously by the Senior Assembly. So have the four Senior Arbiters now present both forgotten their own dictate and that it would take a majority vote to overturn it?"

Suvtrush trailed a pair of unconcerned fingers through the air. "Ultimately, your legal cavils are irrelevant. The human will not be at risk. Further commentary on this resolution is no longer welcome or permitted, Alnduul."

Riordan scanned the alien faces, assessed the value of an aggressive bluff. He rose, waited until the room was silent. "I will not cooperate under these conditions."

Suvtrush's fingers trailed languidly. "That is your affair. We are resolved."

Heethoo touched her index fingers together. "We must avoid such an impasse. I welcome any suggestion that might assist us in ameliorating the contentious trend of our discussions."

Riordan nodded. "I have a suggestion. I suggest you take a day to reconsider excluding Alnduul from my visits. And while you're at it, consider the benefits to be gained from deciding to treat me as an equal. Then, I might have something to say about the Lost Soldiers and their cryocells. Otherwise, we're done. And I'll be sure to report my treatment to the interested parties back on Earth."

Alnduul led the way out of the broom closet. "I do not think they will relent."

"Nor do I," Riordan answered with a tight nod. "But I have a plan."

"Be careful," warned Alnduul early the next day, staring through the interface terminal's transparent walls at the unchanging skyline of Glamqoozht.

"I will," Riordan assured him, then exited the terminal. Because his hands were still shaking, he put them in his pockets. Hopefully the double dose of epinephrine would prove sufficient. but had Caine's traveling medical locker included a dose of combat drug, he would have been sorely tempted to use that, too. He had foresworn such substances on general principles, but today he might need every edge he could get.

As soon as Riordan trotted off the slideway and scanned the concourse, he saw that the Dornaani had not relented. A hundred meters up the concourse, a pair of the pseudo-ungulate quadrupeds he'd seen on his first visit were meandering toward him. This time, he noticed a peculiar stiffness in their posture and movements to which he'd been blind when the *pess*kss* attacked him, but had recalled afterward. Probably a consequence of being under direct and unwelcome control. And whereas the tentacular extensions of their sensory clusters had originally bobbed and roved lazily, those prehensile members were now stretched out into erect fans.

Riordan had done his homework. When this creature, a *yoomdai*, was alarmed or defending its territory, its sensory polyps and tendrils extended into a living radar dish that not only conferred a more focused version of a bat's sonar, but had secondary sensitivities across the entire electromagnetic spectrum. Normally it was a shy herbivore that eluded its prey not only by virtue of its speed, but by its ability to change both the microscopic properties and the shape of its leg-end stumps.

The data in *Olsloov*'s brief computer entry listed one other tantalizing datum about the *yoomdai*'s world of origin, the other worlds on which it might be encountered, and the last confirmed sightings: all were listed as "unknown." Another mystery which Alnduul had demurred answering until "later."

Riordan walked briskly toward the same passage he'd used to quit the concourse at the start of the last attack. The two *yoomdai*, one of which was almost the size of a caribou, either didn't immediately detect his change in speed or direction, or had not yet been informed that he was their target. But after three seconds, the larger one's radar dish of trembling tendrils swung sharply in Riordan's direction, collapsing into a tight cone. Probably getting better target resolution.

Caine ran for the mouth of the passage. The two *yoomdai* swerved after him.

By the time Caine reached the still narrower alley littered with boxlike protrusions, he was surprised to see that, despite his head start, the *yoomdai* were already closer than the *pess*kss* had been. They seemed to fly along the ground, incredibly sure of foot and pushing mightily into each bound as their feet kept altering to achieve optimal traction.

His heart pounding out hard, adrenal thumps, Riordan charged out of the alley and straight into the first mobile's hanging garden of metal, glass, coral, and wood. He swung his arms as he went through it; the resulting clangor battered his ears. Emerging from the far side, he cut toward the hut and the many tools—which was to say, weapons—he knew to be inside.

The *yoomdai* emerged from the alley mouth, each leap a long, flying stretch, but then recoiled, averting their convulsively contracting sensor-fans from the cacophony produced by the sculpture's madly swinging pieces.

Caine felt a sharp pulse of satisfaction. *Hurt and blinded all at once.* He reached the hut, grabbed the door handle, and yanked.

And almost dislocated his shoulder. It was not just shut; it was locked.

Shit.

Behind him, the *yoomdai* began widening their sensor clusters, probably to reduce the concentration of collected sound. They started moving uncertainly forward, giving the wind chimes from hell a wide berth.

Motionless, Caine watched them edge toward him, cautiously, hesitantly. *Probably relying on their infrared-sensitive polyps, now.*

They were still half-blind, but if he couldn't find a weapon, or just something to swing at them…

Riordan glanced at the sculpture, at the fibrous cords that connected the wood chimes to its whirling armatures, and sprinted back toward it.

The *yoomdai* flinched, startled, but followed quickly, the smaller one in the lead.

Caine didn't slow as he got to the structure; he leaped. Grabbing one of the wooden tubes while still in midair, he yanked down with both hands as he dropped back to the ground.

The fiber cord connecting the tube to the overhead armature strained down and against the direction of the armature's spin. It grew taut, groaned, snapped.

Dragging the tube low along the ground, Riordan stumbled through a swaying insanity of other objects. Having been yanked in yet another direction, their oscillations were now unpredictable, manic. He dodged a spinning wand of glass, ducked out past the rest of the erratic chimes, and, resisting the urge to run, moved quickly to the alley-facing side of the sculpture.

Sure enough, the freshly disoriented *yoomdai* were facing almost directly away from him, still scanning along his last known path: into the whirling pandemonium of tubes, bars, and slats.

Keeping a two-handed grasp on the tube, Riordan cocked it back over his right shoulder like an oversized baseball bat and charged.

The smaller of the *yoomdai* was the first to detect either Caine's movement or heat signature, even though it was further away than its larger mate. It spun to face him, its front feet widening, flattening, transmogrifying with alarming speed. The bigger one was just starting to turn…

Guessing that its large body was highly resilient to blunt force blows, Caine aimed low. He swung the tube sharply, snapping his wrists over just before impact.

The tube split as it smashed into the large *yoomdai*'s left leg, just below its hock-analog. A surprisingly loud crack punctuated the creature's staggering fall, but it did not make any sound of its own. Riordan swung the weakened tube around as quickly as his impact-numbed shoulders could roll.

But not in time. The smaller *yoomdai*, startlingly swift, was already in front of him, rising up on its hind legs, lashing out with—

Riordan had a brief impression of the new shape of its front feet—two small spades—right before they slashed at his abdomen.

The first words that Caine heard as he swam up out of unconsciousness were, "He is mad. Or suicidal. Or both." The voice was Suvtrush's.

Riordan kept his eyes closed, tried to assess if he was in pain, if any part of him was numb or missing, and—to the extent possible—determine if he was clearheaded. It seemed so, but...

Alnduul's reply was quiet but sharp. "Do you not see that Caine Riordan is resolved to reject your attempts at inducing a flight-or-fight response? Which, by the way, would not produce the effects you seek. Nor would they persist beyond a few minutes."

There was a long pause. Nlastanl's voice asked in what, for a Dornaani, was a stern, almost arch, tone, "Laynshooz, is this true?"

"Our research was inconclusive on these points," Laynshooz muttered.

"That is not possible. Our data on human physiology and pharmacokinetics are more detailed than their own."

Riordan opened his eyes. "Of course," he said, sitting up, "maybe it was just a simple oversight." The Dornaani around him started. Despite a sharp pain in his abdomen, Caine continued. "On the other hand, maybe the oversight was intentional." Nlastanl's mouth opened...and then closed again as he stole an appraising glance at Laynshooz. *Starting to wonder if your advisors have been telling you the truth about stimulating the poor, slow-witted human, Nlastanl? It's about damn time.*

The stabbing pain in Riordan's abdomen had relented. "At any rate, I apologize for bleeding on your nice, clean concourse." Riordan looked around. The curvature of the room was so pronounced that it seemed as though they were all inside an immense, sterile white egg. Almost no equipment, not even monitors or an IV drip. *Okay, if I'm doing that well, maybe I can startle them a little more.*

Caine swung his legs over the side of the low platform upon which he had been lying. The five Dornaani shrank back, Heethoo emitting a chirrup of either distress or worry.

Alnduul, who was closest, murmured. "Movement may not be wise. Although the lacerations were shallow, they were only closed thirty minutes ago. The fusings may not be—"

"I'll be fine," Riordan assured him.

"And if you are not?" Nlastanl asked in alarmed disbelief.

"Then you'll fix me. Again." Riordan replied, suppressing a wince as he stood and discovered that, although he was wearing his own pants and boots, his shirt had been replaced by what looked like a silver dashiki. It shone a light blue wherever it bent or bunched.

Suvtrush's two index fingers were stabbing toward the floor. "Your intransigence is unacceptable, human. You must comply with—"

"With what?" Riordan stepped quickly toward Suvtrush, who stepped back with even greater alacrity. "Your ridiculous games?"

"Our . . . games?"

"Well, what would you call it? You choose when and where we meet. You choose what you'll tell me and how long we'll talk. You send creatures that almost kill me, even though you've ordered that I'm to be protected. Tell me, how is all that *not* a ridiculous game?"

"But," objected Nlastanl, stepping between Riordan and Suvtrush, "you did not have to fight. You only had to flee."

Riordan shook his head. "I guess that, living in a sanitized world, you've forgotten this basic lesson: if you want to stay free or stay alive, never play by your opponent's rules. Particularly when your opponent is more powerful than you are. Do the unexpected. Turn on the pursuer. Attack the attacker."

"But your survival was never at risk."

"Really? Then who failed to control the smaller *yoomdai* before it could do this?" Riordan patted his abdomen.

"We were surprised—"

"Which almost got me gutted. What will it be next time? A broken control module? A momentary glitch in the lascom? You're kidding yourself if you think you can guarantee my safety. But it doesn't matter one way or the other, because as long as you treat me like a lab rat, I'll turn and bite. And I will keep doing that until you stop or I'm dead. Your choice."

The four Senior Arbiters exchanged long glances. Nlastanl turned back to Riordan, hands folded. "Given that your resolve in this matter could cause you further harm, we shall discontinue our attempts to induce compensatory cognitive stimulation. Now remain here quietly until we have summoned a conveyance for you."

Chapter Twenty-Nine

MAY 2124
GLAMQOOZHT, BD+80 238

Upon exiting the medical facility, Riordan and Alnduul were ushered into a waiting vehicle that rose on vertijets and sped toward a new tower. Riordan glanced at his friend. "Change of venue?" Riordan asked.

"Evidently."

During the forty-second trip, Riordan got a bird's-eye view of the vast, circular bay, spotted a strange structure rising up out of the water two-thirds of the way to the horizon. It appeared to be a split tower of natural rock, a broad hole bored through the narrow gap separating the two halves.

"What is that?"

Alnduul's mouth retracted slightly. "A relic."

"Yes, but from when? And what does it symbolize?"

"I do not know. I doubt anyone does."

"You mean it dates back to before you established the Accord?"

"It might."

The pilot advised them that they would soon disembark upon the tower's roof and to take the elevator down one floor to the observation level.

Riordan smiled at Alnduul. "Sounds like we're out of the basement, at least."

Alnduul did not seem enthusiastic. "That is not necessarily a promising sign."

✧　　✧　　✧

And Alnduul might be right, Riordan thought when he entered the wedge-shaped room that looked out over the bay. Almost all the Dornaani were now physically present. They stared at him as he entered and sat.

Nlastanl raised his small chin. "We have met your preconditions, Caine Riordan. Now, where are the Lost Soldiers?"

Caine shook his head. "I made my cooperation contingent upon *two* conditions. You've answered as much as you can about Elena; I'll take that on faith. But I told you I need to know *why* you want this information."

Nlastanl waved a loose-fingered hand. "If the Ktor can be assured that the Collective knows the location of the Lost Soldiers, can verify they have no freedom of movement, and that their true identity has not been made public, the Sphere's impetus toward a war footing is eliminated."

Riordan shook his head. "Maybe. Or maybe the Ktor won't settle for anything less than your revealing every detail. And given the contempt with which so many of you view humans, why should I believe that you'd keep our secrets?"

Nlastanl folded his fingers together stiffly. "You have no grounds for fearing such a betrayal."

"In fact," Riordan interrupted, "I do." He leaned forward. "You had thousands of years and dozens of Convocations to figure out that the Ktor 'cold environment tanks' were a sham. You had advanced sensors which could show that their occupants were human. But you never bothered to investigate. Which beggars belief. Unless, that is, you decided not to investigate. So if you don't keep faith with your own Accords, why the hell would you keep your word to me? Or anyone?"

The room had been fairly quiet before; it was suddenly as soundless as a tomb.

"The matter you raise," Suvtrush murmured eventually, "is a unique exception that is best explained by a Custodial expert."

Eyes shifted toward Glayaazh. She spread her fingers wide upon the table before her. Her voice was soft, almost entreating. "Caine Riordan, just because the Custodians possess an investigatory capability, it does not invariably follow that it is always wise, or practical, for them to employ it."

Riordan frowned. "Are you suggesting that the Custodians *chose* not to investigate the Ktor, despite suspecting them of misrepresenting themselves?" The patient look on Glayaazh's face told him he'd missed something. "Or is it that the Custodians were *prevented* from conducting that investigation?"

Glayaazh's mouth twisted slightly as she answered his question with one of her own. "Have you not wondered, Caine Riordan, what might occur if the Custodians took a position, or conducted an investigation, to which the Collective objects?"

Riordan nodded. "Reductions in funding, staffing, maintenance. The political equivalent of a preemptive strike."

Glayaazh spoke slowly, carefully. "And if the Ktoran duplicity had been officially confirmed, their flagrant violation of a crucial Accord would have become a matter of *record*, not suspicion. And so, corrective action would have to be taken."

Riordan nodded. "And most Dornaani will do anything to avoid war." *Okay, time to toss a little chum into the water.* "So in effect, the Dornaani Collective aided and abetted the Ktoran violations by ensuring they went uninvestigated."

Laynshooz's eyes were wide. "That is absurd."

"Is it? Once you became complicit, the Ktor had leverage on you. And I've got to wonder: did they use that leverage to get appointed as Assistant Custodians? With primary oversight of Earth? Because if that's true, and humanity ever learned the truth about the Ktor, it's a short step to blaming *you* for enabling them to kidnap thousands of our soldiers and then almost bash us back to the Bronze Age with the Doomsday Rock."

Nlastanl unfolded his fingers. "An interesting but erroneous analysis, since two of your presumptions are incorrect."

Good. Please educate me. "What two facts do I have wrong?"

"Firstly, when the Ktor expressed interest in becoming Assistant Custodians, it was the Custodians themselves who petitioned the Collective to accept their offer."

Huh? Riordan turned toward Glayaazh. She stared back at him, gaze steady, unblinking, almost like a challenge.

That's when it hit him. "Of course. That gave the Custodians a mandate to observe the Ktor serving in that role. So you were able to gather intelligence and evidence without opening an official investigation." Riordan watched her eyes cycle in slow affirmation, then turned toward Nlastanl. "You said I was in error on a second point?"

Nlastanl waved two undulating fingers. "The event you call

the Doomsday Rock was in direct opposition to the policies of the Ktoran Sphere. That is why its initiators, House Perekmeres, were not merely Exiled but Extirpated. They certainly hoped to undermine both the plans and preeminence of the Older Houses by dragging them into an ill-timed war. However, they also intended to drive up the price of the Lost Soldiers by using the Doomsday Rock to eliminate most of Earth's other promising genelines."

Riordan suddenly felt disoriented. "What do you mean, 'drive up the price of the Lost Soldiers'?"

Suvtrush spoke slowly. "This is actually your third error, human. You assumed that the Lost Soldiers were left on Turkh'saar to be activated as a black flag operation. You are wrong. Their abduction was motivated by the economics of Ktoran eugenics. When the Assistant Custodians of House Perekmeres overreached and came under scrutiny, they were unable to bring their genetic prizes back into the Sphere. And so, they cached the Lost Soldiers on Turkh'saar, like buried treasure."

Riordan leaned forward. "And why do the Ktor need terrestrial genetics?"

"Because without unaltered human genelines, the Houses of the Sphere teeter on the edge of eugenic disaster."

Riordan frowned. "No. That doesn't make sense. After the invasion, they had access to almost unlimited cell samples, everything they'd need to prevent their problems with...what? Inbreeding?"

Heethoo raised a finger on either hand. "The Ktor eugenics problem is not inbreeding. At least, not as you mean it."

Caine raised an eyebrow. "Just how many kinds of inbreeding can there be?"

Glayaazh folded her hands. "Many of the alterations made to the Ktor genecode were inelegant and crude, ignored subtler implications and epigenetic connections. These omissions undermine the sustainability of the Ktor as a subspecies, both genetically and behaviorally. Infusions of unmodified, or 'aboriginal' genelines mitigate this trend.

"However, they also dilute or even supplant the enhanced traits of the Ktor. So before their Breedmothers can make use of aboriginal genecodes, they must be 'uplifted' through several generations of carefully managed breeding."

Riordan nodded. "So a simple genetic sample isn't enough.

What the Ktor really need is breeding stock that brings the desired nature *and* nurture to the eugenics program." And hearing himself say that, Caine was suddenly back on Turkh'saar, reliving the moment when one of his team, Peter Wu, turned away from scores of Lost Soldiers still in Ktoran cryocells and asked, *"So, are you saying that the Ktor ultimately wanted to . . . to breed these troops?"* The answer had been right there, but Caine had steered away from it. *"I think we'd need to know a lot more about the Ktor before we can make a guess at that."*

But there was a loose end in all of this. "So how is it that the Dornaani don't officially know that the Ktor are human, yet *do* know that their ruling Houses are teetering at the edge of a eugenic crisis?"

Suvtrush leaned away from the table. "That is a reasonable question, Caine Riordan, but one we may not answer. Like you, there is some data we are not allowed to share."

Caine nodded. "Fair enough. But clearly, you have a conduit that gives you access to the Ktoran Sphere. Unfortunately, that kind of conduit almost never runs one way. Which means that whatever information you get from me could wind up with them." He saw Elena's eyes fade away as he steeled himself to utter his only possible decision. "So I can't share the information you need. Even if I had it."

Chapter Thirty

Hearing Riordan's flat refusal to cooperate, several of the lower-ranking Dornaani rose or reached holographic hands to cut out of the link, but none of the Senior Arbiters showed any sign of moving. "Your decision is unfortunate, Caine Riordan—" Nlastanl began.

"Unfortunate?" interrupted Laynshooz. "The human's prevarication is as outrageous as his insults. I remind this group that we have methods of extracting—"

Nlastanl spoke harshly. "I am this gathering's moderator. If you are incapable of recognizing my authority, recuse yourself. Immediately."

Laynshooz's voice was small, brittle. "I shall be less emphatic."

Nlastanl's attention returned to Riordan. "I am disposed to believe your assertion that you are unaware of the locations we had hoped to learn from you. However, I wish to make a final and more limited appeal that you share peripherally related information that would be of no interest to the Ktor. Rather, these inquiries are solely concerned with your race's ultimate safety. And fate."

Riordan, struck by the sudden gravity of Nlastanl's tone, nodded.

"Among what you called the Ktoran cryocells, some actually preserved their occupants using biodynamic principles, did they not?"

Riordan nodded. "Yes. There were dozens of those units, mostly unopened. They almost looked organic."

"They are. But not in the way you mean."

Riordan frowned. "Organic is organic. How many ways could I mean that?"

Nlastanl assayed a stiff human nod. "Allow me to rephrase. They do not follow the paradigms you associate with any fauna or flora you have ever observed. Those differences could prove very hazardous."

Riordan felt his heart quicken. "Are the occupants in danger?"

Nlastanl waved a lazy finger in the air. "I do not speak of danger to the individuals still in them. I speak of danger to your entire species. It would be profoundly unwise for your researchers to experiment with the biological compounds of those units."

"Why?"

"They may induce unpredictable mutations and other perils."

"You mean, they harbor contagious organisms? Pathogens?"

Heethoo clasped her hands for emphasis. "No, Caine Riordan. It would appear the opposite, at first. The biological compounds would seem beneficial, readily applicable to various vaccines, therapies, even life prolongation. But over time, other effects would manifest."

Riordan felt a vague chill creep down his spine. "What kind of effects?"

Nlastanl waved a hand. "That we cannot say. We know very little about these compounds, and I am not permitted to share more than I already have. But be assured, these symbiopods constitute a greater peril to your race than the Ktor."

Riordan leaned back. If Nlastanl was telling the truth—and the other three Senior Arbiters had become equally somber—then this warranted separate consideration. "How is it that you know what's in a Ktoran cryo—er, symbiopod—and what it would do to us?"

"Because," Heethoo explained softly, "it is mentioned in our histories. If they are what we suspect, we must find the symbiopods and remove them."

Riordan leaned his forehead into his hand. "So these date from the same epoch as the ruins on Delta Pavonis Three?"

Glayaazh nodded. "And earlier than that. From a distant region of space."

Caine's chill intensified. "How distant?"

"We do not know. Beyond our farthest probes."

"And how far have your probes gone?"

"We have explored every system up to fifty light-years from

the Accord's borders. Other probes have been sent as far as three hundred and fifty light-years beyond that."

"And within that total radius of, eh, about five hundred light-years, has there ever been any sign of—?"

Suvtrush straightened all his fingers with an irritated snap. "Nlastanl, be cautious. The human may be simple, but he is crafty. He makes observations. We offer corrections. Those furnish the human with glimpses of the confidential data behind them."

Nlastanl turned back toward Caine. "Are you attempting to manipulate us as Suvtrush suspects?"

Riordan shrugged. "I never ignore an opportunity to learn something new. But frankly, other than getting Elena back, I'm only interested in one type of information."

"And what is that?"

"Finding out which of you might be willing to befriend humans, and which of you would never countenance it."

"So, in short," summarized Laynshooz, "you are trying to discern which of us might be as pliable, as corruptible, as Alnduul. Come, do you deny it? Do you not wish to recruit more like him? Dornaani who will take matters into their own hands to help Earth?"

Riordan shook his head. "I am not here trying to recruit anyone. But if Alnduul had *not* taken matters into his own hands, the invasion of Earth probably would have succeeded. Meaning you would have been faced with a sustained and direct violation of the Twenty-First Accord, which expressly forbids the invasion of a species' homeworld. So you would have had to either fight a war to remove the occupiers or disband the Accord as a sham.

"Of course, the only reason Alnduul had to make those hard calls was because the Custodians failed to provide the support they promised at Convocation. Or was that the doing of the Collective Assembly, pressuring them to stand down while we were dying by the millions?"

Suvtrush waved Laynshooz to silence, took up the argument. "It is not incumbent upon the Collective to conform its sovereign will to serve the mandates of the Custodians. Indeed, the Custodians' lack of autonomy invalidates any assumption that the Accords can be reliably enforced by them."

Riordan narrowed his eyes. "Are you aware that the Ktor representative at the most recent Convocation said the same thing?"

"The Ktor are liars, murderers, and not to be trusted. But that does not diminish the truth when they see it and speak it. Many of us believe them to be correct when they assert that the rules of the Accord contain the seeds of its own inevitable collapse."

"Are you saying it would be better not to have an Accord at all?"

"Many of us have come to think so. I remain undecided."

For Riordan, Suvtrush's assertions weren't half as horrifying as his tone of weary detachment. "And what would you say to those races that have committed themselves to actions and agreements based on the expectation that you shall be as good as your word, that the Custodians will stand as their protectors? What of us?"

Yaonhoyz's mouth tilted slightly. "What of you indeed?" He trailed an unconcerned finger in the air before him. "Your race and the others are merely products of blind evolution. It was foolish to have interfered with you in the first place. We should stop doing so immediately."

Riordan's speciate fear began transforming into rage. "And if that means the deaths of multiple races?"

Yaonhoyz burbled diffidently. "Races are not permanent features of the universe. Nothing is. If it is the fate of your race to be short-lived, we should never have attempted to circumvent that natural outcome."

Nlastanl raised both hands. "This topic is unproductive. Caine Riordan, I must frankly ask for your cooperation on the urgent matter of the symbiopods. Just as you rightly appeal to our sense of integrity and responsibility regarding the fate of your race and others, so, in this matter, do I appeal to the same in you."

Riordan didn't question the Dornaani characterization of the symbiopods. Nlastanl's description of them—organic but not like any other organism in known space—echoed Caine's own uneasiness the moment he'd come within touching distance of them. "I'll help you, but there's not much I can do."

"Explain," demanded Suvtrush.

"I don't know where the symbiopods are."

"We are told most still contain kidnapped troops from your twentieth century."

"As far as I know, that's true. But to protect the Lost Soldiers, I was not given their location."

Nlastanl rested his fingertips against each other. "What became of the symbiopods you turned over to your government?"

Riordan shook his head. "I never had access to that kind of information."

"Very well. How many symbiopods did you turn over?"

Riordan nodded. "Fourteen. All empty."

Dornaani faces were rarely as expressive as humans. Now they went absolutely blank.

Only Laynshooz's face was animated, more so than ever. "It is as I said from the first. This human was not worth meeting. He has neither information about, nor access to, any of the symbiopods. Besides, with so many in the hands of human researchers, the fate of their race is sealed. Unless you can breed both greed and curiosity out of them in two generations."

Riordan flinched. "What do you mean by that?"

Suvtrush put up two didactic fingers. "It is through those traits that the symbiopods are most likely to corrupt your race."

Riordan forced himself to exhale. "Do you also believe that our fate is sealed?"

"No," Suvtrush answered carefully, "but I do not consider the outlook hopeful."

Yaonhoyz looked up from his lazy slouch. "We would be remiss, human, if we failed to express our appreciation for the one matter in which you have been of inestimable help."

Riordan frowned. "And what matter is that?"

"You furnished us with unsolicited testimony that Alnduul not only exceeded Custodial mandates and protocols in aiding your planet, but did so knowingly. Without your comments, our accusations would have mostly relied upon conjecture and hearsay. But, as you were a witness, we now have an unimpeachable account of his violations." Yaonhoyz's mouth rotated almost ninety degrees around the axis of its tapirlike extrusion: a broad grin.

Riordan turned toward Alnduul. The Dornaani's mouth was a skewed, broken crease: a faltering smile. "It was inevitable," he murmured. "Your words have revealed nothing except what my own testimony will assert, once a board of inquiry is convened." He looked away from Caine, glanced around the ring of Dornaani faces. A few—Glayaazh, Heethoo, a few regional arbiters, and now, even Nlastanl—seemed sympathetic or at least saddened. The rest were expressionless. Except Laynshooz—his animation was the Dornaani equivalent of gloating.

Alnduul stood. "I presume these conversations are concluded."

"As is our interest in this human," Yaonhoyz burbled.

Riordan stood alongside Alnduul, copied his friend's elbows-in, arms-out gesture of farewell.

Nlastanl stood, flowing into the same posture. "Enlightenment unto you, Alnduul and Caine Riordan."

By the time Glayaazh and Heethoo had done the same, the remaining Dornaani were exiting the room or had terminated their holographic presence.

When he and Alnduul were alone, Riordan asked, "What now?"

Alnduul's inner lids nictated twice. "Now, we are on our own."

Chapter Thirty-One

Irzhresht looked away from the six holographic readouts that were positioned around her head and reflected in her large eyes. "Third Arbiter Glayaazh is aboard."

"Thank you," Alnduul rose from his cocoon couch. "Please instruct Ssaodralth to escort her to my briefing room. We shall join her presently."

"We?" echoed Riordan, who was studying a holograph that tracked the relationship between powerplant activity, drive settings, and fuel endurance. He had progressed far enough with his Dornaani to decipher occasional labels on simpler controls. This constantly transmogrifying display was far more challenging.

"Glayaazh requested that you be present for her farewell."

Riordan rose, smiling. "I wasn't aware she'd taken such a liking to me."

"She has, but I suspect her visit has a more specific reason."

"Which is?"

The iris valve dilated in front of them. "Let us go find out together," Alnduul said.

Although younger than Thlunroolt, Glayaazh seemed far more elderly. Probably because she eschewed the restorative patches that were *de rigueur* on almost all Dornaani who were middle-aged or older.

However, the slowness of her silent gesture of greeting seemed more a matter of sadness than decrepitude. She stepped forward, one index finger raised. Alnduul mirrored her and their fingertips touched. In all the time Riordan had spent with Dornaani, he had never witnessed any unnecessary physical contact between them.

Glayaazh trailed a finger to the side. "There are no happy meetings without sad partings. As you know."

"As I know."

To Riordan, it sounded like a farewell between a favorite aunt and a beloved nephew.

Glayaazh straightened. "You will soon be summoned to appear before the Collective's Custodial review board."

Alnduul's outer lids cycled slowly.

"The travesty of these meetings will be reprised there. However, you *are* in a position to make a good-faith demonstration that would influence them."

"You mean, bribe them to rule in my favor."

Glayaazh's mouth twisted slightly. "When the stakes are high, review boards become more transactional."

"Surely you are not recommending I avail myself of such opportunities?"

Glayaazh touched the tips of her two index fingers as if she were completing a circuit. "Remain alert to any opportunities that preserve your freedom of action. Which you shall surely lose if you cannot sway some of the board."

Alnduul's expression changed from surprise to deep reflection. It seemed to Riordan that his friend had heard something more specific in Glayaazh's last words than he had.

She turned toward Caine. "I regret that the gathering was not conducive to making a closer acquaintance, to say nothing of my inability to be of more help to you and Elena Corcoran. Perhaps this shall, in some small measure, make up for that." She placed a small, clear tetrahedron upon the table: a Dornaani data crystal.

Riordan raised his left eyebrow. "May I ask what is on it?"

"Many things. Most importantly, complete reports on the investigatory measures taken to locate Elena Corcoran. Beyond the trail left by her medical maintenance module's transfer from one carrier to the next, there are also conjectures about its subsequent destinations."

"And no one has followed up on those?"

"Not for half a year."

Riordan shook his head. "Tell me, Glayaazh, does anything work the way it should in the Collective?"

Caine had been expecting any of a number of responses—irritation, shared amusement, crestfallen agreement—but intense focus had not been among them. "It is interesting that you should ask that, Caine Riordan."

"Why?"

"Because I wonder what you will report of us when you return home."

"I doubt anyone is going to ask me."

"They shall. They have no choice. Since you will be their only source of intelligence, their objections will be overruled by necessity. But at this moment, indulge me. Let us presume that your leaders ask you to assess whether the Custodians can be relied upon to defend humanity as a protected species. What would you tell them?"

"I'd tell them that the Collective will not prevent the Custodians from carrying out their duty."

Glayaazh's eyes widened slightly. "A surprisingly optimistic response."

Riordan smiled. "Not really. The Collective can't risk abandoning Earth. If the Ktor conquer us, they'd become much more dangerous to *you*. But secondly, you'd be breaking your own rules and showing the other races that the Dornaani can't be trusted. That would destroy the Accord more certainly than anything else."

Glayaazh's eyelid drooped in sad agreement. She gestured toward the data crystal. "Your search for Elena Corcoran may lead you down pathways you cannot foresee, require expertise on topics you do not yet know exist. If so, the crystal contains data and contacts that should prove useful. Among them are marginalized experts, scholars, even hobbyists, who will have insights into recondite yet crucial variables that are beyond the purview, or even grasp, of Collective officials.

"And now, as you say in English, 'fare well.'" She said it as two words, thereby emphasizing the original meaning.

Turning to Alnduul, she executed the parting gesture, seemed to stretch her fingers out as wide as they could go. "Enlightenment unto you always, Alnduul."

"And may it radiate ever brighter from you, Glayaazh."

When the iris valve closed behind her, Alnduul picked up

the data crystal, extended it toward Riordan. "It is yours to do with as you please, but be careful with the data. I suspect that some of it may prove...provocative."

Riordan shook his head. "I wonder if you could run that through a translator, first. Make me a copy?"

Alnduul slipped the crystal into one of the small pockets on the abbreviated vest that most Dornaani wore while on duty. "Yesterday, my Custodial oath would have prevented me from doing so, just as I was restricted as to which of your questions I might answer, and to what degree."

It took Riordan a moment to overcome his surprise. "And that has changed? Why?"

"Although you have been dismissed by the gathering, they did not instruct you to depart Collective space, nor did they place any limits upon your travel within it. Yet you remain my *personal* responsibility. Even my Custodial duties do not take precedence over that. Accordingly, while I may not volunteer information, any questions you ask must be answered if, in my judgment, failure to do so could endanger you. And after these meetings, my standards of judgment shall be quite liberal."

Caine cocked an eyebrow. "I suspect I'll be asking you a lot of questions, then."

"So do I." Alnduul moved briskly to the door; it scissored open before him. "We must move swiftly, now. Once I face the review board, I may no longer be a Custodian and so will no longer have a ship. Until then, I shall take you any place *Olsloov* can reach."

Riordan nodded. "Which is probably the only way I'm going to find Elena."

"Yes, but it also exposes you to potential dangers. The Dornaani you seek will also know that you are no longer an official visitor, so I doubt my ability to ensure that your interactions with them are both productive and safe."

"Why?"

"As a Custodian, I can be called upon to bear witness to what other Dornaani do or say in my presence. Consequently, they will only speak freely in my *absence*. Which also makes it easier for them to exploit you."

"Exploit me how?"

"There is no way to know that beforehand. However, much of the information you require is likely to be esoteric, illegal, or both. Purveyors of such knowledge often have unusual motivations. So be cautious."

"I will be. I'd also like to be armed."

Alnduul burbled. "Unfortunately, all materials aboard this ship are the property of the Custodians. You may only use them during an emergency and only under my supervision."

So now I have to start scrounging for my own equipment? "I'm becoming a more problematic passenger with every passing day."

"Perhaps, but with every day passing day, our paths also cleave closer."

Riordan grinned, quipped, "Not if they take your ship away."

Alnduul's answering stare was grave. "Then more than ever."

Yaonhoyz accepted the tight-beam message after ensuring that his thoroughly illegal scrambler was functioning. "I await your orders."

"That is well, since I must convey them swiftly. Have you secured the physical evidence for use against Alnduul?"

"I have," Yaonhoyz replied. "The recordings were difficult to obtain, but even Alnduul has made a few enemies within the Custodians."

"Fortunate. The board must be convened as quickly as possible, that we may put an end to the human's intrusions. In the meantime, I trust our new operative is properly positioned to impede his and Alnduul's further progress?"

"Indeed. All the necessary passcodes and authorizations have been provided as per the operative's requests and were secured without arousing suspicion or inquiry."

"That had best be the case. We cannot be implicated in the neutralization of either Alnduul or Glayaazh. In regard to the latter, has a suitable replacement pilot been secured for service on Glayaazh's ship?"

"Yes, but he lacks experience as a party to illicit actions." An edge of irritability crept into Yaonhoyz's voice. "Suborning him was an imprudent risk."

"Your tone offends even more than your impertinent words."

"My apologies."

"Accepted. I share your reservations regarding operatives whose cooperation must be extorted, but we required a crewperson whose record is beyond reproach. Do you have anything else to report?"

"Just that I abhor dealing with lojis."

"Who does not? But they excel at subterfuge and assassination. More importantly, they are all expendable, especially the black market facilitator through whom you made our anonymous arrangements. She will be eliminated before our plot unfolds. And once it has, and investigators discover her involvement, where will they seek other perpetrators?"

Yaonhoyz felt satisfaction, even pleasure. "Among her loji associates."

"Precisely. All that remains now is for you to give the orders that shall set our plans in motion. Which you will not achieve by reveling in your smug bigotry. This communication is ended."

Chapter Thirty-Two

MAY 2124
WASHINGTON, D.C., EARTH

In the windowless bowels of a ubiquitous Arlington office complex, Richard Downing studied his image on a wall-sized video monitor. The footage was from three years ago. His face was pallid, flabby. His alcoholic self.

He felt an urge for a drink, was suddenly very conscious of David Weber's hulking presence. He pushed down the craving as if it might spring from him, fully fleshed and visible in all its pathetic desperation.

His alcoholic self was surrounded by reporters, halfway down the front steps of the Capitol. "Director Downing," one cried, "there are rumors that Riordan's actions on Turkh'saar could spark a civil war among the Hkh'Rkh. Can you comment on that?"

Downing watched himself turn toward the journalist. "The true state of affairs among the Hkh'Rkh is not known to us in any detail. However, their leader First Voice is still missing, and the Patrijuridicate is divided over whether to replace him. Tensions over when and how they should proceed could indeed prime the Hkh'Rkh for a civil war."

Weber froze the screen. "Your situation is becoming more precarious."

Downing stared at his own image, then at Weber. "Because of this? Captain, that is a three-year-old interview segment."

"Which is receiving widespread replay since word arrived that the civil war you predicted among the Hkh'Rkh may be starting." He tapped a finger on the frozen phalanx of reporters. "The press is using this clip to claim that the government had reason to foresee what is occurring now. That is chum in the water for the sharks in the Procedural Compliance Directorate and their masters over at the Interbloc Working Group." Weber considered the scene again. "They might have been willing to let you fade away, but then you became a person of interest regarding Riordan's suspiciously swift departure last year. And now, new twists in that investigation have put you back in their crosshairs."

Downing heard Weber's leading tone. "New twists?"

"They discovered that Riordan's clearances from the State Department were not actually issued by its employees, but by persons able to access and spoof its system."

"And I presume those persons report to you."

Weber sighed, nodded. "For their sake, and the sake of this office, they have to go out-system ASAP. As do you."

"I beg your pardon?"

"Director," said Weber heavily, tapping the screen again, "your days are numbered. One of the men involved in fabricating the State Department papers also handled the request that I meet you with secure transport outside your safe house. It's safe to assume that they will notice that Riordan's escape commenced within that same hour. If they, or your go-between Kyle Seaver, are interviewed, that leads the investigators to you. Further scrutiny into your actions that day could therefore lead them to me and this office. For instance, the 'taxi' in which I picked you up was untraceable, but a bystander could have taken a picture of it. Once they identify the correct vehicle, they are likely to discover what we really do here in ODINS and gut us. Just the way they did IRIS."

For one brief moment, Downing felt nauseous, but that sensation was quickly displaced by genuine relief. *Hold on, have I been* hoping *for this?* Trying to cover the surprise at his own reaction, he muttered. "Then I suppose I'd better pack my bags."

Weber shook his head. "I'm sorry, Director, but as with Riordan, we have to assume you are being watched. So, no preparations. Within the hour, a location will be relayed to your wristlink. Go there. You'll get each subsequent step only minutes ahead of its necessary execution."

"And if I run into trouble?"

"You won't. Besides, you'll have help from your traveling companions."

Weber waved his wristlink in the direction of the interactive whiteboard dominating the north wall of his windowless office. It slid aside. Three men, one in a wheelchair, looked up from linked dataslates. The tallest of them—white haired, late fifties—straightened. "Adding a few last bells and whistles to the shell game we'll be playing with our cryocells, sir. It will be months before anyone notices the shift in inventory." He glanced at Downing, smiled broadly. "Director, we've never met, but I'm a big fan."

Downing almost sputtered in surprise. "Are you? Well, that's very kind. I suppose." He turned to Weber, tried to modulate his voice so that he sounded surprised, rather than alarmed: "These are my... my traveling companions?"

The tall white-haired one was not in bad shape, but had passed the age for field operations. The fellow in the wheelchair was in his twenties and quite fit, but, unless the wheelchair was a cover, it meant that he was one of the few individuals whose body refused to sync with smart prosthetics. The third was in his late thirties and carrying just enough extra weight to make him an operational liability in circumstances where speed, rather than wide shoulders and a broad chest, would be crucial to success.

If Weber noticed Downing's concern, he gave no sign of it. "You won't see them, of course, but they'll be nearby. Larry—er, Mr. Southard—will be reanimated occasionally to maintain ops oversight and make any needed corrections to your itinerary." The white-haired one nodded, still smiling. "Mr. Ryan Zimmerman"—Weber nodded to the young man in the wheelchair—"is, to put it succinctly, an all-purpose computer guru. And Angus Smith is to electronics what Ryan is to computers."

Downing glanced at the burly man. "I must ask, your last name is Smith? Truly?"

Angus may have smiled behind his beard. "Truly."

Downing cocked an eyebrow at Weber. "First genuine Smith I've met in this line of work."

Weber grinned faintly. "Me, too."

"I don't suppose you can tell me where we're heading?"

"No, sir," Southard answered. "Opsec. And we're not all going to the same place, at first."

"So, that's the shell game you were talking about, seeding us into military cold 'banks.' Mixing us in with normative redeployment traffic, I wager."

Larry smiled. "You'd win that bet. Given our taps into the service databases, we'll just look like four more grunts being shuttled around in refrigerators. The folks trying to tail us won't start out looking for that. Once they do, they'll have to show sufficient cause for access to those records: more delay. By that time, we'll be at our destination."

Downing nodded, saw the three men afresh. Not merely as fellow fugitives, but as humans about to cut all ties with everything they knew and loved. "I'm very grateful, chaps. I can't begin to guess the sacrifices you're making, to leave Earth behind, but—"

"Don't bother yourself about that," Ryan said sharply. "I don't have anyone. Not anymore."

Angus nodded. "Pretty much that way for all of us." He nodded toward Weber. "That's part of why we were chosen. If this day ever came, we don't have baggage." He stepped forward, extended a furry paw toward Weber. "It's been a great ride. And a genuine privilege, sir."

Weber had to clear his throat before he could answer. "Likewise, Angus. And the same goes to all of you gentlemen. One day, when these witch hunts are behind us, I'll send word that you can come in out of the cold. But until then..."

Zimmerman nodded. "We'll make our way in the world—well, worlds—Captain. No reason to worry about us."

Larry nodded, led the others back into the small room, touched a wall control. The smartboard sealed the opening.

Weber, still looking at the blank surface, murmured, "I suspect it will be hardest on you, Director. You have a wife, a daughter."

Downing put on his best ironic smile. "Captain, you need to keep your intel current. I *had* a wife. My daughter has been well and properly poisoned against me. And given what is likely to come"—he gestured toward the reporters frozen in the posture of wolves about to take down prey—"leaving is the best thing I can do for them." He put out his hand toward Weber. "Well, I suppose this is—"

The big man shook his head. "One favor, if I may."

"Certainly."

"Kyle Seaver. What do you think of him?"

Downing thought. "Never had reason to get a complete dossier. Before the war, he was studying to go into the entertainment side of the sim business. Enlisted the day after his father was killed in an elevator free-fall during the Arat Kur EMP strike."

"Sir," Weber repeated patiently, "what you *think* of Seaver?"

Ah, that *kind of assessment.* "Solid fellow. Could have used him in IRIS. Doesn't make waves, doesn't miss a trick. Mother was Nolan Corcoran's much younger sister, you know." Downing paused, reflected. "Actually, if you recruit Seaver, I wonder if you might give him a small side assignment."

Weber smiled. "I will neither confirm nor deny, now or later, that any such person reports to me. Nor can I confirm or deny any assignments that might be given to him."

Downing smiled back. "If you can, do have Seaver, well, watch over Connor Corcoran."

Weber frowned "Do you believe Riordan's son is on someone's target list?"

Downing nodded. "Might be. More superstition than logic, mind you. But some of our adversaries... Well, their motives have occasionally been as mysterious as their methods."

"I understand, Director Downing. But as I said, no promises." And Weber winked.

Downing smiled. "I'll see you in a few hours, then."

Weber shook his head. "Actually, sir, you won't. You'll get a message on your wristlink. Just do what it says." He stuck out his hand. "Goodbye, sir. And Godspeed."

Chapter Thirty-Three

In the same drab Arlington office complex, Kyle Seaver held the elevator door open for Lorraine Phalon. "Such chivalry," she said with a roll of her eyes.

"Just trying to get on the boss's good side, get a bigger raise."

Now Phalon did laugh. She was neither Kyle's boss nor in position to give him a raise. "Manual," she instructed. The elevator's previously blank display illuminated, showing virtual buttons. She pushed "B2" and the elevator headed briskly for the subbasement.

The doors opened moments later, revealing a single security guard in a gaudy rent-a-cop uniform. She was chewing her gum loudly and looked bored. But when the guard saw who it was, she dropped the act and rose into parade rest. "Commander."

"At ease. Are we expected?"

"Absolutely, ma'am."

Phalon and Seaver went through the only door, where they found a waiting room furnished with dull paintings. After two minutes, they were buzzed in.

After navigating a dogleg in a short corridor, the real nature of the facility became evident. They went through a battery of scans conducted by men and women who were well-armed and looked like they'd be pretty deadly even if they weren't. After passing the print, retinal, and DNA checks, Phalon and Seaver were ushered into a long, plain hallway. There were no numbers on the doors. Either you knew where you were going or you didn't belong there. Phalon crooked a finger at Seaver, led him to the left.

"We can talk business, again," she muttered over her shoulder. "Do you have anything more on the surgical records of Downing's past operatives?"

He caught up, paced her. "No, Commander. But there's something else you should know about Trevor Corcoran. The witch-hunters aren't going to bypass him this time."

"Why not? He wasn't at Turkh'saar, never had anything to do with the Lost Soldiers or Riordan's disappearance."

"No, ma'am, but he and Riordan were the only two humans captured during the Arat Kur sneak attack at Barnard's Star II C. So until two years ago, the only person who'd logged more hours with the Arat Kur was Caine Riordan. And some of what they saw and heard is now becoming highly sensitive."

"Mr. Seaver, I prefer my information without a side helping of suspense."

Seaver sounded apologetic. "Yes, ma'am. Trevor Corcoran had a ringside seat to the frictions that not only existed between the Hkh'Rkh and their Arat Kur hosts, but among the Hkh'Rkh themselves."

Phalon bit her lip. "So the Procedural Compliance Directorate will lasso him as a resource to help the Interbloc Working Group decode recent events in the Patrijuridicate."

Seaver nodded. "But ultimately, that will just be window dressing to conceal their real motivation: to use Corcoran's reputation as leverage over his godfather, Richard Downing."

Phalon frowned. "And how would they do that? Corcoran is squeaky clean."

Seaver shrugged. "Once the Directorate is authorized to get a look at his *full* dossier, they're going to find confidential after-action reports from his early career. Specifically, from surgical strikes conducted in countries that are now major members of the Developing World Coalition."

"Yeah, well, that was then and this is now."

"Yes, ma'am, but with respect, the news venues won't care. Which means the Directorate can threaten a public pillorying of Corcoran unless Downing explains how Riordan left so quickly. And that will lead them to Weber and ODINS and rejuvenate their efforts to, er, 'find,' the Lost Soldiers."

Phalon nodded. "Good catch. Get in touch with Trevor, tell him that if he's approached by either the Procedural Compliance Directorate or Interbloc Working Group, he is to deny or disavow and then report to us ASAP."

"Yes, Commander." They stopped before a large black door. Seaver's eyes widened. "Is this it?"

"This is it," she confirmed as the door opened. A man in street clothes stepped out before they could enter. "It's an honor to meet you, Commander Phalon. Mr. Seaver, if you would please follow me."

Phalon made to fall in behind them. The man stopped, shook his head. "Just Seaver, Commander."

She let slip an ironic smile. "You do know I've been inside before, right?"

"Yes, ma'am. But at that time, things were less... complicated."

So it's come to this. She nodded. "So now protecting yourselves means keeping me out?"

"We're not just protecting ourselves, Commander. We're protecting you, too."

"Is that so?"

The man, whom she had never seen at ODINS before, folded his hands. "Let's presume that our office comes under investigation for some unforeseeable reason." He almost smiled. "The more contact we've had with you, the more likely you'll get swept up in that investigation. And the more likely those investigators will then push their inquiry to the levels above you."

So you're not really protecting me. *You're protecting Silverstein, Rinehart, Sukhinin. Everyone, all the way up the tree.* Which was, of course, the smart move.

Phalon shrugged. "Yes, well... I was just dropping Mr. Seaver off."

"Yes, ma'am," replied the man. "I hope we'll meet again." Which sounded an awful lot like, "Goodbye forever."

As the door closed behind Seaver, another door opened: the one by which people exited ODINS. Richard Downing emerged, saw her. He smiled. "Hello, Commander Phalon."

Well, well. Just the guy I need to talk to. Probably here to get his own one-way ticket off Earth. "Hello, Director Downing. I wonder if I could have a moment of your time. Lieutenant Seaver recently turned up some very interesting information."

Downing stopped in front of her, shrugged. "I'm sure Mr. Seaver turns up interesting information every day. Why don't you tell me about it as we head to the elevators?"

"Happy to, sir." They started, very slowly, to their joint destination. "Mr. Seaver has been conducting some precautionary background research into the operatives you employed during the final weeks of the invasion."

"Old news, I'm afraid."

"Yes, sir, mostly. Except in the case of Major Opal Patrone, whose medical records were gutted by redactions that date from months *before* the invasion. That led Seaver to wonder if they were motivated by something other than her classified contact with exosapients."

"Oh? And what does Mr. Seaver propose as the actual reason for the redactions?"

"Ongoing operational security, sir. Specifically, he suspects that Major Patrone was not just Riordan's bodyguard, but that she, too, had been equipped with a scrambler to bring down the Arat Kur's C4I network."

Downing smiled faintly.

"Seaver speculates that there had to be contingency plans in case Riordan never got in range of the enemy's systems. So he went back through the records of your other operatives and discovered a number of surgical events—staged opportunities— similar to the one used to implant the Dornaani scrambler in Commodore Riordan's arm when he was ostensibly attacked on Mars.

"Specifically, it appears that Trevor Corcoran was also fitted with a virus transmitter during his treatment for a fracture on Barney Deucy. Opal Patrone's was evidently implanted during an interruption of her cold sleep while returning from Convocation."

Downing nodded. "Mr. Seaver is to be congratulated. Of course, we knew that the redactions themselves might attract undue attention. But given what we had to conceal ... well, it was Hobson's choice from the start."

So Seaver was right! "I will pass your kudos along to Mr. Seaver. However, my immediate concern is that the Directorate's witch-hunters will eventually piece together the same information and come to the same conclusions. If they do so just as Trevor's past service record in DWC countries comes to light, they'll use that against him. Or more likely, against you. And if, as I suspect, you are in the process of expediting your own exit scenario..."

Downing stopped. "They'll only have Trevor left. And they'll crucify him."

"Sir, it could go further than that. The authorities could compel him to undergo surgery to have the implant remov—"

"No!" It was the first time Phalon had ever heard an edge of desperation in Downing's voice. "That would kill him. Only the Dornaani can remove an implant safely. In Caine's case, the procedure was performed during the same operation in which their surgeons repaired the injuries to his spine and liver."

Phalon felt her brow heating. "Director Downing, given the danger, was it wise to allow Trevor and the others to remain unaware of their implants?"

Downing shook his head sharply. "Commander, we've all been under intense scrutiny since before the war. If I had tried, and failed, to inform Trevor or the others surreptitiously, leadership would have insisted upon removal. I'd have been killing my own godson. That's why I intended to warn him to leave Earth soon after I did, to take an extended holiday until they're finished ranting about me."

Downing raised a palm to his forehead. Phalon had a fleeting impression that he might faint. "But now I'm... I'm out of time, Commander. There's no safe way to tell him about the implant or even get a message to him."

"Then I'll be your courier, Mr. Downing."

"You? You'll get him a message?"

"All things considered"—*and given what all of you did for all of us*—"I think it's the least I can do. So if you have the time to come with me..."

Downing checked his wristlink. "I do. Just barely."

Chapter Thirty-Four

MAY 2124
WASHINGTON, D.C., EARTH

Seaver took the indicated chair in Captain Weber's office. He tried to radiate cool, collected competence while his head whirled with all he had just been told and shown. *But still, why* me?

Weber tossed out the answer to Kyle's silent query. "Mr. Seaver, you are both an extraordinary opportunity and an extraordinary risk for us. The risk is obvious: you are young, not widely experienced, and have drifted into your current line of work rather than seeking it out. However, that is also a large part of what makes you an opportunity. Your connection to ODINS will not be anticipated by the watchdogs tasked to detect an organization like ours."

He smiled. "I get it, sir. They'll never expect that spooks like you would put any trust in a kid like me."

"Exactly," Weber replied flatly, crushing Kyle's hope that his self-deprecating comment would earn a few brownie points or at least a smile. "But you present an even more unusual advantage. And no, it's not the fine head on your shoulders; it's good, but there are others that are comparable."

Jeez, just drop my ego down the toilet while you're at it.

"Rather, your job already requires that you contact individuals with whom we, too, must coordinate: Director Sukhinin, Assistant Director Rinehart, and Admiral Silverstein."

"So recruiting me as a liaison to IRIS's uncompromised gate-keepers doesn't trigger any alarm bells. Sir."

"As I said, you *do* have a fine head on your shoulders." He waved in the quiet man who'd walked two steps behind them throughout Kyle's introductory tour. "This is Ed Peña. He is our on-site security chief and the person who has the most frequent contact with the outside world. Memorize his face. If you ever meet him again, you can be certain that we have a crisis."

"Well, except when I see him here."

Weber frowned. "Perhaps that fine head is getting weary. You will not see me, nor the inside of these offices, ever again. That is how we remain beneath the radar of those who are looking for us. Contact procedures will be explained before you leave. Do you have any questions?"

"Just one, sir. During my tour, you mentioned that you'd like me to 'keep an eye' on Connor Corcoran. Why?"

"Because too many members of his nuclear family have been targets for assassination."

Seaver sat up. "Sir, I know the DWC isn't fond of Riordan or anyone who was connected with IRIS. But... assassination?"

Weber gestured to Peña, who tapped the room's smartboard. Diagrams of a space battle appeared. "This is the most recent attempt on Riordan, mounted just as he was about to enter Dornaani space."

Seaver realized he had been gawking at the screen. "Jesus!" he breathed. "That system is outside our borders. It's not even part of the land grab."

Weber frowned at Seaver's profanity, but nodded. "Yes. How do you know?"

"I remember most of what I read."

"Interesting. Go on, Ed."

Peña didn't even nod. "The investigation into who ambushed Riordan and *Down-Under* has been a dead end. The combat drones are Arat Kur models we arrogated from the roaches at the end of the war. But during this battle they were controlled by human milspec systems."

He snapped the display off. "If the Dornaani hadn't ridden in like the cavalry, we'd have lost a lot more than two people and a refueling shuttle. The captain, Schoeffel, couldn't afford the time or the risk to search for the ship that brought in the drones. So all we had were serial numbers from the wreckage to backtrack them to one of our research labs."

Seaver nodded. "Where you found a person of interest who made the drones disappear from the lab's inventory the same day they performed their own vanishing act. And who is now in places unknown, either with a suitcase full of credits or a bullet in the back of their head."

Weber nodded. "One final caveat. Whoever sent Riordan's assassins could also be unwitting pawns of the Ktor. You need not look so surprised, Mr. Seaver. You know better than to believe the media assurances that our counterintelligence services have apprehended all the megacorporate executives suborned by our enemies."

"So are those the players you want me to watch most closely when it comes to Connor Corcoran's safety, Captain Weber?"

"For now. There will be others."

"When do I start?"

"You already have."

Trevor entered the Bosun's Chair, not entirely convinced that he should have left his sidearm at home. The call for the meet was untraceable and had come from a burner wristlink.

He squinted into the subdued lighting, took a step inside...

Abruptly, a woman rose from one of the booths opposite the bar. She was dressed in service dress blues. Not an uncommon sight in Annapolis, but also no guarantee she was actual Navy. She marched straight at him...

...at which point Trevor recognized her as Caine's counsel during the Turkh'saar hearings: Lorraine Phalon.

Before he could wave or utter a greeting, she had brushed past him toward the door, snapping, "Excuse me." Then, over her shoulder, "You're welcome to my seat."

And then she was gone, her walk instantly more casual when she reached the sidewalk.

Trevor slid into the booth she'd vacated and discovered three cocktail napkins laid in a row. An eager busboy arrived, leaned forward to sweep them away. "No," Trevor said, "those are mine."

The busboy glanced doubtfully at the napkins, shrugged, and moved on to the next table. Trevor put his shoulder against the wall so that, as he turned the napkins over, they could not be seen by anyone to his rear or flanks.

Phalon's handsome script on the first explained the other two: they were copies of a message from Richard Downing. Damned melodramatic, Trevor thought.

Trevor turned over the second napkin and instantly realized

that what he had dismissed as melodrama was actually a desperate attempt at secrecy.

A list of bullet points laid out a startling new reality. Downing was fleeing the Procedural Compliance Directorate's witch-hunters, they'd be coming for Trevor next, no one involved with IRIS during the invasion was safe, careers and lives were being overturned and frozen.

Downing resorted to another bullet-point list to explain why official resistance to the witch hunt was unlikely. In summary, its immediate objective was not to destroy or ruin, just fix its targets in place. Consequently, every investigatory initiative could be made to sound routine, even dull. The majority of politicos would not realize that the ultimate aim was the removal of reliable personnel so that, once the process was over, a very different intel apparatus could grow into the organizational vacuum.

The third napkin presented Richard's flatly declared intent to leave. Probably for good. To help Caine retrieve Elena. And lastly, if Trevor wanted to follow, he could do so by looking in the classified ads.

That final line was not just a hasty bit of advice. It reprised a lesson Downing had imparted to Trevor about using classified and want ads for passing intel. It was old school but reliable, his godfather had proselytized a year before the invasion, a fourth glass of holiday cheer in his unsteady hand.

It was also the last time they had really talked, Trevor reflected. At least until after the war, after Opal was dead, after Elena was gone. After everything had gone to hell.

Trevor crumpled the napkins in his large, corded hand, jammed them in his coat pocket, and flinched as his palmtop paged. He fished it out of the same pocket, tapped in his security code, frowned when a blizzard of promotions started scrolling past.

What the—? This can't be. My account is totally blocked from—

And then he realized: he was looking at classified ads. He remembered Richard's voice, even the words, from that yuletide exchange. "Want ads, lad. They're your best friend for receiving and sending precoded messages. Properly constructed, no computer can detect them, no algorithm unpack them." He had smiled, put a finger against his nose. "No matter how our work may change, my boy, this much will always be true: if you absolutely must hide something, hide it in plain sight."

Trevor scanned the ads. Mostly furniture, vehicle leasing, and travel offers, several of which were offworld. But as he skimmed one for Epsilon Indi, a phrase jumped out at him from the otherwise predictable and tiresome copy:

> Stuck working the same dull job? Seeing the same scenery? Living the same boring existence, day after day? Well, look up to the stars. Because the start of a better life could be right up there, hiding in plain sight!

"Hiding in plain sight?" *No. It* can't *be a message.*

But it was. As Trevor combed through the ad, he found phrases of particular significance to him and Uncle Richard:

> So come to NovOz, where we're waiting for you with smiles, shrimps on the barbie, and a big glass of chablis!

"Shrimps on the barbie" had been Uncle Richard's call to dinner at the occasional Corcoran-Downing cookouts, howled in an awful Aussie accent. To which Trevor's mom Patrice had always added, "and a big glass of chablis!"

Trevor discovered he was choking back tears, not for what the war had done to his relationship with Richard, but for simpler days. Happier days. Days when Dad still got to cookouts. Days when he'd still been alive.

Okay, so Richard is passing through Epsilon Indi. Logically then, when Trevor got to Epsilon Indi, he'd find an ad in the NovOz colony with another phrase from shared memory. The ad would cycle, of course, through automated variations—enough changes to elude any bots trained to look for simple repeats. But every version would point to the next destination, where Trevor would discover yet another ad with a family reference—a pet name, a memorable event—that would guide him onward to the next system, and the next ad and ultimately on to...

To where? And to what? God only knew. But hell, it was a path forward.

And that was all that Trevor Corcoran ever asked for.

PART THREE

Collective Space
June 2124

SOMNIA

Somnia vana
(Empty [delusional] dreams)

Chapter Thirty-Five

Unable to sleep prior to the shift out from HD 2401 A, Caine Riordan's eyes were fixed on the small, bright disk in the aft view: in actuality, the huge orange star they were about to leave behind.

The heavy gee forces cut out. His limbs started to drift upward.

"Preacceleration complete," announced Ssaodralth from the pilot's couch.

"Shift drive ready," Irzhresht put in from navigation.

Alnduul leaned back into his cocoon couch, prompting Riordan to do the same. "Commence transit."

The universe rushed away, pulling Riordan after it. He had a fleeting impression of being sucked down a drain...and then his perception was abruptly normal again, as if he'd blacked out for the sliver of time separating the two sensations. He wasn't aware of any post-transit vertigo until he sat forward. Even then, it was only a fraction of that which followed human shifts.

After the world stopped its faint wobbling, Caine checked the holosphere. BD +76 351, another main sequence K-class star, floated at the center of the display. Three potential courses were already linking the tiny likeness of *Olsloov* to the second planet: a green world that Dornaani characters labeled as Issqliin. "'Old park?'" Riordan translated doubtfully.

"Park of Antiquities," Irzhresht corrected flatly.

"However, a reasonable effort at translation," Ssaodralth added as he chose the second of the three approach vectors and engaged thrust.

Alnduul expanded the navplot's field of view until it also displayed the closest gas giant, two orbits further out. "Computer, inquiry," he said, waving his hand in the air, a ghostly fingertip alighting upon the large planet. "Antimatter supply?"

"None," replied the computer. "Bunkers depleted."

"Refurbishment cycle?"

"Automated fueling facility is nonfunctional. Report and repair request has been relayed."

"How long ago?"

"Two thousand one hundred forty-six days."

If Alnduul noticed Riordan's surprised stare, he gave no indication. His finger moved to the Mars-sized planet just sunward of Issqliin. "Secondary antimatter facility: status report."

"Also inoperative, as per last report. Solar arrays have sustained additional damage. Storage rings now unsafe."

Alnduul leaned back into his couch. "We will have to produce our own antimatter. Again."

Riordan rose into the gee forces. "That's four times since we left Rooaioo'q. Isn't this, well, odd?"

"We deferred fueling at HD 2401 because *Olsloov* no longer qualifies for priority service. We would have waited almost three months."

"Okay. And the other three systems where we came up dry?"

"Malfunctions, similar to this one." Alnduul let a finger droop. "It is increasingly more commonplace, particularly in less trafficked systems."

"But this system has easily accessed volatiles, multiple facilities."

Alnduul lifted his head. "Computer, time since last shift in or out of this system?"

"Three hundred and twelve days."

Riordan glanced at green-blue marble orbiting the primary star. "So this system has been abandoned? Even though Issqliin is a green world?"

Alnduul raised a finger. "For a while yet."

"What do you mean?"

"It was heavily terraformed. Being at the outer edge of the habitable zone, Issqliin was one of the first worlds we improved during our reexpansion. The average planetary temperature was increased five degrees centigrade by several centuries of carbon dioxide generation. This vastly reduced the polar caps, producing larger oceans and significantly increased habitable tidal shelves. It became an ideal world for establishing what you think of as a combined nature preserve and theme park."

"A theme park for what?"

Alnduul looked at him. "For our original way of life, such as you saw on Rooaioo'q. At the time, Issqliin was the superior planet for that project."

Riordan did not have a command tip on his finger, so he reached into the holosphere itself, touched the image of Issqliin, spread his hand. The view of the planet enlarged. Ice caps covered half of it. "It's backsliding. Why?"

Alnduul waved a lazy hand at the other planets in the navplot. "For the same reason there are no antimatter supplies: neglect. Our terraforming is rarely self-sustaining. In the case of Issqliin, its gravity cannot permanently retain the thicker atmosphere it was given, resulting in a diminished greenhouse effect."

Riordan folded his hands. "You said that Issqliin is a product of Dornaani terraforming. Is there another type?"

Alnduul blinked slowly. "That is an excellent question to ask of the one who waits on Issqliin."

"And who is that?"

"The Caretaker. Let us contact him."

After an hour of unanswered radio messages, Alnduul tried a different approach. "*Olsloov* sending to Issqliin port authority auton. The Caretaker of record, Uinzleej, is not responding, may be deceased. Require priority override for emergency refueling. Custodian authorization code is being relayed now. Commencing planetfall in twenty-four minu—"

A voice—raspy with disuse?—interrupted sharply. "*Olsloov*. Delay descent. This is Uinzleej. There are no longer any refueling facilities planetside. Divert."

"Uinzleej, I am pleased to hear your voice. My mentor has spoken highly of you."

"Eh? Who is your mentor, Custodian?"

"Thlunroolt." There was no immediate reaction. "Of Rooaioo'q."

"Him. Yes. You should have said so immediately. And you are ...?"

"Alnduul."

"*Senior Mentor* Alnduul, in charge of the Earth Oversight Group?"

"I am he."

"Then I repent my terseness. I am not accustomed to visitors. Or company." It sounded as though Uinzleej had also lost any ready facility with normal conversation. "So, you are not here simply to refuel. What brings you to my park?"

"The hope that you will share a small measure of your unique knowledge."

"What knowledge? Why do you need it?"

"Actually, it is my friend who needs it. I will allow him to explain." Alnduul gestured toward the nearest audio pickup.

Before Riordan could jump in, Uinzleej was sputtering irritably. "What friend? What is so important that—?"

"Uinzleej, my name is Caine Riordan. Thank you for allowing us to intrude upon your preserve and your privacy."

The Caretaker, whose voice suggested considerable age, fell silent. Then, "You are human."

"I am."

"And you have *two* names."

"I do."

"Hmm. Things have changed. You must be quite remarkable, if Alnduul calls you a friend. Speak quickly. I am busy but I will take the time to hear your request."

You're busy? Riordan glanced at the image of Issqliin turning slowly, lightless and forlorn. A faint network of transit lines that met in urban nexi were almost completely lost amidst the encroaching greens and reds of the local vegetation. "A Senior Arbiter instructed me to expand my understanding of Dornaani history if I wish to find my mate, who is located in one of your systems."

"I perceive no logical connection between increasing your knowledge of local history and improving the chances of locating your mate."

"I shall clarify. Given my mate's dire medical condition, finding her will largely depend upon determining which systems might have the technologies and expertise to preserve her. But in order to do that, I must better understand the history of several of your most esoteric, and, er, unsanctioned technologies."

"I presume that your mate's present injuries were incurred during her work as a factotum?"

"As a what?"

The longest pause yet. "A factotum. One of the humans we breed and retain for interacting with your race."

Riordan stared at Alnduul, whose inner lids nictated twice as he spoke toward the audio pickup. "No, the human's mate is not a factotum."

A shorter pause. "So, she too is a native of Earth. What has befallen her?"

Riordan told him, ending with, "To discover where her body is being housed, I am told it is essential to acquire an understanding of virtuality's origins and its operation."

"Its origins, yes. But beyond that, it is not the technology you need to understand. You must understand, to the extent you are able, the mind and the purpose of those who built it."

"What do you mean by that?"

"That would require too much time to explain. Indeed, your request is entirely too time consuming. Unless..."

Alnduul made encouraging finger-trailing gestures at Riordan while Uinzleej paused.

"...unless you agree to assist me with a study of historical value."

Damn it, back to being a lab rat. "What does this study involve?" Visions of vivisection flitted through Caine's glum imagination.

"You must complete a simple task. Alone, and without any modern implements."

Alnduul's eyelids seemed to tighten. "Uinzleej, as a Custodian, I am responsible for the safety of Caine Riordan during—"

"Yes, and being a Custodian, you may be compelled to report whatever you hear or observe. I will not tolerate that."

"So," Caine interjected before a dispute could arise, "I alone will be conveyed to whatever coordinates you specify. How long will it take for me to complete this task?"

"A few hours. At most."

Well, that's not so bad. So the catch is something else. "And what must I do?"

"Prove your fitness. Then cross a river."

Too easy. "What must I do to cross it? Build a boat? A bridge?"

"No. You simply need to cross a ford."

Riordan was quite sure that walking across the ford would be anything but "simple," but he had to move forward. "Tell me more," he said.

Chapter Thirty-Six

Caine checked his wristlink, only to realize, for the third time, that it was gone, along with every other bit of technology he had unthinkingly worn down to Issqliin. Drawing a deep breath, he ran toward the last defunct robot between him and the end of the obstacle course.

Riordan had only been planetside half an hour, but Uinzleej's remote-controlled proxy had already tested his endurance and agility and now required that he navigate a dry river bed while striking targets: a collection of rusty, dilapidated robots. They all appeared to be inert, but Riordan wasn't taking any chances. As he drew within two meters of the final one, he feinted, dodged, and then bashed it with his bludgeon: a manipulator arm from the first defunct bot he'd attacked.

The rusted bot almost fell over, but ultimately its low center of gravity rocked it back upright.

Riordan, looking back over the three ruined bots he'd felled prior to this one, asked, "Good enough?"

At the end of the shallow streambed, Uinzleej's proxy bot—a smoother design, clean, and fully functional—swiveled its "head" toward him. Uinzleej's voice emerged from the small speaker where a real Dornaani's mouth would be. "Adequate."

Riordan stared at the tall vegetation hemming them in, caught sight of a familiar silhouette: a goldenrod tree, identical to the ones on Rooaioo'q. Maybe the species had originated on Dornaan. "So, do we go to the river now?"

The Uinzleej-robot turned and began rolling back toward the lightly built vertisled that had carried them from where *Olsloov* had landed.

"Your fitness is satisfactory," Uinzleej's voice announced. "We may proceed to the river-crossing scenario."

Riordan looked after the robot from which the uninflected statements had emerged, wondered if Uinzleej was actually alive or if all that was left of him was a brain in a high-tech jar. Still, Glayaazh's data chip indicated Uinzleej as the essential first step in Riordan's search, not only because of the Caretaker's specialized knowledge, but his connections among the Dornaani expert hobbyists most likely to guide him to Elena.

When Riordan began comparing the relative martial merits of the robot arm he had just wielded to a leg from his last target, the robot-proxy—called a "proxrov" among Dornaani—halted. "We must depart." Its "head" rotated toward the goldenrod trees. "Hurry, human."

"Just deciding which limb to take."

"You may not take any."

"What?"

Uinzleej's proxrov rotated back to "face" him. "The use of any modern artifacts would drastically decrease the authenticity of the final scenario."

Oh for the love of—

Three hulking shapes burst from the closest stand of goldenrod trees. Quadrupeds with immense chests and shoulders, they resembled outsized gorillas with wide, multieyed heads.

Riordan gauged the distance to the vertisled, which suddenly looked as fragile as a cubist rendering of an origami dragonfly. No way he could reach it in time. He snatched up the robot arm, cocked it back over his shoulder—

With twinned whispers, two drones popped up from the vertisled and turned innocuous looking tubes toward the creatures. Each tube spat three times, a crackling, electric sound.

In less time than it took to blink, ugly mauve craters erupted on the shoulders and head of each creature. A spray of similarly colored blood and chunks flew out behind them, marking the trajectories of exit wounds. Two of the shaggy ogres tumbled aside, limp. The third yowled, scrabbled in a crippled circle to retreat back toward the woods.

The drones each spat once.

Gobbets of ruined flesh, and dusky-colored bone exploded from the injured creature. It fell, suddenly as still as the others.

Riordan panted, a receding wave of terror colliding with a sudden surge of relief. "What . . . what the hell were those?"

"Feral specimens. The park is impossible to maintain properly. They grow desperate as suitable game becomes sparse." Uinzleej's proxrov resumed moving toward the vertisled. "I repeat, we must depart, human."

Riordan started following gratefully.

"Leave the implement. You must cross the river without any advanced tools."

Riordan tossed the robot arm aside, but only after he had set foot on the vertisled.

Riordan stared across the river. Uinzleej's proxrov stared back. Or seemed to.

Caine examined the length of goldenrod tree he was clutching in both hands. The splintered trunk probably had little chemical similarity to terrestrial wood, but the familiarity was soothing.

It had not, however, proven soothing to the herpiform crawling away from him, trailing yellow-green slime as it did. He'd only landed a glancing blow upon the seven-foot ciliated worm-snake, but his first target had fared less well. A two-handed swing had caved in that one's hideous head: a fang-lined sphincter ringed by pupilless black eyes.

Riordan cautiously followed the wounded one before slashing down again with the driftwood trunk. The sharp edge of its splintered end sliced into the flank of the animal, lopping off a few cilia before it cut through the belly and smashed down into the shallow stones of the ford. The sphincter-mouth shrilled and writhed away. Two of the other herpiforms, alerted by the sound, roved in its direction, either smelling the blood or sensing its impaired movement. As they tore into it, Riordan tossed the shattered trunk away and reassessed his situation.

With the exception of the two herpiforms now devouring the wounded one, the rest remained as they were: a bridge of bloated, half-submerged caterpillar-shapes that spanned the river. Although not immediately dangerous, they'd shown surprising energy swarming in Caine's direction when he'd first entered the water. They had retreated with equal alacrity after discovering that he was anything but an easy meal.

So, a standoff. Riordan dominated his bank of the river, but the sphincter-mouths controlled the shallow waters of the ford, maws aimed upstream to catch whatever small prey the current brought them. Caine eyed the remaining driftwood on his side of the river. Not enough to bash his way across. Besides, they were sure to swarm him if he waded back in.

Nor was there any other means of crossing the river. After the proxrov had deposited him in this narrow gorge half an hour ago, Caine had quickly discovered his lack of alternatives. The river both entered and exited the ravine over waterfalls. The upstream cataract fed a current too strong and swift to cross before being pushed into the gaping maws of the sphincter-mouths. Downstream, the river frothed around jagged boulders before becoming a cliff-plunging flume. And whereas the far, or eastern, ridge that paralleled the river appeared scalable...

He turned. The steep western slope at his back was crested by an overhang of split and uneven rock: a troubled gray brow, brooding over the gorge. No way to get over that rim.

As if to warn Caine against trying, the mass overhead grumbled, groaned, sent a few small stones bouncing down to join those around the ford. Riordan's initial gut-stab of fear was tempered by a sharp, logical riposte. *What are the odds of a geological shift occurring just half an hour after I arrive?*

Frowning, he checked on the proxrov. It remained inert, as it had been since piloting the vertisled to the other shore.

Riordan turned and reconsidered the escarpment behind him. So, the test wasn't just to find a way across the ford; it was to do so before getting squashed by a rockslide. Uinzleej had certainly chosen the right place for it. The soil-and-stone composite of the western slope showed signs of heavy erosion, undermining its rocky crest. That was probably what had created the ford in the first place: every time a bit more of that fractured mass gave way, it rolled down and—

Riordan's mind stopped, swerved on to a new track. He was no geologist, but it did indeed appear the slope's flinty skirts had been mercilessly pounded, even pulverized, by multiple rockslides. The few solid outcroppings further upslope appeared scarred and cracked, again consistent with heavy impacts from overhead.

But with his life on the line, Caine couldn't afford to leave that hypothesis unconfirmed. He scrambled up to the nearest granite protrusion, examined it closely for several minutes.

Satisfied, Riordan picked his way back down slowly, taking particular care not to dislodge any of the rubble that had proven stable enough to bear his weight. Stopping two meters away from the ford, he lowered himself into a squat. It would have been more comfortable to sit, but it took too long to get up from that position. So, hunched forward, he stared across the river at the motionless proxrov and waited.

And waited.

Without a wristlink, Riordan had no way to mark the passage of time; the cloud cover was absolute. However, after two stand-and-stretch routines, and what Caine guessed was a little less than half an hour, there was another rumble from the craggy crest of the slope behind him. He wondered how Uinzleej managed that trick. Probably something he'd embedded deep in the rock formation long ago. But Riordan didn't allow himself to get distracted by pondering the specifics; Dornaani always seemed to have plenty of near-miracles up their sleeves.

The next episode of stony groaning and cracking occurred about ten minutes later. Granite chunks broke away from the lip, crashed down the slope, were reduced to pebbles after impacting each other or the outcroppings. Riordan turned back to face the proxrov, didn't even try to suppress a yawn.

There was no way of knowing if Uinzleej understood what a yawn was or what it signified, but he might have. Within a few minutes, a third rumbling began, but this one built slowly and along a wider section of the overhang. Sections of the shelf cracked, fell away, showered down, raising small explosions of dirt wherever they impacted. Riordan yawned again.

The rumbling built into barely suppressed thunder, punctuated by sharp lightning cracks as the splits in the crest widened and new ones appeared, cleaving previously solid masses of stone. Caine smiled. *Not long, now.*

Even though he was expecting it, Caine flinched at what sounded like pile drivers colliding directly overhead. Without wasting time to look, he jumped up...and fell. His left leg had gone to sleep. Cursing, he rolled to his feet, and hobble-sprinted up the slope.

Straight at a massive landslide.

The lighter rocks expelled by the shattering lip flew over him into the river; a few even hit the far shore. Heavier ones rained down around Riordan as he leaped from one spot of solid footing to the next. The main wave of boulders was not far behind, the smaller ones leaping up high wherever larger ones smashed into them from either side, squirting them above the mass of rushing stone.

Riordan realized the landslide was moving faster than he'd anticipated just as his bounding run brought him within three meters of the nearest outcropping: a crooked fang of broken granite. He threw himself toward it, rolling into the narrow furrow underneath as the approaching roar grew into deafening thunder.

Abruptly, Riordan was hemmed on both sides by a torrent of rocks, some the size of buffalos as they tumbled and spun and leaped past his shelter. One crashed on top of it: the mass shielding him groaned, dipped slightly, but held.

The drumming of the smaller, following stones increased as the leading edge of the landslide raged down toward the river. Slabs that had collided higher up the slope now streamed past as fragments trailing in the wake of the bow-wave of destruction. Some caromed sideways, were flung under his shelter. One the size of a fist struck a glancing blow against his left thigh: probably not a break, but Riordan expected he'd have a grapefruit-sized contusion and limp to go along with it.

And then, along with the scree and gravel that flowed and chattered in the aftermath of the stones, came the dust. Gray, white, choking: it was as if Riordan had been thrown into the exhaust plume of a quarry's grinder. Coughing, he scrambled from beneath the outcropping, sleeve across his face as he picked his way down toward the ford, mindful of the new rockfall's treacherous footing.

At the bottom of the ragged, reconfigured slope, the dust began thinning where it encountered the water, the sediment sinking instead of remaining airborne. Riordan emerged from that fog near where he had started, but the ford was unrecognizable. Its once-smooth apron was buried under almost a meter of large, jagged stones. And further out...

The rockfall had not merely devastated the ford, but also the sphincter-mouths. Pools of bile welled up from where herpiforms either lay inert or still thrashed fitfully. The new rubble narrowed into a causeway as it progressed from the shore, stretching most of the way across the river.

A few of the most distant sphincter-mouths were only moderately wounded and still capable of feeble movement. Riordan watched them writhe away from the new rocks and wallow in the disrupted current.

The proxrov remained motionless, just beyond.

Riordan turned, began picking his way along the upstream shore toward the cluster of driftwood that had been beyond the landslide's path.

With any luck, he wouldn't need more than one or two stout clubs to finish making his way to the other shore.

Chapter Thirty-Seven

Uinzleej met Caine at the entrance to the last intact building in the small, fortified Caretaker's compound. He clasped his hands in excitement, eyes assessing his visitor from head to toe. "At last, a successful *and* valid test subject." His entire torso bobbed as they made their way into Uinzleej's home. "Your performance was most satisfactory. Please, be seated." He waved absently around the dingy oval room.

Riordan glanced after his host's gesture: nothing but the saddle-shaped "chairs" designed for the buttock-free physiology of a Dornaani. He lowered himself to the floor, took in the wild clutter of stacked tables, control platforms, holosphere pits, and shelves of unrecognizable gear. It looked like an explosion had gone off in the middle of a Dornaani rummage sale.

Uinzleej swung unsteadily into his seat. He was very old, possibly the oldest Dornaani Riordan had yet seen. "Your participation today definitively refutes all doubts regarding the ability of unaugmented humans to succeed at atypical survival challenges. Idiotic cavils, really, but they could not be dismissed without modern proof of your species' primal capabilities." He fumbled after a bottle designed for his extrudable lamprey mouth.

Okay, so today I'm not really a lab rat; I'm a knuckle-dragging specimen of Cro-Magnon. "So your work is focused on whether primitive humans were able to survive without genetic enhancement or exosapient assistance."

Uinzleej sat erect and stared, as if Caine were a dog that had suddenly spoken quite clearly but had said something absurd. "No. My only concern is with measuring how vulnerable primitive humans were to unusual challenges. I do not expect you to understand why that is important."

Riordan struggled to make a connection, flung out his best guess. "You're trying to determine how much the traits and instincts of risk takers and innovators improved early humanity's odds of survival."

Uinzleej sat straighter, as if the talking dog had said something intelligent.

Riordan followed his hunch to its probable conclusion. "And therefore, you're hoping to determine how statistically prevalent those 'change agents' were in primeval breeding populations."

Uinzleej sat silent for three full seconds. "I did not expect you to be able to adopt so detached an evolutionary perspective on your own species."

Riordan smiled. "I did not expect to discover that you were so interested in humanity."

The old Dornaani leaned back on his saddle seat, folded his hands together and rested them on his small, wrinkled potbelly. If he had had spectacles, he would have resembled a stock character—specifically, the gnomish professorial type—from a Victorian comedy of manners. "The more one knows of Dornaani history, the more one discerns that it is ineluctably entangled with your own, human." Uinzleej's mouth twisted. "Have you not wondered," he resumed in an almost coy tone, "at the strange density of intelligent species in this part of space? Why, beyond the borders of the Accord, there is nothing but silence?"

Riordan nodded. "I have wondered if it is a result of intent, rather than chance."

The Dornaani's mouth straightened. "Intent may be too strong a word. Excepting humanity, which is clearly native to Earth, there is little to suggest that the rest of us were seeded here as part of a plan. Rather, this was simply a fortuitously remote haven for those who dwelt or fled here when the prior historical epoch imploded."

Riordan folded his arms. "That certainly explains the co-located human and Slaasriithi ruins on Delta Pavonis Three."

Uinzleej leaned forward. "As hostility between the mentor

races grew, we Dornaani implicitly understood that resisting such advanced powers would be tantamount to defying the Great Wave of Fate itself. The community that ultimately grew to become the Collective was swollen first by migrants who foresaw that flood, then by refugees seeking as distant a corner of space as could be found. What little evidence exists all points to this conclusion."

Riordan frowned. "That still doesn't explain the absolute silence almost twenty millennia later."

Uinzleej dropped a dismissive finger toward the floor. "You fail to deduce the logical answer: that only this pocket of sapience survived the conflagration that we call the Final War. That is consistent with the proposition that this region of space attracted migrants and refugees because it was remote from the centers of power."

Riordan knew a circular argument when he heard one. He leaned back against a deactivated robot, smelled dust rise up. Time to shift gears, hopefully move Uinzleej in a more useful direction. "Do you know what caused the Final War?"

"There were bitter disagreements over life prolongation, conferral of equal rights for all species, constraints upon exploration, exploitation of primitive societies, and the legal standing—if any—of virtual beings." Uinzleej rubbed his hands fretfully. "It was not a war that began or was waged swiftly. For the better part of a millennium, there was sweeping, unthinkable destruction..." He stopped when he noticed Riordan's unintentional frown. "You doubt my account?"

Riordan shook his head. "No. I'm just trying to reconcile why, if it remained untouched, your 'homeworld' does not have a more complete record of the war."

Uinzleej's reply was sharp, irritated. "Extrapolate, human. If this astrographic region was at great remove from the centers of power, then it was equally distant from major information repositories. The result resembled your Dark Ages, except imagine that it was global and that every community was rapidly and utterly isolated.

"Picture it as an extreme version of that terrestrial analog. Ships no longer make port or appear on the horizon. Fearing marauders, city fathers burn docks and collapse mountain passes, praying that the epidemic of war will burn itself out before it can arrive in their darkened streets. Let a millennia pass. Then another, for good measure."

Riordan frowned. "But surely every community kept records—"

Uinzleej leaned forward abruptly. "They were records that ceased to have meaning as the centuries passed, that succumbed to the vagaries of time and folly. Consider another, albeit earlier analog from your own history. Only a single library burned in Alexandria, but you still feel the loss of it. In what detail can you now recount the movements and machinations of Rome? Of Athens? Of Egypt, Sumeria, Assyria and the many states with which they contended? You have only scraps from which to infer the greatest deeds, let alone daily activities, of the empires which first shaped your world. Data from what we call the Times Before is exponentially more rare and fragmentary."

Riordan's frown persisted. "At least you Dornaani retained some of that data, some memory of those times. The rest of the species were... what? Primitive tribes brought along as a labor force?"

Uinzleej's eyelids opened wide as he looked at Riordan. "Those species were much more than a mere labor force." His gaze became thoughtful. "The term the Elders used for all of you, collectively, was Seedling Races."

Seedlings? "Just how widely were we seeded?"

The old Dornaani's gills fluttered briefly. "There is no quantitative data on that. But the Elders' records do indicate that the Arat Kur were the least widely seeded, as they were used solely for subterranean resource exploitation on gray worlds."

Riordan's breath caught in his throat. "So when everything collapsed..." Caine shut out the scene conjured by his imagination: an airless world, its rocky depths filled with cranky, industrious, wry Arat Kur trapped in their caves, dying, no chance of reprieve or rescue. "And the other races?"

"When left to manage their own affairs, the Hkh'Rkh tended to revert and savage each other to the point that they lost communal viability. However, there may be some pockets of fully recidivistic survivors somewhere."

My God, feral Hkh'Rkh. Not intelligent, just canny, vicious predators over two meters tall. It was a scene from a horror movie. "And the Slaasriithi?"

"They were seeded more frequently and successfully. But since their reproductory and social complexity makes their communities particularly fragile, their fate was usually the one you witnessed on Delta Pavonis Three: profound devolution."

Caine swallowed. "And us?"

"Humans. You were the great triumph. And the great tragedy."

Riordan frowned. "Why that?"

"Why which?"

"Why both? Either?"

Uinzleej sputtered; an almost human sound of dismay. "Surely the tragedy is obvious. The Ktor genecode is human and their atrocities are innumerable. They also demonstrated a corresponding tendency to destroy themselves in internecine strife. Of course, on that point, your own history hardly warrants pride."

"So then how are humans a triumph?"

"Is it not equally obvious? The Ktor are but a genetic aberration of your species. However, your *unaltered* genecode mitigates strong aggression-protection instincts with equally powerful tendencies toward cooperation and innovation. Of particular value was your flexibility in rebalancing these extremes as circumstances dictated."

Riordan smiled bitterly. "So we were simply the Elders' most self-regulating tool."

Uinzleej squinted. "There is nothing 'simple' about that quality, human. You were aggressive if required but inclined toward consolidation and group cohesion in the absence of adversity. That quality was highly attractive to the Elders, not merely because it made you versatile, but because it made you self-sustaining. You took possession of your own fate. You were naturally inquisitive. You were productive. You were excellent explorers." Uinzleej's voice faltered. "In point of fact, you were to replace us."

Riordan recoiled in surprise. "As the Elders' assistants?"

"That and more. When the war arose, the Elders were grooming us to become what was called a 'peer race.' Upon making that transition, our tasks would have necessarily passed to another species. Fragmentary records suggest that the Elders considered humanity best suited and that we agreed." His voice darkened. "However, others disagreed. Pointedly."

Riordan nodded. "One of the war's catalysts?"

"It was what prompted the Oldest Ones to very nearly annihilate my race."

Riordan frowned. "How did you survive their attacks?"

"They did not attack us themselves. They used proxies."

Caine nodded, suddenly understanding. "The loji."

Uinzleej raised three emphatically rigid fingers in affirmation. "The Oldest Ones had long aided and abetted any low-gee natives who vigorously rejected Dornaani culture's presumed primacy of a planetary existence. Within half a dozen generations, few of them were physically capable of surviving, much less reproducing, in a gravity well.

"By the time the Final War commenced, our forces were fully engaged repulsing loji insurgencies. Ironically, that may be part of the reason the Oldest Ones did not bring their doomsday weapons here: the internecine strife left us too paralyzed to influence outcomes elsewhere."

Riordan saw an opening to shift the conversation closer to topics that might ultimately lead to finding Elena. "Do you have any details on these advanced weapons?"

Uinzleej pointed a single desultory finger toward the floor. "That knowledge is lost to us, along with many other wondrous accomplishments and devices."

And there's the opening. "Yet I have seen that not all the knowledge of the Elders has been lost. And much of what remains is not fully understood."

For a moment, Uinzleej seemed disoriented by Riordan's observation. Then his mouth twisted slightly. "So, we come to it. Virtuality. Yes, it was originally created by the Elders. However, what you call virtuality is merely a shadow of the greater miracle they achieved."

Riordan straightened. "What do you mean?"

"Seek my colleague, Oduosslun. In the Sigma 2 Ursa Majoris 2 B system. She will tell you, or maybe show you, something useful."

"Something useful?" Not good enough. "I wish I had time to visit Sigma 2 Ursa Majoris 2, but I am compelled to restrict my travel to systems where I might pick up the trail left by my mate's abductors."

Uinzleej's gills popped softly: mild exasperation. "Then Sigma 2 Ursa Majoris 2 B *is* the next logical step on your journey. Oduosslun will acquaint you with the miracle I mentioned. It is, I suspect, the therapy of last recourse for your mate, one that would both maintain her cognitive functions and sufficiently stimulate her nervous system. Find where such miracles are still performed, and you will find her."

Before Caine could get his mouth open for another question,

the old Dornaani slashed two rigid fingers through the space between them. "No. We have come to the limit of my expertise. Our discussion is over." He paused. "Except ... I *would* welcome observing you at greater length. I could offer considerable inducements. I can arrange for a new mate who is, in all meaningful measures, superior to the one you are currently pursuing. You look unimpressed. Ah, multiple mates, then? Within reason, I am quite certain I can procure—"

Riordan was careful to keep his interruption calm. "I am not interested in other mates."

"Ah. Well. I am also able to provide you with material riches. I believe your species persists in its obsession with gold? To use your idiom, I would pay you handsomely for any successful breeding activity. Even if you do not wish to stay afterward."

Riordan forced his molars to unclench.

Uinzleej moved on to his next offer. "What else—ah! Many of your species enjoy hunting. This world is full of creatures you may kill for your gratification. To use another of your idioms, you would be lord of all you survey."

Lord over a decaying, backsliding world. Is he serious? Well, given his opinion of humans, he probably is. "Uinzleej, your offers are not enticements. On the contrary, they repel me."

"They *repel* you?" Uinzleej looked crestfallen. "That is most distressing."

Riordan could not resist one last, ironic comment. "I'm sorry you're disappointed. It must come as a shock that most humans are actually civilized, now."

The old Dornaani started. "Civilized? You? Absurd. I am disappointed because you have misled me. Despite your adequate demonstration of primal abilities, you now claim to be repelled by your species' primal value-objects. That strongly suggests you are a defective specimen. My test results are ruined. Begone. You are of no further use to me."

Alnduul stood when Riordan reentered *Olsloov*'s bridge. "You seem unharmed," he breathed.

"I told you I was." *Four times since I left the surface.*

"And your leg is ... ?"

"Just fine." But Riordan was careful lowering himself into his couch.

"I must apologize for Uinzleej's inability to accept humans as a truly sapient race. And for his willingness to expose you to such dangerous conditions."

Riordan didn't care when the couch conformed to his posture. "You warned me he might. And I never expected any different."

"Even so, I am grateful for the patience you have shown when dealing with the many . . . idiosyncratic Dornaani you have encountered thus far."

Riordan smiled. "I waited three and a half years for a chance to bring Elena home, so I've had a lot of practice being patient. Still . . ."

"Yes?"

"I'll be a lot happier when we're one shift closer to her."

Alnduul turned to his crew. "Irzhresht, calculate navigation values for shift sequence to Sigma 2 Ursa Majoris 2 B. Ssaodralth, commence preacceleration."

Chapter Thirty-Eight

Shortly after *Olsloov* came out of shift near the smaller, orange star of the Sigma 2 Ursa Majoris 2 binary system, Caine Riordan had the uneasy feeling that everything was going too smoothly. They had reexpressed just twenty-two planetary diameters from the main world of Aozhoodn, received an immediate reply to their arrival hail, and were cleared for refueling in less time than it took to complete the formal request.

Very soon, reasoned Riordan, something *had* to go wrong.

But refueling proceeded without mishap, and Alnduul accessed Oduosslun's comm code without any delay or difficulty. She picked up on the second page but, as had Uinzleej, answered in voice-only mode. "We have not met, Alnduul, master of the *Olsloov*."

"That is true, but we have a common acquaintance."

"And who is that acquaintance?"

"Uinzleej, keeper of Issqliin. He asks us to convey his regards."

"Does he? That is most unlike him. Do you know him well?"

"No, Oduosslun. Our personal contact was brief. It was my companion who spoke with him at greater length."

"Then why is it you, rather than your companion, who elects to contact me?"

"My companion's command of our language, and mastery of our customs, is somewhat basic."

A pause. "So, your companion is a human. From Earth, not a factotum."

"That is correct."

"Is he too fearful to speak for himself?"

Caine moved closer to the audio pickup. "I was simply waiting for an invitation to speak, Oduosslun." Formal Dornaani introductions required using a common acquaintance as an intermediary.

"That was cannily worded, human. You seem to have a passable understanding of our customs, after all. When you have learned more, return. Perhaps I would be sufficiently interested to speak with you then—"

Alnduul interrupted. "Oduosslun, I suspect you will be interested in speaking with him *now*. Given your interests."

"And what do you know of my interests, Alnduul?"

"Various sources consider you the preeminent independent expert on Dornaan's modern era. And Uinzleej has implied that you have facilitated your research with esoteric research tools." Which Riordan understood as a euphemism for gray market virtuality access.

Oduosslun's reply was arch. "And did Uinzleej tell you that my insistence upon using those 'tools' cost me my post as Academician?"

"He did not."

"At least he is not a shameless gossip. Very well. So you know who I am. Now explain why I would wish to meet this human at all?"

Alnduul's nostril pinched: a frown, probably because Oduosslun had still not asked Caine's name nor invited him to speak. "My friend has been directly involved with significant events in recent history."

"Name one. Be sure that it will, as you claim, interest me, or we are at an end."

"He is the human who made contact with the devolved Slaasriithi on Delta Pavonis Three, and later reported his findings and analysis at Earth's Parthenon Dialogs. At which he suggested that humans had been taken from Ea—"

"Enough," Oduosslun interrupted. "I know this human." The gray haze of the comms holosphere brightened. The Dornaani imaged there was of indeterminate age but unusually well muscled for her typically slender species. "Congratulations, Caine Riordan. You must be quite proud of yourself." Her tone suggested he should be anything but.

"I simply did the job I was sent to do, to the best of my ability."

Oduosslun's mouth pinched into an unsightly squiggle. "I am not speaking of you personally, but of your entire, intemperate species. We Dornaani maintained relative calm among the races of the Accord and deflected inquiry away from the origins of the Ktor for thousands of uneventful, uncomplicated years. But now, a short-lived creature, a half-witted mayfly, simply skims across these subtly complicated seas of statecraft for a few short months and leaves a typhoon of chaos roiling in its wake."

Caine knew better than to start a point-by-point debate. Win or lose, that was likely to make her an adversary who would be unwilling to aid him. So he turned the argument around. "I agree. It is a strange turn of events, Oduosslun. I wouldn't think a mere mayfly was capable of discomfiting so many purposive patterns and profound plans."

Oduosslun's response was sharp, but also eager, engaged. "The smallest creature can cause the greatest changes if it happens to be in just the right place at just the wrong time. As you were."

"Of course. But why was *this particular* fly in the right place? Again and again?" Riordan expected Oduosslun to ask what he meant by "again and again," and so, open a wider door that touched upon the other historical events to which Caine had been a party.

But instead, the Dornaani stared intently at him. Then her eyelids flickered. "That is an interesting question. I have wondered it myself. But presently, I am wondering why you need to speak with me at all."

Riordan nodded. "Uinzleej indicated that virtuality was an invention of the ancient races and that a more sophisticated version still exists."

"It is called Virtua. Why do you wish to know more about it?"

"I believe my mate is connected to or embedded in it. I need to find or at least contact her."

"So. You need to know where you may enter Virtua."

Riordan nodded again, then remembered that the Dornaani might not understand the motion. But Oduosslun returned his nod. "I have the information you seek. But it is not free."

Here we go again. Riordan shrugged. "What do you want me to do?"

"Land at the primary downport. You will find a headset waiting for you. Put it on. Then travel to these coordinates."

"That's all?"

Oduosslun's mouth twisted. Wickedly, Riordan thought. "Once we meet, I will require proof that you are who you say you are."

"What kind of proof?"

"Cell and tissue samples. Painless. Harmless."

Riordan glanced at Alnduul, whose eyes were grave. Caine met Oduosslun's unblinking gaze again. "And how does that prove who I am? Do you have access to the CTR's genetic ID database?"

"It is not your DNA that will prove your identity."

"Then what does?"

"Your willingness to give the sample at all. It demonstrates that your need is genuine. You would not risk sharing it otherwise."

Riordan raised an eyebrow. Whatever Oduosslun knew about him, it clearly didn't include his near-gutting on Glamqoozht, where physicians had taken *plenty* of tissue samples. On the other hand, Oduosslun and her peers were operating with little or no oversight. They could easily use his genes to create some kind of doppelganger or clone or god knows what. But right now, that didn't matter. Getting Elena back did. "Very well. And once you've confirmed my identity, what is it that you want?"

"A complete account of everything that you did, saw, or spoke about during your visit to Issqliin."

Riordan frowned. "I'll comply as best I can, but I'm not sure I'll remember everything that you—"

"I do not trust recollections. They are intrinsically distorted by subjectivity. Rather, I shall record your memories."

Record my—? Riordan looked at Alnduul, whose eyes seemed to droop as their lids cycled once, very slowly: the equivalent of a resigned shrug. Caine looked back at Oduosslun. "Do I have your word that you will record *only* the memories from Issqliin?"

The muscular Dornaani's mouth twisted around its axis once again. Again, her "smile" was marked by a sardonic ripple. "If you wish."

Riordan nodded, kept his face as expressionless as he could. "Then I accept."

Oduosslun's tilted mouth remained as it was. "Of course you do. Make haste. I am on a temporary hiatus from my research. Before long, I shall regain access to the 'special research equipment' I require." Her mouth wrinkled ruefully after the euphemism had slipped from her. "If you are not here by then, I will be unavailable for several months. Of course, if that occurs, you are welcome to sightsee in our extensive junkyards while you wait."

"Understood. I will—"

"On your journey," Oduosslun interrupted, "be sure to note the corpses of miracles scattered along your route. A visitor should see them, even if the visitor is only a human."

Before Riordan could suppress his indignation enough to inquire what Oduosslun meant by the corpses of miracles, her face and holographic connection dissolved.

Olsloov's shuttle had been out of the bay less than a minute when port authority warned Irzhresht that she was deviating from the planetfall flight corridor designated for Aozhoodn's equatorial downport. In the shuttle's small holoplot, a tube marked by bright white guidons flashed into existence. A tiny holographic image of the shuttle appeared on top of one of the boundary guidons. It flashed orange.

Correcting course, Irzhresht's handling of the controls was more brusque than usual. "Oduosslun might have warned us that we cannot travel directly to the coordinates she provided. They are far outside the landing corridor."

Alnduul, seated in the passenger and cargo section with Caine, agreed in an almost soothing tone. "Most inconvenient. I will request a flight path from the downport to Oduosslun's coordinates as soon as we—"

Irzhresht flung a hand at the deck without turning around. "Not possible. Only preauthorized or official vehicles are allowed beneath forty kilometers altitude. And the downport's dedicated airspace is only ten kilometers in diameter at its widest, and highest, point."

"And below that?" Riordan asked.

"It collapses down to a ground zero diameter of three kilometers, centered on the terminal." Irzhresht checked the rapidly scrolling data next to her. "However, there is an automated application for free access. Or we can submit specific flight plans for approval."

Alnduul spoke toward the ceiling. "Computer, access port authority data feed. Submit my credentials and operator authorization to request direct access to Oduosslun's coordinates."

There was a much longer silence before the port authority answered. "Cannot comply at this time. Special requests are backlogged."

"How long is the estimated wait time?"

"Approximately eighty-five weeks."

Alnduul's eyes closed, his mouth scissoring in irritation.

Riordan sighed. So, no direct air access to Oduosslun's coordinates. He checked the planetary map holo. "Computer, measure distance between equatorial downport and coordinates provided by Oduosslun."

"Six hundred forty-two kilometers."

"And a walking route?"

"Eight hundred and twelve kilometers. Warning: overland route intersects several significant terrain obstacles."

Alnduul's eyes had reopened. "You plan to walk there?"

"Not exactly." Riordan glanced at a screen showing *Olsloov*'s keel view: towers and domes were racing up at them. "There seems to be a lot of junk just beyond the city's perimeter."

Although Riordan hadn't intended it as a question, the computer answered. "Confirmed. Debris field ringing the city ranges from one hundred to three hundred meters in width."

Interesting. "Size of individual debris objects?"

"Largest is 1591 cubic meters. The majority are too small to measure accurately at this range."

"Condition of the debris?"

"Inquiry too general. Please narrow parameters."

"Scan for active electronics in debris."

"Multiple results. Primarily sub-utile power levels."

"Huh?"

Alnduul interceded. "That usually indicates a device in what you call 'sleep mode.'" Alnduul's large eyes fixed upon Caine's. "What is your interest in this?"

Riordan barely heard the question. "Irzhresht, are there any restrictions on using *Olsloov*'s sensors?"

"You mean, to examine the surface from orbit?"

"Yes."

"There are no restrictions."

"So if you surveyed that debris from orbit, what level of detail would you be able to acquire?"

"Despite the power of *Olsloov*'s arrays, detail would be limited. At best."

Riordan thought some more. "Then what about the shuttle's sensors, if it was hovering at an altitude of one kilometer?"

Irzhresht turned a questioning gaze upon Alnduul, whose mouth twisted as he answered. "At that range, it is likely we could resolve each item's serial number. What is your plan, Caine Riordan?"

"It's still a work in progress. I'll figure out the rest on the way down."

As Caine emerged into Aozhoodn's intensely humid air, a garishly painted proxrov approached to confirm his identity. *As if there is any other human within two dozen light-years*, Riordan reflected while responding to the robot's various queries.

Satisfied, Oduosslun's fuchsia-and-lime automaton handed him a headset and marched away from the downport's landing pads. Riordan called after it. It didn't stop. Catching up and jogging alongside, he asked about the planet, about accommodations, and about food.

No reply. The proxrov continued marching away.

Riordan set aside his annoyance. Best to find a live Dornaani, anyhow, someone who could direct him to lodgings before the shuttle returned to *Olsloov*.

However, as he wandered the uncomfortably warm streets, he encountered even fewer Dornaani than he had on Glamqoozht. Worse yet, the first two only stared when he asked for directions to a government office or visitor's bureau. Riordan was fairly certain that it wasn't his atrocious pidgin Dornaani that had startled them. Rather, they seemed convinced that he was a malfunctioning, freakish bioproxy. He pressed on, deeper into the city's cluster of spheres, domes, and glass-sided parabolas.

Unfortunately, when Caine finally discovered a building complex with a steady stream of Dornaani foot traffic, he could neither understand the locals' clipped replies nor decipher the holographic signage near the entrance. So, feeling vaguely like an eight-year-old who had run way from home, Riordan contacted Alnduul, whose shuttle was still dirtside, waiting his turn to lift.

His friend arrived at the building complex shortly thereafter, explained who Riordan was and what he needed. Surprisingly, they treated Alnduul little better than they had Caine, but provided directions to what sounded like a visitor's hostel. It was close enough that the pair decided to walk.

The building turned out to be a small, worn dome, its concierge system slow to awaken. Once inside, they understood the immense lag: the hostel had not been used in years, perhaps decades. Despite small, automated caretaking robots, the ceilings and higher reaches of the walls were dim with layers of dust. At first, the water dispensers spat only stale air and a grit-clotted slurry. And in one room, they came upon the shriveled remains of a single, indeterminate creature: a bioproxy, judging from the control device still embedded in its desiccated neck. Alnduul expressed no surprise, no anger, no indignation at the state of the facilities, merely resignation tinged by embarrassment.

As the sky began darkening toward dusk, he offered Caine a ride back up to *Olsloov*. Riordan demurred, explaining that in addition to getting used to life on Aozhoodn, he had a plan that required that Alnduul be standing by in low planetary orbit from tomorrow morning onward.

When Alnduul's departing shuttle had dwindled to a bright-tailed speck, Caine took off the outsized and outdated headset provided by Oduosslun. He replaced it with the circlet he'd been issued from *Olsloov*'s stores. That, along with food, was all that Custodial protocols allowed him to take from the ship. He began heading toward the outskirts of the city.

Riordan was approaching the sharply demarcated urban boundary when the circlet emitted two rapid tones: Alnduul's comm link. He activated the plasma HUD; the Dornaani's face appeared, concerned. "Do you not intend to stay overnight in the hostel, Caine Riordan?"

"Yes, but I figured I'd start scouting the junk at the edge of the city."

Alnduul's eyes became grave. "The preliminary scans conducted during landing show that much of the debris is machinery that may still be functional and could self-activate if you approach. Depending upon the device, that could put you in considerable danger."

"Alnduul, I'm not going to approach. I'm just surveying.

Nothing else." Riordan paused, smiled. "Until you bring the shuttle back down tomorrow."

Alnduul was silent for several moments. "So that is why you inquired about the accuracy of the shuttle's sensors from one kilometer. So that we may provide you with precision imaging, information, and instructions during your activities near the downport."

"Including tomorrow's salvage operations," Riordan agreed.

"Salvage operations?" Alnduul echoed.

"Of course," Caine replied. "You don't think I'm going to *walk* eight hundred and twelve kilometers, do you? See you tomorrow morning. We have a lot of work to do."

Chapter Thirty-Nine

"Caine Riordan, I must once again advise caution. You have inserted the new relay module correctly, but until you activate it, we have no way of knowing if the octobot's onboard computing is corrupted. It could become erratic. Dangerous."

Wiping his brow, Riordan stepped away from the inert, spiderlike machine, glanced a kilometer behind him. *Olsloov*'s shuttle hung motionless over Aozhoodn's main downport, its vertijet exhausts glowing a faint blue. "Have you tried the remote activation signal?"

"We have, but the unit is protected by user-defined access codes. The only alternative is to bypass the robot's processor and activate it manually. However, it may have a security protocol to attack anything that attempts unauthorized manual access."

Riordan reconsidered the strange device. More than four meters across, its visual invocation of a spider was decidedly imperfect, primarily because the legs were spaced evenly around its round cargo bed. On the underside of that disk was a cluster of the small and phenomenally efficient Dornaani batteries that Caine had encountered frequently during his three days of crawling through the junkyard. Alnduul was obligated to remain silent about their engineering specifics. Which was fine, since Caine barely understood the underlying physics. A tiny field effect generator pulled subparticles from antiprotons, that were themselves extracted from a microscopic but almost infinite supply of what sounded a lot like

266

antideuterium, but apparently wasn't. The annihilation of each antisubparticle was contained by that same field effect generator just long enough for the energy to be transferred to a capacitor that seemed to defy several rules of physics. Bottom line: a single reaction was enough to power the big bot for a day of moderate use.

After assessing, removing, and reconnecting several of the robot's batteries by following Alnduul's instructions and schematics displayed on his HUD, Riordan circled around to the machine's rear access panel. A similar panel, the site of the control relay he had already replaced, was open at the front. But whereas that one held a checkerboard matrix of receptacles for logic elements, the rear panel revealed a snaky morass of Dornaani "wiring" that recalled fiber-optic cables. Caine let his right hand follow along with the diagram being superimposed upon his HUD's view of the actual wiring. "Alnduul, please confirm: depressing this toggle will connect the batteries directly to the processor core."

"Yes, as well as to all other primary systems. But if the new control relay is not recognized, you will not be able to control the machine through your circlet. Manual deactivation would be the only option and could prove hazardous. I strongly recommend you do not attempt to repair this device."

"It's the only one we've found that might get me to Oduoss-lun's coordinates in time."

"Caine Riordan, that will not matter if you are not alive to make the journey. I counsel—"

Yeah, I know what you counsel. "Please monitor and keep transmitting control codes. Manually connecting the battery... now."

The instant Caine pushed the toggle, the fiber-optic wires flared into multicolored life. The octobot jerked forward, as if flinching away from Riordan's hand. Probably just a residual command being finished. But still... "Alnduul, are the control codes—?"

"Not recognized!"

The octobot's two rear legs were already closing toward Caine.

Riordan grabbed the rim of the rear panel, yanked himself into a forward leap that ended atop the cargo bed. The octobot's rear legs crashed together where he had been standing, then hovered a moment as if surprised to find nothing between them.

Riordan reasoned he had maybe half a second to decide what to do next.

The biggest problem was the structure of the legs themselves. Each was a jointed sequence of eight rugged spheres that could twist and turn in any direction. And the front two legs were already beginning to arc back toward him. He couldn't stay where he was, but if he jumped clear, there'd be no way to reaccess the octobot's control loop...

Wait, that's it! The control loop. When he replaced the faulty relay, there hadn't been any power in the system. But what if the relay couldn't initialize, couldn't reactivate the controls, unless the system already had power in it?

As the front legs grabbed for Riordan, he slid under them and off the front edge of the octobot. He spun, grabbed for the new control relay. It popped free.

The front legs were already reversing their spin, their terminal spheres swinging back at him.

Riordan wrestled the relay back into place, pushed down hard. It engaged with a click and illuminated.

The front legs abruptly froze in mid crush. Lights began to chase each other around the gridwork of modular logic elements.

Riordan slipped out from between the legs, stood back from the octobot. "Alnduul, is it—?"

"I recommend you try the HUD controls now, Caine Riordan."

Caine called up the remote operation interface, which autodetected the configuration of the octobot. Riordan, feeling dampness under each arm, marveled at just how much sweat the human body could produce in a few seconds. "Legs to default position."

The octobot's front and rear legs reconfigured themselves to match the other four. The machine was now a symmetrical eight-pointed star, the cargo platform perfectly level. Riordan exhaled, blowing out a case of the shakes. As he started walking toward the next piece of salvage, he ordered, "Unit. Follow user."

Legs cycling with a smoothness that belied their long disuse, the octobot trailed after Riordan.

Who, for the first few minutes, felt an atavistic reflex to keep that nightmare shape further back than its default follow mode dictated.

Once online, Anansi (because who could keep calling the mechanical beast "octobot"?) gathered the remaining salvage in just two hours.

Riordan was pleased with the haul: a handheld broad-spectrum scanner from a medical diagnostic system; an animal suppression weapon analogous to a carbine-sized coil gun; a remote control actuator that worked as both trigger and safety when slaved to the carbine; batteries of various types and sizes; a four-hundred-liter cargo container coated in molecular-level velcro that allowed it to be fastened anywhere; a mesh that could emit and absorb high levels of infrared; a dozen working lights; four working speakers; a remote-operated industrial turntable; and last but certainly not least, a holographic viewfinder that was the functional equivalent of a multispectrum, range-finding scope.

Once Anansi was loaded, Riordan led it back toward the downport. The rusted bones and warped bodies of the discarded machines through which they moved evinced two noteworthy properties. They varied wildly in form and style, which imparted the impression that this was the junkyard of several species, not just one. Yet they all had identical interfaces for data and electricity.

Caine's circlet emitted a now-familiar double tone. "Connect," he instructed the device. "Hello, Alnduul."

"Caine Riordan, I see you are returning. I recommend you alter your current heading thirty degrees left."

"Why? Another pack of the bug-eyed borzois who were shadowing me yesterday?" Which, as a descriptor, really didn't do justice to how shockingly weird the creatures looked.

"Yes. They have chased wounded prey into the dense debris just ahead. If you approach any closer, they are likely to detect your scent and investigate."

Which, since Riordan had no functional weapon, would be problematic. "Turning thirty degrees left."

"We shall monitor their movements until you are within the city's patrol boundary. Do you intend to pause for a meal, or shall we begin repair and assembly of your salvage?"

"I had a big breakfast, so let's get straight to patching this stuff together. I want to be on my way tomorrow."

"That may not be feasible."

"Maybe but I'm going to operate on the assumption that it is."

"As you wish. I shall see you soon." Alnduul's channel snicked off.

As Riordan led Anansi further to the left, he glanced at the horizon: mounting layers of green, as far as the eye could see. Every square inch of Aozhoodn seemed eager to send up a shoot, a flower, a vine. With seas covering just over eighty percent of its surface, and with landmasses more numerous and smaller than Earth's, the equator's narrow tropical biome was flanked by two broad temperate bands. The planetary datafile indicated that there were a few rain-shadow deserts somewhere in that collage of blues and greens, but too small to spot from orbit.

The planet's three urban centers were almost as hard to detect: pinpricks of light that only appeared when the terminator line rolled beneath *Olsloov,* dragging the blackness of Aozhoodn's night-side behind it. There was no evidence of outlying communities, transit networks, or nearby facilities. The one time that Riordan had openly wondered where all the inhabitants were, Alnduul had allowed a finger to drag downward. "They are there, Caine Riordan. But you will not see them."

Riordan had seen plenty of their proxrovs, though, cycling between different destinations before turning their backs on the city and marching back out through the encircling boneyard to god-only-knew-where. Hidden retreats of the unseen Dornaani, whose daily activities were—what? Being tended to by various automatons while staring at their nonexistent navels? Or was their involvement in virtuality so extreme that they had ceased to venture out of their homes? That thought, of thousands of Dornaani lying lost in dreams of places and events that never were and never could be, sent a chill dancing down Riordan's spine.

As he approached the edge of the city's patrol boundary, a ubiquitous swarm of cookie-sized sentinel drones collected at his projected entry point. However, this time, a robot on treads was moving to join them. When Caine was five meters away from the automated welcoming committee, the bot uttered what sounded like a question in Dornaani.

"I'm sorry," replied Riordan. "Could you please speak slowly and use smaller words?"

It was a full ten seconds before the bot tried again. In English. "Human. You may not enter."

Riordan frowned. "But I have exited and entered at this point for the past three days."

"This has been recorded. However, you may not enter at this time."

"Why?"

"You have salvage, but you lack a salvage license."

Riordan sighed. Anansi was almost out of power, and the harvested gear couldn't be refurbished without the tools on the shuttle. "How do I get a salvage permit?"

"You must apply for one."

"Where do I do that?"

"This unit is equipped to dispense salvage permits."

Well, why didn't you just say so? Riordan walked across the line, stopped in front of the robot. "I wish to apply for a salvage permit."

"Do you require a daily, weekly, or yearly permit?"

"Daily."

"Collector or salvage operator?"

"Collector." Riordan wondered who the regular salvage operators might be, imagined lojis combing through the wreckage.

Sensor panels emerged from the robot's back, swept Anansi. "Total mass of salvage remains under maximum daily collector limit." The panels retracted, the robot hummed, and then a chime sounded in Caine's control circlet. "Daily salvage permit, collector class, has been conferred. No fee. Travel safely, visitor."

Riordan walked back to Anansi, ordered it to follow him, and recrossed the boundary. As he passed the robot, he wanted to ask, "Why are you so stupid? Why are *all* you Dornaani robots so stupid?"

The answer, or at least a partial one, hit him in mid stride: because the robots were *designed* to be stupid, even though Dornaani computers were incredibly sophisticated. Which made no sense, unless...Riordan doubled his pace toward the downport.

The octobot was still scrambling to keep up when they arrived at the shuttle. Alnduul, emerging from its hold with tool kit in hand, stopped. "Caine Riordan, you appear to be agitated."

Caine ignored the comment. "Does the Collective have laws limiting the sophistication of robots?"

Alnduul blinked. "Yes, as well as computer autonomy."

"Why? What happened to make Dornaani so fearful of robots, of autonomous machines?"

Alnduul's lids cycled very slowly. "That is not a question I may answer for you. But I suspect Oduosslun will."

"I hope you're right."

Alnduul's nictating lids flicked. "You misunderstand, Caine Riordan. In the process of helping you find Elena Corcoran, Oduosslun *must* answer that question. And others related to it."

Riordan frowned. "I don't understand."

"No, but you will. Now, if you still intend to commence your journey tomorrow, we must begin transforming this rubbish into the devices you require."

Chapter Forty

Riordan commanded Anansi to slow to one quarter speed. "*Olsloov,* are the crocodactyls still circling me?"

Several moments passed, then, "They are." *Olsloov* herself was not directly overhead, so all comms were routed through one of the overwatch satellites she had seeded before Caine set out three days earlier. The comm lag was significant enough to be a tactical concern.

"Well," Riordan sighed, squinting into the rising sun, "maybe these crocodactyls will keep their distance like the last ones."

"Perhaps," Alnduul answered, "but that flock nested near the downport and had a healthy respect for machines. The three following you now are native to the wilds. Their movement is more confident; they are circling you more closely."

Riordan glanced around at the still-dim horizon: heliotropic clusters of huge, canopy-linked chrysanthemums—Aozhoodn's equivalent of trees—hemmed him in on the east, south, and west. To the north, oddly jagged hills framed a narrowing valley that was part of the shortest path to Oduosslun's coordinates.

Riordan scanned through every point of the compass. "I still can't see them."

Alnduul explained why. "The creatures are staying below the tops of the trees and the crests of the ridges. I suspect they will remain concealed until they close to attack distance."

Which was certainly what they seemed to be doing, Riordan

allowed. Beneath him, Anansi plodded on with insensate relent-
lessness. At his back, the micro-velcro box was still three-quarters
filled with provisions. The audio and lighting units were clipped
to its sides; that array had already repelled more than one group
of nocturnal predators. The faint chill of those nights had been
amply warded off by the IR emitter upon which Riordan sat, rid-
ing at the front of the cargo disk, the coil-carbine across his lap.

But now, Caine was beginning to think the better of wielding the weapon himself. "Alnduul, I think it's time to set up the
automatic targeting system."

Alnduul's silence was longer than the lag interval. "Although
the system functioned properly during tests, I do not recommend
relying upon it now. It would have to engage three targets."

Riordan nodded for the benefit of the wilderlands around
him. "Yes. Three *flying* targets. Much harder for me to hit, even
with the smart targeting interface between the scope and the
HUD." He checked the holographic viewfinder he'd lashed to the
side of the coil-carbine as its "scope." Like most optics, it was
finicky about rough handling and had required resighting twice
since Riordan had ridden Anansi out beyond the downport's
patrol boundary. "I'm not a professional marksman, you know."

"Yes," replied Alnduul with minimum delay. "That is quite
clear."

Ouch. And that's not entirely fair, you facetious little—

"However, using the automatic targeting device would require
the octobot to remain stationary. You would also have to remove
the container from the cargo bed."

"Only if I planned to mount the system on Anansi. Which
I don't."

"That is even less advisable. It would be best to—"

Riordan caught a flash of movement above the trees to the
west. Holding his carbine steady, he reached over and scooped
up the handheld multispectrum scanner. It had proven to be a
reasonable, if energy hungry, substitute for electronic binoculars.
He swept it along the tree line, saw the tip of a crocodactyl wing,
then nothing more. The scanner did not have a dedicated range
finder like the scope/viewfinder, but it was able to give distance
approximations by actively pinging selected objects. After returning
an estimate of four hundred seventy meters to the tree line, Caine
surveyed his intended path, especially where the woods converged

from the facing skirts of the saw-toothed uplands. Presuming he kept to the smoothest ground at the center of that pass, he'd be within one hundred meters of the trees on either side.

Riordan frowned, interrupted Alnduul's stream of cautious advice. "I'm going to stop here. I've got almost five hundred meters of clear ground in every direction. But up ahead, that pinches down to one hundred meters on both flanks. At that range, they can fly unseen at treetop level until they swoop in for the kill. Neither I nor the automatic fire control system would have enough time to engage them all."

"Agreed. However, if you stop now, they may become more aggressive."

"I'm counting on it. They already seem determined to attack, so I want them to do it here, where the sightlines are longer."

Riordan knew that Alnduul would not agree, that Ssaodralth would become anxious, and that Irzhresht would not give a damn. But just as predictably, Alnduul's eventual reply was, "What can we do to assist?"

Riordan reached behind to ready the components of the automatic fire control system. "Alnduul, keep monitoring the satellite feed and tell me what you see."

"I could simply patch the visuals through to your HUD."

"No. I can't rely on updates that are ping-ponging through a second and a half of relays. I need your eyes on the situation, and your judgment about what you think the crocodactyls are about to do next. Ssaodralth, be ready to operate the remote systems that I won't have time to oversee." *Or might forget.*

"Such as—?"

"Lights. Sound. The IR generator—"

"The IR generator?"

"Yes. They're predators with heightened IR sensitivity and a tendency to flinch away from anything unexpected. So a big IR pulse might blind and scare them off for a few seconds. And Irzhresht, I need you to drop down to forty klicks, directly overhead."

"That will take time."

"That's fine. The closer you get, the less lag."

"Understood. Complying."

Riordan exhaled hard, then breathed in deeply. *Here we go.* "Anansi, stop."

The octobot halted.

Riordan grabbed the automatic targeting system's platform—the turntable, its integral clamps, a few extra batteries—and jumped down. "Command circlet, assume local control."

"Warning," it told him. "Local computing assets are less than one percent of those available from *Olsloov*."

Yeah, and they're a second and a half too far away. "Understood. Confirm: command circlet to local control."

"Local control established," the circlet announced. "Safety protocols may be compromised."

No kidding. Riordan set the turntable on the ground, "Zero-balance turntable. Raise to maximum elevation."

"Complying," replied the circlet. The platform gimballed slightly, then rose up on its six telescoping legs until it was two-thirds of a meter off the ground.

Riordan used three of the turntable clamps to hold the carbine, ensured that the weapon's makeshift remote controller-and-handgrip had clear traverse in all axes. "Execute special command Ack-Ack."

"Executing," answered the circlet. Riordan watched as the substeps began compiling on the left-hand side of his HUD:

Control link to weapon scope: confirmed.

Control link to turntable: confirmed...

"Caine Riordan," Alnduul said calmly, "the three aviforms are altering course. They are now spiraling in toward your position from the east."

Integrated feedback loop between subcomponents: confirmed...

"Alnduul, start feeding target azimuths to the circlet."

"But the lag—"

"Doesn't worry me. I just need pretargeting updates so that the carbine leads the targets as they approach."

"Understood." The turntable immediately swiveled through one hundred degrees to face east, then tilted so that the carbine was slightly elevated.

Control link to weapon functions: confirmed...

The turntable cheated slightly higher, then a bit more to the left—

—just as the three crocodactyls came rushing over the eastern treetops, half a kilometer away. They were not massive animals: less than three meters from the chins of their toothy maws to the ends of their broad, flat aileron tails. However, they were capable of extraordinary bursts of speed and their hypertrophied barracuda jaws had severed Dornaani arms with a single bite.

The circlet simultaneously announced and scrolled out, "Special command Ack Ack completed."

Riordan shouted, "Circlet, scan three incoming aviforms." He jumped over to Anansi.

At two hundred and fifty meters, the crocodactyls swooped lower and began spreading out. The turntable adjusted, became slightly more level.

"Scan complete."

"Designate aviforms as targets. Lock on closest target." As Riordan gave the orders, he slipped his only other weapon—a makeshift spear—out of the rack he'd affixed to the side of the cargo container. It might have started out as a tent pole; it had a wicked spike on one end.

At one hundred meters, the two flanking crocodactyls swung away from the largest's direct attack vector: a pincer movement.

The circlet began to report, "Closest target is now—"

"Engage closest target. One round per second. Once hit, shift to next proximal target. Repeat cycle."

The coil carbine's shots—each a sharp *spat!*—were as steady as a double-time metronome. In his HUD, Riordan watched as the turntable struggled to keep the viewfinder's reticle on the largest crocodactyl.

The fourth bug-zapper report produced a wide spray of amber-brown blood that briefly obscured the creature. Then it was tumbling forward, revealing the gruesome wound that had been inflicted; it had been split down its spine, wings spasming as its body peeled apart like an opening hinge.

Alnduul's voice. "From the south!"

Riordan turned, poked his spear in that direction.

But that flanking crocodactyl was still thirty meters out. Directly behind Caine, the turntable was already accessing this next target; it spun around, reduced elevation, achieved target lock...

...that left it trained on Riordan's midriff.

Shit!

Caine dove left and down, toward Anansi's legs—and felt a short, sharp gust as the first round went downrange just above him.

The onrushing creature balked at all the rapid movement: the spinning turntable; the close miss of a projectile; Caine's desperate dive. Its wings flared and it veered toward Riordan, jaws gaping.

That slower, wider target silhouette was evidently all the autotargeting system needed. At eight meters range, it spat a second time.

A gaping hole blew through the crocodactyl's leathery left wing. It flapped harder, widening the wound as it swerved to fly away. Directly over the turntable.

The weapon elevated rapidly, fired at the same instant the predator swept over.

The rear half of the crocodactyl erupted into a mist of sienna-colored gore. It fell like a stone, its tail glancing the turntable and knocking it over.

"Automated targeting off-line," the circlet announced, just as the third creature swooped in toward Riordan, who thrust his spear out between Anansi's legs. The crocodactyl slowed, swooped low, snapped at the end of the spear as it passed.

It banked, the three eyes on the right side of its long head moving asynchronously, assessing, measuring—right before it changed tactics and came at Riordan over the back of Anansi.

Unable to swing his spear around in time, Caine ducked and shouted, "Noise!"

The cargo box on Anansi's back abruptly emitted a staggering wave of sensory madness. Sirens yowled. Lights pulsed in eye-gouging detonations of lurid color. Horns hooted. Electric banshees shrieked. Blue-white strobe effects exploded like clustered star flares. And the IR emitter blasted a wave of heat straight into the crocodactyl's face.

Wings suddenly reversing, the creature turned, soared away.

"Track target," Riordan panted.

"Distance and altitude increasing, both rates steady." A pause, then, "Both rates declining."

Alnduul interrupted the circlet. "It is angling back."

Yeah. Stupid creatures tend to be stubborn creatures. "Keep giving me updates." Riordan scrambled out from between Anansi's legs, reached the turntable. Like most Dornaani gear, it was tough: no sign of significant damage. But there wasn't enough time to set it up again.

Riordan popped the clamps holding the carbine, reached for the combination handgrip-remote-controller.

It was gone. Nowhere to be seen.

Shit. "Anansi, belly down."

The octobot kicked its legs out straight, came to rest on its undercarriage.

"The creature is at three hundred meters," Alnduul announced.

"Circlet, confirm command link to weapon."

"Confirmed."

Alnduul's voice was slightly less calm. "Two hundred meters."

Riordan jumped onto Anansi's cargo bed, crouched behind the cargo container, saw the crocodactyl approaching out of the corner of his left eye. "Circlet, confirm weapon operational status."

The pause was unpromising. Then, "Power supply intermittent. Probable damage at coil-battery interface."

Riordan looked, saw the weapon was slightly crooked in the middle. He pushed upward on the muzzle; the carbine was somewhat straighter.

"Weapon operational," the circlet reported.

"Fifty meters," Alnduul wheezed.

Riordan shifted the muzzle carefully toward the oncoming creature. "Anansi, activate defense protocol 'Steeple.'"

As the crocodactyl swooped down, Anansi's eight legs swept up to meet at a point directly over the center of its cargo bed, securing Riordan within a tall, tapering cage. The creature tried to arrest its dive toward the sudden barrier, reversing the cycling of its wings. It managed to decelerate enough to merely bounce off and flop to the ground.

Riordan, holding the damaged carbine tightly, cheated it in that direction, aimed between the stacked spheres of Anansi's legs. "Target guidon."

An orange guidon appeared in Riordan's HUD, arrow indicating he should nudge the muzzle to the left. As he did, the guidon became a square orange reticle, painted on the creature's rising body.

The circlet announced, "Target lock—"

"Fire. Four times."

The coil carbine spat rapidly.

By the fourth discharge, the computer could no longer tell which of the creature's remaining parts were to be designated as the target.

Five seconds passed before Alnduul spoke. "I recommend

delaying further travel until the weapon is repaired and the automated control system is overhauled and retested."

"I knew you were going to say that. And Alnduul?"

"Yes?"

"Thanks."

"You are welcome. Repair schematics are being relayed to your HUD."

Trying to keep his hands from shaking, Riordan got to work.

Chapter Forty-One

Two hours later, Riordan commanded Anansi to stop at the mouth of the northern valley. What had appeared to be a sward of low, level grass was in fact a bog. Further on, surly mists hung low over the rank expanse, which stretched from the foot of the eastern slope to the base of its western counterpart. There was no sign of solid ground, so no way for Anansi to pass. Reduced visibility increased vulnerability to ambushes by predators. And the combined stink of rotting vegetation and swamp water was overpowering.

Turning Anansi west, Riordan surveyed the slopes there, first with the naked eye, then the HUD's reified visuals. It would be hard, slow going for a while, but according to *Olsloov*'s mapping, the mounting foothills eventually levelled off into an extensive tableland that skirted the long, fen-filled valley.

Which was a rather strange terrain feature: although the lowland was a natural drainage basin, it did not seem to have enough inflow to sustain a marsh. Mysterious origins notwithstanding, Riordan literally and figuratively turned his back on it and ordered Anansi to ascend the foothills to the west.

Although neither particularly steep or craggy, the slopes were uneven enough that Riordan had to remain especially watchful; the bug-eyed borzoi scavengers gathered for collective mating frenzies in upland dens. Caine had no desire to turn a blind corner and interrupt one of their orgies.

As Riordan neared the rim of the plateau, he finally allowed himself to anticipate an imminent opportunity to stop, relax, gulp down some lunch, and stretch his legs. But as his eyes drew level with the upland plain, all such thoughts disappeared.

Just over three kilometers away, an immense, mostly leveled structure lay half-buried in dirt and debris. *Olsloov*'s initial, low-res scans had suggested that the tableland was simply covered by the spoor of long-past landslides. But at this range, other features became visible. Low corners of otherwise vanished buildings and an unnatural plenitude of shards with at least one right angle radiated outward from a vast, shattered platform made of a slate-like composite. After commanding Anansi to climb higher on the western slope in order to give the ruined expanse a wider berth, Riordan raised his hand scanner to study it in greater detail.

From that vantage point, it was evident that the entire plateau had been some kind of sprawling complex A slightly elevated central region still extended few stunted claws up at the sky. And, as Anansi's ascent continued, further surprises were revealed.

At the northern end of the tableland, the wide-ranging destruction became a narrower path of absolute annihilation. It was as if some impossibly powerful tornado had touched down heading northwest, tearing apart rock faces and drilling into the plateau itself. However, as Anansi continued upward, Riordan discerned that the cause of the destruction had not been a natural force at all, but rather, something even more extraordinary.

Where the path of annihilation descended from the plateau, Riordan saw toppled sections of what had either been a titanic tower or a stack of monstrous tubes. The behemothic remains continued along the same northwest heading, eventually disappearing between two small hills. But on reexamination, Caine realized that the gigantic objects hadn't fallen *between* the two hills: they had crashed down and through the crest of what had originally been one larger hill.

Further on, the wreckage had blocked and diverted a river, its new course marked by a distant, serpentine glimmer. Riordan traced its original downriver course to the northernmost end of the swamp. Its desiccated bed was now a channel that collected runoff from all the surrounding hills and shunted it into the low-lying valley.

Caine leaned back, tried to take in the full footprint of the past catastrophe. The debris had toppled down from whatever facility had once dominated the plateau. But even if there had been an impossibly high and heavy tower rising up from the central platform, it still would not have had enough force to smash through terrain features. That would have required a much longer fall.

Wait. Olsloov *made planetfall in Aozhoodn's equatorial downport. So, could this have been a—?* "Circlet, display current global coordinates."

The data flashed on Riordan's HUD.

He stared at the numbers, particularly the unexceptioned string of zeros in the second value, and leaned back against the cargo container. He reached into his breast pocket, activated the headset that Oduosslun had sent to him. "This is what you meant by a dead miracle, isn't it?"

Oduosslun's response was immediate, as if she had been waiting on the other end. "It is but one corpse from a whole graveyard of them."

"This was a beanstalk, a space elevator?"

"And it has been over fifteen hundred years since it fell. Now, only a few curiosity seekers ever see it. And then, only from a distance."

Now that Riordan knew what to look for, he realized that the ruined tubular colossi were the cars that had traveled along the elevator's length, ferrying cargo and passengers from its equator-straddling mooring point on the plateau to its terminus in space. "Where is the cable itself?"

"Too narrow to be seen at distance. But your question tells me you understand the real miracle here: a substance that was strong enough, inexpensive enough, and pliable enough to bear the mass and stresses of ground-to-orbit cable transfers. Indefinitely."

Riordan stared at the long, ragged, trail of debris. "Indefinitely?"

"With proper support and maintenance, yes. But we became too distracted, too apathetic, to caretake even the Elders' greatest achievements. To say nothing of our own."

"But I thought those kinds of problems only started about five centuries ago."

"Our decline is not recent. It has only become more pronounced, more noticeable, in recent times. The seeds were sown even as we reached for greatness."

"You mean, during your first wars with the loji?"

Oduosslun snorted, a surprisingly human sound. "Whose

tutelage led you into those fishless waters? Uinzleej, I will wager. He is too enamored of the ancients to see the real truth: it was the Elders, not we, who set us on the path to lethargic timidity and from whose scraps we built our 'Golden Age.'"

Riordan smiled sadly. "You're starting to sound like another Dornaani I know."

"Yes. Thlunroolt. Why are you surprised? Do you think I could possibly be unaware that Alnduul was his prized pupil? Or that I could be ignorant of his many declamations before the Senior Assembly half a century ago? And yet, while I disagree with Thlunroolt on many matters, we are of one mind on this: our reemergent civilization 'flourished' not because of what we created, but because of what we exhumed from the mausoleums and derelicts of the Elders. And because of that, we never mastered the knowledge that built the miracles now crumbling to dust around us."

"And is that what I shall find at the coordinates you provided? One of those miracles?"

"Yes. Continue on your current path, toward the headwaters of that river you see far ahead."

"What should I be looking for?"

Oduosslun's voice was at once coy, ironic, and bitter. "You will know it when you see it." The hiss of the headset's carrier wave died out.

"Oduosslun was certainly right about knowing the miracle when I see it," Riordan muttered into the circlet a day later. "Are you receiving visuals, *Olsloov?*"

"We are. But we must end this conversation, Caine Riordan. Oduosslun will know that you have arrived at the coordinates and may wish to communicate with you. However, she will not do so if she knows we are still comm linked. We shall only intervene if you are in danger."

"Aren't you even going to wish me good luck?"

"We do not believe in luck, Caine Riordan. However, I wish enlightenment unto you. In every passing second."

The connection to *Olsloov* faded. Riordan dismounted Anansi and approached the object before him.

Two hundred meters high, it looked like a pyramid that had been stretched skyward: taller than its base was wide, and also thinner in cross section. The upper half of the mirror-black object was cooled by breezes, giving it a shiny coat of condensation that ran in rivulets down its unnaturally smooth face.

Bisected face, Caine mentally corrected. A split three meters wide began where the object's apex should have been and descended to a point only two meters above where it seemed to rise out of the native rock. At the midpoint of that vertical gap was a perfectly round hole that cut straight through the object. And in the center of that twenty-meter-wide hole was a perfect black sphere, ten meters in diameter. Floating in midair.

Looking at that motionless, lightless sphere, Riordan felt his sense of reality begin to fall away... until he reaffixed it to the certainty that everything had an explanation. Neither the hand-held multispectrum scanner nor the carbine's scope had detected anything unusual about the structure during his descent into the shallow dell that it dominated.

His study of the floating sphere became more exacting, clinical. How to reach it? He had no way to fly up, and certainly no way to climb, those slick surfaces...

Wait... no way to climb?

Riordan looked back at Anansi, wondered if his emerging idea was too bizarre to work. *Well, only one way to find out...*

"Anansi, lower cargo bed to one meter." As soon as the octobot kneeled, Riordan began emptying the cargo box.

Caine glanced down at his piled supplies and equipment, now far below him.

The octobot was suspended seventy-five meters above the ground. It straddled the edifice's central slit, locked in place by six of its legs, three of which pressed against either side of the channel. Anansi's last two legs stretched straight out into midair, ready to shift and maintain an optimal center of balance in the event of insufficient traction on either side.

One last chimney-climbing push and Riordan would be able to scramble out onto the near rim of the hole and discover how the black sphere was being held aloft at its center. But the moment he reflected upon doing so, the voice of reason calmly deafened him with, *You are mad. You're one slip away from becoming a high-impact meat-pie.*

But the part of him that kept seeing Elena's face reiterated the countervailing facts: *Oduosslun didn't contact me when I got here, didn't answer when I tried reaching her on the headset. So it seems my choices are to go up or to give up.*

There was no way either of those voices were going to relent. So he ignored them and ordered his control circlet, "Assess surface for next ascent routine."

The circlet spent a moment accessing the handheld scanner he'd clipped on the box, facing upward. "Surface moisture on left is two percent greater than on prior ascent surface," it reported. "Surface moisture on right, three percent greater."

Taken as a total, this last ten-meter ascent would exceed what Riordan had approximated as the traction safety limit. But he hadn't come this far just to give up.

"Ascend," he ordered.

Anansi repeated its chimney climbing motions. Of the three legs maintaining full outward pressure on each side, first the middle one on the left withdrew slightly. Its spheres contracting, it then curled slowly upward until it contacted the channel's wall approximately half a meter higher than before. The leg flexed and stiffened, exerting full pressure against the slick surface. Then the other legs took turns at completing identical motions: first the right middle leg, then the right front, then the left rear, then the left front, and finally, the right rear. At which point, Anansi was once again balanced.

So far, so good. "Ascend."

The right center leg moved up.

Riordan studied the increasing dampness of the surface above him.

The left center leg moved up.

How close should I get before trying to scramble up to the rim of the hole? A meter? Two?

The right front leg curled upward, then reextended to lock itself against the wall...

Except it didn't.

With a squeal, the leg's contact, or pedal, sphere slipped down a few decimeters, throwing Riordan to that side. Which caused the leg to slip farther.

Anansi's programming compensated. It pulled the right front leg back quickly in order to reposition and regain balance. But when it came away from the wall, the sudden load increase overcame the right middle leg's traction. Its pedal sphere also squeaked, skittered, and then stopped. But the leg's servos started groaning.

Fear raised the hairs on Riordan's forearms as he assessed his predicament. Anansi was listing sharply to the right. The right front leg was dangling in midair, unable to get solid contact with the wall because of the extreme angle. And now the servos of the right rear leg were groaning in chorus with those of the middle leg: a consequence of carrying more than double its normal share of the load. Any moment, it might give and Anansi would go down—

Wait! That's it! Go down*!* "Rear left leg, descend."

Anansi obeyed; it was no longer tilted so far forward, but the right rear leg was still groaning.

"Left middle leg, descend."

Anansi obeyed, Riordan watching for the leg to reextend to the wall. But as it did, he could hear a grinding where the right rear leg's pedal sphere was pressed against the surface of the channel. It began to quiver.

"Right middle leg, ascend to match left middle leg."

Anansi complied. The right rear leg shook, and then stopped quivering.

Riordan breathed heavily. "Right front leg, establish contact with surface."

With Anansi's tilt reduced, the right front leg was finally able to connect with the wall again.

"Equalize legs. Minimal movements."

After about thirty seconds of the pedal spheres pushing slightly upward and downward, Anansi was once again balanced.

Riordan stared at the distance to the hole. He'd lost about half a meter. He sighed. "Circlet, reduce distance of individual ascents by eighty percent."

"Reducing current ascent interval by eighty percent: confirmed."

Okay, baby steps, now. "Ascend."

Chapter Forty-Two

After ordering Anansi to lock itself in place and enter sleep mode, Riordan pulled himself up and over the rim of the hole and checked his wristlink.

The climb had taken slightly more than an hour. At this rate, it might be dark by the time he got back down to the ground. So, whatever was keeping this ten-meter sphere in the air, he'd better figure it out quickly.

Seen up close, its utter motionlessness was even more striking. If it was being held up by electromagnetic forces, they would have to be as finely tuned and nearly as powerful as those in an antimatter containment chamber. But that required megawatts of power, which his hand-scanner should have detected.

Whatever the trick was, though, there had to be forces acting upon the sphere. Logically, to overcome the planet's gravity, the most likely candidates an attractive force pulling upward, a repulsive force pushing upward, or both.

But testing that hypothesis could prove dangerous. Whatever was projecting those forces was probably equipped to eliminate any obstructions between itself and the sphere. And, given the sphere's pristine surroundings, Riordan conjectured that those means of elimination were kinetic enough to discourage local avians from nesting in or even visiting this natural eyrie. So, step one: test for a safe approach.

Caine undid one of the cargo straps he'd been using as a

288

safety line. He swung it gently through the space beneath the sphere.

As the strap traversed the midpoint, which was also the centerline of the channel in which Anansi was perched, Riordan felt its mass drop significantly. But it wasn't the result of a mysterious field effect. Severed, the strap's further half fell toward Anansi. Riordan studied the length of strap still in his hand: an industrial laser could not have cut the end more cleanly. Frowning, he lowered himself to examine the space directly under the sphere.

Only when Caine was perfectly still and focusing carefully did he detect a very thin wire, perhaps three millimeters wide, running down from the bottom of the sphere into the emptiness beneath. Although its core was round, the wire was veined by four ridges arrayed around its circumference like the points of a compass rose. Despite the active camouflage that concealed the rest of the wire, the peak of each ridge shone like polished chrome, so fine that Riordan couldn't really fix his eyes on the edge itself. It was just a hair-thin line of brightness.

Riordan stood. So, the strap had not been severed by the main wire, but one of those four edges, each of which might only be a few molecules thick. Which was pretty impressive but didn't bring him any closer to learning what held the sphere aloft.

Caine studied it closely but to no avail. There were no visible emitters, and the sphere did not move when Riordan pushed it. Had he missed something underneath, surprised and distracted by the almost monomolecular edges he had discovered there? He lowered himself again, saw nothing new, but then realized that if the wire ran all the way down the channel, he and Anansi should have encountered it during their climb. By getting sawed in two.

It took a full minute of careful examination to solve that mystery. The cable terminated in a perpendicular junction with another, identical cable just above the rim of the hole. Which Caine had fortunately avoided by mere centimeters when he had clambered up.

Riordan stood, tried to see the floating sphere with fresh eyes. *What if it isn't floating at all? What if it is simply—?*

Riordan aimed his scope at the nine o'clock point of the hole's rim, magnification set to maximum. Sure enough, almost completely invisible, a wire emerged from the midpoint of that surface and disappeared into the center of the facing side of the sphere. It took some effort to work around to vantage points that allowed him to examine the three o'clock and twelve o'clock positions of the rim, but again, he discovered similar wires.

Which meant that the sphere was simply being held in place by four incredibly strong and almost invisible wires.

Riordan shook his head, laughed, and as he did, the headset provided by Oduosslun crackled. As soon as he had it on, her voice asked, "Shall I tell you the true tragedy of this dead miracle?"

"Please do."

"No one else remembers that this construct is here. And no one knows who built it."

"Do you?"

"It is almost certainly Dornaani. A Golden Age homage to the wonders of the Times Before."

"So were the Elders *actually* able to control gravity?"

Oduosslun appeared in the side monocle "I doubt we will ever know. At this epochal remove, it is often impossible to establish the provenance of the few fragmentary accounts we possess. So one cannot reliably distinguish between exaggeration, misperception, and invention."

"You said this structure is 'almost certainly' Dornaani. Why are you uncertain?"

"Because the real miracle of this object—the wire—is something we Dornaani no longer know how to make. It, like the rest of the ruins around you, is yet another reminder of how far we have fallen."

Riordan looked out across the hills, saw hints of other forgotten objects: a series of broken stelae, some inscribed with glowing sigils, some dark. Still further, he spied the mist-cloaked phantom of a needle-shaped tower, three ghostly spheres floating in a stack directly above its point, eternally frozen in the instant preceding their impalement.

Caine nodded. "I think I understand now why both the Collective and the Custodians are so insistent"—*more like manic*—"about preventing the spread of advanced technology."

Oduosslun raised a single emphatic and approving finger. "Yes. Because we are living examples of how socially destructive it is to routinely employ devices that you cannot build, or even imitate, yourself. That is how we Dornaani went from being rag pickers to night watchmen. We forsook becoming soldiers or explorers because we settled for being caretakers of prior races' legacies and younger races' futures."

She paused. "But, after all, that is nonsense. We could have been explorers and soldiers, both. But we *chose* not to be."

"Why?"

"Because, despite all of our bitterness and resentment, this truth persists: it is not our nature. It is yours. Now, descend and study the sides of the channel near the base of this edifice."

"What will I find there?"

"The final miracle. And the way to reach me."

Riordan didn't find the final miracle with his eyes, but his fingertips. A perfectly round three-meter section of the western side of the channel looked exactly like the rest, but had a faintly different texture: smoother, glasslike. At first, it didn't react, but when Caine laid his palms flat against it for several seconds, the surface retracted slightly.

A small hole appeared in its center and widened until the entire outline had become an aperture. Riordan leaned forward, inspecting its edges. Perhaps it was an iris-valve comprised of so many and such fine leaves that the mechanism could not be detected by the naked eye. But it worked, and looked, like magic. He stepped through the portal into the space beyond: a three-meter wide tube, bored into the monument's faux rock.

The instant Riordan's foot crossed the threshold, a light appeared: a neon blue ring that outlined the perimeter of the far end of the tube. Riordan approached it warily, wondered if this was how a wild animal felt when approaching a human device, unable to discern if it was a trap, something useful, or simply an unfathomable object.

The glowing blue circle was neither mounted on or emanating from the wall. It seemed to be separate: a ring of pure light that was snugged up against the black rock, close as a coat of paint. Riordan leaned forward to examine it ... and smelled the ocean.

Caine jerked back. *The ocean? Here?* But upon leaning forward again, he detected the same scent, as faint and fleeting as the olfactory equivalent of a ghost. Hell, was it even there, or was it just his imagination?

Riordan leaned closer to the ring. The odor became stronger, persistent.

Riordan took the severed strap out of his pants pocket, spooled it into a tight disk, and carefully advanced it toward the blue light.

Just before it should have touched that bright, narrow ring, the coiled strap was pushed away, like the matching poles of opposed magnets. Except this push moved the strap toward the black surface inside the ring.

The part of the coil that touched the rock. Riordan advanced the strap farther: the blackness continued to swallow it.

Caine flinched back, irrationally fearful that he might lean too far forward, lose his balance, and fall into...

...into what? A void? A hole in the fabric of time and space? A different reality?

At the same moment that Riordan realized that the strap was still intact, he also discovered that his armpits were every bit as wet as they had been after the crocodactyl attack. But instead of heat surging along his brow, he felt a wave of cold moving out from his gut.

This was not a confrontation with a familiar enemy; this was an encounter with the unknown. He cleared his throat. "Oduosslun, I think I've found that last miracle."

No reply.

Which meant the journey, the test, was not over. Riordan stared at the lightless hole framed by the bright ring. To get to Elena, he had dodged assassins, fought wild animals, endured the gibes and contempt of diffident Dornaani, and damn near been killed by the octobot that was now his servant. But this? To walk into the unknown? It was the oldest, most primal fear of humankind, inculcated by eons of brutal lessons which, titrated down into their purest form, became age's invariable advice to youth: beware the things and places you do not know. Because out there, beyond the flickering ring of the tribal fire, on the unlit streets of concrete cities, in the unending depths of space—there lay an unquantifiable, unbounded potential for death.

Riordan breathed deep. All of that was true. But it was also true that, out in the same darkness, lay the unseen opportunity, the untouched wonder, the undiscovered country. And although venturing there meant courting risk, or even annihilation, it was the only way that humanity had ever moved forward, beyond huddling—unwashed and fearful—in cold caves. And in that moment, Caine reheard Oduosslun's pronouncement upon the difference between the nature—and thus, the fate—of their respective races. *"We could have been explorers and soldiers, but ... that is not our nature. It is yours."*

Before he had time to reflect any further, Caine took a long step forward.

Riordan blinked against sudden sunlight. He smelled brine, heard surf, squinted into the glare. A few meters beyond and below his vantage point, dark blue breakers rolled in, flattening into sheets of foam that spent themselves upon a long stretch of beach.

At his feet, a widening skirt of the structure's black pseudo-rock sloped down sharply and disappeared beneath the sand. Riordan glanced behind: the ring of blue light was still there, but surrounded by sand. Swathes of dune grass waved behind it. *Christ, is this a ... a gate to another world?*

As if she had been reading his mind, Oduosslun's voice was in his headset. "There is no danger. Walk around, if that interests you. Or return. The portal is not temporary. It is permanent."

Riordan frowned. "How is your signal getting through to me?"

Her reply was almost mischievous. "I called it a *miracle*, did I not?"

Riordan sat on the black fan-shaped ramp. It was too steep to descend on foot, so he slid down. As he did, he noticed that not only was the sky a cloudless cobalt blue, but the star was the same blinding yellow-white of Earth's sun. So, he was definitely not on Aozhoodn, where the sky had hints of aquamarine and a more proximal yellow-orange sun. And yet Oduosslun's signal was coming through what she had called "the portal." Or getting to him some other way.

Caine rose to his feet, dusting sand—real, honest-to-god sand—off his duty suit. White, cigar-shaped aquaforms leaped among the swells beyond the breakers, their body-length fins flaring as they did. He walked down to the edge of the surf, felt the water roll over and soak into his boots, squinted against the fine spray that coated his cheeks, his lips. The instinct to lick it away was almost too fast for his learned reflex: never let anything from an exoplanet environment into your GI tract until exobiologists have approved it.

Except ... the spray that had landed on his lips didn't quite match the brine in the atmosphere. The ocean's odor was exactly what he had expected: the faint sulfur funk, backed by smaller hints of iodine and a fresh-fish tang. But the miniscule misting on his lips, and particularly the smaller amount that leaked through to a few tastebuds, was nothing more than saline.

Riordan smiled and glanced at the horizon, appreciating it one more time. "Okay, Oduosslun," he said at last, "you can turn off the simulation."

The environment faded away. Riordan was in a small chamber, lying on a foamy surface that was inclined at forty-five degrees, and snugged just to one side of a round entry. This room was the other side of the black-surfaced "portal" that he had passed through. "So tell me, why do you consider this parlor trick a miracle?"

"The simulation is not the miracle, human."

Riordan reflected, discovered his oversight, smiled again. "No, of course not. It's the *transition* that's the miracle, the fact that I believed I had walked through some kind of telelocating portal. How did you do it?"

Oduosslun's tone had reverted to its default: dismissive. "Firstly, the illusion was no more my handiwork than the monument in which it is housed. But to answer your query..." Deeper in the small chamber, a hologram shimmered into existence: it was Riordan himself, leaning toward the black portal, the coiled strap halfway through the bright blue ring. But from this perspective, the entirety of the strap was visible.

Riordan's smile widened as he remembered the entry into Alnduul's hidden facility on Rooaioo'q. "So, the side of the 'portal' I was facing is lined with your light absorption materials."

"So you are already familiar with that technology? Interesting. However, this is a far more powerful version than the limited versions we build today."

"Another product of your Golden Age?"

"Yes. And by the time you passed through and entered this room, your mind was linked to virtuality."

"That fast? And without physical contact?"

"Physical contact is unnecessary if the virtuality equipment is sufficiently sophisticated and the brain and mental patterns of the subject are fully mapped beforehand."

Riordan glanced at the tube from which he'd entered. "And you were able to do that while I was dawdling on the threshold."

"Yes. There are thousands of the remote mapping sensors embedded in the entry tube's walls, and its shape is optimal shape for such scans. However, keeping the subject immersed requires that they lie down without being aware of doing so. If they were to remain standing, they would ultimately become aware of muscle fatigue or the need to actively maintain balance."

Riordan glanced at the inclined surface upon which he had been resting. "That's why you put in the black stone ramp leading to the beach. By sliding down to the beach, I voluntarily initiated the process of putting myself into that resting position within the sim." Riordan rose and exited the virtuality chamber. "Still, I don't believe this is the final miracle."

"No?" Oduosslun sounded simultaneously irritated and... hopeful?

"No. The final miracle is that these *trompe-l'oeils* were made at all. The final miracle is the social phenomena that built them, that has shaped your species' culture. You spent so much time living among and using the actual artifacts that you became obsessed with imitating them. Or, in the end, just creating the illusion of them."

"An acceptable insight. I wonder if humans can generalize from that insight, to appreciate the very different forces shaping you, albeit toward radically different ends."

Yeah, that would be great, but first, Elena. "So now—?"

"Now we shall meet."

"Where are you?"

"Back in the downport."

Oh fer Chrissakes...

"You should depart immediately. You are modestly intriguing but if I am granted access to the special research equipment before you arrive, I shall not wait."

By the time the carrier wave hissed out of existence, Riordan had already swapped his circlet for the headset and was loading his gear back on Anansi. "Circlet, establish commlink to *Olsloov*."

"Expediting. Link established."

"Alnduul?"

"We have been awaiting your contact, Caine Riordan. Have you completed Oduosslun's tasks?"

"I have. But now I need to meet her. Back in the downport. And the clock is ticking."

"That is most irritating. How may we assist?"

"The only way to cut travel time is to keep moving. Nonstop."

"Through the night, without sleeping?"

"Yes, through the night. But not without sleeping."

"How do you propose to direct the octobot while you sleep?"

"I don't. But given the quality of your remote control from orbit, I can strap myself to the cargo bed and sleep while you do the nighttime driving."

"It is a strange plan, Caine Riordan." A pause. "But then again, so many of yours are. I recommend you start back at once. It will take us some time to calibrate the controls."

Chapter Forty-Three

In a crowning—and perhaps intentionally malign—irony, the entry to Oduosslun's urban residence was through a hidden passage in the traveler's hostel where Riordan had spent his first nights on Aozhoodn.

Ushered into a subterranean level by two proxrovs and a swarm of flying eyebots, Riordan noted stark distinctions between this retreat and Uinzleej's. The aesthetic was minimalist, and if there was any dust or rust, Riordan was unable to detect it. After three days of nonstop return travel, he was by far the dirtiest object in the facility.

He was led into a sparsely furnished room as another bot arrived and offered him water and what looked and smelled like a ham sandwich. He hastily consumed both and leaned back in a comfortable human chair to wait.

He awoke with a start when Oduosslun entered. Her long strides were incongruous for her species. "I require the genetic sample I stipulated during our first exchange," she announced without preamble.

Riordan checked his wristlink, discovered an hour had passed, frowned. "What about my memories from Issqliin?"

"Those were recorded as you slept."

So the refreshments hasn't been simple hospitality, after all. *Hell, why did I expect any different?* "In case you are unaware, humans get upset when you drug their food and drink."

"I am aware. I am also aware, as you are not, that had I announced my intentions, you would have been in a heightened state of anxiety and watchfulness. That interferes with the depth of sleep required for a clean and useable recording of your memories. Now, the genetic sample."

You arrogant bastards. Always ready to justify every violation of privacy. I have half a mind to—but no. Elena. Remember Elena.

Another robot entered, bristling with what looked like medical implements. Riordan extended his arm silently. One of the instruments grazed across his cheek, then his arm, then stopped, poised over his thigh. Without warning, it shot a hair-thin needle down through his pant leg, retracted it just as swiftly.

Riordan jumped. "What the hell was that?"

"Stem cell sample from your femur."

"You just took a bone sample?" Riordan's anger gave way to surprise at how little it had hurt.

"The osteoid materials are of no interest, but stem cells offer subtle genetic data absent in other tissues. The extraction site may be tender for two days, but there is no cause for concern. The aperture in the bone has been resealed. I shall now address your queries regarding Virtua.

"The information and directions you seek cannot be safely imparted unless you understand both the origins of Virtua and our society's problematic relationship with advanced automation. Logically, we must first examine the events that first brought these two factors into friction with each other."

Riordan almost smiled. "You sound like another historian I know."

"Historian?" She stiffened. "I am an observer. I do not claim to convey a unified story, just the pieces for which I have data. Such as this." Oduosslun waved a hand at the walls. A high-quality hologram of a starfield materialized. They began moving through it erratically. "Our earliest shift drive was like yours: each shift must start from and end upon a stellar object. But a millennium after the Final War, we reattained the more advanced form of this technology."

The zigzag advancement through the starfield became an almost straight line. The journey that had taken eight shifts took only two.

Riordan nodded. "Those are deep-space shifts. No need to start or stop in the vicinity of a stellar object. That's how the Custodians helped us counterattack the Arat Kur." He glanced at Oduosslun. "Another miracle you inherited from the Elders?"

"Only in the sense that we knew it could be done. We had to rediscover the technology independently. But once we had, we were faced with a quandary."

Riordan nodded. "You had the means to easily expand far beyond the one hundred and fifty-light-year globe that defines the Accord."

"And beyond the fifty-light-year buffer zone, as well. This was the catalyst for our fateful debate over the Collective's potential loss of political coherence."

The starfield view rotated. Bright green lines connected the stars of Dornaani space in a chaotic cat's cradle of shift routes. "History teaches that the longer the communication time between a polity's capital and its borders, the more likely it is to either become an empire or dissolve into petty states."

The cat's cradle of links expanded beyond its earlier borders, became so immense that it resembled a cubist ball of yarn. "We rejected those outcomes by staying within our original limits. However, there was another reason to do so."

Riordan nodded. "The uncertainty of what you might find beyond: the remains of the Final War."

"More than the remains, human. Dormant threats. Sleeping giants. Every shift beyond the limit was fraught with uncertainty. What would we find there? A virgin system? A brace of blasted planets? Or the malign beings that had reveled in Armageddon, even as it consumed them?"

The holosphere showed brief, incomplete scenes of planetary bombardments that made whole continents conflagrations. Fleets of silver specks raced toward each other in deep space, brightening like fireflies before vanishing. Lush green worlds rotated to reveal hemispheres as densely cratered as ancient moons.

Riordan stared at the frozen tableaux of dying green worlds. "It reinforced your instinct to turn inward, to more fully resign yourselves to—"

"—To rag picking. Which caused such a continual loss of vigor, of drive, that now, we are no longer effective Custodians." She leaned forward, pointed at the hologram. "This—*this*—was what undid us. Once we truly believed we *had* to be rag pickers and night watchmen, thus we remained." She stalked away from the image. "This is what caused our descent into Virtua and the danger it represents. To all of us."

Chapter Forty-Four

Oduosslun waved her hand at the wall again. The scene in the holosphere changed to Glamqoozht, the regional capital. The skyline was the same. The bay, despite a few changes in the shoreline, was easily recognizable. But the streets were busy, brisk and uncluttered in the manner of a smaller European city.

And there wasn't a single proxrov in sight.

Nor were there any bioproxies or floating eyebots. Riordan leaned forward, studying the scene more closely. "How long ago was this recorded?"

"Four thousand seven hundred sixty-one of your years ago. The physical similarity is a consequence of our penchants for thrift and familiarity: our buildings are built to last indefinitely. But as you can see, we were still a community."

"But the lack of automation?"

"It was deliberate. Accounts of the Final War's last years depict robots, drones, and even computers becoming erratic or responsive to enemy commands. Millennia later, as the loji wars concluded, automated systems were again purged, for much the same reasons." In the holosphere, the landing field of a large spaceport was being filled with wrecked and gutted automatons of varying shapes and sizes. A final actinic blaze vaporized them.

Oduosslun flicked a finger; the image froze. "These events fostered a deep and abiding distrust of all robots and computers able to control the actions of other machines. Those we did allow

were built with overlapping safeguards and emergency discon-
nects. The most stringent restrictions were put upon nanites and
similar microbots, although a few medical models were retained
as therapies of last recourse."

Holographic depictions of Dornaani cities and machinery
resumed whirling past. The inhabitants' personal devices changed
in shape, but the sphere-and-needle architecture, and the Dornaani themselves, were—from a human perspective—freakishly
consistent. However, toward the end of the montage, two new
types of visitors appeared. Loji, wearing what looked like gee-
compensation suits, were occasionally shuttled about in small
vehicles. More infrequently, humans strode swiftly through the
scenes, but always as lone individuals, never groups.

Riordan pointed at one of them. "Are the humans factotums?"

"They are. Now, attend closely."

At first Riordan didn't notice any differences in the scenes,
but slowly, he began seeing the trend. "There are fewer Dornaani
in the concourses."

"That is the first visible effect of Virtua: detachment from
community."

"So is this when Virtua was, er, reinvented?"

Oduosslun froze the time-lapsed images. "Virtua has always
been there, human. As I said, it was the greatest miracle of all."

Riordan shrugged. "Well, I grant you that it's very impressive—"

"Human. Be silent. Until you have experienced Virtua, not
mere virtuality, your opinions only demonstrate your ignorance.
Virtua was neither conceived nor built for entertainment. It was
used for planning, for modeling."

"Okay, but if it was 'always there,' does that mean you activated it during your Golden Age?"

"Human, listen more carefully. It was *always* there."

Riordan sat straighter. "You mean, the Virtua in use today
is the original? Was built by the Elders?"

"Either them or one of the other ancient races. Virtua is
fundamentally different from virtuality because it is not simply
a scenario; it is an entire universe. Its sophistication and immersivity exhilarate, edify, terrify. Yet few Dornaani knew of it until
five centuries ago."

"So it was an underground phenomenon?"

"To adopt the closest human term, access to Virtua was a

gray market commodity. The cost to use it increased as average persons began acquiring permits for access. That spawned the development of imitations—virtuality—and a tremendous surge in users." Oduosslun reactivated the holosphere. The wide slideways and concourses were increasingly populated by proxrovs instead of actual Dornaani.

Riordan sighed. "So as increasing numbers of Dornaani spent time in computer-controlled fantasy worlds, they started accepting more automation in their lives."

Oduosslun's outer eyelids opened and shut slowly. "A sane being cannot both surrender their senses to virtuality and retain an aversion to the technology that drives it. In particular, its users accepted those technologies that addressed their physical needs. Proxrovs were the first sign of this trend." Automatons now constituted three-quarters of the traffic on city slideways, most of them bearing loads. "Originally used to run errands and fetch food from our public commissaries, remote-operated proxies became the primary means whereby virtuality devotees interacted with the world."

Riordan, eyes riveted to the holosphere, felt a sympathetic horror rising in his chest. The great cities of the Dornaani were now rarely visited by the descendants of their builders. "And so now most of your population won't leave their virtual worlds."

Oduosslun's left hand flopped loosely upward: despairing affirmation. "Other factors intensified the trend. Four centuries ago, budget analysts proved that the combined costs of virtuality, autonutrient delivery, and proxrov-assisted mobility were drastically less than any other form of geriatric care. Furthermore, the recipients experienced less pain and depression."

A chill running down his spine, Riordan watched as a withered Dornaani—limp, lifeless—was carefully removed from a maze of machines by two proxrovs.

Oduosslun's gills burbled. "Our older populations were glad to accept this as a subsidized alternative to traditional late-life care. Since then, the trend has spread to younger generations. Every age cohort is impacted."

The holographic images now matched Riordan's own experience of the Collective: proxrovs and bioproxies moving through mostly deserted streets. Dornaani scuttled like cautious interlopers among them.

Oduosslun waved the images away. "A comprehensive census is now as hard to accomplish as anything else. However, best estimates place our total non-loji population, which once numbered in the tens of billions, at only eight hundred million. The number of traditionally active individuals are estimated between seven to nine million. Roughly twenty times that number of partially active. The remainder spend at least ninety-five percent of their time in some form of virtuality, and defer an equal percentage of all social and physical interface to proxrovs, bioproxies, or other simulacra."

Riordan discovered he had been holding his breath. A whole race shriveling, decaying, disappearing into a digitized opium haze. Leaving a desperately factious and unready Accord to fend for itself. "It . . . it's terrifying," he murmured.

"It was inevitable," Oduosslun countered brusquely. "Be warned, human. Your species could suffer a similar fate."

Riordan remembered the naked streets, shook his head at the contrast with Earth's megalopoli. "If it *can* happen to us, I think it's a long way off."

"Do not be obtuse. I do not refer to virtuality. I mean you are equally susceptible to the curse of self-fulfilling prophesies. Ours was to be dutiful rag pickers and here you see the endgame. Your challenge will be different. Whatever destiny we assign to ourselves also defines our doom. It is there, lurking, waiting, from the instantiation of sentience. It is the antipodal defect of the virtue we call 'foresight.'"

Riordan shook his head. "I'm not sure that humanity has any self-fulfilling prophesy that—"

"Then watch." Oduosslun swept her hand toward the wall. "Is this not the validation, the affirmation most humans long for, like primitive hand-wringing penitents?"

And Caine saw himself standing, like Abraham, before a burning bush, its outline reminiscent of the pear-shaped Dornaani silhouette. A voice suspiciously like Oduosslun's emanated from the crackling flames. "You have expiated the genocidal sins committed by your half-sibling Ktor twenty millennia ago. For lo, when you floated above the homeworld of the Arat Kur, you held righteous apocalypse in your grasp, and yet you stayed your hand." The voice became avuncular, more human, more like . . . Nolan's? "But your species can be mercurial, and wayward in following any course for long." A pause as the Caine-shepherd bowed, almost dovened, as the pronouncements washed over him. "So we shall watch and measure how you acquit yourselves when you take up the duties, the burdens, you will soon inherit from us."

Abrahamic Caine looked up.

Damn, I am never *growing a beard...*

Fear and longing brightened the simulacrum's eyes. "But surely you cannot mean to confer such terrible power and such terrible responsibilities upon us?"

The voice from the bush was now a mix of many Riordan had heard since arriving in the Collective: Oduosslun, Suvtrush, Glayaazh, Thlunroolt, Uinzleej, and even Alnduul. "We can no longer shape your fate, can no longer intervene, either to protect or constrain. Old secrets become the new truths with which you must contend. Our stewardship of the Accord is at an end. Yours must begin."

"But we barely survived the first invasion of our lands." Caine's image waved desperately toward a wide, flat valley where flocks and tents were clustered. "Our weapons are crude. Our numbers are as a few drops of rain compared to the vast ocean of our foes."

The bush burned low. "And yet, these are the challenges that ennoble your kind. The peril and the promise of new races and worlds. They will call forth the best from you. Go now, and prepare yourself."

The vision ended; Caine discovered he was running a palm along the underside of his neck, assessing three days' worth of stubble.

Oduosslun waved at the empty space where the scene had unfolded. "As if the reasons and motivations of any species could ever be so pure. But that does not prevent us from wishing and then believing that they are." Spittle rasped in her extruded mouth. "It is in the nature of social creatures to crave approval and approbation, to build a temple out of what they have told themselves they are and must be."

Oduosslun stared at Riordan. "Reject that reflex. Reject the simplistic narrative. Reject the opiating allure of presuming you know your own destiny. Rather, embrace the ineluctable truth that you are not preordained saviors in the midst of a mythic cycle, any more than we were the guardians and guarantors of civilization. Like us, you are simply another species living out the consequences of what came before."

Oduosslun turned away. Riordan had a fleeting image of her words rising up around her like a suit of armor, of wicked spikes and razor-edged flanges protecting a raw, flayed body that was somehow still alive, despite the agony. "Why are you telling me all this?" he asked.

Oduosslun seemed not to have heard; her response seemed more like a distracted musing. "One of your myths—Pandora's Box—is especially instructive. For all of us.

"We Dornaani ultimately chose to leave that box of knowledge and challenges unopened. Indeed, we put it far away, taught generations to forget it. That choice did not just determine who we were to become; it revealed who, at the core, we truly are.

"Conversely, in order for Pandora and your rude forebears to become truly human, they had to *open* the box. They had to grapple with the ruinous and petty passions it released. That is how humanity's character was established: not by some Olympian deity, but by a young woman who could no longer resist the allure of forbidden secrets. Her act exemplified the defining characteristic of your species, a trait that is far stronger in you than it is in us: curiosity."

Oduosslun's fingers rolled in a slow cascade. "Most humans cannot resist the desire to know and act for themselves. We could resist and did. We were arguably wiser, choosing the warm safety of our hearth over the glimmering possibility of greatness. Conversely, one never achieves greatness by staying safe at home." Her gills pittered faintly: an ironic chuckle. "Yet, no one ever inadvertently destroyed the universe by staying at home, either."

Riordan leaned back. "Do you believe a species can alter their intrinsic traits and characteristics, to change their outcomes?"

Her mouth twisted slightly. "No race has ever been capable of observing itself from such remove, so I lack data for assaying an answer. However, that question would greatly interest the Virtua expert to whom I shall direct you. His focus in not on recorded events, past or present, but in greater patterns. All such speculations are nonsense, of course, but he can doubtless answer your most urgent question: if and where your mate has been immersed into Virtua. And what you must do to extract her from it."

"And where will I find him?"

Oduosslun waved at the ceiling. "On a planet orbiting the

primary star of this binary system. I have just sent him a request on your behalf. He will be easy to find."

"And will he, too, require journeys or tests?"

The twist of her mouth became slightly wrinkled: a hint of sardonicism. "Nothing that will inconvenience you." There seemed to be an unspoken gulf, and warning, behind her words.

Oduosslun gestured toward the door. "You have what you came for. My research and investigations resume soon. I must prepare for them. I recommend you do the same for yours."

As soon as Anansi and the rest of the salvage from Aozhoodn was secured in *Olsloov*'s forward cargo bay, Riordan went to the bridge. Alnduul was standing watch alone. His voice and face were solemn. "It is gratifying that you are back, Caine Riordan."

"Likewise. Now all I need is a shower. Or maybe an hour-long bath in one of those big wading pools you relax in."

"We require the pools for hydration. Relaxation is an incidental benefit. For now, do use your stateroom's shower. At least until your body is . . . free of contaminants."

Jeez, if I'm too sweaty, just say so. "Oduosslun showed me how recently the Collective started using robots. And why."

Alnduul finished plotting their course to the system's primary. "Since your inquiry involved Virtua, it was inevitable that she would do so."

Riordan nodded. "You know, when I repatriated Tlerek Srin Shethkador at Sigma Draconis, I noticed that Ktor ship designers apparently share your ancestors' aversion to autonomous or remote systems. There were none on their bridge or in their corridors, nothing voice-actuated or -operated. Everything was run through direct, physical controls."

Alnduul slowly drew a finger through the space between them, like bait trailed in a sluggish stream. "That is consistent with what we have heard. Logically, they would only forego automation if it entailed great risk."

Riordan nodded. "So robots and computers turning on their users might have a parallel in Ktor history."

"Which underscores the importance of acquiring additional perspective on Virtua before you seek it directly."

"Oduosslun made it sound indistinguishable from reality. Is it?"

"I do not know. Indeed, I *cannot* know."

"What do you mean?"

"Custodians foreswear direct interface with any form of virtuality, but most expressly, Virtua itself. Under normal circumstances, we are not even allowed to confirm its existence."

"And that's all you can tell me about Virtua?"

"That is all I *may* tell you. The best way to facilitate your inquiries is to commence our journey to the fifth planet of Sigma 2 Ursa Majoris 2 A. Please secure yourself in the couch. We shall be accelerating briskly."

Chapter Forty-Five

Riordan watched as the blast covers retracted from *Olsloov*'s wide bridge blister and revealed the mostly barren surface of their destination: Zhashayn, the furthest moon of the gas giant Sigma 2 Ursa Majoris 2 A V.

Alnduul rose into the lower gees of the diminishing thrust. "We have reached our parking orbit. Your host, Laaglenz, has signaled that he anticipates your arrival."

Riordan turned, stared at Alnduul's serious tone. "What's wrong?"

The Dornaani did not turn to look at him. "I am ... discomfited by the necessity that you proceed alone."

"Why? Is Zhashayn another dangerously neglected world?"

Alnduul shook a dismissive finger at the deck. "Zhashayn is neglected but quiescent. It has a rudimentary biosphere and it maintains its security robotics with local resources."

"So the residents actually care about the condition of their world?"

"Its residents command more resources than usual," Alnduul answered carefully, "and insist that their access to the rest of the Collective, and the services upon which they depend, are both reliable and secure."

Riordan frowned at Alnduul's carefully oblique reply. "What's the danger you're not explaining and that I'm not seeing?"

"There may not be any danger, Caine Riordan." His Dornaani friend's gills rippled restlessly. "But Laaglenz is said to be ... unusual."

308

Damn it. What does that even mean *when it comes to Dornaani?* "Unusual in what way?"

Alnduul's lids drooped. "You have been told that Laaglenz is singularly knowledgeable regarding Virtua. Have you been told why?"

"I assume he's another hobbyist researcher who also happens to be an expert."

"He may be that also."

"'Also?' What else does he have to do with Virtua?"

"He is a facilitator." Seeing Riordan's perplexity, Alnduul added, "Although access to Virtua is not strictly illegal, it has never been authorized as a *public* resource."

Riordan leaned back. "You mean Laaglenz is...is some kind of middleman for the black market?"

"*Gray* market," Alnduul corrected. "But there is speculation that he procures access to Virtua for various individuals, and for almost all the residents of Zhashayn." His voice became a murmur. "Although you are unlikely to encounter any."

"Because they are all hooked into Virtua?" Caine prompted.

Alnduul waved stiff, anxious fingers as he looked away. "Observe particular care in your dealings with Laaglenz. His expertise with Virtua may derive from extensive personal experience within it. Such exposure can change behavior, perspective. Values."

"So you're saying not to trust him?"

"I am saying that you should be careful. The shuttle is ready for you. Laaglenz's proxrov is waiting at the downport with transportation." He turned to regard Riordan with large, unblinking eyes. "Enlightenment unto you, Caine Riordan."

Zhashayn's downport was perched on the side of a high volcanic cone that afforded an arid but marginally livable biome. Not that the residents cared. The dust-swept concourses were deserted, except for endlessly circulating patrol drones and proxrovs. As Laaglenz's robot servant prepared their aircar for departure, Riordan wondered what happened when one of the city's ancient Dornaani slipped away into a coma. Did their personal proxrovs continue to cycle through the same tasks, having no one to check on them and no one to report to? Even as the aircar lifted and the lightless community dwindled beneath them, Caine continued to watch the plodding progress of the dust-caked automatons. How many of them were already executing just such perpetual and pointless errands?

Despite the local investment in Zhashayn's infrastructure, its biosphere was the least welcoming of any that Riordan had encountered in Dornaani space. The primary, a whitish-yellow F class subgiant, appeared to be the same size as Earth's own sun, even though it was half again as distant. Its intense rays were slow to burn their way across Zhashayn's scorched middle latitudes; the moon-world was tidally locked to the ringed gas giant tilting down behind the opposite horizon. Several times during the silent flight, Riordan watched green-white aurorae dance in the gathering dusk ahead, lighting their way to the north pole, the world's only consistently temperate region.

An hour after leaving the downport, they began descending into the darkness of a valley. The faint light of the perpetual midnight sun cast just enough shadows to reveal that they were dropping toward a cluster of dim, regular shapes: a compound of some kind.

Lights snapped on abruptly, outlining a landing pad, several squat buildings, and a dome. If the aircar had started to slow, Riordan could not detect it. He glanced at the proxrov autopilot, clutched his seat-straps—

—and exhaled when, at only fifteen meters altitude, the small thrusters rotated downward and roared, slowing the aircar to a full stop in less than three seconds.

"Did you enjoy the trip?" asked a nonmechanical voice from the proxrov.

"I found it . . . exhilarating," Riordan replied as the car settled gently to the ground. "Am I speaking to Laaglenz?"

"You are. Follow my servant. You will be offered refreshment, a change of clothes, and a circlet that will record your memories. Move quickly. Even though the sun will not go much lower, the air will become uncomfortably cool."

Riordan removed his straps, started clambering out of the aircar. Well, at least Laaglenz didn't *sound* dangerous.

Laaglenz's residence—it was the only Dornaani home in Riordan's experience that warranted the term—admitted only one adjective: eclectic. Although still minimalist by human standards, its outer rooms were de facto galleries of unusual objects either hung on walls or displayed on platforms. A few drew his attention: an ancient, short-handled paddle; the hide of a large, scaled animal; a painstaking model of a mysterious mechanism; holostills of varied planetary surfaces; a parade of small animals and

geometric shapes cut from glass or crystal; and finally, a mummi-
fied Dornaani—whole, uncovered, and perversely foetal in death.

When Riordan declined Laaglenz's remotely offered hospitali-
ties, the proxrov led him to a broad descending staircase and
produced a heavy control circlet similar to the one Caine had
worn during his first experience with virtuality on Zhal Prime
Second-Five. Gesturing down the stairs, the proxrov headed back
toward the entrance.

As Riordan reached the bottom of the stairs, a Dornaani of
indeterminate age emerged from an archway at the other end of
the massive underground chamber. "You are Caine Riordan," he
announced. He left no time for Caine to confirm, deny, or otherwise respond. "Your Custodial chaperone may not be contacted
while you are here."

"I have no communication devices."

"Prudent. All communications are blocked. Nor may you have
any recording devices."

"I presume you have enough for the both of us, particularly
since you intend to record my memories."

"Do not interrupt. It disorients me. It slows the exchange.
It is unwelcome. Your memories are the least of what I shall be
recording. I explain. My existence is without physical needs or
foreseeable end. Thus, only the products of a mind remain both
important and interesting. In a limited mind such as yours, the
greatest value resides in your undiminished capacity for primal
reactions. I require your express permission to record your experience of Virtua. Or you must leave."

Riordan was not surprised by the request. Hell, after having
Oduosslun record his memories, Caine presumed Laaglenz's prerequisite would be at least as intrusive. But this meant agreeing
to real-time psychic voyeurism. Which felt like taking a step
closer to the ancient rite of selling one's soul.

As Caine's consciousness recoiled from that concept, an even
deeper reflex summoned Elena's face, Connor's and Trevor's lurking
just behind. Her smile—swift, genuine, playful—bore into his heart,
conveyed no reproof. If she had been suddenly, magically, awake
and in his mind, he knew exactly what she would tell him: to flee,
as fast as he could, back to *Olsloov*, and then across the border into
human space, soul and self intact. Because she loved him. Because
she loved Connor. And that, ultimately, was why he so loved her.

Caine nodded. "You may record my experience of Virtua."

"Put on the circlet." The Dornaani glanced at the cumbersome device. To Caine, it looked more like the lower half of a helmet.

Riordan complied, discovered that it was even heavier than the similar-looking interface he had worn before. "I don't understand how recording my moment-to-moment experiences will provide you with useful data."

"It has been centuries since I have been interested in 'data' or other discrete items of information that can be argued, proven, or disproven. My interest is in impressions and possibilities, the imponderable maybes of past, present, future."

"So you have no interest in actual history? Or in contemporary events?"

"Only insofar as they fuel and refine my work as a speculator." He stressed the word "speculator" as if it might have been a formal title. "The Dornaani who directed you to me have wasted their—and thus, your—time focused upon narrow questions of what, where, when, and even how events transpired. My focus is upon the only question that is truly infinite: *why* does a thing occur? Why does it not occur differently? Why does each actor make the choices they do? And ultimately, why is each factor in the total causal equation essential to produce the outcome?" One eyelid fluttered briefly. "A true speculator might have to create a whole world to adequately test that question. A true speculator would revel in that labor."

Riordan nodded. "I've been told that Virtua is the ultimate tool for exploring strategic scenarios."

"Not just for strategic scenarios. For everything. Your species' speculators fumble about with computer modeling as if they were panhandlers in your American West. With the thinnest veneer of empirical observation and report, they scoop wildly at any current of possible causality. And they call that process 'research.'"

Walking deeper into the room's maze of suspended reflective arcs and rings, Laaglenz waved a finger at the vaguely symmetric array. "Virtuality, but Virtua most particularly, leaps beyond guesswork and weakly informed hypotheses. To evolve the analogy of your panhandlers, Virtua does not merely produce gold. It produces the *perfect* gold that your ancient alchemists called the philosopher's stone: the only substance that confers perfect knowledge."

He gestured to a smart couch that had already reshaped itself into a human-friendly recliner. "General virtuality removes guesswork and even live experimentation from fields as diverse as social evolution and genetic manipulation. However, in Virtua itself, *all* elements and conditions are defined. Consequently, all variables and interactions in the simulation manifest as natural byproducts of the total environment, just as they do in life. You may then alter any baseline value you wish, introduce whatever variable you like, and then test that revised scenario repeatedly. Infinitely."

Riordan forced himself to sit. "And are Virtua's outcomes always correct?"

Laaglenz studied Riordan more closely. "Your facial expression is... disapproval? You think we are, to use your phenomenologically infantile expression, playing God?"

"No, but if a deity does exist, then you are certainly trying to duplicate its workshop."

"A timely turn of phrase, since you require a preliminary exposure to its output. A brief preconditioning interaction facilitates full immersion in Virtua, accustoms you to the intense fidelity of the experience."

"So what are you going to show me?"

"Show you? Human, it is so much more than that." Laaglenz stepped out from under the gleaming rings and partial parabolas and waved his hand.

Riordan's vision blanked. His consciousness seemed to plunge away into darkness and then, at what felt like the nadir of his awareness, sprang back upward.

Upward toward a burgeoning light...

Riordan threw up a hand against the brightness, discovered his fingers were wrapped around the grip of a weapon: an old-fashioned semiautomatic pistol, the kind that fired brass cartridges. The smells—smoke and a marshy funk—were as full and nuanced as anything he'd ever experienced. So were the voices that were shouting instructions and warnings.

Riordan lowered his hand.

Washington, D.C. Next to the Reflecting Pool. Almost in the spot where Downing had buttonholed him a year ago. But that was where any resemblance to memory ended.

The Capitol Dome looked as if some gargantuan monster had taken a bite out of it. The Reflecting Pool was green with algae, weeds along its margins, runners from the overgrown walkways draped over its sides and down into the water. The grassy margins of the Mall had grown thigh-high wherever it wasn't pocked by craters. And, vertijets screaming in terminal approach, a sleek black transatmospheric lander was plummeting out of the sun.

"Run!" yelled a woman in a much-patched USSF duty suit. A rabble of tatter-clothed civilians with rifles of every type and epoch sprinted after her, making for the tangled trees. Several disregarded her order, kneeled and started firing at the approaching craft.

"No! Run!" Riordan shouted, and in that moment remembered, *This isn't happening. This can't be happening. But the sounds, the smells, even the salty taste of that bead of sweat on my lip...I can't tell that they're not real.*

The lander's braking thrust kicked up dust from the craters the same moment that its chin-mounted barrel swiveled toward the few civilians who had stood their ground with outdated caseless assault rifles and antique shotguns. Riordan, caught between knowing that he could fight alongside them without any actual risk and raw terror of the hovering death machine, experienced a novel mental state: paralyzing indecision.

The lander's weapon made a familiar grating hiss: a coil gun. Civilians fell. Some disintegrated into upright smudges of dark red vapor.

Riordan felt his hand tighten around the grip of the pistol. There was nothing that he could do for them, no way his weapon could hurt the attackers. And besides, none of it was real. It *couldn't* be, he kept telling himself. But still, he didn't run.

Because that's what you'd like me to do, isn't it, Laaglenz? To show me, by my own actions, just how primitive and easily herded I am. So, no. I'm going to stand my ground. But not against the lander. Against you.

The lander settled and a side ramp lowered. Tall, fit humanoids in full combat armor trotted down in assault crouches, all of them wearing—improbably—knee-length, open-fronted robes. They swept the landing zone with their rifles, and then one of them saw Riordan. The figure stopped, stood, touched the side of its helmet. The reflective faceplate seemed to fold away, revealing—

A Ktor. Even at this range, Riordan recognized the exquisitely chiseled features, the impossibly wasp-waisted decathlete's build.

He could even see the bright amber eyes, crinkling in mortal amusement.

The one next to him swung around, saw Riordan, raised his rifle: another coil gun, from the look of it. But the first Ktor pushed it down with his free hand and, smiling more broadly, spoke into his helmet's communicator.

A moment passed, during which Riordan reflected. *If this was real, they would have gunned me down as a matter of principle. Or reflex.* Which meant that Laaglenz was pushing the simulation past the point of believability. That reassured Riordan, gave him a sense of control.

Until a saber-toothed tiger came prowling down the landing ramp, a brightly lit mechanism embedded in its muscle-rippling neck. At a gesture from the leader, the beast—its massive shoulders even with the Ktor's chest—swiveled its steam-shovel head toward Riordan, lifted its nose to catch the scent.

Riordan's resolve not to react flitted away like a swift. He brought his other hand up to steady the already-cocked pistol. It was two hundred meters to the nearest cover and, simulation or not, there was no way he was going to outrun a saber-toothed tiger. Which hesitated, uncertain for a moment.

But only a moment. Riordan hardly saw its first long-legged leap in his direction: despite its size, the creature was startlingly quick. It came on, shoulders bunching and releasing, mouth open slightly. Caine sighted the gun, kept it steady and low, wished he'd had the presence of mind to check the rounds remaining in the magazine, and tried not to see an oncoming saber-toothed tiger, just a steadily expanding target.

He held his fire until fifteen meters—he'd intended to hold until ten but, shit, that cat was *big!*—and then fired steadily. He couldn't tell if any of the first three shots hit, then a dark patch erupted on the creature's shoulder. It didn't even break stride.

Riordan kept squeezing the trigger, even as the creature launched into its final leap, jaws widening, monstrous claws sliding free of their beds, hide spotted red where at least four of his rounds had hit.

The first paw raked across his chest.

Raw impact. Flying sideways. A deep slash of breath-robbing pain. And then—

Chapter Forty-Six

Gasping, Riordan found himself sitting bolt upright in the smart couch, hands clutched to his intact chest. "How—?"

"I will answer all your questions about Virtua later," Laaglenz interrupted. He studied Caine from beyond the orrery of the interface apparatus. "Next time, allow yourself to be immersed in, rather than questioning of, the experience. Regardless, you seemed to find Virtua quite realistic."

Riordan exhaled raggedly, releasing the terror and tension of the death spasm. "Everything except for the scenario itself."

Laaglenz's mouth twisted. "How ironic. It is one of our assessment models."

"Of what? A Ktor invasion of Earth?"

"Occupation would be a more accurate term, but yes."

"Well, I've never seen Ktor wearing robes. And I doubt they keep extinct terrestrial predators as pets."

"Interesting, but tangential. However, it is crucial that you appreciate the dangers of behaving recklessly in Virtua."

"I thought there weren't any physical consequences to using virtuality."

"Virtua is not 'virtuality.' Not only is the data and sensory infusion infinitely more dense, but the neural connection is correspondingly more complete. It is rare, but lethal trauma in Virtua can cause cardiac arrest. So caution is required. Also, you would normally be given an exit code to break the link to what you would call Virtua's 'server.'"

Of all the supercilious, impatient, and dismissive Dornaani Caine had met, Laaglenz was rapidly developing into the one he liked least. "Still, I'm surprised that so many users keep going back. An exit code and caution can't eliminate all the danger."

Laaglenz let the fingers of one hand roll lazily to the side. "Yet that is the unavoidable cost of participating in Virtua. Because it is a shared rather than personalized experience, its simulations cannot be easily started or stopped. Nor can they be edited to remove the quotidian necessities of daily life.

"Virtua's origin as a testing platform *requires* it to duplicate reality in every detail. Only a scenario that contains every potential variable has the power to test every possible permutation and every possible outcome. Because we can adjust any variables along an established timeline, we can create alternate pasts, presents, and futures, and so, assess *why* each one's outcome is different. Without this flawless modeling capability, we would not be able to identify and refine long-arc metaconcepts."

Caine broke in as Laaglenz paused to inhale. "Define metaconcept."

Once Laaglenz's inhale was completed, it reversed into a long sigh. "Very well, we shall progress at human speed."

And suddenly, Riordan wasn't seeing the room anymore, he was floating inside a transparent orb. Laaglenz was in an identical sphere alongside him. Beneath them, the trailing arms of the Milky Way glittered, adorned with an infinitude of stellar sequins the size of dust motes.

"Metaconcept," Laaglenz began flatly. "Explicatory example: the baseline rarity of intelligent life in the universe must obey a calculus. We can explore this metaconcept and its dynamics heuristically by positing relevant variables and then refining them for testing within Virtua." The Milky Way turned slowly. They began rushing in toward the stellar cluster that was the home of all five known races.

"We start with a single pertinent variable that may be broken into opposed propositions: either all intelligent species emerge spontaneously, or some percentage of them are the products of uplifting." Their bubbles plummeted to the surface of a green world where an unknown exosapient species—mind-bending agglomerations of tentacles, eyes, and flipper-feet—were spreading out from a large orbital lander, cataloguing and gathering local fauna.

"The concept of uplifting brings forth a multitude of other questions. Do all intelligent species have an equal predisposition to experiment with it? If not, why do some evince a greater tendency than others? More subtly, what determines the type and extent of uplifting that they employ?"

Their bubbles were suddenly inside a laboratory. One of the exosapients was artificially fertilizing two different creatures. The first was a skinny, big-eared, big-eyed badger analog. The second was a six-legged amphibian. "Two examples of possible variations in uplifting," Laaglenz said in a bored tone. "In the first creature, uplifting assists a species hovering on the edge of intelligence to cross that divide. In the case of the second creature, uplifting occurs at an earlier stage, providing a less certain but subtler push toward eventual sapience."

Their bubbles flew up through the ceiling of the laboratory. In an instant, they were in deep space, high above the system's ecliptic. They watched the planets spin feverishly around their yellow star, then dove back down after several centuries had elapsed.

In the same marshland of the same planet, the badger analog's now-distant offspring were exploring further beyond their burrows. Their front paws were slightly more articulated, so they handled objects more adeptly. Several showed a nascent interest in the possibility of scaling a tall fern. In a nearby stream, several of the modified amphibians ventured ashore and stayed there longer, their lungs expanding far more than their ancestors' had.

Caine's bubble dissolved along with his immersion in Virtua. Laaglenz was now seated in a saddle chair, just out of reach. "I presume you see how this applies to the races of the Accord."

"I do." Actually, Riordan wasn't at all sure that he *did* see the significance, but memories of Uinzleej's hypotheses were inspiring a vague hunch. "Whether or not some, or all, of the species of the Accord are uplifted, each presents an opportunity to search for signs of it. But in doing so, we will immediately notice a statistical aberration in our sample. We shouldn't have that many opportunities, that many races, in so small an astrographic region. And we have a concrete basis for that assertion.

"The Collective's survey fifty light-years beyond the Accord found no additional exosapient species, nor did it detect any radio emissions originating within a further thirty light-years. So there is a 'sapient-free shell' around the Accord that is eighty light-years thick and nine times its volume. Consequently, either the concentration of sapient species that occurred in Accord space is extraordinarily dense, or there is a surrounding volume of space almost ten times its size where the concentration is extraordinarily sparse."

"Or—" Laaglenz began.

"I'm not done. The third, and far more likely, scenario is that the incidence of intelligent species within Accord space has been dramatically increased by external factors. Uplifting could be the cause, but there is a second likely variable: transplantation. Lastly, I dismiss the possibility that the dead zone surrounding us was depopulated by the Oldest Ones' xenocidal sweeps because your survey found no signs of such destruction." Riordan leaned back, arms crossed. And waited.

If Laaglenz was impressed or surprised, he gave no sign of it. "The metaconcept requires consideration of additional uncertainties. How many species that uplift others are themselves products of earlier uplifters? How many races have received uplifting from both? Is humanity itself an example of that phenomenon?"

Riordan's surprise at the last broke forth as an exclamation. "Why would humanity be an example of double uplifting?"

Laaglenz waved a didactic finger from side to side. "A particularly promising branch of the hominid evolutionary tree may have been the recipient of late-stage uplifting to give it dominance over the others. And in terms of early-stage uplifting, we should revisit the strange fortuity of the extinction-level event that shattered the dominion of Earth's dinosaurs, yet left its biosphere primed for small proto-mammals that were better able to survive the aftermath."

Riordan shook his head. "There must be some chance in the universe. Some luck, both good and bad."

"Yet how, from this distant vantage point, may we discriminate events of intentionality from those of happenstance? It is imponderable. Let us instead evolve the metaconcept to include the corollary your conjectures imply: that because the Accord's concentration of sapient species is statistically abnormal, it is probably a tainted sample. Many or all of the races may have been uplifted, transplanted, or both. But note how all these speculations ultimately bring us to the most important, and tantalizing, mystery of all: *why*?" Laaglenz's lamprey mouth lingered upon, almost seemed to taste, that final word.

Riordan shrugged. "If the Elders foresaw the Final War, they might have moved some species out of its path."

"If true, then transplantation, rather than uplifting, is the variable most responsible for the tainting of the local sample of sapience. It also implies that the transplantation was not haphazard but purposive. Logically, the Elders would have chosen to preserve complementary species, to create what I call an optimum blend." Laaglenz indulged in a smug pause. "Which is, of course, precisely what we observe.

"Consider. We Dornaani, as the most advanced, were to serve as guards and mentors. The Slaasriithi were included to bring life to as many worlds as could support it. The Arat Kur would exploit the resources of lifeless worlds to maximize industrial productivity. The Hkh'Rkh may have been intended as defenders. And humans were to have served as explorers, pioneers, and, ultimately, to ensure synergy between the races."

"And the Ktor?"

Laaglenz's mouth crinkled irritably. "The Oldest Ones may have insinuated them to disrupt your part in this mixture, just as they groomed the loji to disrupt ours."

Laaglenz leaned far back in his saddle seat. "This illustrates the value of metaconcepts." Riordan's puzzled look elicited another burbling sigh. "We began with the question of the rarity of intelligence, a vague wondering as formless as a lump of clay. But by broadly interrogating that question itself, we have sculpted our curiosity into a nascent theoretical shape that defines a general metaconcept.

"On its own, it does not reveal or convey anything of substance. However, it stimulates narrower inquiries that build toward a more concrete analysis and understanding. However, the more exacting our examination becomes, the more it points us to a fundamental mystery. What criteria did the Elders use in choosing these specific races?"

Riordan understood, nodded. "And if the local species are complementary, then you should be able to reason backward to those criteria. That, in turn, provides hints about how the Elders thought about different kinds of intelligence, and maybe, their motivations for earlier uplifting."

Laaglenz rose. "This is where the modeling power of Virtua becomes indispensable: positing and testing the different origins of intelligence, the shapes they impart upon species, and how those different species may be integrated into an optimal blend. A detailed articulation of such hypotheses involves concepts that are both multilayered and multivalent. You would be unable to track them. However, because of Virtua, I can simply show you that process in action."

Riordan shook his head. "And how do you 'show' the process of examining the hypothetical complementarity of species?"

Laaglenz sounded surprised. "Surely it is obvious. Even to you." When it was clear that the answer was not obvious to Riordan, the Dornaani exhaled and waved his hand at the dangling metal mobile overhead.

Chapter Forty-Seven

Riordan was suddenly roving between worlds of the Accord, some that he had visited personally, most of which he had not. But rather than being there himself, he was a spectator inside some other person's mind, yet fully aware of all their sensations and intents. The scenes were as diverse as the locations.

—Wielding primitive hand-tools, Arat Kur labored in the subterranean reaches of what was apparently a lush Slaasriithi world...until, in the distance, Riordan saw the dim outline of distinctly human ruins: the iconic New York skyline.

—Slaasriithi and Arat Kur worked a lichen-blanketed plain beneath the midday ghost of gas giant Epsilon Indi Two. But they did so under the watchful eyes of Hkh'Rkh, who held their traditional two-handed *halbardiches* at the ready as humans in dark gray uniforms observed impassively from a distant VTOL.

—A pack of feral Hkh'Rkh bounded through a dense clutter of yellow and teal foliage, two of their number exploding into mauve smears. Before their remains spattered to the ground, an open sled powered by six gimballing, ducted propellers whined overhead, safari-garbed Ktor laughing, pointing, reloading rifles that were almost the size of rocket launchers.

—From the margins of the Capitol Mall, Riordan saw himself sliced to ribbons by the saber-toothed tiger. As his shredded body fell into the Reflecting Pool, the robed Ktor turned their weapons upon the scattering insurgents. They fell in windrows, swallowed by the waist-high weeds...

Riordan started as he came out of the hurried montage of experiences. "What...what?"

"These are not random scenes, human. These are but a few of the outcomes that result from introducing slight changes to the same model."

"And what were you modeling, the failures of the Elders' 'speciate blend'?"

"No. This was a much narrower, short-horizon model designed to explore possible outcomes after Nolan Corcoran discovered the Doomsday Rock. However, since the model's timeline and causal chains have been overtaken by subsequent events, it is now offered primarily as an entertainment scenario."

"As entertainment?" Riordan tried to reconcile a Dornaani's enjoyment of the scenes he'd just witnessed with the horror he'd felt being in them.

"Yes. Although it still provides us with useful data points for how events of the last ten years may determine the fate of the Accord. In this case, after running the post-Doomsday Rock Discovery scenario through dozens of iterations, we discovered a number of watershed events. Identifying such inflection points, even in retrospect, improves our ability to detect new ones in advance."

"So you're trying to predict the future."

"I suspect not even the Elders believed that was possible. But it improves our understanding of the variables and interactions that led to the present, and therefore, helps us foresee the places, people, and events that are likely to significantly *shape* the future. For instance, the larger model from which this variant scenario was developed is called the Accord Endgame Assessment. In all its variations, it has been run uncounted thousands of times, now mostly by open-use participants."

"Open-use participants? Are they the ones who visit it for, er, entertainment?"

"Yes." Laaglenz rose from his seat. "They elect not to follow the experimental restrictions upon behaviors that deviate too greatly from the prevailing social norms."

Riordan frowned. "But can't you just edit out their actions, replace them with something statistically normative?"

Laaglenz was genuinely disoriented for a moment. "Do you not understand, human? There are no *a priori* assumptions, no limits on activities, no scripts. Virtua is a total system, a world that provides complete freedom of action to its users."

"So how do you build that? Do you start with modular game shells that Virtua expands by generating new details in response to user actions?"

Laaglenz's eyelids sagged: impatience, boredom. "All of Virtua's scenarios and simulations are ultimately derived from the Prime Model, the only universe left in finished form by the Elders. However, they also left behind partially completed models. We expand, change, or adapt these worlds by altering their fundamental values or variables. Their scope ranges from discrete regions to nearly complete universes."

Riordan held up a hand. "Wait. Are you saying the Prime Model is a complete universe?"

"I am."

"What the hell does that even mean?"

"It means exactly what I have now repeatedly told you: there is an entire, fully-iterated universe bounded within the Prime Model. Significant portions of others are bounded within what you call the limited 'shells' we use."

"So you are saying that the world, the entire universe, of Virtua is already fully generated, down to the last subatomic particle?"

"Human, do you derive some strange pleasure by using different words to reiterate the same misperceptions? The universe of the Prime Model has *always* existed, complete and whole. There is no generation involved. The only alterations to its dynamic cause-and-effect chains are those imposed by user actions."

Riordan shook his head. "That's impossible. How can Virtua—a finite system within the real universe—contain a subset of information as infinite as the universe itself? How can any program, any system, hold and manipulate so much data, track so many separate functions?"

Laaglenz's expression did not change, but the gills on the left side of his neck rippled. Asynchronously. "How indeed?" he breathed in a tone Riordan had never heard in a Dornaani's voice: distracted ecstasy. One of Laaglenz's eyelids fluttered.

Riordan wondered if being in Virtua too long could cause madness. "So," Riordan resumed carefully, "there are multiple users active in any given iteration of a model, at any given time."

"Of course."

"But how is that coordinated? Your users must be widely separated, have different lag times, might even be on different planets."

"User proximity is not essential. Real time interplanetary and interstellar participation is effected through connection nodes in different star systems."

"Real-time *interstellar* participation?" Riordan was about to rebut with "No, not possible," and then remembered the crash of the Corcoran simulacrum. It had been instantly reported to overseers twenty light-years away. "So these nodes are...what? Some kind of wormhole communication network?"

Laaglenz made a dismissive gesture with the falling fingers of one hand: a bored confirmation.

"But how?"

"As I said at the outset, 'how' is invariably a dull question. So dull, in fact, that I will only answer one of the following: how Virtua operates, or how to find your mate."

At last. "Tell me how to find Elena."

"A typical human choice, selecting personal attachment over greater knowledge."

"Actually, no choice was required. You've already promised to answer all my questions about Virtua."

"I did no such thing." But Laaglenz sounded less than positive.

"You were probably distracted"—*by the sound of your own voice*—"but when you brought me out of the first sim, I asked you how it worked. You interrupted by promising me that, 'I will answer all your questions about Virtua later.'" Riordan shrugged. "But I would have chosen Elena, anyway. Because when all is said and done, she's real and Virtua is just make-believe."

Instead of becoming angry, Laaglenz lowered his head. He seemed to stare at his midriff. "Given your limited ability to understand what Virtua is and does, I suppose I cannot flaw your reasoning. Indeed—" His sudden pause became a full stop, succeeded by a vacant stare.

Riordan leaned into the Dornaani's wandering field of vision. "Laaglenz? Are you well?"

"I am...reflecting."

Caine was prepared to regret his next question. "Reflecting upon what?"

"Upon the irony of what I just said. 'Given your limited

ability to understand what Virtua is and does, I cannot flaw your reasoning.'"

"Yes, what about that?"

"I might as well have been speaking of myself." Laaglenz glanced at Riordan; he looked more sane, but also, deeply haunted. Terrified, almost. "There is much validity in an earlier question you posed. 'How can a discrete system in the real universe contain within it a subset of information that is as infinite as the universe itself?' It cannot, of course. That is how I started on this path, this life: by asking that same question."

"And?"

"And I was...'discouraged' from pursuing it too far. That is why I am here. On the margins. Asking 'why,' rather than 'how.'" His voice darkened. "Asking how can be much more dangerous."

Riordan was at once eager and wary. Eager because he could sense that Laaglenz was on the verge of revealing recondite, and possibly crucial, knowledge. But Caine was equally wary, because one wrong word could cause the Dornaani to recoil back into the protective shell he had built to shield himself from whatever impossible truth he had grabbed hold of... and that he could not let go. "I did not think," Riordan murmured, "that enlightenment was ever discouraged among the Dornaani."

"It never is." Laaglenz's voice became hollow. "Yet this was. And so I fear—" He looked up, his eyes suddenly clear, intense. "Human. When you enter Virtua, be mindful of worlds that no longer resemble ours in any meaningful way."

"But isn't that kind of change inevitable once users alter the event paths of—?"

"No, no!" Laaglenz interrupted anxiously. "I mean a world, a universe that is so changed that it is unrecognizable, where history has no overlap with ours, or where the rules of physics may have branched away from those we know."

Caine started, as much at the Dornaani's sudden earnestness as the bizarre change of topic. "Are you referring to"—Riordan struggled to remember the term—"the many-worlds model of parallel universes? From first-generation quantum theory?"

Laaglenz flapped annoyed fingers in his direction. "Yes. Maybe. Sedge and muck! I do not know what label you hairless apes gave it! But I have wondered..." His voice grew faint. "If a branching incident in a temporal stream—that instant when a symmetry split occurs spontaneously—could be induced, even controlled, then..." His pause became a protracted silence, then a distracted stare.

"Laaglenz?"

"Yes?" He blinked, as if surprised by his surroundings. "You are correct. I promised to tell you how Virtua works. Ask your questions." There was no indication he had ever been diverted from their original, almost combative exchange.

Riordan leaned forward. "So, Virtua's instantaneous connections are facilitated by something you call 'nodes'?"

Laaglenz poked a finger at the floor. "Incorrect. 'Node' does not refer to the *means* of instantaneous transmission. A node is any star system in which those means are present."

"Okay, so what do you call the *means* of instantaneous transmission?"

"The closest rendering in your language would be 'keyhole.'"

"And are they some kind of wormhole, or...?"

"Understanding Virtua does not require that I help you understand the physics of keyholes."

"Nor their impact upon Dornaani culture, apparently."

"Your meaning is unclear."

Riordan shrugged. "These keyholes sound like yet another reason that Dornaani don't have to leave their homes anymore. And I'm guessing that as use of Virtua became more widespread, an increasing number of these keyholes were reopened."

Laaglenz did a poor job of mimicking confusion. "'Reopened?'"

"Look, it's pretty clear that the first keyholes had to be created by the ancients." Riordan shrugged in response to Laaglenz's stare. "Hey, you're the one who said that Virtua has 'always been there.' Logically, then, so have its keyholes. And back when Virtua was turned off or boxed up, I suspect its connections were either ignored or forgotten. But as modern users started discovering it again, you had to find those keyholes. And then, as it expanded, you had to create new ones, just so that the system could run properly."

"Again, your meaning is unclear. 'Run properly'?"

"Virtua sounds way too big to run on what we would call a single platform. I'm guessing it requires a distributed network. So by increasing the number of nodes, you weren't just expanding the user base, you were increasing Virtua's computing power.

And you couldn't have done that unless you learned how to make keyholes yourself."

Laaglenz's face was carefully expressionless. "A provocative assertion without any supporting evidence."

"You're a speculator, so you know that when you don't have complete data, that's *precisely* when you have to rely on thought experiments. And here's mine.

"Even if your race was the heir apparent of the Elders, they wouldn't put nodes only in *your* star systems. Because if your metaconcept of an optimal speciate blend is accurate, then they had to distribute the keyholes evenly. Eventually, that communications parity would become essential to political stability among the races.

"But if the Elders had left behind *lots* of keyholes—say, as many as you now have for Virtua—then some of the other races should have already stumbled across at least one, particularly the tech-savvy Ktor. But since they haven't, it seems likely that the Elders left behind relatively *few* keyholes.

"Of course, you Dornaani now have a major advantage they didn't foresee: you are the only race that remembers their existence. So you're the only ones who have records showing where some of them were located. That, together with your advanced science and technology, allowed you to study them for a few millennia and discover how to make your own. That's how you've been able to grow Virtua's nodal switchboard." Caine spent one brief moment appreciating the surprised look on Laaglenz's face. "Now, tell me how to find Elena and how to get her away from the monster that's got hold of her."

"'Monster?' What do you mean?"

"I mean Virtua. And in order to retrieve her, I suspect I'll to have to face it myself."

"'Face' Virtua? Human, to influence its outcomes, you have to be *inside* it."

Caine nodded. "As I've come to realize, thanks to you. So if I'm going to free her from the belly of that beast, you have to tell me where I can jump down its gullet."

Chapter Forty-Eight

Caine drift-walked slowly beside Alnduul as they moved along one of *Olsloov*'s less-used passageways. The Dornaani had been waiting for him when his shuttle returned from the surface of Zhashayn, but had remained uncharacteristically quiet as they made their way forward. "Where are we going?"

"A restricted area. But first, let us stop in here." He waved at an unusually large iris valve. It opened and they walked through into a gallery with a mural-sized view of space. Well aft, a speck of intense yellow-white light—Sigma 2 Ursa Majoris 2 A—silhouetted the gas giant in orbit eleven. Alnduul spent a moment gazing at it. "We will shift in two days."

Riordan nodded, resisted the impulse to reply *I'll believe it when I see it.* Cynicism had become habitual while traveling in the Collective. But, the sensors showed nothing in range that might interfere with the preacceleration and outshift to the K-type orange star known to human astrographers as BD+75 403A. "It's hard to believe that I might finally see Elena."

"You may see her, but it is unlikely that she will be responsive."

Riordan nodded. "Sometimes it's important just to be close to someone, Alnduul. Even if they aren't conscious."

Alnduul let air leak slowly out his gills. "I am acquainted with the human desire for closeness, although we Dornaani have no analog. But we do feel strong regret when we are parted from a close friend." He looked out at the stars. "It is as I shall soon feel regarding my departure from you, Caine Riordan."

"You're going somewhere?"

"Yes. That is why I wished to speak to you alone, while contemplating a view that encourages us to keep our vision broad and far-reaching."

Riordan replied with a rueful smile. "When you start speaking in cosmic superlatives, I start getting worried." Caine let a few moments pass. "So, what's happened?"

"As anticipated, I must return to Glamqoozht to face a board of inquiry. They shall determine whether or not I shall remain a Custodian, let alone the Senior Mentor for the Human Oversight Group."

"What do you plan to say to them?"

"Very little. The board is comprised of many of the same persons who met with you, and as Glayaazh pointed out, they have already made their decision. Besides, if obeying my oath as a Custodian has become cause for dismissal, what may I hope to say?"

Riordan nodded. "Maybe this is a better question: what would you *like* to say to them?"

Alnduul stared at the unwinking stars before his reply came out in a fervent rush. "I would tell them that, after half a millennium of growing detachment and moral relativity, their greatest shame should be that they no longer feel shame at all."

Alnduul's equivalent of teeth—shearing plates that worked like an iris valve—scissored rapidly. "For a culture to remain coherent and viable, it must declare what it opposes just as clearly as it declares what it embraces." Alnduul's mouth relaxed. "It is implicit in the belief structure professed by the Corcoran simulacrum: integrity is essential to the continuance of virtue, just as hope is essential to the continuance of life. We have forgotten these truths."

He turned away from the stars. "I have made provisions to ensure your continued safety. Accordingly, Irzhresht shall remain behind with you."

Riordan's left eyebrow climbed before he could stop it. "Irzhresht doesn't seem particularly fond of me."

Alnduul trailed a finger. "Irzhresht displays little fondness for anyone. Lojis learn early to suppress signs of need, affinity, or particularly, trust."

"Okay, but can I trust *her*?"

"You may trust that she will not wish to displease *me*."

"That's not very reassuring."

"Perhaps not, but it ensures that she will be a reliable assistant." His tone darkened. "Her circumstances were dire when our paths first crossed. It was my sponsorship that brought her into the ranks of the Custodians."

"So she, too, will be excluded from private meetings."

"That is why I have arranged for another assistant, one with fewer social constraints." He waved a finger over his vantbrass: the image of another loji—smaller, grayer, more covered with tattoos—appeared before them. "This is Hsontlosh. He is accepted in both Collective and loji communities, and has been invaluable in brokering cooperative relationships between them."

"You know him personally?"

"I have met him, but cannot claim to know him. However, two Dornaani Arbiters sympathetic to your cause have often retained him and place their highest confidence in his discretion and reliability. You met one of them on Glamqoozht. Heethoo."

Riordan nodded. "One of the few friendly faces around that table. And the other?"

Alnduul moved toward the exit. "Glayaazh." He motioned for Caine to follow.

Well, I can't ask for a better recommendation than that. "So Hsontlosh can accompany me wherever I go."

"Yes. And he is also your—what is your term?—'back up.' A puzzling idiom, since it also means to reverse direction."

Riordan was too concerned to find Alnduul's linguistic confusion amusing. "Why do I need back up?"

Two of Alnduul's fingers traced a fretful arabesque in midair. "Irzhresht is loyal to me, but has always traveled under my direct protection. It is unlikely, but a loji from her past could learn that she is more vulnerable now, and seek to extort her into betraying you."

"And you think she would be susceptible to that pressure?"

"No, but she is proud and secretive. She might not inform you of attempts to coerce her."

Riordan nodded. "But Hsontlosh would see the signs and warn me."

"Yes," Alnduul drifted a single finger into an upward curl. "Lastly, you will have a guide that is particularly adept at Dornaani customs and concepts, and at explaining them to a human."

"That sounds too good to be true. Who is this guide?"

Instead of answering, Alnduul approached and waved at an iris valve outlined in orange: restricted access. He entered, stood aside to allow Caine to pass.

Riordan stopped after two steps. A human was rising from a cocoon couch near the opposite bulkhead. He was of early middle age, brown hair, brown eyes, plain-featured with a medium skin tone that could be encountered amongst humans of almost any ethnotype. He smiled. "I am Eku. You must be Caine Riordan. I am pleased to meet you."

Riordan nodded, scanned the compartment. A Dornaani cold cell was snugged against the far bulkhead. "So, Eku, I see you've just come out of cryogenic suspension."

"That is correct."

Alnduul moved closer to Eku, watching Caine...who was suddenly wary. *So there's been another human on board the whole time. Nothing technically wrong about that, but I wonder...* "How long have you been in cold sleep, Eku?"

"Just over forty-six terrestrial years, Mr. Riordan."

Caine nodded. "And of the places you've visited on Earth, which is your favorite?"

Eku seemed to relax. "I was quite fond of the Crystal Palace in London." Eku's smile became thoughtful. "Not so much for its beauty as for what it represented."

Riordan nodded. "Dreams, hopes, aspirations, joy."

Eku returned the nod, his smile widening. "Yes. All those things."

Riordan returned the smile. "Well, I imagine you have a lot of catching up to do. It's been a pretty lively half century." A nod at Eku—"I'm glad we had the chance to meet"—and then Riordan stepped back through the iris valve.

Eku called after him. "I am also glad, Mr. Riordan."

Riordan nodded as the iris valve closed, started back toward his quarters.

It took Alnduul half a minute to catch up with him. "I had hoped this would not be necessary."

"You mean, having me meet a factotum?"

"No: that I would need to rouse Eku at all. But you will require his assistance." An awkward pause, then, "You are to be congratulated on how swiftly you discerned his origin."

"Oh, drop the bullshit praise, Alnduul. Firstly, why would

another human be on board *Olsloov,* particularly one whose appearance is optimized for multiethnic infiltration? And secondly, there's no other reason you'd have a human on board who's been in cold sleep for forty-six years, forty years earlier than humanity knew that you or any other exosapients existed.

"But the clincher was the Crystal Palace. That's been gone almost two hundred years. So it seems you've been popping Eku in and out of his cryogenic kennel for centuries."

Alnduul recoiled. "The deployment of a factotum is never a casual matter. It requires the highest level of permission within the Custodians, since they become familiar with many of our most confidential activities and technologies in the course of their operations. But I understand your anger."

Riordan sighed. "I'm not sure you do. First the ancients decided to grab some of us as interstellar breeding stock. Then the Ktor land on Earth to grab the Lost Soldiers. Now it turns out you Dornaani have been dropping off your own human infiltrators for so long that some of them may still remember watching mastodon migrations." He shook his head. "Being a protected race apparently hasn't stopped anyone from scooping up humans whenever it suits them. Including our so-called protectors."

Alnduul folded his hands. "We have never 'scooped up' anyone. Our factotums are descended from humans whom the Elders removed from Earth. Their sole mission has been to assist us in safeguarding your race without any noticeable intrusions or cultural disruptions."

Translation: without sending us into a panic about aliens among us. Which, all things being equal, was probably a good idea. But still... "I'm not even sure why I should trust a highly obedient, confidential agent you keep on frozen standby more than I should a loji." They arrived at Riordan's stateroom. He turned to face Alnduul. "I'm going to rest a while." He wasn't sure whether it was a white lie or if, in fact, he might lie down in the cocoon to process this latest surprise.

Alnduul, looking forlorn, held out a small, featureless sphere. "Since our paths will soon part, you must keep this, Caine Riordan."

"What is it?"

"An emergency beacon. Compress its opposite poles and an activation tab will appear. Activate and deploy it in the event that something goes amiss."

Riordan took the sphere. It was the size of a tennis ball and matte black. "Deploy it where?"

"Free space is best, but it will function anywhere."

Riordan raised an eyebrow. "And it sends you a message?"

"If you deploy it in a system with a communications node—a keyhole of any kind—its code and point of origin will be relayed throughout the Collective. I should receive that signal in hours. Possibly minutes. Otherwise, it will be relayed to any passing ship running an authorized transponder. It will be automatically rebroadcast by all ships whenever they enter a new system or encounter another vessel."

"And that message can't be blocked or purged from their systems? Or decoded?"

"Decoding is impossible. This beacon only emits its location and identification code and only I know what its activation signifies. As far as blocking or purging its signal, a precondition for all Dornaani ship transponders is that they remain available for relaying such messages. If that availability is terminated, the transponder's signal is automatically altered to reflect that violation."

Riordan stared at the night-black tennis ball with greater appreciation. "That's a pretty impressive parting gift."

Alnduul's response failed to match Caine's shift to a more lighthearted tone. "I wish I had a better one to offer. I hope our parting is only temporary."

Riordan nodded, pocketed the device, and discovered he was already repenting his annoyance over Eku. Alnduul had been a steadfast friend, and if Caine had not always agreed with his propensity toward information control rather than transparency, the Dornaani had unswervingly supported his interests and those of humanity. So much so that it now threatened to end his career. "I hope you'll be back soon."

"So do I." Alnduul did not sound particularly hopeful.

Riordan did not want to ask for another favor, but was realizing that if he didn't, hundreds might pay for his reluctance. Caine folded his arms. "Alnduul, if something happens to me while you're away…"

"I will seek Elena Corcoran. Once she is safe, I shall seek justice for you."

Riordan waved those concerns aside. "Thank you, but there is a larger matter, one that transcends my personal concerns. I have to ensure the safety of the Lost Soldiers, the Cold Guard, and my crew. But if I am unable to do so, please give them whatever help you can. I'm sorry to ask, but I have no one else to turn to."

Alnduul's nictating lids closed and opened very slowly. "Only a true friend, both to me and to them, would ask such a favor. I accept. Gladly."

Riordan sighed, smiled, put out his hand. "I know this not your custom, but..."

Alnduul extended his much thinner hand, the birdlike bones delicate where Riordan's enfolded them. "I regret that Dornaan has no analog for this gesture of bonding." He withdrew his hand. "I shall leave you to your rest, Caine Riordan."

Caine watched him turn and dwindle down the corridor, wondering when, after Alnduul dropped him at the next and hopefully final destination, they would meet again.

If ever.

Eku stood as Alnduul entered his compartment. "Has Mister Riordan become sufficiently acclimated to having a factotum assistant, Alnduul?"

"No, but he shall. Riordan is highly adaptive. We must discuss a different matter."

Eku nodded. "Corrupt loji."

Alnduul sat on one of the cocoon couches. "Their tendrils reach much further, much deeper, than you remember. Be wary."

"Have they become openly restive, hostile?"

"No, and that is what worries me. They are not exploiting the full scope of their growing leverage." Alnduul felt weary. "The masters of the Ten Great Rings teach patience, particularly before commencing an ambush or a betrayal."

Eku was frowning. "Then mere vigilance is not sufficient. I must ensure that Riordan can survive even if am separated from him. Or slain."

Alnduul raised a sad finger of affirmation. "Which is why you must hold this in trust for Riordan." Alnduul gently extracted a universal access key from a pocket on his utility vest.

Eku took the device: an innocuous-looking fob. "I do not presume to challenge your decision, Alnduul, but... is this wise?"

"It is necessary." Alnduul drifted his fingertips in the direction of the access key. "Entrust it to Caine if his circumstances become ... inauspicious."

"But he will not know what to do with it."

"Correction. Riordan most certainly will know what to do with it, once you have explained its function. But he will not know *how*."

Eku looked crestfallen. "I shall instruct him. But if he is unable to act, rest assured, I will make prudent choices on his behalf."

Alnduul streamed two fingers. "I know this. Riordan's choices will be no less prudent, although they may be unorthodox. However, it is crucial that it is his will that determines how the fob is used. Whether he means to or not, he represents his people as he moves among us. He—they—must have agency in whatever transpires next."

Eku stared at the fob resting in his palm. "And if, after your hearings, the Arbiters ask for the fob's return?"

Alnduul gestured beyond the bulkhead. "Then I will tell them I have lost it."

Along with everything else.

PART FOUR

Collective Space and Zeta Tucanae III ("Dustbelt")
July–October 2124

CAVEAT

Caveat Emptor
([Let the] buyer beware)

Chapter Forty-Nine

Eku touched his left hand to his ear. "*Olsloov* has shifted."

Riordan checked his wristlink, nodded. "Right on time." He stepped aside to allow a slowly advancing robot to pass, its avoidance sensors apparently defunct. Given its antique patina of dust and rust, Caine was impressed that it functioned at all.

Eku pointed toward the northern horizon. "There are the ruins of which Alnduul spoke."

Riordan followed Eku's index finger, descried a huge arch in the mist, two small yellow moons rising over it. The arch shone like burnished bronze in the late afternoon light of BD+75 403A, the K 8 star that the Dornaani called Leltlosu. "The ruins date from the Times Before?"

"Beyond all doubt. This is often the case in systems with original keyholes."

Their control circlets highlighted a path that took them through mostly dark complexes of domes and spheres. Another robot, a hexaped, limped across the broad promenade they were approaching. "I expected a world with functional Elder technology to be, well, different."

Eku nodded. "You expected superior maintenance, cleanliness. That was the case until approximately a thousand years ago."

"So interest in maintaining historic sites began fading even before virtuality became widespread?"

"Yes, but it was due to frustration, not disinterest."

"Because the Dornaani could not repair or duplicate the Elders' achievements?"

"Worse. They could only approximate them using cruder methods." Eku led them into a poorly lit avenue that appeared not to have been trafficked in years. "The newer keyholes are an example. Keyholes exploit a phenomenon closely related to the one utilized by shift drives. However, creating a keyhole requires greater mastery of theoretical physics and high-energy engineering."

"Which the Dornaani must have achieved, since they learned how to create them."

"They have only created lesser, impermanent imitations, Mr. Riordan."

"Please, just call me Caine."

"Very well, Caine. The plaza ahead is where we are to meet Hsontlosh. After you have been properly introduced, I will have to leave you."

"I thought you were coming along as my local eyes and ears."

Eku nodded. "That would usually be the case. But in this instance, it would be unwise. Like many Virtua node administrators, the one here on Leltlosu-shai expands her influence through the acquisition and sale of information.

"As a native of Earth, your mere arrival will unavoidably attract her attention. The nature of your request will especially pique her curiosity. However, appearing in the company of a factotum would reveal that Alnduul places extraordinary importance upon a positive outcome. She could use that as leverage."

"How?"

"A factotum should not travel without a Custodial overseer. Consequently, the departure of *Olsloov* would lead her to correctly deduce that I am now operating without one. If she reported that infraction, I might be removed from your service, and Alnduul's legal problems would likely be aggravated."

So everything on Leltlosu-shai has to be kept at arm's length, then. As Alnduul suspected. "Being a factotum sounds like a pretty tricky existence, Eku."

"From my perspective, the uncertainty of life on Earth seems a much greater challenge. Here, all my needs are met, and the only threat is that I, or my family and friends, might perish. But that is now a very, very rare occurrence. Upon our retirement, we live out our lives with each other before a final immersion in Virtua."

Riordan stared. "Factotums are allowed to use Virtua?"

Eku was surprised by the question. "Why, yes, of course. When we become too old or infirm to pursue our duties, we are courted by node administrators to enter their simulations. Permanently. We..." Eku stopped, squinting ahead into the amber dusk. "There. That is Hsontlosh."

The loji Eku indicated was supported by an exoframe that absorbed most of the burden of Leltlosu-shai's point-seven-three-gee environment. Moving slowly, carefully, he met them at the entrance to the plaza. "Enlightenment unto you," he said, offering a labored version of the traditional elbows-in, hands-and-fingers-out gesture.

Riordan returned the greeting. Eku, who seemed surprised, lagged a moment behind.

Hsontlosh slumped in his exoframe. "Caine Riordan, I regret that our first meeting allows little opportunity to become acquainted, particularly given the delicate matters we must now address together. But our host is impatient and we dare not delay."

"I understand. However, you come very highly recommended."

Hsontlosh's eyes half closed and his mouth retracted fully: a Dornaani bow. "I am honored by the high regard of those who recommended me." He turned to Caine's companion. "I presume you are Eku."

"Correct."

"Thank you for accompanying Mr. Riordan to this place. I am sending the location of my ship and its entry code to your control circlet. You shall be able to await us there in relative comfort."

Eku scanned the data in a plasma monocle suddenly thrown out by his smaller circlet. "Thank you. Your ship: it is not shift capable."

"No." Hsontlosh's mouth twisted slightly. "It appears I am far richer in reputation than I am in resources. If we must travel beyond this system, we will either charter a berth on a liner or await Alnduul's return."

"Understood. I must apprise you of the precautions that have been arranged for Mr. Riordan's entry into Virtua."

Hsontlosh's eyes cycled twice, rapidly. "At the node-mistress's urging?"

Eku shook his head. "No. From my familiarity with humans who have spent extended periods of time in Virtua."

Riordan wondered just how extended those—and his—might ultimately be.

Hsontlosh's lids remained wide open. "This node-mistress does not typically accept requests or advice."

"True, but I conveyed Alnduul's absolute resolve that special provisions be made for extended immersion. These include automated muscle stimulation, nutrition, hydration, and waste removal, as well as other supportive therapies. In addition, the node-mistress has agreed to respond to in-sim user signals."

As if anticipating Caine's puzzled frown, Eku turned to face him. "Because time passes ten times as fast within Virtua, you will be able to signal your need for two or more days of uninterrupted sleep. It is the recommended minimum for every seven in-simulation days."

Riordan nodded. "Because even if my brain can keep up with events at ten times normal speed, my brain can't *sleep* ten times as quickly."

"Correct. By sleeping through two consecutive simulation days, you will have approximately five hours of uninterrupted sleep here in the real world. You must also remain mindful of the correlation between long stays in Virtua and negative effects."

"What kind of negative effects?"

Eku frowned. "The effects usually diminish with complete rest and the passage of time, but postimmersive pathologies include disjointed thought and rapid behavioral swings. Mania has been reported. And while the length of recuperation can be reduced by postimmersion therapies, it cannot be eliminated."

Great. Riordan nodded. "Thank you for the warnings, Eku."

"You are welcome. I shall be present when you exit Virtua. Farewell." Eku bowed to both of them, retraced his steps briskly. Riordan followed Hsontlosh in the opposite direction.

As soon as they were out of earshot, Caine asked, "Why was Eku surprised when you greeted him?"

Hsontlosh's gills rippled. "He was surprised that I used the greeting customary among so-called 'core' Dornaani. Most lojis utterly reject the core's cultural forms." He paused. "Of course, most lojis utterly reject factotums."

"Why?"

"There are many reasons, but the most galling is that the Collective takes better care of factotums than it does of loji. To fashion an analog from your planet's past, it is analogous to the resentment that neglected and overworked slaves must have felt toward their masters' pampered dogs." Seeing Riordan's reaction, Hsontlosh expanded. "These are the harsh realities of our species, Mr. Riordan. There are many inequities and ancient, unthinking grudges. The loji attitude toward the factotums is one such: nothing more than inherited bigotry that has long outlived the conditions that engendered it."

Riordan nodded as he followed Hsontlosh along a narrow passage between tightly clustered domes. "The Collective itself no longer seems receptive to factotums."

"That drastically understates the situation, Mister Riordan. Factotums used to have communities on several worlds, but are now constrained to one. Furthermore, it has been centuries since they have operated in truly challenging or unpredictable environments. As a result, they have become less decisive, bold, independent. They no longer excite hatred so much as scorn among lojis. The Collective's attitude is different but no better. Most wish to quarantine the factotums' last world and then seed it with sterilization agents. A few advocate immediate euthanization. We are here."

Hsontlosh tapped a featureless plate set in the side of a small, dust-covered dome. An iris valve opened swiftly, its scalloped plates so fine that it appeared to be a magically expanding hole. *Just like the portal in the monument on Aozhoodn.*

Entering, they found themselves in a lightless room. A voice spoke through their control circlets: "Be seated." Riordan began feeling about, was on the verge of objecting that they couldn't see or feel any seats when the same voice ordered, "The floor will suffice. Sit. Now."

Riordan lowered himself, back against the wall. As soon as he was still, both the wall and floor clutched at his duty suit like a combination of fine-spined burrs and glue. He turned in Hsontlosh's direction. "What is—?"

The room abruptly accelerated down and sideways. Heavy

gee-forces pushed at Caine, but the smart surfaces in contact with his clothes kept him pinned in place.

The acceleration continued to build. They twice changed direction sharply, without any perceptible pause. From the dark beside Riordan, Hsontlosh muttered, "I assure you: this is not how one usually enters a Virtua node."

"If it were, no one would use them," Caine grunted as the room pulled what felt like a hairpin turn. Eku's warning about the mistress of the local node came back to him: a powerbroker always trying to get more leverage. Which evidently included tactics as primitive as shaking up her visitors before dickering with them.

The room finally settled into a slowing, diagonal descent. Riordan controlled his breathing. Even if he left the room disheveled, he wasn't going to give the node-mistress the satisfaction of seeing him dizzy.

The room settled and the far wall opened. A brace of shining drones, hovering on thrusters, were waiting in a bright room. The walls and floor released his clothing, and the same voice from his circlet. "Arise and exit. My drones will guide you." As Riordan and Hsontlosh complied, the floating robots parted and then reformed around them in a diamond pattern.

The right-angled rooms through which they moved were far more reminiscent of a research station or military base than a home. They passed storage bins; racks of waiting or recharging robots of various sizes and shapes; data centers where holographic solids representing information streams whirled, pulsed, fused, separated.

After several hundred meters, they were led down a side corridor into a typically Dornaani room: egg-shaped, indirectly lit, white. And empty, until a female Dornaani stepped straight out of the far wall.

Riordan started at her sudden appearance, was immediately annoyed at himself. It was just another cheap holographic parlor trick. On the other hand, it was hard not to assume that what appeared to be a wall was, in fact, a wall.

The node-mistress was adorned with control devices: a double circlet, vantbrasses, even glowing rings. She waved at the floor before her. It rose up, reshaped itself into a large Dornaani chair. Another wave and, just beyond it, a wide but low cocoon emerged.

She settled into the chair and her mouth twisted slightly. "Loji, you have finished your errand. Go."

Hsontlosh lowered his eyes as he spoke. "I have been asked to stay with this human, whom I have the honor of introducing to you as—"

"I know the human's name, and I know yours, Hsontlosh of Ullshyand's Fourth Ring. I also know your reputation for obsequious politesse and spineless catering to every opinion that is at odds with your own. Assuming you have any. You are of no interest to me and you are not welcome here. Leave. I will not speak with Caine Riordan nor oversee his immersion into Virtua until you are gone."

Hsontlosh's tattoos had darkened profoundly. He glanced at Riordan. "I am duty-bound to stay with you, but..."

Riordan nodded, imagined Elena's sleeping face, somewhere in the vast complex around them. "If you don't go, I can't accomplish what I came for."

"A human more perspicacious than a loji," the node mistress observed. "Already, this promises to be memorable entertainment." Her mouth twisted as Hsontlosh turned, face pale, tattoos almost black, and exited. Two of the robots followed him.

Riordan nodded at the Dornaani. "Since you already know who I am, and why I am here..."

"You wish to learn something of me. But that is neither necessary nor desirable. It is enough that I consented to receive you. You may call me by a name from one of your own languages: Kutkh."

Riordan hoped that one day he'd find it easier to control his temper when confronted with Dornaani disdain. "Then I shall be blunt. You wouldn't have allowed me to come here unless you wanted something. What is it?"

"A question worthy of an answer," pronounced Kutkh. "I want you to try to kill me."

Riordan had several simultaneous reactions: that he could not have heard correctly; that Kutkh couldn't be serious; that he wished he was armed; and that the two floating robots suddenly looked extremely dangerous. But all he said was, "Please repeat that."

"I see your perspicacity has profound limits, human. To clarify, you will attempt to kill me while we are both in Virtua."

Which is still damned risky. For both of us, exit codes not-withstanding. "But why would you wish to—?"

"I seek insights. You need know nothing more. Do you accept?"

But if she controls the model . . . "I assume you can't keep track of my actions if you're in Virtua, also. Otherwise, there would be no point to this exercise."

"Perhaps your perspicacity is not so stunted after all. While immersed in the model, my perception and knowledge are limited to that of the persona I have adopted."

"But if my attack takes you by surprise, if you don't have time to use your exit code—"

"Human, I cannot discern if you are indirectly attempting to gather additional information or express a quaint but ludicrous concern for my well-being. Either way, your inquiry is unnecessary and unwanted. Perhaps it would be wiser to worry about your own safety, instead."

"You're not going to provide me with an exit code?"

Kutkh's mouth twisted slightly; it was a malicious, not amused, smile. "You shall have an exit code. But if you use it, your quest is over. Permanently."

Jesus Christ, Kutkh is making this a game? *For Elena's life?* Before Riordan could stop himself, the words blurted out, "So this is just another stupid test."

The twist of Kutkh's mouth became more pronounced. "As is everything."

"That stupendously specious evasion still doesn't explain or justify threatening my life—and ultimately, my mate's—just to gain a few new 'insights.'"

Kutkh's eyes opened slightly wider. "You may prove a worthy opponent, after all. However, debate and discussion are pointless. I have something you need. You are either willing to pay my price, or you are not.

"I shall explicate the dangers once, human. Virtual trauma can trigger a fatal seizure or arrest. But it is far more likely to cause memory loss. The same is true if your stay in Virtua exceeds one real-time month. The longer the immersion, the more extensive the loss and the more likely it will affect long-term memories." Kutkh gestured toward the cocoon bed. "Do you have further questions?"

Riordan thought. "I need to know your identity in the simulation."

"When you awake, your pants pocket will contain a note revealing my persona."

Riordan nodded, laid down on the platform. The surface on either side of his head rose toward his temples.

"Are you sure you haven't forgotten anything, human?" Kutkh's voice was a broad taunt.

"Such as?"

"Your own exit code."

Riordan paused. What if he used it by reflex, before he could stop himself? "No. Don't need it. Let's go."

The last thing Caine heard was the burbled huffing of Dornaani laughter.

Chapter Fifty

JULY 2124
LELTLOSU-SHAI (VIRTUA), BD+75 403A

Riordan awoke to the sound of feet thumping overhead.

He opened his eyes to a wood plank ceiling. Sitting up, he swayed, momentarily unsteady. A side effect of immersion into Virtua, maybe?

But no, the swaying was not in his head but in his surroundings. Which, given the brackish sulfur stink, meant he was on a boat. Then other sensory impressions arrived in one great rush.

Small compartment, below decks. A narrow passageway to his right, flanked by two fuel bunkers of charred briquets the size of his fist. An odor of burned wood coming from a large companionway to his left. Faint shouting. A distant gong. Intermittent gunshots—hoarse blasts, not the sharp reports of modern firearms.

Riordan rose, headed left toward the sound and the smell of smoke, felt something on his head. He swept off a brimmed cap, tucked it in his back pocket, noticed the coarseness of his pants the same moment he felt his calves start to itch. Woolens. A sturdy vest, practical coat, and worn linen shirt completed his attire. He checked his pants pockets. His probing fingertips grazed a folded piece of paper. Kutkh's message . . .

A scream from beyond the companionway, followed by the shrill, truculent voice of a young girl. Regretting the dull clomping of his worn brogans, Riordan climbed up into the light.

The top of the companionway was framed by boat hooks racked to either side and led out to an afterdeck four meters across. Pushed back against the stern was a cluster of shoddily clothed people, crouching away from two menacing men. Both were dressed in rough but newer clothes, and kept the group corralled against the transom, their swords—*swords?*—raised. But not against the crowd. Their intended target was a young girl who was scrambling out of a toppled barrel, midway between the swordsmen and those cowering before them. However, instead of dodging away, her eyes widened as, between the legs of the men threatening her, she saw Caine emerging from the hold.

Time slowed long enough for Riordan to see how the next few seconds would unfold. In a moment, the people behind the girl would also see him. A sliver of a second after that, the two sword-bearing bravos would notice that too many pairs of eyes were now focused behind them, and they'd turn. From that point, it was a toss-up whether they'd bother to demand that Caine surrender, or simply skewer him on the spot. But if by some miracle they didn't notice him, they certainly meant to cut down the girl.

So Riordan seized the only advantage fate had given him: surprise.

Caine grabbed one of the boat hooks, and with a long leap, brought it down into a two-handed thrust. It punched against the spine of the closer swordsman. He sprawled forward. Directly into the desperate crowd.

Without stopping to reassess, Riordan leaped back as hard as he had jumped forward. A thin, fast current of air cooled the tip of his nose as the second swordsman's blade swept past. Riordan shifted his grip on the boat hook, holding it like a staff as he circled away. The bravo followed cautiously, sizing up the unexpected enemy.

But only for a moment. The large man leaped forward with a yell, sword coming over his shoulder.

There was no time or space to do anything but block. Riordan, hands wide upon the boat hook, realized he couldn't trust the wood to stop the blow, Caine twisted the pole to the right as he stepped out to the left.

The sword sliced into the shaft at an angle, splitting it along the grain. But Caine's twisting parry diverted the force so that the edge of the cutlass jammed between the splintered halves of the handle. The rapid change in momentum tore the weapons out of their wielders' hand, sent them clattering down the companionway.

Again, the men circled each other warily. Riordan kept his face expressionless, assessing. *He's bigger and more experienced. I'm* probably *smarter and better trained. So...*

Riordan sidestepped away, right foot cheating back slightly.

The bravo interpreted the move as indecision. Right fist cocking back like a meaty hammer, he charged and let fly a roundhouse punch.

Riordan leaned forward as he slammed an outside block sideways against the inrushing forearm, felt bone bruising bone. Only partially deflected, the blow tore skin off Caine's left ear as he countered with a right punch of his own. His opponent raised his right hand to block...

Caine checked his punch, rocked back on his right heel, brought up his left leg and kicked forward into the man's right knee.

Caine did not hear the sharp, decisive snap he had hoped for, but the effect was similar. His opponent fell with a groan, sweeping a broad paw at Riordan as he dodged past, grabbed the second boat hook, spun back around...and stopped. And smiled.

Unable to stand, the bravo stopped cursing long enough to see that Caine was not smiling at him, but at something over his shoulder. He turned. The crowd at the stern was inching forward, a heavily built woman holding the bloodied sword of his fallen friend.

Caine leaped in, swinging the boat hook in a wide, smooth arc. Years of baseball made it second nature to power the bat all the way through the ball. Or in this case, the head. The force of the blow splintered the wood against his opponent's temple. He fell forward like a sack of potatoes.

Holding the shattered handle in his right hand, Riordan raised the other in both greeting and caution...and realized with a start that the crowd at the stern was speaking English. But in an accent and idiom that was almost indecipherable:

"Step to that painter and cast off! We'd best give it the buttock downriver while we can."

"Hang on, these two aren't flannel-jackets. They're naught but common carvers. Crew could still be aboard, hey?"

"Yeh, an' 'oo's the well-fed bloke in the brogans?"

"Never mind that. Gwynnie: use that great chiv! Snuff that red-eyed bastard's candle, just like t'other!"

Riordan dropped the remains of the boat hook to raise both hands: an appeal to pause, to stay the blow. But, in that critical moment, when calming words should have been coming out of his mouth, Caine glimpsed what lay beyond the stern... and was struck dumb.

Beyond large docks and ramshackle wharfs, a great dome rose above a disorderly stew of buildings, few of which reached as high as three stories. Which was why the unmistakable edifice that was St. Paul's Cathedral loomed even more majestic here than it did in modern day London. In the near distance, the Southwark and Blackfriars bridges drew his eye up the Thames, to where its southward bend obscured Westminster Palace. From that same direction, a boat chugged toward them, white smoke belching out of its funnel. Although it was still too far off to make out many details, the figures clustered at the bow were carrying what appeared to be long, thin, sticks: shoulder arms of some type.

A nearby blur of motion and a meaty thump pulled Caine's attention back to the afterdeck. The woman with the sword was straightening up from the inert thug. There was a smile on her face and fresh blood on the blade.

"No!" Caine shouted, realizing that his long second of amazement had been the last second to save the man. "You didn't need to—"

Just as the woman's expression of puzzlement began to become irritation, her eyes snapped away from Riordan's, looked past his shoulder...

A roar deafened his right ear the same instant an ugly red crater appeared just below the woman's collarbone. She slumped sideways, sword falling from nerveless fingers.

Riordan instinctively spun away from the blast, glimpsed a cluster of short barrels just before they swung into his cheek like a hammer.

The blow muddled what was left of Caine's hearing, left behind a muffled roar. He was falling but couldn't stop it. His skull was heavy with pain, seemed separate from his body. He didn't feel himself hit the deck, was unaware of the position of his arms and legs—

Then, the sense of being in his own body was back. He was

slumped sideways on the deck, his left cheekbone a blinding ache. A large man stepped past him, working the heavy cylinder of a pepperbox revolver. He wore a black armband, had a long scabbarded dagger on his belt. The crowd retreated from him until their rumps pressed against the boat's transom.

"Anyone else want a go?" he shouted. "No?" He cocked the pistol's hammer. "I've as many barrels as you 'ave bodies. I figure 'at's fair odds for traitors what will slice open the 'eads of senseless men." He gestured at the two dead bravos, then returned his attention to the crowd. They leaned away as the weapon's six muzzles swept across them, the little girl with her hands in her pockets.

The man stepped toward her. "An' what about you, y' little mudlark? Somethin' t' hide? Let's see your dabbles, then." When she shook her head and pushed her hands deeper into her frayed pockets, he grabbed her elbow roughly, hauled savagely at it. She screamed.

Caine tried to raise up on one elbow; the world tilted sharply. His face smacked down on the deck again. A lightning bolt of agony shot from his left cheekbone to his left temple, then arced across to the right. He thought he might vomit.

The man's strength finally prevailed; the girl's hand popped out of her pocket. The narrow, balled fingers were stained gray, cuticles and nailbeds almost black. The ogreish man grinned horribly, pistol coming up. "Not a mudlark, but a cinderscamp! Filchin' coal from the king 'Imself!"

She yanked her hand away. "Can't steal from a man 'oos already been robbed of ever'thing!"

He grabbed her by the shoulder. "Shut yer sauce hole! I've a mind to—"

She swung at him. He saw it coming, grabbed her fist as it flashed toward him. "Eh, but ye're a bricky one, ahn'tcha?" Now holding her wrist, he pulled upward. Her feet left the deck. She screamed, this time in agony.

Riordan rolled on his back. "Let her go."

The man looked around. "Wot? You still breathin'? I can fix that."

Seeing that the man had momentarily forgotten the girl, Riordan did his best to spit. "I'll bet you can."

Suddenly florid, the patch-haired ogre took a step toward

Caine, then halted. The color bled back out of his jowls. He smiled. "Nice try, climber. Keep yer place and you might even dodge the noose. But this little cinderscamp, she'll be learning 'er lessons at the end of a rope."

The dangling girl shrilled at him. "Lessons? From *you*? Ye've bollocks for brains, y' pillock!"

"Oh, but I've wits enough to understand the new catechism." He laid the barrels of the pepperbox against her forehead with a gentleness and a grin that made Caine shiver. "No good tryin' to fill yer pockets with a little coal...because Coal has already pocketed every little thing. Including you."

She spat at him. "Piss off!"

The man rubbed away the slimy gobbet that had landed in his left eye, using the back of his pistol hand. "Right, then. Time to shorten the gallows' queue." He hauled her up higher, until her head was level with his own.

Caine pushed himself up through vertigo and nausea, swaying on his elbows. "Bastard! Coward!"

The big man sighed, shook his head, dropped the girl. She fell flailing to the deck as he turned toward Riordan. "Now, see: I try to be a reasonable man. To scare rather than kill. But there's them as just won't let that be. Like you, f'rinstance." He paced toward Caine. "An enemy of the state."

"And how did I harm the state?"

The ogre grinned. "Why, by rubbin' me fur the wrong way, ye sorry bastard." He raised the pistol.

And in that instant, Riordan realized what he'd *actually* done. He'd saved a girl that didn't exist, had brought on a virtual death that might actually kill him, and had ruined his chances of saving Elena. All because Virtua felt so utterly real that he'd become lost in it, had believed what his senses told him...

His self-recriminations were obliterated by the sound of the expected gunshot. But at the very moment he expected the scene would fade to gray, the pistol-wielding brute fell his length on the deck, the left side of his head a ruin of bone and blood.

"Becca!" a new voice shouted from above and behind.

"Uncle Pip!" the girl shrieked back.

Riordan turned his head carefully.

A rangy man hopped down from a scaffolded stone piling alongside which the boat was moored. He landed on the small top-deck behind the smokestack, raced toward the stern. Caine didn't know what surprised him more, his unlooked-for rescue, or that he had never noticed that the boat was mostly sheltered under of the arches of a long, low bridge.

The man slid down the ladder to the afterdeck, one hand on the railing, the other holding what looked like a short musket. Becca ran to him, the rest of the crowd coming away from the taffrail far enough to bend over the sword-wielding woman whom the ogre had shot.

Niece on his hip, "Uncle Pip" crossed to Riordan. "I'm in your debt, sir." He extended his hand, the angle of which suggested it was both a gesture of introduction and a practical offer of help up from the deck. Riordan took it, accomplishing both. The man smiled. "I'm Steven Robinson. Pip, to my friends." He waited. "And you'd be called—?"

"I'm Cai—"

Riordan caught himself in the middle of his reflexive reply. *Careful! Keep your distance. Keep reminding yourself this isn't real. Don't even use your own name. Use your grandfather's.*

"Cei. I'm Cei."

"That's it?"

"Just Cei."

Becca looked up at him, pushing a strand of red-gold hair out of her eyes. "That's a funny name. Is it like chi, the Greek letter?"

The unexpected question prompted Riordan to raise an eyebrow; the resulting tug at his lacerated cheekbone made him wish he hadn't. "No. It's C-e-i."

She frowned. "Well, that's not right. That's a Welsh name, usually. And 'Kay' is how it's said." She considered Riordan thoughtfully. "Then again, you're no Welshman. You're a climber, right?"

Riordan frowned. "A 'climber'?"

That drew stares, even from the group around the dead woman.

"You know," Becca urged, "an American."

"My parents were from there," Riordan answered truthfully. "Where did you learn about Greek letters, Becca?"

She smiled up at Pip. "M'uncle. Back before he had to leave." She hugged Robinson. "But now he's back, and he'll show those Blackhands a thing or—"

Robinson, moving again, shook his head. "I'm not here to stay. I'm here to get you. Just heard about your mum a few weeks ago."

He kissed her sadly on the head, then leaned into the compartment where Caine had first awakened. "There's enough wood to get down the Thames, but I'll wager there's no starter coal on board. Here now, Mr. Cei, are you handy with a steam engine? Or a gun?"

"More the latter than the former."

Robinson stared at his reply. "You've been to university, have you?"

Caine shrugged off the question. "What kind of gun?" He glanced at Pip's musket, which had a handle protruding from the left side of the action.

Pip saw the look, shook his head. "No, not this. We'll need something heavier to keep them at a distance." He nodded toward the boat closing in from upriver.

Riordan shrugged, discovered that the field of vision in his left eye was shrinking as his cheek continued to swell. "What do you have in mind?"

"A customs cutter like this one should have an old Puckle gun on board. A fine fit for our purposes."

"What's a Puckle gun?"

Another stare from Robinson. "Are you quite all right, Mr. Cei?"

"I'm fine. Show me the gun."

"In a moment. Becca, I don't know why all those people thought it was a good idea to jump down to this boat."

"Better'n being shot in the street by the Blackhands!"

"Well, yes, I suppose so. Here's their choice: they climb back up the scaffolding and make for the bank quickly, or sail with us right now. I'll let them off downstream, as soon as we've given the blaggarts the slip."

"Right you are, Uncle Pip!"

"Good girl. But Becca, be sure they understand: anyone who gets off must *run* to the bank. No shilly-shallying on the bridge." Becca saluted and ran to the others.

Riordan looked up at the bridge as he followed Robinson forward. "Why do they need to get off the bridge?"

"Mr. Cei, do you remember the ditty, 'London Bridge is Falling Down'?"

Riordan looked back at the low stone arches again, recognized the outline, and nodded. "I understand. Charges hidden in the scaffolding?"

Pip nodded.

But Caine, following him along the portside gunwale to the pilot house, kept staring at the mighty pilings beneath the bridge. Although not a demolitions expert, even he knew that it would take dozens of barrels of black power to bring down a stone bridge, particularly without any way to direct the blast upward into the structure. *But, if the year here is slightly more advanced than it looks...* "Nitroglycerine?"

Robinson stopped, looked at him with a smile. "We, Mr. Cei, are going to get along famously, I wager. Now, duck in the storeroom back of the pilot's station. There's the Puckle gun. We'll need it up on the top deck. I'll help you get it up the ladder."

Chapter Fifty-One

Once it was set up, Riordan remembered reading about the Puckle gun. Essentially a tripod-mounted small bore cannon that operated like a revolver, it had been created in the early eighteenth century, saw little use, and even less adoption. However, in this version of Earth, it had apparently been adopted and improved. Its original flintlock action had since been refitted to use far more reliable percussion caps. With a bore of just over three centimeters, this model's ten round drums were thicker and heavier, mostly because each chamber held more powder, thereby increasing range and lethality.

After Riordan fixed the weapon's tripod in place, he quickly checked the reloading mechanism. A breech handle unlocked a hinged rear plate, allowing the gunner to demount the spent cylinder and mount the next one.

Below him, through an open panel in the roof of the pilot house, he could hear Robinson calling instructions back to the escapees now working as the stokers and tenders of the customs cutter's boiler. As they pulled slowly away from the foot of London Bridge's midriver piling, Pip's makeshift crew proved to be highly motivated. They had been involved in that morning's coal riot, and none of them were first time offenders. For many, the gallows were a distinct possibility. However, their natural inclination—to heave as much wood into the burner as fast as they could—had to be restrained. The cutter could not afford to run out of fuel until they were quit of London and well beyond any downriver towns that riders could alert in a timely fashion. Which meant that the following boat, its boiler already hot with a full head of steam, would catch them before they could match its speed. Unless, that is, Caine could dissuade them.

He examined the Puckle's sights: conventional v-notch and post. No tangent for estimating the drop of a projectile over range, but there was a series of four even marks on the sights and four corresponding notches for raising the barrel. "Pip, what's the range interval on the elevation marks?"

There was a silence before Robinson shouted up his reply. "Base setting is for one hundred yards. Each notch adds another hundred. But the last one is bollocks."

"So beyond four hundred yards or so, it shoots like a rainbow."

"Yes. You've done this before, haven't you?"

"Not exactly, but I'm familiar with the principles." Riordan glanced at the pursuing boat. Although angling toward them, it was devoting most of its speed to drawing abreast. Probably to give its musketeers a broader and easier target. "Are you planning to run straight or add some evasive maneuvers?"

"Bloody hell, Mr. Cei. You sound like an officer. We've no time to do anything but run."

"If you change your mind, let me know how and when you're going to zig or zag. I don't want to waste ammunition."

"Right-o. Might want to stand-to, now. They're nearing four hundred yards."

"I'm letting them come to three hundred before I even try a ranging shot."

Another pause. "That's a bit close, don't you think?"

"Not with a gun like this. If we shoot early and miss by too wide a margin, they could become more confident and come on harder. But if our first shot is close, and by the third, we're hitting their hull, they're more likely to back off."

Pip's laugh was a rich baritone. "Well, I'll leave off giving advice to the chief gunner!" He raised his voice for everyone to hear. "Stay out of sight. Under the gunwales, if you can. Stray shots will go through the sides of the pilot- and engine-houses."

Leaving the Puckle concealed under a tarp, Riordan crouched low behind the upper deck's weather siding. He studied the oncoming boat through the gaps between its waist-high sections. "Pip, if that ship is like ours, where's its Puckle gun?"

"That's a new cutter. Smaller and faster, but not enough room for any deck guns. I wouldn't want to bet the same about the two just joining the chase back near Blackfriars."

"Nor I," Riordan agreed. Their immediate pursuer had closed the range to three hundred and fifty yards.

Apparently Caine was not the only one gauging the distance. Two narrow, horizontal plumes of smoke jetted over the enemy's gunwale, trailed by the barks of twin musket discharges. One ball raised a divot of water almost fifty meters off the starboard quarter. There was no sign of the other.

Staying beneath the rim of the weather siding, Riordan crept back to the Puckle, worked his way under the tarp, lifted it an inch off the barrel. Azimuth was not hard to fix and hold. Although the enemy boat was going faster, it wasn't changing relative position that quickly, and the Puckle's free traverse enabled minute adjustments.

However, the same was not true of the elevation. If Pip was right about the unreliability of the range marks, there was a good chance that the gun would undershoot even at the three-hundred-yard setting. Time to find out if it did.

Riordan eased the Puckle's hammer back to full cock, rotated the cylinder clockwise until the first chamber's percussion cap clicked into place. Sighting along the barrel, Caine cheated the aimpoint just forward of the enemy cutter's midship line, slid the tarp off, leaned away, and squeezed the trigger.

The Puckle's report was not as loud as Caine had expected; it was merely an amplified musket. The recoil, however, was enough to make him glad that he'd secured each leg of its tripod to the topdeck. A small geyser marked where the round hit: fifteen yards short of the enemy's hull. Ducking down, Riordan spun the breech handle, rotated the cylinder until chamber two locked into place, refastened the handle, laid flat, and waited.

Two seconds later, the crackle of distant musketry reached his ears but no sound of balls hitting the cutter. Not surprising. Firing a long arm from a moving boat, even using a braced rest, was difficult. And he could also count on reloading taking more time than usual. Unless... "Pip, that rifle of yours, is it a muzzleloader?"

Pip's first reply was a startled laugh. "Shite and eggs, Cei, are Americans really raised in caves? Cor, I haven't seen a military muzzleloader since I was a lad. We're just lucky this lot are still armed with muskets."

Wait, a musket that's not *a muzzleloader?* "So, you use, er, breech-loading muskets?"

A long pause. "If we get out of this, Cei, I'm bringing you round to a doctor, find out if that pistol whip cracked your brain pan. The London Irregulars use Lorenzonis. Us, too. Ball and powder for eight shots in closed ports behind the breech. Surely you've at least *seen* one."

Lorenzoni. A vaguely familiar name from firearm history. A Florentine gunsmith. "How many shots a minute, Pip?"

"Out here? Maybe four. Besides, most London Irregulars are just hoodlums with guns. Never trained a day in their life."

Riordan crept back alongside the Puckle, cocked the hammer, and nudged the azimuth. Probably about two hundred sixty yards, now. The rate of closure was decreasing as their own cutter's speed increased. Leaving the elevation at the three-hundred-yard mark, he pulled the trigger.

The Puckle barked, flinching against its deck moorings. A white spout appeared ten yards beyond the enemy boat. Caine frowned. *So, if the three-hundred-yard mark shoots to about two seventy, the two-hundred-yard mark will probably shoot to about one hundred ninety.* He turned the cylinder to the third round and cocked the hammer.

As he finished, enemy musket fire sputtered in reply to his last shot. One ball clawed a few splinters out of the starboard gunwale. As Riordan waited for the range to close, he checked the percussion caps on the four spare cylinders: firmly seated, no sign of moisture. He leaned toward the opening that communicated with the pilot-house. "Pip, how long does it take to fully reload one of those Lorenzonis?"

"Moving on the water and with spray flying, it could take a minute, maybe longer." He glanced toward the enemy boat. "They'll be given the order to fire at will quite soon, now."

"I'm counting on it." *Hell, I'm going to provoke it.* Riordan crept back to the Puckle, dropped the elevation to two hundred yards, and raised his head to sight along the barrel. He shifted its aimpoint to the enemy's bow and squeezed the trigger.

A white jet appeared a few yards beyond and in front of the cutter's prow.

A wave of musket fire answered as Riordan ducked down. He heard a few faint zipping sounds, well overhead. The Irregulars were overcompensating, aiming too high.

Caine reloaded hastily, jumped up, made a small adjustment, cheated the aimpoint a little further back along the bow, squeezed the trigger.

A puff of dust and paint blossomed out from the enemy's forward gunwale. Spalling wood and splinters erupted inboard where the round exited on the other side. Riordan reloaded quickly, staying low. Now that he had the range, he had to lay down fire as quickly as he could.

A second, more ragged wave of musketry swept the cutter, balls spatting the length of its gunwale. A few hit the pilot house and smokestack. One punched through the weather siding a yard away from Riordan as he checked his aim and fired again.

And missed. The round passed over the foredeck, clipping the far gunwale.

Riordan hated wasting the time it took to reload from a crouched position, but now that the enemy was closer, he couldn't allow them to draw a steady bead on him. He rose just high enough to sight down the barrel, musket balls whining overhead, a few plunking into the hull and pilot house.

Pip's shout was incongruously calm. "Mr. Cei, if you please..."

"Working on it," Caine muttered, fired the gun, unlocked the cylinder...

...and saw his round hit the enemy's pilot house. There was no way to tell if it had inflicted any casualties, but the pursuers' reactions became excited, urgent. And most important, distracted.

At last.

Riordan stood so that he could reload and fire as quickly as possible. One of the next two rounds hit, just above the waterline. He leaned on the barrel for the next several shots, three of which hit just at or below that mark.

More excitement on the enemy ship. A mad flurry of poorly aimed return fire, and then the bow of the pursuer started swinging away. But even though they were trying to open the range, the inertia of the Irregulars' ship would keep them in Riordan's firing envelope about a minute longer.

Riordan did not rotate the cylinder this time. Instead, he yanked it off the mount, slapped a fresh one into place, and began firing.

Sometime between the third and fourth round from that new, ten round cylinder, the pursuing boat pulled hard to starboard, opening the range even faster. Caine maintained his rate of fire, but paid the predictable cost in reduced accuracy. Several rounds plunked harmlessly in the water, as far as five yards from the enemy hull. But the reward was three more hits at or just beneath the waterline. And it was now clear that at least a few casualties had been inflicted and that the Irregulars were shaken. They were no longer reloading quickly nor coordinating their fire.

"Rum show, Mr. Cei!" Pip called up. Becca's addition was a cheer, soon taken up by the engine-tenders.

"Not done yet," Riordan shouted down as he tossed aside the third cylinder and started mounting the fourth.

"But they're running!" Becca objected.

Pip's reply proved he was no stranger to military engagements. "Running does not mean they won't eventually come about and dog us at a safe distance. Until we know they *can't* chase us, we've not made good our escape."

Riordan resumed firing at the receding boat as rapidly as he could. He might have scored another two or three hits, but he hardly cared once he saw the distinctive motion of men bailing water.

He was mounting the last cylinder as a precaution when Pip emerged from the wheelhouse, carrying a tightly wrapped package under his arm. Riordan glanced warily back along the port quarter. Behind them, the Tower of London was still in range. If the garrison had Puckle guns or heavier pieces—

Pip grinned up at Caine. "There's nothing coming from there, Mr. Cei. We took care to ruin their powder this morning. Inside job, as it were." He undid the bindings on the package. The wrapping fell away, revealing a pair of signal rockets.

Riordan nodded. "I think I know why you're not worried about the other two boats catching up to us."

Pip grinned. "I *knew* you'd done this before, Mr. Cei." He clamped a sleeved bracket to the cutter's short foremast, fitted a rocket's launching stick into the sleeve. A quick strike of a friction match lit the fuse. Robinson strode back to the cover of the pilot house, where Becca had been keeping a steady hand on the wheel.

The tail of the rocket flared. It leaped away as if scalded. In a moment, it had hissed high overhead and burst—a faint pink color.

Pip appeared on the afterdeck with Becca and two others, watching as the bridges of the Thames shrank into the distance. Riordan looked back along the same vector, wondered what year it was in this strange version of Earth, remembered he probably had an answer in his pocket. He fished out the note from Kutkh and read:

> *Welcome to London, 1869 AD, twenty-two years after the conclusion of the Great Coal War. You have been inserted into a place where you have a more than "sporting chance," to borrow the local idiom.*
>
> *My persona is Lord David Lawrence Weiner the Third, Earl of Greater Connecticut. You will have no problem gathering information about me. The accuracy of that information is another matter entirely.*
>
> *Kutkh*

Caine crumpled the note and tossed it into the wind, which carried it over the transom. With the crisis passed and the adrenaline fading, he became aware of the throbbing ache that was the left side of his face. Riordan sat heavily on the roof of the pilot's house, looked up at the gray sky, closed his eyes...

And realized that, until he read Kutkh's note, he had once again been halfway to forgetting that this world—all the people, pain, and death—were just an illusion.

Far behind the boat, a wide jet of smoke shot up from London Bridge, followed almost instantly by a long rumble that growled toward them over the wavelets. Chunks of stone and the skeletal remains of scaffolding flew up out of the cloudy chaos. As Riordan watched the fragments soar higher, a widening froth ran outward, the shock waves and small debris pummeling and churning the Thames into what looked like wild, flat rapids.

Those troubled waters seemed to resonate with what Riordan sensed of this world: that it was even more grim, more brutal than Earth's actual nineteenth century. But regardless, this was home now, at least for a while. *Maybe a long while,* Caine reflected. *So*

I'd better get used to it, at least until I kill one of this imaginary planet's most powerful imaginary men.

Caine frowned. Imaginary world or not, being an assassin was a damn lousy business. Unfortunately, he couldn't just accept that role; he had to excel at it. Or he would never see Elena again.

Riordan sighed, recalled a resigned lament muttered by the Brits among the Lost Soldiers, and now a favorite expression of their present day commander, Bannor Rulaine:

In for a penny, in for a pound.

Chapter Fifty-Two

JUNE 2124
DUSTBELT, ZETA TUCANAE

Bannor Rulaine stared out the pitted window at the equatorial dustbowl that was the least attractive, and thus safest, region of Zeta Tucanae Three. There was nothing to see except swirling curtains of grit and sand. As usual.

He glanced at his wristlink, instead. It was the same one he'd worn four years ago, back when he and the others who now called themselves the Crewe had started traveling with Caine Riordan. Back when they had left Earth to take the fight to the Arat Kur homeworld. *And back then, who could have guessed that would be the* simple *part of this job?*

The entry chime brought Bannor's awareness abruptly back to the wristlink that was still staring up at him: 1356 hours local. *She's four minutes early*, Rulaine thought. *The military version of right on time.* He stood. "Come in."

The prefab panel slid aside revealing a person he'd never met in person but about whom he'd come to know quite a lot over the past week: Ayana Tagawa. She stopped in the doorway, eyes widening slightly when she discovered her new CO already standing. She came to attention. "Colonel Rulaine!"

Bannor waved away the formality. "Captain, in this outfit, we're pretty relaxed about titles and rank unless there are bullets or bombs inbound. Normally, I'd just sit you down for an introductory chat, but we're already late for a meeting. Come with me." He led her out the still-open door.

A short corridor brought them into the cavernous warehouse where Bannor and his team had managed to spend two years hiding in plain sight. Robots crisscrossed the dirty flooring, piling spoor from a central excavation against the walls before returning for another load.

Tagawa cleared her throat. "Colonel, those piles of soil..."

"Reinforces the walls against the wind." Bannor shrugged. "Not an uncommon precaution here in the equatorial zones. We get some pretty ferocious dust storms. But the real reason for all the dirt up here is because we had to dig down there." He gestured toward the central hole being covered with false flooring. "We've created a sublevel to hide the cold cells of both the Lost Soldiers and the Cold Guard. Stuck *Puller* down there, as well."

Tagawa frowned. "After you finished your subcontracting missions at Epsilon Indi, I know you went entirely off the grid, but—"

"We didn't just go off the grid, Ms. Tagawa. We shut down for six months before any of our cells reactivated. Since then, we've been reconsolidating."

"I'm sorry. I do not know what you mean by that."

Bannor nodded. "After Turkh'saar, the Slaasriithi dropped teams of us in four different places. With over three hundred cold cells, there was no way to store them in one place, not right away. We sent a clandestine survey team out here to find a bankrupt facility in a dismal place." He looked around. "Perfect hideout for us."

"I presume the survey team was led by Captains Wu and Phillips?"

Bannor smiled as they entered the warehouse's transition chamber to the outdoors, sealed the door behind them. "What gave that away?"

"They are well liked yet not exactly well known on the main world. They use all the regional slang, know every local detail."

Bannor nodded. "They ought to." He opened the outer door. They emerged into a twenty-kilometer-per-hour haze of dust-thick wind. "When they got to this system, Zeta Tucanae was the tail end of the Big Green Main. Zeta Tucanae Two—called TouTwo then, Rainbow now—barely had a population of thirty thousand, most on government 'trailblazer' contracts. Now, with nine-point-four shift ranges on most of the ships that come out this far, Rainbow gets about eight thousand new colonists a month." He smiled into the gale-force grit. "So most of the locals consider Peter and Susan to be original settlers.

"Peter stays in the shadows because his personal data is all over the grid and hot as hell. But Susan's last ID dates to 1942, so she doesn't have to keep her head too low."

Bannor led Tagawa toward an unpressurized hab module as they approached the far side of two windswept landing pads. "But Earth bureaucracy will be right behind the new settlers, bringing a brand new postwar database. At that point, having no ID will become just as bad as having the wrong ID."

"So you are on borrowed time."

Bannor nodded as they went through the hab module's outer hatch. Once the vents had sucked away most of the dust, the inner door sighed open. Captain Christopher "Tygg" Robin smiled down at them. "So this is the new talent, boss?"

"Yup. We'll do the introductions later."

"Right." Tygg led them along the module's single, central corridor. "Our visitor is getting antsy. He's concerned about being detected."

Rulaine couldn't help smiling. "As cautious as ever. Is everyone assembled?"

"Everyone on the list, boss."

"Colonel," murmured Tagawa, "Captain Phillips told me I would meet the team's leadership today. Is that—?"

"Change of plans, Tagawa. Susan is satisfied you are who you say you are. Your contact protocols on Rainbow were perfect, no one is tailing you, and we know you don't have an embedded bug."

"How could you know that?"

"Because you were medscoped while you were snoring through your second night in the bag; Peter Wu doctored your tea. So welcome to the team, Tagawa."

"When will my duties begin?"

"Right now. I need your intel-trained eyes and ears at the meeting we're about to walk into at the end of this hall. Because unless I miss my guess, our visitor could be changing our lives here. In a big way."

"And who is our visitor?" she asked.

Bannor opened the door. "Him."

Seated at the far end of a table that was too big for the small room, a Dornaani rose from a makeshift, species-friendly seat.

"Hello, Ms. Tagawa," he said. "I am gratified to meet you. My name is Alnduul."

Ayana Tagawa bowed, sensed the room was crowded, then realized why.

It wasn't because six humans were seated cheek-by-jowl around the table. It was due to the two-meter monster whose bulk took up almost a fifth of the available space: a Hkh'Rkh. Because of his height, he was bending at the waist, as if poised to consume the other occupants in a single gulp.

Ayana realized that her breath had caught in her throat. Annoyed, she exhaled sharply. She had faced death, lived on a razor's edge for over a year among the Ktor, but she had never been in the presence of a true exosapient. And Hkh'Rkh, the most daunting species of all, were particularly imposing in person.

The being's head—if you could call it that—swiveled toward her, completely contiguous with its pony-neck. Black, pupilless eyes poked outward from under the bony protective ridge that was its streamlined skull, the only irregularity in the widening column of muscle that blended into its broad, barrel-shaped torso and spine. Patches of fur ran along the crest of its shoulders and the ridges of its conventionally jointed arms, forming a spiky stripe that narrowed down to nothing as it reached the tip of a tail shaped more like a caiman's than a mammal's.

But the greatest surprise was what emerged from its mouth: a trembling black garter-snake of a tongue, followed by wholly understandable words. "I am pleased to meet you, Ms. Tagawa. I am Yaargraukh. It is good fortune for us all that you passed Captain Phillips' security checks. Your skills and training make you a most valuable addition to our team. I bid you welcome."

Ayana nodded an acknowledgement. "Forgive my initial reaction, Yaargraukh. I did not anticipate meeting a member of your species."

The black tongue swished. Amusement? "I suspected as much." His tongue stilled. "Although that, too, was a test."

Bannor slipped past her, nodding. "The people in this room probably have humanity's most diverse and extensive experience with exosapient species. Although as I understand it, no free human has spent more time with Ktor than you."

One of the humans seated at the table—a youthful man of medium build—nodded at her. "That's why Captain Phillips was so thorough in vetting you. We had to be sure you didn't have a permanent tail." He smiled. "I'm Duncan Solsohn. Glad you're with us."

"As I am honored and grateful to be among you. Had Commodore Riordan not directed me here, I suspect I would be dead by now."

Strangely, her mention of Riordan prompted all eyes to turn toward the Dornaani. Eventually, Duncan, still smiling, said, "Our assessment agrees with yours, Alnduul; neither *Olsloov* nor your shuttle has been spotted. But why did you enter CTR space via Tau Ceti? That system has a lot of traffic."

"As I intimated, Captain Solsohn, time was of the essence and that route was the swiftest. Due to my precarious status as a Custodian, I may soon be unable to protect Caine Riordan."

A women whose lithe fitness recalled Ayana's own, threw up a hand in dismay. "And you think any of *us* can help him? How?"

Alnduul touched his fingertips together. "Prior to making planetfall, I put a proposal before Colonel Rulaine and Major Solsohn: to bring a group of you to join Caine Riordan as assistants, aides, possibly expediters." He noted the restless reactions around the table, turned toward the woman who had spoken. "I understand your reservations, Ms. Veriden, but such a plan would relieve many of your group's problems, as well. During my journey here, I had occasion to scan relevant communications among certain terrestrial governments that remain highly motivated to locate you or, more narrowly, the Lost Soldiers. However, since the Consolidated Terran Republic never had access to the Lost Soldiers or the cryocells in which they were transported, the governments in question remain unable to track them. So, their new focus is upon those of your team who belonged to, or conducted operations for, the Institute of Reconnaissance, Intelligence, and Security."

"Damn IRIS alums, again," Dora Veriden groaned with a roll of her eyes. "You spooks will be the death of us yet."

Alnduul's large eyelids cycled rapidly. "Ms. Veriden, your own arm's-length association with the Institute has resulted in your being included in that group."

A plain-looking middle-aged man in a light blue Commonwealth Survey and Settlement Office duty suit patted her arm. The sympathy seemed both genuine and ironic. "If you can't beat 'em..."

"Shut up, Karam," Veriden muttered.

"Yes, dear."

Bannor, who remained leaning against the wall since there were no seats left, raised a quieting hand. "Look, Alnduul's plan could be a triple win. Those of us whose IDs are on the intel grid need to leave the CTR. If we do, the rest of you remain much harder to find. And once the Crewe is in the Collective, we'll be in place to help Caine. Although"—he glanced at the Dornaani—"I've got the same reservation as Dora. I can't see how we'd be of much use to him on your turf."

One finger on each of Alnduul's hands raised. "Those of you associated with IRIS are a formidable and—forgive me—markedly aggressive group, one that would disincline any Dornaani who might think of further obstructing Caine Riordan's quest to find Elena Corcoran. Our technology may require some familiarization, but your diverse and adaptable skill set will more than compensate for any temporary loss of efficiency."

Bannor nodded thoughtfully. "Still, there's one drawback if everyone from IRIS leaves."

A short, somewhat stocky Asian man nodded. "There won't be many people left who were born into this century."

"Less than a dozen of us by my count, Pete," agreed the man Dora had called Karam. "And almost no one who's familiar with the way CTR spooks operate."

Bannor nodded. "So while leaving helps everyone here stay hidden, it also reduces their ability to see trouble coming." He rubbed his hands together in what Ayana read as frustration. "The goal was always to get us all over the border, into the new landgrab systems. But Alnduul's offer may be the best we can do right now, because after three years, I still haven't found a way to make that happen."

Ayana allowed several seconds of silence to elapse before she raised her chin. "I do not mean to be impertinent, but have you inquired if our esteemed guest might be willing and able to do us the honor of providing such assistance?" She kept her eyes on Bannor.

Who looked sideways at Alnduul.

Who allowed the fingers of one hand to droop. "If I had the means to transport your personnel to a safe haven, I would already have offered it. Unfortunately, my own predicament precludes such action, Ms. Tagawa. As I informed Colonel Rulaine and his officers prior to planetfall, I must appear before a board of inquiry immediately after transporting them. The process and outcome is likely to be more akin to one of your courts martial. If so, I will be unable to assist myself, let alone anyone else."

Ayana inclined her head. "When such leaders act in opposition to their sworn duties, they compound injustice with disgrace."

Alnduul's eyelids flickered twice. "I am aware that you have suffered a similar fate, Ms. Tagawa."

She offered a shallow, sitting bow, aware that the other eyes in the room were now fixed on her. "And like me, you may be compelled to seek refuge from superiors who would make you a scapegoat for their own failings and dishonor."

"I cannot. I have taken an oath."

Tagawa held Alnduul's gaze. "So have I. However, in violating their own oaths of service and honor, such leaders dissolve the obligations of those who were oathbound to them."

The eyes in the room swiveled toward Alnduul.

Who stared at Ayana for a long moment. "That is a perspective worthy of lengthy consideration, Ms. Tagawa." He turned to Bannor. "Colonel Rulaine, once your team is reunited with Caine Riordan, I will seek a means of evacuating your entire command."

Bannor nodded, looked around the room, was answered by more nods. "I guess all that's left is to finalize our departure roster."

Duncan grinned. "Actually, Missy Katano and I have already come up with a list."

One of Bannor's eyebrows raised slightly. "That was fast."

"That's because a lot of it was inevitable." Duncan glanced at Katano, one of the few Lost Soldiers who was not, in fact, a soldier. According to Susan Phillips, she'd been an intel liaison between the covert operatives and commandos operating in Somalia at the end of the Twentieth Century. Since Missy now managed the group's logistics and information distribution without flaw, Phillips considered her to be worth her weight in gold. Literally.

Katano started ticking names off the list. "We started with the IRIS must-go's, Colonel. That means you, Duncan, Peter, Newton, Dora. Next..."

"Hey, Missy!" shouted diminutive Miles O'Garran from out in the corridor. "Forgetting someone, maybe?"

She smiled. "And Miles," she added. "We realized that Ms. Tagawa had to go, too, so—"

Bannor held up a hand. "Whoa and wait a minute. No offense to Ms. Tagawa, but she just got here."

"And she's too hot to stay," Duncan countered. "She spent a year with the Ktor, knows they're human, that they've been abducting our people, and that they started scheming to bring us down before we split the atom. Besides, if her meeting with Caine ever comes to the attention of our pursuers, they're going to follow her trail. Hard."

Ayana bowed slightly toward Bannor. "I would be honored to accompany you. And I have a debt of gratitude and honor to repay to Commodore Riordan."

Bannor shook his head. "I know Caine. He wouldn't want you arriving here, finally safe, only to run off and risk your life helping him."

"Honor is weak if it shuns risk," she replied mildly, staring into the colonel's hazel eyes.

Bannor was surprised by Ayana's frank, unwavering gaze. She might be a child of the neo-Edo traditions, but for all those formalities, she was no wallflower. *Hell, if she were a little closer to my age, I just might... Christ, stop that!* "Okay, Ms. Tagawa: you're in. Who else?"

Missy Katano was ticking names off her fingers. "We figured Yaargraukh was a logical choice. No offense"—she added, leaning toward the Hkh'Rkh—"but you're *really* traceable if anyone ever sees you."

His thin black tongue popped out, snapped back in. "I quite agree."

Missy smiled, went back to the list. "We've got to get Katie Somers out of CTR space, too."

Dora Veriden frowned. "Somers? Who's she?"

"One of the Cold Guard."

Tagawa frowned. "Your pardon, please, Ms. Katano, the 'Cold Guard?'"

"Elite troops thawed out of cold sleep to help on Turkh'saar." Missy turned to Dora. "Katie's a specialist in drones and cyber-weapons. Her higher clearance puts her intel signature way above the background noise."

Bannor frowned. "That's a pretty big group, Missy."

She shook her head. "Sorry, but it gets a little larger, sir. You should really have a grease monkey and a trigger-puller, too."

Bannor was tempted to reject the proposal outright, but hell, no harm in hearing it. "Who and why?"

"I'm recommending Rodriguez and Capdepon, sir."

Bannor shook his head. "Vincent Rodriguez is far more than a grease monkey. He's the only Lost Soldier qualified on all the modern machinery. He's needed here. And while Joe Capdepon is a fine soldier, we already have enough trigger-pullers."

Missy frowned. "Yes, sir. But then you've still got a problem: all your trigger-pullers are chiefs, not Indians. Sir."

Bannor ignored the unfortunate archaic axiom. "I know that look, Ms. Katano. You've got an alternate solution."

"Yes, sir. We could send the two Lost Soldiers whose cold cells failed. It not only helps you, it helps them. And the rest of the unit."

Bannor folded his arms. "Convince me."

"Well, sir, you yourself said that if Murray Liebman can't be stuck back in a freezer, we'd better stick him in a combat zone."

"Yes, well..."

"Sir, he's outstanding in the field, but the longer he sits around, the more likely he is to become a major discipline problem. Again. Not good for morale. Or opsec."

Peter Wu nodded. "Specialist Liebman was under my command on Turkh'saar. I can vouch for him. As long as he has something to do, he'll be fine."

Katano smiled her appreciation while keeping her eyes on Bannor. "The other Lost Soldier is Craig Girten, sir. He's been requesting any assignment that would take him off-site. For two years, now."

Rulaine nodded. "I am aware." Bannor was also aware why. Girten, of all the Lost Soldiers, had become a "black rabbit's foot": the guy who had, again and again, been the sole survivor in his unit, from the Ardennes all the way to Turkh'saar. The only persons who hadn't bought into the inevitable graveyard superstitions were Riordan and his original crew. Or as Bannor and the others in that group preferred, "the Crewe."

"Okay," Rulaine murmured. "tell the two of them to grab their gear. Anyone else with IRIS or intel affiliations? Karam? Tygg?" As he mentioned Tygg's name, his wife, Melissa Sleeman, leaned back, her jaw suddenly taut.

Duncan shook his head. "Neither of them were actually IRIS. They're not of interest to our pursuers."

Bannor unfolded his arms. "Well, then, I guess we'd better start packing."

Chapter Fifty-Three

As Caine Riordan opened the French doors to the balcony, a light breeze spun the last tendril of smoke rising from the extinguished oil lamp on his night table. The large house, a genuine Victorian, was quiet. His *ronin* bodyguards were too stealthy to be heard.

Another step carried him into the cool quiet of his bedroom's balcony. Out beyond Willard Bay, the moon was rising over Long Island Sound.

Caine leaned his weight upon the oak railing and winced. Although healed, his left hand was still sensitive around the scarred knuckle where his fourth finger had once been. Last year's escape from Rangoon had been entirely too close. Of the two steam gunboats flying British colors, the one that they hadn't disabled with gunfire ran them down and attempted a boarding. After Riordan emptied his second revolver, there hadn't been time to do anything but fight back with katana and sai. Frankly, they were lucky to have made it out of that long, narrow bay alive.

Well, virtually alive. After more than three local years, it remained a challenge to keep that distinction in mind. But his time in Virtua was finally coming to an end, one way or another. The basic strategic moves he had plotted while escaping from London—which had sent him on an incognito circumnavigation of the globe—had ultimately brought him to this place, this confrontation with Kutkh. Or, more accurately, with her local persona: Lord David Weiner, Earl of Greater Connecticut.

However, the details of Riordan's plan had sharpened as his knowledge of this strange alternate Earth of 1872 broadened.

The first clear deviation from Earth's historical timeline was that the spate of mid-eighteenth-century pluralist revolutions had not taken place. Instead, Europe had transitioned straight into a more energetic and ruthless Imperialist phase. The majority of its wars were colonial clashes fought by the familiar empires of Earth's equivalent epoch. But here, their reach was so absolute that every patch of land, every tiny atoll and islet, now belonged to one of these leviathans, either directly or through their innumerable satrapies and client states.

However, as Riordan had asked more questions and read more histories, it became evident that although these empires had never been weakened by popular revolts, they nonetheless retained only a fraction of their autonomy. Here, their dominance had been undermined with finesse and subtlety by a very different set of change agents: businesses. But how and why had early industrial magnates become the power behind the age's various imperial thrones?

The answer turned out to be coal. Or more specifically, its arresting scarcity. Anthracite, the lifeblood of Earth's early heavy industry, was rare. More energy-dense fossil fuels were entirely unknown.

Tracking backward, Riordan discovered that, in consequence, the Industrial Revolution had not arrived as a wave, but a slowly rising tide. The markedly greater costs of manufacturing were exacerbated by constant increases in the price of coal as known seams were exhausted more swiftly.

Prospectors roved across the globe to find more deposits. England's discovery of the North American fields gave it an economic boost almost as great as the Spanish discovery of silver centuries before. Indeed, the American colonies became so prized for their coal reserves that, by 1770, they had attracted droves of new and well-subsidized settlers and workers. Before long, the businesses that consumed New World anthracite decided to build their factories on site, rather than shipping the fuel across the Atlantic. The industrialization of America had begun half a century early.

Those empires that could followed England's lead. A redoubled frenzy of prospecting sparked colonial wars, even as coal's increasing value and scarcity slowly but surely transferred the power and prerogatives of empires to the industries that controlled the mines and colliers. Those few nations that chose to cling to traditional sources of energy were swiftly relegated to second-tier status or the dustbin of history. And although the polities that embraced this new reality survived, they did so under the increasingly overt direction of the globe's real power: the Capital and Coal Council.

The 3C, or simply "Coal," rapidly consolidated into a consortium which demonstrated marked propensities for both ruthlessness and avarice. However great the historical injustices of Earth's nineteenth century had been, they were dwarfed by the 3C's unrelenting and nightmare of brutality.

Caine's reverie became a reflection upon characterizing Coal's reign of terror as a "nightmare." After all, here *everything* was just a bad dream. And yet, this world had remained utterly and flawlessly believable in every regard. His struggle to remember, minute to minute, that this was a virtual space had not become easier, but harder. It was now populated by simulacra whom he had known for years, whose joys and tragedies moved him, who laughed and wept and hoped and despaired. Worse yet, he still had to remind himself that sensations—such as tonight's skin-cooling sea breeze—were just a blizzard of electric impulses, tricking his brain, his nerves.

Which, he had begun to fear, might not just be the endgame for Dornaani civilization. It could be in humanity's future as well. Conceivably, those seeds were latent in electricity itself. Given how it ultimately expanded each individual's sphere of contact and control, its utility was inseparable from the allure of its power. *We summon heat and light without having to create it ourselves. We communicate across continents and oceans. We operate machines that labor in our stead. We keep opponents at a safe distance with remote sensors and drones.* Is that how the long, subtle slide into speciate senescence began, that the more a species distanced itself from direct action, the more unfamiliar the natural environment became?

Riordan drew in a lungful of night air that wasn't really there. If humans completely insulated themselves from all physical effort and risk, that could erode the mental resilience required to contend with emotional and psychological challenges. And if that, in turn, led them to minimize contact with those whose different ideas were the most frequent source of such challenges, what would become of social bonds? Of courage, of love, of hope?

Riordan shivered, wondered if his actual body was covered by the same thin sweat of dread that chilled his virtual one. *So will we, too, come to rely upon virtuality to rediscover this smell of dark pines, this cool buffeting of a crisp night wind, and the siren call of spray-capped swells rolling on a moonlit sea?*

Riordan quit the balcony, shut the French doors, wondered if any tangible benefit would result from his sojourn in Virtua. He'd spent over a year readying his body for the coming confrontation, even while chafing at the certainty that his new muscle mass would not follow him back into the real world.

But what of the rest? Would the engagement at Rangoon, and a dozen others, better prepare him for actual close combat? Would the training and the skills he had acquired in Virtua translate into actual competencies? Maybe so; maybe not. Only time and real-world experience would tell.

Riordan shuttered the windows, drew back the covers of his bed. He slipped under them slowly, arranged them to lie loosely upon his body. All that remained was for him to signal the machinery of Virtua that this sleep cycle was to last for two local days. Caine lay back slowly. He blinked five times.

He paused. Three blinks.

Another pause. One blink. And...

Blackness.

Chapter Fifty-Four

"Cei!"

Riordan leaned sideways to look into the next baggage car, felt the crisp November wind lash into his face, much colder than the breeze off the bay three nights ago. Standing in the rear doorway of the car ahead of his, Pip Robinson gave a thumbs-up. "Target's departure is confirmed."

"Wire test?"

"Circuit is good."

"Operational security?"

"Semaphore from over the river signals that our observers remain uncompromised. No sign of enemy security forces. Routine defense contingent is traveling with the target. It's just Weiner's standard Boston to New Haven run."

It was indeed typical in all particulars. Lord David Lawrence Weiner's special train, which shuttled him back and forth between his offices in Boston and New York several times a month, was right on time. At approximately 1:10 PM, it would finish crossing the dual-track rail bridge that stretched across the Connecticut River. A coded telegraph from observers in Lyme confirmed that the train was in its normal configuration.

This meant that a small security car—essentially a four-wheeled fort—was positioned ahead of the armored locomotive, which was in turn followed by two reinforced corridor cars with steel-shuttered windows: duty stations and billets for the protection

378

forces, as well as Weiner. Then the observation car, which in most trains would have been either first or last in line. But that made it excessively vulnerable to derailings and attacks, so this observation car was a custom design. Slightly convex mural-sized windows provided the central viewing gallery with a panoramic view of the passing scene. The tail of the train included two more reinforced corridor cars and, finally, a battery car: an iron-sided box with one cannon trained behind and one to either side.

It was said that Weiner's train was the safest conveyance on the planet. Evidently, his many foes believed that assessment. It had never been attacked.

Riordan responded to Pip Robinson's sitrep with a thumbs-up and, "Execute."

A moment later, the floor beneath Caine jerked into motion. Their own train's relic locomotive staggered forward against the weight of the five muddy baggage cars that had been unceremoniously shunted into this unused siding two days ago. The cars groaned slowly toward the eastbound track.

Eight hundred yards to the west, three of Riordan's operatives, wearing railroad coveralls, would already be raising signals indicating a line closure ahead. It would be unusual if anyone challenged them inasmuch as they were positioned between stations. Just in case, one of them was an easygoing, glib American who could deflect any but the most insistent of inquiries. Which was fortunate, since his two pals didn't even speak English. The strike team had been chosen for boldness and resolve, not multilinguality.

As the shabby train began to pick up speed, Riordan turned to face the thirty men behind him, clustered around several blocks of ice. Each of the frost-sided cubes was belted with numerous cloth bandoliers. "Load tubes," he ordered. "Then check your gear."

The group split. Half of the men retrieved small, partitioned boxes from the drafty cargo apron near the open rear door. The other half checked the fittings and straps that held their swords, percussion-cap revolvers, and ammunition. There were even a few custom-built wheelguns, which in this world meant percussion cap shotguns fitted with revolver actions.

Caine's own readiness review was markedly different. He began by checking his armor: a full suit of two-hundred-year-old Italian field plate. Cuirass, greaves, cuisses, vantbrasses, the rest: he made sure every exquisitely crafted piece moved smoothly.

Although designed for optimal distribution of weight, Riordan had trained in the thirty-four-pound suit for months, just to be sure of moving swiftly for a few crucial minutes today.

He scanned the men's equipment, spotted a holstered pistol without a lanyard affixed to its grip, nodded at it. The owner, a Prussian by the name of Heidl, murmured a quick apology and fumbled with awkward hands after the leather lead that should have attached it to his belt. "Heidl," Caine muttered, "*die neuen Handschuhe. Nicht so schwer.*"

Heidl blinked, then smiled as he slipped off the heavy, lined gloves he'd been wearing and replaced them with light leather ones that made handling the lanyard much easier.

Riordan pulled on his own shooting gloves, smoothing them so that they fit snugly beneath the back-hand armor of his demi-gauntlet.

The men carrying the partitioned boxes from the car's cargo apron deposited them near the ice. As they began checking their own gear, those who had just finished doing so slipped the bandoliers off the frost-covered blocks. From each pouch, they carefully removed a heavy-walled vial half filled with frozen, and therefore inert, nitroglycerin. Storing it against the ice had kept it well under the requisite fourteen degrees centigrade.

The delicate part of the work began. Several men drew small, clockwork firing mechanisms from the boxes' partitions, confirmed each one was fitted with a primer cap, and passed it on. The next man inserted it into a waiting vial and armed the device by turning its top-mounted key until the striker was cocked and tabs had extended to lock it in place against the inner walls of the tube. Which, if broken, would release the tabs and striker simultaneously.

Once the last tube had been sealed and reinserted into one of the bandoliers' many well-cushioned loops, Riordan flipped back the cover on the inside of his left vantbrass. He read the pocket watch fastened there. "Seven minutes. Weapons check."

His men made sure that their swords cleared their scabbards smoothly, that the spare cylinders for their revolvers came readily out of the other pouches on their bandoliers. In Riordan's case, there were no extra cylinders. He wouldn't have time to reload. Instead, a brace of three pistols rode low on his left hip. He drew them one by one, ensuring that there were no snags.

As he reholstered and secured the last, he glanced up. The men's eyes were upon him. Expectant, fearful, eager, and, above all, deadly earnest. They had all lost something—livelihood, family, dreams, pride—to the 3C. Ever since the Great Coal War, its plutocrats had dictated economic policy, reshuffled wealth according to their own interests, and seemed well on the way to establishing the corporate equivalent of serfdom.

And always at the forefront of those who espoused and enforced such policies was Lord David Lawrence Weiner, Earl of Connecticut, coal and steel magnate of the Greater British Empire, and the most powerful man in America.

Lord Weiner was also invulnerable, or so Caine had often been told during his escape from London's waterfront. That opinion was loudly reprised by the dissenters who stashed him and Pip in one of Amsterdam's shadier dockside taverns. There, in a secret basement that smelled of old tobacco and stale gin, he had been assured that none of the world's disparate resistance movements had any hope of attacking or assassinating Weiner. Better to stick to humbler targets.

"Such as London Bridge?" Riordan had wondered aloud.

"That was madness," a smuggler from Santander had opined over his gin. "I mean no disrespect to Commander Robinson, but the plot was too bold, too uncertain. And too costly." The Spaniard's eyes shifted sideways toward Pip. "How many did we lose? The two who set the charges, three of the agitators who ensured that the riot would distract the Blackhands, and then dozens more who knew no better than to attack the Irregulars? All to destroy one bridge in a city with half a dozen others?"

"Not just any bridge," Pip said thickly. "London Bridge. A symbol. And so, a message."

Antanas Voldermaras, a fatherly, gray-bearded Lithuanian, shook his head sadly. "A message that we haven't the means to send again."

Riordan shrugged. "Actually, I think you can repeat the message. And louder. But there are other actions you have to take first."

Bram Prins, a Jewish banker from Mittelberg, leaned his index finger alongside his temple. "Such as?"

Riordan smiled. "What do you need most?"

Pip sighed, tossed back his beer. "Everything. But mostly, money and weapons."

Caine looked around the table. "What about security?"

"Security?" The Spaniard transitioned from scowling skepticism to intense interest. "What do you mean?"

Riordan spread his hands. "Does your movement have trouble with infiltrators and informants?"

Dark looks were traded around the table.

Caine nodded. "So you need better counterintelligence. And then..."

"And then we are ready to strike!" The Spanish smuggler's eyes gleamed.

"No," Riordan corrected. "Then you need to recruit people who are willing to join, or already are part of, your enemy's infrastructure. Their job is not to attack Coal, but to carry its information out to you."

Prins glanced meaningfully at Voldermaras. "We don't get many people like that."

The fatherly Lithuanian stroked his beard. "Recruiting such persons would require large organizational changes."

"And large amounts of money," Prins sighed.

Caine shrugged. "I might be able to help with that, too."

One of the Spaniard's saturnine brows arched high. "You can make money for us? How?"

Riordan smiled. "The stock market."

Prins glanced at Caine. "Friend, that is not as easy as you might believe."

"It is if you know that a disaster of your own making is about to hit a company. For instance, what if you had a purchasing agent who knew—*knew*—that a certain coal shipping line would soon lose several of its ships in a dock fire?"

"Colliers?" exclaimed Pip. "Caine, the 3C's Blackhands guard those cargos like a mother cat guards her kittens."

"I'm talking about when the ships are *empty*, Pip."

"Well, that would be easy enough, I suppose. But how do we make a profit from that?"

Caine paused. Trading mechanisms that were commonplace on his Earth might not yet have been formalized in this one. "Are you familiar with the term, 'short sell?'" The blank expressions around the table had been more eloquent than any answer.

The memory was jogged aside momentarily as the baggage car swayed, then bumped sharply. It was on the main track now, soon to head over the Old Saybrook bridge.

Superimposed upon Caine's quick mental image of that extremely conventional span were dozens more: bridges in Paris, Prague, Stockholm, Florence. In Indian cities with names he still couldn't pronounce. In jungle-hidden villages with names he had never learned. Wherever he went, there were always bridges. Over the past three years, how many had he crossed? How many trains had he ridden? How many roads had he traveled? He couldn't recall and hadn't tried to keep count while circling the globe as an unofficial liaison among resistance groups.

After his short-sell strategy tripled the operating budget of the movement in Amsterdam, "Mr. Cei" had been summoned to Prague. There, various resistance leaders had grilled him on both his bona fides and his future plans. Many had balked at his refusal to share the details of his background, but his successes and practical outline for greater coordination among the globe's scattered insurgencies impressed them.

However, it was his unprecedented knowledge that ultimately won them over. In a world where petroleum and its byproducts were unknown, much of the transformative chemical research of the second half of the nineteenth century had never taken place. Against that stifled scientific silence, Riordan's calm explanations of how to efficiently and economically produce large quantities of nitric acid, white phosphorous, and hydrogen were a revelatory thunderclap. Laboratory confirmations of his claims, and their ready weaponization, led the resistance leaders to ultimately trust the calm, mysterious stranger who they codenamed "The Professor."

The European resistance grew in size and confidence. Its leadership reached out to other regions, transformed localized dissent into a global insurgency. In every country, new groups arose, eager to join the fight but unsure how best to do so. Visiting and developing cadres for those fledgling resistance cells soon became the most crucial job in the movement. A job to which the Professor was tirelessly dedicated.

Riordan had also laid the technological and logistical foundations for an operation that ultimately marked a turning point in the conflict: a conventional battle against Coal's armies. Fought at the end of the summer just past, the engagement had stunned the world. The reports were everything that Caine had hoped for. "Mere peasant farmers" armed with "impossibly sophisticated weapons" had routed both Imperial Chinese regiments and stiffening troops sent along by the European cantonments in Tianjin.

And so Riordan's challenge to Coal had finally drawn both Lord Weiner's assets and attention to China. Weiner/Kutkh had been forced to reconsider. After years waiting for Caine to attack directly, all the signs now pointed to a different, maddeningly indirect, strategy. Riordan meant to destroy the world order, and with it, Kutkh's wealth, power, and invulnerability.

Accordingly, Weiner had sent spies and troop ships across the Pacific to eliminate the human who had orchestrated this global revolt.

And whose actions had kindled a deadly resolve in the grim-eyed men standing in the swaying baggage car, waiting to intercept Weiner's personal train.

Riordan nodded at them. "Stand to your positions." He flipped a switch linking a small telegraph handset to a bank of wet cells. "The command circuit is live. Wait for your signals. Listen for Pip's whistle in case of a line failure. And good luck."

Chapter Fifty-Five

As most of the men tramped back to the third, fourth, and fifth cars, Riordan leaned out again, waited to catch Pip's eye. The Englishman was double-checking the springs of a self-unfolding wood lattice that left little room for the eight men with him in the lead car. "Too late to worry about it now," Caine shouted above the wind and the wheels. "Either it works or it doesn't."

"That's right enough!" Robinson howled back with a grin. "Three times over!" Similar devices were coiled in readiness in cars three and five.

"Is the target in sight?"

Pip turned to his observer at the car's lead door, who had a clear view past their dilapidated switcher engine. There was no coal or wood car. "What're yeh seein', Jock?"

Pip strained to hear the reply, relayed it loudly. "Weiner's train is just on the bridge."

"And the final 'go' sign?"

"The bedsheet is still flapping from the trusses on the eastern span. The strikers are primed and the circuit is ready."

Riordan nodded, grateful but not really relieved. He'd yet to see a plan where *something* didn't go wrong.

Their train rattled as it ran out on to the rails of the bridge. It was a pratt truss with three spans: the west one that they had just entered from the Saybrook side; the center that towered over the deepest part of the river; and the eastern span, which Weiner's mighty locomotive was traversing as it left the Groton side.

385

The team in Riordan's car finished removing the weather tarp from the third-generation Puckle gun they had secured to the floorboards in front of the loading door. The chief of the crew, a French journalist by the name of Pompogne, caught Riordan's eye. He'd had been a war correspondent until running afoul of the 3C-controlled Ministry of Commerce and Credit. That, and his reputation for unflappability in the face of certain death, had served him well in the resistance. But at this moment, the Frenchman's renowned sangfroid seemed less than absolute. "Monsieur Cei, a word, if I may."

"A quick word, if any, Pompogne."

"*Oui.* May we truly hope to escape, or is that a fable to stiffen the courage of the men?"

Riordan took an extra second to fix the Parisian's gaze. "Pompogne, I do not lie to my troops. Nor do I believe in suicide missions. The ropes lashed to the middle pier lead down to the water. Two of the boats that will come out from Groton are ours. If you've put on your armband, they'll pick you up and make for Fishers Island. A ship is waiting there. Now, just follow the plan and remember your training."

Pompogne nodded and returned to the crew of the Puckle gun.

Their locomotive's whistle shrilled twice. A standard greeting between trains, but also a signal for Caine's men: the enemy engine was now within a hundred yards.

Cradling the command relay, Riordan moved to the steel-lined side of the baggage car and uncovered the crude periscope affixed there. Its wide-angle lens was concealed under the rain cap of a false ventilation pipe and provided a one-hundred-twenty-degree field of vision. To the far right, he could see Weiner's train approaching.

As expected, the squat, four-wheeled iron security car was at the front, but if it was carrying its Puckle gun—rumored to be mounted on internal rails for quick repositioning—there was no sign of it. Just behind, the armored locomotive belched black smoke: coal. Only the best for Weiner, whose arrogance had evidently rubbed off on his crew—his chief engineer did not deign to return the hail of their approaching rust-bucket engine. Which was why Riordan had told his men to purloin the ugliest, oldest pug of a locomotive that they could. If their little train seemed unworthy of a second look, all the better.

At the midpoint of the bridge, Weiner's juggernaut rushed past. Caine nudged the periscope to view the track ahead of it, glanced down at his watch and looked back up...

...just in time to hear a thunderclap from the western end of the bridge and see trusswork and rails flying high into the gray sky. Cheering started along the cars of Riordan's train—*damn, didn't see that coming*—but there was no way to silence his men now.

However, their voices were abruptly buried beneath the iron-on-iron screeching of locked wheels as Weiner's locomotive slammed on its brakes. The big engine and heavy cars bucked against the sudden deceleration, shimmied, but stayed on their tracks. Again, as expected. Weiner's staff were the best at what they did.

His private guards had a particularly fearsome reputation, which was why some of Caine's associates had preferred a different plan: to rig the *whole* bridge with explosives and detonate them from a safe distance. But Riordan surprised them by insisting that Weiner had to be killed in personal combat, preferably by Caine himself. It was a more profound statement, he calmly explained to his speechless colleagues. Besides, if they did not *see* Weiner die, then there was no way to be sure that he *had*.

Four seconds after the first blast, a matching detonation shattered a good part of the eastern span, lumber and twisted iron spinning upward and outward over the Connecticut River. Riordan's own locomotive braked hard, wheels squealing. But it was a lighter train with plenty of safe track ahead; their stubby switcher engine came to a halt with a hundred yards to spare. After ten seconds, Riordan's engineer, a singularly taciturn fellow from Turin, began reversing carefully away from the ruined rails in front of them.

Riordan swung the periscope back toward Weiner's motionless train. A handful of men in overalls had descended from its immense locomotive. A few others in gray dusters were swinging down from the steel-shuttered corridor coaches, rifles in hand. No Lorenzoni actions, here—their weapons were late model break-breech percussion carbines. Too easily fouled or damaged to be trusted on a conventional battlefield, but for short, intense firefights, the gun's preformed paper loads delivered a dramatic increase in rate of fire. One or two of Weiner's guards noticed the small baggage train now reversing toward their end of the bridge, waved to get the attention of their engineers.

Riordan gauged the distance. Approximately one hundred yards between the rear cars of the two trains, so about forty seconds.

Another engineer hopped down from the cab of Weiner's locomotive, started running toward Riordan's switcher engine, waving a red flag. A few moments later, through the firing ports of the battery car at the end of Weiner's train, he saw the partial shadows of the gun crews moving energetically. Not good. But again, not unexpected.

Riordan leaned away from the periscope and back into the doorway. "Pip!"

The Englishman's head popped around the far side of the folded grid of four-by-fours. "They on to us?"

"They will be soon. We need more steam, then a hard brake." Robinson nodded and went forward to pass the word to the engineer.

Caine snugged his eye back against the periscope's eyepiece as the first flag-waver was joined by another. More ominously, the muzzle of the last cannon in the battery car was swinging in their direction.

The floor jerked under Riordan's feet. He reflexively grabbed the armor plating in front of him. The engineer had yanked open the throttle to steam backward, beyond where the enemy gun could traverse. Caine swayed back toward the periscope. Twenty yards between the trains. They just might make it if—

The cannon roared. A deafening explosion answered and suddenly, all sound was an indistinct rumble muffled under a loud, painful ringing. Riordan staggered away from the periscope, glanced down the length of Pip's car. Through the door at the far end, he saw a vertical jet of steam gushing from a wide tear in the top of their engine's boiler: a wound inflicted by the cannonball, which, after hitting high, had exploded an instant later, blowing the smokestack off. Even as the engineer from Turin slammed on the brakes, the hiss of venting steam soared into a metal-shuddering howl. Riordan ducked back.

The boiler blew apart. The world went sideways. Fragments shrieked through the first car, ripping away the restraints that held the self-unfolding gridwork compressed. The springs uncoiled with a screech, flipping open the three-piece boarding ramp. It smashed against the car's left side, which, modified to hinge open along its bottom, was flung outward by the blow. As the train began to slow, the wooden gridwork extended upward and outward, began to drop... and kissed the roof of one of Weiner's armored coaches.

Wood shattered as the initial impact bounced and twisted the ramp's gridwork. Beams shivered apart. Bolts tore out as it dragged along the coach's roof... and then dipped into the gap between cars. Snagged, the end of the ramp flew apart in a shower of ruined planks and braces. Its amputated stump fell, twisting as it scraped and splintered along the siding until Riordan's train finally rolled to a stop, its baggage cars well beyond the rearward traverse of the enemy cannon.

"Pip?" Riordan shouted.

"Here," came Robinson's response from the jumbled ruin of the first baggage car. "I'm all right. So's half of my team. We'll join the ground attack."

Which meant that Riordan's total boarding force had been reduced by a third. So, an even harder fight and even more casualties. He leaned back toward the periscope. *So, while they're still surprised...* Caine pumped the command circuit's clacker, yelled "Go!" and, just to be sure, got his whistle in his teeth and blew a long blast.

The sides of the third and fifth cars fell outward. Springs were released, freeing the last two boarding ramps. They unfolded at an angle, like self-extending fire ladders until their teams yanked out the elevation chocks. The ramps crashed down on the roofs of the armored coaches opposite them. A moment later, the loading door of fourth baggage car slid open, just before the one in Riordan's own, second car did the same.

Caine clacked the command circuit twice, blew his whistle in unison with it.

The first assault wave—light, nimble men—swarmed across the ramps toward the roofs of the enemy train less than four yards away. Weiner's marksmen opened the shutters of their armored coaches, aimed upward at the boarders, and promptly came under fire from the shielded Puckle guns shooting from the side doors of baggage cars two and four.

The chaos was total. Falling bodies. Flashing weapons. Coaches and baggage cars rapidly riddled with holes. But the greatest madness was the tidal wave of sound: hammering weapons, shrieked orders, sharp detonations. All roiling in the hellishly narrow gap between the two broadside trains. Again deafened, Caine struggled to think, to stay alert for signs that the boarders had breached Weiner's well-armored cars.

Riflemen in the lead security car, partially blocked by the locomotive and its coal tender behind, shot the second and third boarders from baggage car five off its ramp. One fell into the gap between the trains and exploded the instant he hit the ground. Streamers of clothes and flesh spattered against the sides of both trains, just as the first boarder reached the roof of the lead coach. He gently lobbed an entire bandolier of vials over the short coal tender and into the cab of the locomotive. The back-to-back explosions—first the bombs, then the engine's boiler—almost jolted him off the roof.

The savage firefight raging between the middle cars of the two trains was dominated by the Puckle guns, which pounded through the side armor and sheet steel blinds of the sleeper coaches. More boarders swarmed over the grids; more were shot down. Another, in the heat of combat, forgot the detonators' sensitivity. As he tore a vial from his bandolier, it triggered. He vanished without a trace.

The remaining boarders hurled vials in front of them to blow holes in the cars' unarmored roofs, lobbed others down into the interiors. One coach burst outward, spraying steel debris into the facing baggage cars, slicing through several of Caine's waiting wave of ground attackers.

But the armored coaches had been multiply breached. Riordan jammed on his open-faced helmet and clicked the command circuit three times—the signal to unleash the final, suppressive volley.

The Puckle guns began pounding out rounds feverishly. Although less carefully aimed, they blew additional holes in the already weakened sides of the passenger couches bracketing Weiner's observation car. The gun battles raging between the roof-perching boarders and the defenders still huddling inside the coaches intensified. A few more of Riordan's men toppled as they leaned forward to unload their revolvers and wheelguns down into the shattered metal boxes.

Riordan turned away from periscope, nodded to the waiting troops in his car, then clacked and blew his whistle four times: close assault. He drew his saber, his lowest-hanging revolver, and stepped to the side door where Pompogne and the other Puckle gunners were pulling the weapon aside. "Follow us," he ordered, then jumped down to the siding.

He almost stumbled—jumping in the armor was still a gamble—straightened, saw half a dozen men following Pip over the cubist wreckage that was the remains of the first car's failed boarding ramp. Several of Weiner's guards from the battery car fired out the ruined windows of the nearest corridor coach. One of Pip's men went down with a cry, clutching his leg. Another slumped, hit the ground as limp as a rag doll.

Robinson and his team wheeled into crouches, returning fire with less accuracy but greater vigor. One of the guards dropped just before a boarder leaned over the roof and arced a vial into their firing position. The explosion blew through the side of the car, left a jagged hole where the guards had been sheltering. A survivor, covered with dust, crawled feebly out of the smoking debris, trying to reach its ragged edge and roll down to the ground. The tail man of Pip's team lagged a moment, raised his wheelgun, fired. Blood splattered out from the side of the guard's neck. He collapsed.

Similar scenes played out along the length of Weiner's ravaged train as Riordan neared the coupler between the observation car and the following coach, his pistol trained upon that gap. As he reached the step-up, a wounded guard leaned out the doorway of the passenger car. Bloodied and swaying, he brought up a sawed-off double-barreled shotgun.

Riordan stopped, fired three fast rounds. The second hit the man in the gut, ruining his aim just as both barrels discharged. The buckshot churned the gravel rail bed a yard beyond Caine's left foot.

The staggering guard grasped at the porch rail, trying to remain upright. Riordan dropped his lanyarded revolver, seized the grab bar, and pulled himself up in one long leap. He landed on the top step. The man's holster flap was back, his hand on his pistol. Leading with his sword, Caine kept his forward momentum and thrust from the hip.

The point of his saber punched through the guard's sternum. The black-uniformed man fell back, sliding off the sword but still moving, still trying to reach his pistol. Riordan aimed and plunged the saber in again, closer to the heart. The man slumped, gargling a sigh before blood ran from his mouth.

He's not real; none *of this is real,* Riordan told himself as he cleared his saber and caught up the revolver he'd let swing on its lanyard. He cocked the weapon just as another guard came out the rear door of the observation car.

This was an easier shot; the man was only four feet away, had no cover, was framed in the doorway, didn't have a weapon ready. Riordan aimed, cheated the barrel lower, and emptied the three remaining chambers in rapid succession.

A rough triangle of large, bloody craters—typical of .44 caliber lead bullets—erupted on the guard's solar plexus.

As the man fell, Riordan tore the pistol off its lanyard and let it drop. Pompogne leaped up the stairs and over the body, followed by one of Robinson's men. Pip, just behind, waved others into the observation car. The steady outgoing gunfire suddenly shifted to furious, internal fusillades as Weiner's men hammered at the boarders coming in both the forward and rear doors.

Riordan pulled his second revolver, considered his sword, sheathed it.

Pip, grinning despite the carnage, nodded at the pistol. "Glad you practiced every day?"

Riordan nodded. "Let's go." They followed the last of Pip's men into Weiner's observation car.

Bodies. Blood on the jagged remains of windows, on shredded silk blinds. Smoke so thick it hung in drifts. More than a dozen frantic, dodging men. All firing. Never more than four yards away from each other. Missing far more often than they hit.

Arms akimbo and miraculously unscathed, Weiner stood with his back to the rear gallery window, watching the slaughter. He smiled when Caine entered the shooting gallery that had been, only a few minutes before, his opulent and spacious lounge.

Riordan ignored the magnate, brought his left hand up to steady his aim, and began firing, cocking the hammer after each shot. Those slivers of extra time did not only pay off in accuracy; he was twice able to hold fire when one of his men charged past and into the fray.

After the fourth shot, one of Weiner's personal bodyguards stopped targeting the other entrance to the car, head turning, seeking the source of the slow, steady reports that had killed one guard and wounded two others. A small man, he was not only competently wielding a pistol in either hand, but was now drifting their barrels in Caine's direction, as if they were divining rods that would reveal the source of the unacceptably effective fire.

Riordan hastily fired the last two bullets in his revolver at the veteran shootist—missed with the first, only winged him with the second. Caine presumed himself to be as good as dead.

But grazing the small man's arm had put a hitch in his machinelike precision. That was all the opportunity that Pompogne and Heidl needed. They aimed hastily, fired until the gunman went down.

Riordan pulled his final revolver, cocked it, crouched as he moved forward. Pip dodged over to his side, drew a bead on Weiner, even as the earl's last few guards began collapsing back into a tight, protective knot. "Pip," Caine warned, "remember. *I* kill Weiner."

Robinson nodded, gesturing to remind their men of the plan's final protocol. It was unlikely any saw or understood. The volume of fire had decreased, but both sides were still playing hide-and-seek with pistols at point blank range.

Pushing back the stubborn terror of standing up into an imaginary firefight, Riordan rose, aimed, squeezed the trigger twice.

One of the two guards covering Weiner stumbled aside, clutching his wrist. Caine cocked the pistol and closed the distance. A flurry of shots from Pip took down the last guard.

Leaving Caine standing four feet away from Weiner, no obstructions between them.

Lawrence Weiner was not the titan that the newspapers and portraits made him out to be. He was not much more than five feet six inches and was more stocky than he was imposing. His facial features were not as fine and commanding as on the front page, but were actually rather genial. The sort of guy with whom you could share a few drinks and laughs.

None of that mattered. Riordan raised his pistol and squeezed the trigger.

Misfire.

Which is why I insisted on double-action revolvers. Riordan squeezed the trigger again.

This time, against all probability, the action jammed. As if the mechanism that turned the cylinder had hung up.

Weiner-Kutkh smiled more broadly, even as his last guard fell, gutted by three rapid rounds from a wheelgun.

The room was silent, eyes moving between Riordan and the dreaded Earl of Greater Connecticut. Caine hauled back on the revolver's hammer with both thumbs, hoping that would unjam the mechanism.

The hammer resisted, began to give way—and the mainspring broke with an audible *pang*.

Weiner-Kutkh waved airily. "I seem to have been born lucky."

"Said every cheater who's ever lived," Caine retorted. He leaped forward, arms outstretched.

Weiner's smile became open-mouthed astonishment as Riordan did not stop to grapple, but rather, caught the smaller man in a bear hug and kept charging forward.

They crashed through the rear gallery window and plummeted like a many-limbed millstone toward the frigid river below, Riordan's armored arms still locked around the man he had to kill.

If not by gunshot, then by drowning or hypothermia.

Chapter Fifty-Six

Riordan awoke with a start, expecting a crushing blow and icy darkness instead of the dim white room of Kutkh's underground bunker. His heart was racing, but not arrhythmically.

He sat up sharply. Not only did he lack any memory of dying, he also didn't remember the long fall to the Connecticut River. But if the fall hadn't killed him, then why...?

As if appearing out of nowhere—*or had it?*—a robot rolled toward him. It proffered his duty suit.

Kutkh's voice erupted from the robot. "Attend me! Immediately!"

Just as polite as ever. "Can't, if I don't know where you are."

"Follow the robot, human."

Riordan maintained a leisurely pace as he complied. He carefully observed the familiar surroundings until he was led into a large, wholly unfamiliar room. Kutkh was lying on an elaborate couch that looked more like an escape pod. "Human!" she cried. "You are reckless! Suicidal!"

Riordan smiled. "And you're not really here. Nor am I. We're still in a simulation. But it's not Virtua. This one has"—he looked around—"flaws."

The room was abruptly gone, gray nothing in its place. Kutkh materialized, apparently standing on a flat surface in the midst of the void. "I misspoke. You are not merely dangerously suicidal. You are insane. Your actions are without logical coherence. You

395

allow years to pass without any attempt to kill me. But finally, just as you are poised to ruin the entire model with a popular rebellion, you mount a crude and outlandish assassination attempt."

Riordan smiled. "Which killed you, just the same. Or would have, if you hadn't stopped the simulation."

"I did *not* stop the—"

"I can understand your frustration, of course. On the one hand, you couldn't overreact to the growth of the global resistance movement, even when you started getting impatient, wanted to be able to leave the model. But you couldn't ignore the other leaders of the 3C when the rebels openly challenged Coal in a place where your control was weak and large, and angry armies could be raised: western China.

"Besides, you've had enough of your 'game.' You wanted to get on with your own life. So when I beat you in China, you decided that enough was enough. You devoted your forces, and focus, to getting rid of me." Riordan smiled. "You took your eyes off the ball, Kutkh."

"So, the uprising in China...that was all a ruse?"

Riordan nodded.

Kutkh's eyelids flickered: incomprehension, not anger, this time. "But why? Threatening the world order was entirely unrelated to your objective: killing *me*."

Riordan smiled. "Not if it made you pay less attention to your personal security."

"I did not change my security precautions. I remained—"

"Kutkh, once I kept you in the model longer than you expected, or wanted, your attention to terminal defense started slipping. First you started traveling more. Then, when you realized I wasn't coming for you directly, you started relaxing surveillance on your routes, your associates. All because you believed you had my persona figured out: an opponent who relied on guile not strength, who struck you where you were weak and avoided where you were strong. I wasn't the half-evolved savage you expected to try murdering you on your throne. I was a patient adversary who had resolved to kill you with a death of a thousand cuts."

Kutkh blinked rapidly. "So your plan, from the first, was—"

"To make you so certain that I was determined to defeat you strategically that you would no longer expect a brute-force blow to your face. Like the one that just killed you. Or should have, several times over. But I guess you couldn't stand being bested at your own game."

"You did *not* best me! I was simply—"

"Kutkh. I had my pistol aimed at your heart and took three shots. You caused three misfires. In a *revolver*. Then we were falling eighty feet toward the Connecticut River. You were too weak to escape and I weighed enough to sink us straight to the bottom. But you either stopped the simulation, forced it to defy physics, or both."

Kutkh's lamprey mouth writhed for a moment. "I understand your suspicions, Caine Riordan, but your accusations are incorrect. Firstly, I did not alter or terminate our encounter. Virtua itself did that." Seeing Caine's doubt, she explained. "All designated observers of the model are impervious to both intentional and chance terminations. This is usually achieved by plausible alterations of events."

Riordan managed not to roll his eyes. "So Virtua kept my revolver from killing you three times by 'altering outcomes.' It's still cheating. But when we crashed through the gallery window and started falling, it stopped the whole program. Why didn't it just adjust the outcome again, keep the window from breaking?"

"Physics."

"I beg your pardon?"

Kutkh's gills warbled in exasperation. "In the case of sudden and unforeseeable threats, the only way to avert an observer's death may be to halt the program. When you rushed Weiner in the observation car, Virtua no longer had sufficient time to insert a natural event that both saved me *and* remained in compliance with the laws of physics. If it violates those laws, Virtua loses both its experimental validity and its immersivity."

Kutkh allowed several fingers to droop. "So Virtua paused the model for a millisecond—just long enough to extract us. To anyone observing, we continued our plunge into the river and disappeared. We will be reinserted into the event stream at a place and time of our choosing." Kutkh stood slightly more erect. "Your willingness to hear my explanations is gratifying. I hope it signals your willingness to restart our contest."

"*Contest?* Virtua won't allow you to be killed. You said it yourself: you're a 'protected user.'"

"We can alter the terms of the challenge so that—"

"No. I'm done."

Kutkh's face and voice hardened abruptly. "If your participation is at an end, then so are your hopes of finding your mate."

Riordan smiled. "Kutkh, you just admitted that Virtua had to save your life. That's the same as admitting that I killed you, that I won. So you *are* going to honor our agreement."

"What makes you so sure?" There was slightly less hauteur in her tone.

"Because if you don't, I will inform your users why the model had an interruption today: that you are tampering with Virtua."

Kutkh's voice became dismissive again. "Finding the users of this model would prove extremely challenging."

"For me, yes, but I'll bet Uinzleej, Oduosslun, and Laaglenz could locate them easily. And political power players like Glayaazh, Heethoo, and Nlastanl might want to investigate further. I suspect that forcing me to participate in your little death match isn't strictly legal.

"Either way, the scandal of an investigation, and the loss of privacy, will drive users away from your model. And you'll become an object of scorn once they learn that, after setting me an impossible challenge in a rigged game, you still had to cheat to win. Against a human."

By the time Caine finished, Kutkh's posture was rigid. "I shall not be baited by you, human. But since *you* are willing to stoop to extortion"—Riordan had to suppress a chortle at her hypocrisy—"I shall give you what you wish: contact with your mate." Then her mouth twisted slowly. "Of course, you may be so changed that she will not recognize you. Or will not wish to."

Riordan wondered if it was his real or virtual extremities in which he felt a sudden chill. "What do you mean? I haven't changed."

"No? I shall demonstrate. Wiggle the fourth finger of your left hand."

Riordan grew angry. "I can't. You know I lost it during the fight in—" But before he could finish with, "Rangoon," he discovered that the missing finger was not only back on his hand but wiggling.

The chill in Caine's extremities expanded, ran the length of his body. Which made him wonder: *the length of my real or virtual body?*

The twist of Kutkh's mouth tightened. "As I asserted, you are changed. The discrepancies and uncertainties will increase. You will labor to suppress habits you acquired in Virtua, will fight against muscle memory natural to that body but which makes you clumsy in your real one. You are already missing 'persons' you met in Virtua, though you are also telling yourself that they are not real, that they are simply a collection of impulses sent to your brain."

Kutkh's smile was that of an assassin giving the knife one final twist. "And so, with every passing day, you shall wonder at, and be changed by, this question: is there really any difference between the impulses and waves that create your experiences here and those that created them in Virtua?"

Riordan, suddenly weary and disoriented, struggled to fight against the conceptual undertow of Kutkh's assertions. Which was why he was caught off guard when her tone changed from condescending to eerily earnest. "The inevitable implication is that we are not defined by the crude particulars of our physical existence. Rather, we are creatures woven from strands of time and consciousness. We have no true self independent of those strands, whether they are spun in this world or in Virtua."

Riordan's instinct told him that Kutkh was leaving something out of this relentless cascade of assertions, but if even a fraction of what she said was true... "So, the simulacra in the model," Riordan said carefully, "have, well, a reality of their own."

Kutkh's fingers fluttered aimlessly. "The starting population of any model is drawn from real templates. Their consciousnesses are complete matrices of actual minds from that world. Anything less would invalidate the analytical value of the model and make complete immersion impossible for later users."

Riordan could not trust himself to speak. Myriad realizations came at such speed and in such disorder that any attempt to articulate them would simply result in disjointed babbling. And pushing up unbidden through that riot of contending thoughts came the memory of Laaglenz explaining, *"The universe of the Prime Model exists, complete and whole, when you enter it. There is no generation at all.... Just as it is in reality."*

So were these "models," well, *copies* of the original universe? It seemed impossible, but it agreed with Laaglenz's claim that, *"the entire universe of the simulation is fully defined, down to the last subatomic particle.*" Which made a terrible kind of sense. Elder miracles notwithstanding, there was no way to pregenerate a whole universe. It *had* to be a copy. But it would still be impossible to control it, to productively manipulate and track a dataset as big as infinity itself. Unless...

There *was* one elegant solution to both seeming impossibilities, but what it implied about the nature of reality, and the Elders' mastery of it, was the stuff of nightmares.

If every "model" was a copy of a universe that *actually existed* somewhere, then Virtua didn't have to process all its data, just read and manipulate select parts. Still, it was staggering to imagine any system able to even compass the dataset for a whole other universe.

Riordan froze. *Wait, a* whole other *universe? That was one of many* parallel *universes? Like the theory of the same name?* Is that why Laaglenz had wondered, *"What if a branching incident in a temporal stream—that very moment where a symmetry split occurs spontaneously—could be induced, even controlled?"* Was Virtua some unthinkably powerful mechanism capable of forcing splits in a timeline? Did it—could *anything?*—make whole alternate universes?

But wait, maybe it wasn't necessary to "make" new universes at all. If one followed the many-worlds theory to its logical conclusion, all things that could happen *would* happen, in some parallel universe. So maybe Virtua *wasn't* creating anything. Maybe it simply located and accessed those *already-extant* other worlds. If that was true, then each new "model" was just a data tap into an alternate world that had branched in precisely the same way and due to the same causes, that the model's "designers" had chosen to study. Which would mean that Virtua didn't really process or manipulate data at all; it was more like a multiverse switchboard. But if so, then Riordan was faced with an ethical imperative upon which he had to act, no matter how surreal it seemed.

Caine forced himself back into the moment. "I need assurances that you will not destroy the world I just left."

Kutkh looked surprised by Caine's change in demeanor. "Why?"

"Because I owe that to the...the simulacra I am leaving behind." Even as he said it, Riordan tried to imagine that Pip's smiles and Becca's laughter had been nothing more than convincing simulations.

The Dornaani's face was blank for a moment, then disbelieving comprehension reanimated it. "Human, these are not real beings."

"Your description of them indicates otherwise. To use your own terms, they are 'actual minds.'"

Kutkh's eyes closed. "You are being maddeningly obtuse. These consciousnesses do not derive from protean sources. They are activated within a machine and may be turned off along with it. Can you not see the implicit distinction?"

Riordan shook his head. "What I see is a *lack* of distinction. If both worlds are populated by independent intelligences descended from those of the original model, how is turning off the Virtual world different from destroying the actual one?" When Kutkh's only response was a bored sideways stare into Limbo, Riordan discovered that he didn't merely dislike her: he hated her. "Whatever you might do to other worlds in other models, I insist you leave this one alone."

Kutkh's expression became one of canny assessment. "I refuse." Her tone was firm, but more in the way of setting the ground for a negotiation, rather than making a declaration.

Riordan considered, and hated, the words he had to utter next. "I'll trade for it."

"And what do you have that I could possibly want?" Her tone was one that Riordan imagined a spider would use to invite a fly into her web.

Caine swallowed. "You tell me."

Kutkh paused. Her mouth twisted. Not wry; cruel. "What I want from you is you. A full patterning. Well, as full as this system can manage."

"You mean...me, in this machine? Forever?"

"Correct."

Riordan had to remember to breathe. To comply didn't cost him anything, but it might create an eternal hell for a Virtual iteration of himself. "And will my Virtual self keep my memories from this world *and* from the model?"

"Yes." It was a surprisingly frank reply. "As I understand it, a complete duplicate *must* be an unedited and total consciousness or it will not work."

Well, that's reassuring. If it's true. "My agreement is contingent upon three guarantees. First, that you insert my virtual self back into Virtua as soon as we finish here. No long delays or interruptions."

"Very well."

No surprise that she had agreed to that demand "Second, you will not adjust the world to help or hinder me or my friends in any way."

Kutkh let the fingers of one hand roll languidly. "That does not guarantee safety, you realize."

"No one's safety is guaranteed in the real world, either. I just don't want virtual-me to have crosshairs on his back."

"And your third request?"

"My third *demand* is that I may return here, whenever I wish, to verify that you've kept your word."

Kutkh's eyes bulged. "Unacceptable. I shall not compromise the privacy of my own—wait!"

Riordan had envisioned walking out of Limbo. As he did, everything faded to charcoal gray. He remained hovering at the cusp of departure. "Yes?"

"What you ask is impossible. There is no way to prove that events involving simulacra are natural outgrowths of the virtual weave, rather than a result of operator manipulation."

"You make recordings of the simulations, don't you?"

Kutkh blinked once, involuntarily. "I . . . we can. But recording of the entire event stream is not only extremely data intensive, but is diffic—"

"Bullshit. Virtua was designed to study the progression of star-spanning events. Logically, it had to record every detail for researchers to examine. So, you're to keep a full recording of the 3C world. And if I return and suspect you manipulated events, I'll alert Senior Arbiters and former Custodial leaders about your abuse of this node."

Kutkh tried to maintain an expression of impatient indifference.

Riordan smiled. "Of course, if you can't agree to my three conditions, we can just skip all this and I'll start contacting—"

"No. I agree to your terms."

"Excellent." Caine drew a deep breath. Or at least felt as though he did. "I'm ready to join Elena now."

Chapter Fifty-Seven

Caine waited. There was no change in the featureless, soundless gray around him. "Kutkh, you promised—"

"Patience, human. She cannot be contacted immediately. We must wait."

"For what?"

"For your mate to sleep. You are a conscious mind, still within Virtua. Your mate is an unconscious mind in a different model—the original model, which we call Ur Virtua. Establishing a conduit between the two can be challenging."

"You mean I can't even see Elena in Virtua? Can't hold her hand while I talk to her?"

"It would probably kill her. And it would surely kill you to try. Only a complete mind may enter Ur Virtua. To do so would leave your body brain-dead."

"So how did Elena get into it?"

"She was not registering any higher brain function when she was inserted."

"Was she in a coma, or—?"

Kutkh interrupted, annoyed. "These are particularities of which I was not apprised, in which I have no competence, and about which I have no interest. Her caretakers were possibly careless with her medical maintenance. Again, I lack that information. Whatever the cause of her condition, they obviously knew that Ur Virtua, which is exponentially more detailed than its other

403

expressions, might reach her remaining cognitive and reactive functions and spark them back into activity. I did not believe such a process could work."

"So why would my appearance in Ur Virtua kill her?"

Kutkh replied through an exasperated gill-sigh. "We do not know the circumstances of how she first became aware within Ur Virtua. She may have awoken into it. She may have been living in it as one passes through a convincing dream: uncritical and untroubled by any contradictions with her real life because she never recollected it, or has not thought of it in years. Your appearance in that world could inflict a fatal cognitive shock."

"She's so frail that she could die of surprise?"

Kutkh's eyelids half closed. "She is probably in a state of both mental and bodily semisuspension. The more shock your appearance incurs, the more likely that a cascade of cognitive dissonance will convince her that her world is an illusion and throw her out of Ur Virtua. Once conscious, her first reflex will be to use various voluntary muscles. That will cause her autonomic nervous system to reactivate.

"This would be catastrophic. She remains alive because her body's activity is precariously balanced between minimal autonomic functions and cryogenic suspension. If she regains consciousness, that balance cannot be sustained. She would die in minutes. Seconds, given the extreme cryoshock."

Riordan nodded. "So the only safe alternative is to put me in one of her dreams."

"Yes."

"I'm ready."

"So is she. You may proceed."

"Not with you here."

After a pause, Kutkh said, "That may not be wise. You have no experience in—"

"I won't take any undue risks." *And I don't trust you.*

"As you wish. I shall return when the link is broken. Either one of you may do so at any time. But remember, her conscious mind is only partially active. She may be too sluggish to protect the coherence of her world, to close the link before damage can be done."

"I understand. Leave. Now."

Kutkh vanished. After a long moment, Riordan saw the gray infinity in front of him begin to thin. What began as a translucent oval slowly became transparent, like condensation fading from a window.

Through which he saw Elena, as beautiful as he remembered. Or maybe she wasn't. He didn't know because it didn't matter. It never had. It was Elena. As serene in sleep as she was vivacious in life. He murmured her name.

She stirred. Her face—cheek on pillow, long dark hair flowing over it—filled the aperture like a cameo wreathed in fog.

"Elena," he repeated, "do you remember my voice?"

Her eyes were still closed. "Hmm? You?"

"My voice. Do you remember my voice?"

"I... Nice voice."

"Do you remember it?"

"Yes. Maybe? Who are...?" Her lips slipped over the last word. She was falling back into a deeper sleep.

"Elena. Listen to my voice. Listen. It's me. It's Caine."

Her eyes opened; they were blank, focused on nothing. And yet... "I know your face."

"Yes. I'm Caine."

"Cain." A long pause. "Bible?"

"No. We know each other from... from before. We met on the Moon."

"Man in the Moon. Cain. Blood moon."

Riordan frowned. In a borderline dream state, Elena's memory, imagination, and desires were likely to mix, merge, transmogrify. The best he could do was shepherd her toward reliving sensory impressions from her old life, without pushing her so far that she awakened.

Her mumbles were faint but did not stop. "Blood in the moon. In Jakarta. On the streets. On Caine's back." She started, her eyes widening but still empty. "You, you're not Cain. You're *Caine.*"

Riordan tried to keep his breath steady, failed dismally, was too relieved and happy to care. "Yes, Elena. It's me, it's Caine. Can you see me?"

"No. Wait. Yes. You... you're a... ghost?"

Riordan swallowed the reflex to shout *"No!"*; that might jolt her closer to consciousness.

Before he could think of a safe reply, Elena's tone transitioned from questioning to declarative. "You're Caine. From my old dreams. Dreams I've forgotten."

Her words pierced him like an impaler's stake, the weight of his first, brief hopes dragging him down. Fighting to avert a disemboweling slide into despair, he grabbed at a topic likely to awaken the lost memories. "You remember Jakarta. And me. Do you remember what happened?"

"So much blood." A tear slipped from her eye. "You died."

"So you *do* remember."

She inhaled. "I do. So clear. Like an earlier life."

What? Elena was not a believer in reincarnation...or was she? "What else do you remember about that other life? Do you remember our times together?"

"Yes. No. Some." Her lower lip twisted painfully. "You were gone. Mostly."

Too true. They'd only had a few days on the Moon before overzealous security agents put Riordan into cold sleep. For thirteen years. When he finally regained his lost—*stolen?*—memories, the brief window of time in which they might have reconnected was nailed shut by two Ktor blades—one in each of their backs.

In the end, almost all of their love, passion, and hope had been spent in the imagination, not the actual experience, of each other. And however powerful such longing might be, it was ultimately intangible, left no physical impress. So he had to focus on more vivid sense memories. But carefully: the more intense or poignant they were, the likelier they'd snap her out of Ur Virtua. "Do you remember Connor?"

Elena's mouth opened, then buckled as tears filled her eyes. "Oh. Connor. Connor. Where is—?" A choked sob stopped her.

Riordan kept his tone soft, soothing: "Connor is fine. He's with me. He misses you." *Take a chance.* "He wants to see you."

"I miss him. Connor. I want him...I want...I..." Her hands caressed the air, then settled close to her. As if she were cradling an invisible infant. Tears ran in rivulets down her cheeks.

Caine became aware of his own wet eyes and his tightly constricted throat. He wiped his face, turned back to her...

...and discovered Elena's blind eyes fixed on his own, wide and wondering. "Connor. He...he looks like you. He's..."

"Yes, Elena. He's our son. You remember."

"Ours. Ours! I want...want to remember. But..." Her arms moved restlessly, one hand pawing after the vanished dream-infant, the other reaching, trying to bridge the impossible gulf between them. "I can't. Can't remember. Only pictures. Flashes. Like an old dream. A dream." She sobbed. "Just a dream..."

"It's not a dream. It's a... a different world." Which was probably how and why Elena's mind had vaguely latched on to the concept of reincarnation. What else could explain such clear, powerful memories of two entirely different lives? "Tell me what you remember about the other world."

"I remember... but it's broken. Into pieces. Pieces of a mirror. Showing other times. Other places." A long, pained sigh. "I miss you. Both of you. Everyone. Places near water. My dad." She stopped suddenly. "He died. Dad is dead." Her eyes shone. "The pain. How does it fit? In one dream? One world?"

She paused long enough for new tears to well in her eyes, and for Caine to steer her back toward the most vivid and positive memories. "You never told me: why did you name our son Connor?"

"I... I don't remember. No... it was someone in your family. And mine. Our grandfathers. Same name. I remember."

"You see? You *do* remember."

But she hadn't heard, spoke over him. "I remember. Making love. On the Moon. Shouldn't have. No prophotabs." A small frown. "Didn't need. Didn't want." Her empty eyes found his again. "I was wrong."

"And after the Moon?"

"No more. No you. Missing. I hoped. Too long." The pooled tears overflowed. "Just Connor. All I had. Of us."

Riordan had to wait a moment before he could speak. "I wanted that, too. More than anything."

"Hard. So hard. Alone." She sighed away a final tear. "I want to sleep. Too hard... to remember. To want. No dreams. Just sleep."

"Soon, Elena. But we have to—"

"No. Please. Too real. Always too real. Then empty. When I wake up. Alone." Her face pinched again. "Please. Let me sleep. Easier. Than wanting dreams."

Caine's throat almost closed. "But Connor and I, we're not dreams. We're—"

"Like life." Her breathing became more rapid. "It mixes. Dreams. And life. All of it. Can happen. They told me. When they called me. To watch. To be the Watcher. Because I dream stories."

Riordan frowned at her intense, inchoate declarations. "Who told you? What did they say?"

Elena may or may not have heard him. Her tone shifted, as if she were recalling something portentous, even fearsome. "The Watcher exists on the edge of every reality. And at the crossroads of all dreams. Never knowing which is which. Others' dreams. Or my own. Dreams like you. And Connor. Please. Too much pain. Let me sleep."

"I can't lose you again. You can't just—"

"I must sleep. You and your stories are not . . . cannot be . . . real."

"Elena—"

"No! *You . . . are . . . not . . .*"

Suddenly, Riordan's view into Elena's world widened, became as crisp and clear as normal vision. Elena had straightened from the waist and was upright in bed, her chin still drooping toward her chest, her long raven hair a shining silk curtain that hid most of her face. She was in a small, round room of close-fitted stone. A narrow casemate window admitted a shaft of dim light from a blue-green crescent moon, against which a wheeling bird cut a fleeting, wide-winged shadow.

Elena's speech was suddenly collected, severe. "Hold and desist. Are you a malign spirit, that you keep me in this dream?"

Chapter Fifty-Eight

Riordan blinked at the change in both Elena's tone and her environment. "Am I a... a *spirit*? No! I—"

"You are earnest." Elena may have frowned. "We may have met before. A past life, perhaps. Other worlds, other realities. But I cannot be sure. When one looks beyond the shimmering surface, faces—of the dead, of spirits, of nightmares—may look back."

"I'm not a spirit. I'm real. Connor's real. We were—we *are*—a family."

"You speak what cannot be. Yet you seem to speak truth. One or both of us are deluded. Or you are a canny spirit. And bold, to tell a such a lie. If lie it is. Do you mean to enter this world?"

"I... I can't."

Elena's nod was still that of a somnambulist. "Few can. Only malign beings, or those who once walked into the beyond from this world: rebels and iconoclasts, dream-striders and question-askers. In every epoch, the keepers and makers of history have been happy to let them pass through the shimmer and be gone. But common folk are often saddened to see them go. Some spirits return out of longing, rather than iniquity. Are you one such, seeking to return to the world in which you were born?"

Still trying to track Elena's swerve into almost Shakespearean idiom, Riordan was unsure how to respond. An incorrect reply could brand Caine as a duplicitous, and therefore malign, spirit. So, the simple truth and a bit of redirection. "Elena, I know

409

nothing about the world you are in. I only know we miss you, here in the world where I met and loved you, and where we have a son. Where Connor is waiting for you."

Elena stood slowly, walked in a shuffle toward what looked like a pool of glittering water, except it stood upright, defying gravity. "They were right," she murmured as she started to circle it. "It was an ill omen that I looked back when I walked out of the shimmer." She paused. "You are a familiar spirit. Your words find purchase in my heart. All the more reason I must say, enough. Begone."

"Elena, please; it's me, Caine. I'm real."

She raised her arms as if they were immensely heavy, the folds of her snow-bright nightgown expanding like wings. "This is the robe of the Watcher. I am no addled widow in white weeds, unable to remember a husband though his voice calls from beyond the shimmer. You deceive. No spirit that loved me in life would ask that I join it in death."

Riordan fought to find a reply. "Wouldn't one who truly loves you also travel long and far to remind you of your earlier"—*No! Too risky!*—"your *other* life? A life unfinished, and with so many left grieving behind you?"

Elena shook her head slowly. Her black tresses hardly moved. "You urge me to enter a world of dreams. To walk through that watery door into your realm. But if I do, it shall not fail to consume me, just as it does the others who hazard it."

Riordan shook his head. "No. That door is not how you will reach me." *Or is it?*

"Then you speak riddles. There is no other portal that links this world to those beyond the scope of mortal understanding. You are trying to trick me, spirit. But I forgive you: it is in your nature."

"No, Elena. I am not asking you to step through that door. I just want to talk to you, to—"

"To tempt me with tales of our life in some imaginary otherwhen? To use my dreams against me? No, to listen further can only seduce me to my death." She resumed her circuit of the vertical pool.

"But Connor will—!"

"No." Elena stopped again "Too much pain." She did not move; the salt statue that had been Lot's wife could not have been more still. When she spoke again, she did so without turning, her voice so soft that Riordan had to strain to hear it. "I am of this world, you of some other. I release you, spirit, of whatever troth or duty may bind you to me."

As she resumed her slow circuit of the room, Elena looked over her shoulder at Caine. "Spirit, if this other world exists, and if you are truly some extension of my loved one, then bear this message to him and to our child: should they ever teeter upon the brink of oblivion, seek me."

"Seek you? How? Elena, no—"

"I could wish, so easily, that you were not a ghost, not a..." Her voice trailed off, thickening as her eyelids drooped and her smile faded. Gray mists crowded in around her, shrinking the window into Elena's world as she began another slow orbit of the vertical pool of water.

"No!" Caine shouted as the slate-colored nothingness of Limbo surrounded him... and he started up from where he was lying: the couch he had first laid down upon in Kutkh's subterranean domain, now surrounded by instruments and medical machinery. He tore off the leads and osmotic pads attached to various parts of his body, glad that none of them were IVs. Not that it would have stopped him.

Caine leaped up from the couch... and fell awkwardly on the floor. Robots wheeled in to both help him up and restrain him. The room spun, his limbs felt weak. Then he saw them and realized why.

He had lost a startling amount of weight. His hair fell into his eyes, almost blinding him. "Kutkh, Kutkh!" He hated even having to call for her, to say nothing of the edge of desperation he labored to keep out of his voice. But pride had to wait upon what really mattered: saving Elena from Ur Virtua, finding a way to get her stabilized and homeward bound. "Kutkh!"

"Be still, human," the Dornaani snapped as she drifted into the room in a chair kept aloft by a quad of rotors.

"Elena... didn't know me. She won't..."

"I am aware of the general outcome of your visit with her, human. It is unfortunate. But what may I do? You wished access and it was granted."

"Take me to her."

"You cannot wake her safely."

"I accept that." *For now.* "But I need to see her."

"How touching."

"Not to hold her hand," he half-lied, "I want to see her condition. With my own eyes."

"I did not know you were qualified as a physician."

Riordan wobbled to his feet, alarmed by the changes in his sense of balance. He had moved differently in Virtua, had become accustomed to far more muscle mass, a slightly higher center of gravity. "I can read enough Dornaani to examine the readouts, maybe see if she can still be revived. Or restored by regeneration therapies or organ cloning."

Kutkh cycled her inner eyelids slowly. "Very well."

"Then let's get going."

Kutkh pointed a finger to either side. "We have not yet completed our business, human. You agreed to provide me with a copy of your consciousness. We must do that immediately. By the time the process is concluded, you will begin experiencing the after-effects of your long immersion."

"I'm experiencing them now."

"You have been in Virtua for one hundred and twenty days; the exhaustion will become much worse. I will provide stimulants to maintain you during the trip to your mate's virtuality support pod. But I make no promises regarding the sequelae."

"All right. Just hurry."

"I will be swift." Kutkh gestured toward the ceiling. A hole appeared in it and a silver-streaked globe descended toward him.

"How long does it take to copy my consciousness?"

"An hour, possibly less."

"Does it hurt?"

The node mistress's lamprey-sucker mouth twisted. "Not usually."

Kutkh's spearhead-shaped aircar traversed half the continent in less than an hour. Riordan climbed down, striding toward the dome in which a small fraction of Leltlosu-shai's Ur Virtua participants were housed.

A large iris valve opened in its side. Caine pushed past the security robots that swerved away at a wave from Kutkh. "Where is she?"

"According to the contract made on her behalf, she is in

cell 9-1845." Kutkh pointed toward the other end of the soaring dome. "Back there."

"Back there" turned out to be another cathedrallike rotunda, built out from the first. As they rode the lift to its ninth tier, Riordan stared around. Every surface was lined with inward-facing hexagonal hatches of cryocell storage tubes. It was like rising up through the center of a hollow beehive-mausoleum.

The lift stopped. Caine jumped out, glanced at the ninth tier's directory, located the section that held cell 1845, ran, and started counting. Bile came up in his mouth. He spit it out and kept running past the green lights of active cells.

1843, 1844, 1845—and a red light.

Riordan clutched himself, mute with confusion, terror rising up behind it. "What does it...it...?"

Kutkh murmured, "Very odd," and tapped a control panel alongside the hexagonal hatch. It sighed open. The virtuality support pod slid out.

It was empty.

Chapter Fifty-Nine

Riordan staggered, caught himself on the rim of the pod, the world corkscrewing around him. "Where... where the hell is she? How is this possible? What's going on?"

"Evidently, your mate's body is gone."

Thanks for stating the obvious, asshole. "But she was embedded through this node. Don't you—?"

"Human, I am a node keeper. That is all. I am not responsible for biohousing the users or other participants. That is a separate activity, performed, as you see, in a separate facility."

"But she's still in the simulation."

"Human, this is simply where she was initially embedded into Ur Virtua. She could have been moved quite easily, particularly once she was medically stabilized."

"Wait. You said that she had to stay in Virtua to survive. That without it—"

"That is not what I said. I said her survival would be threatened if she became *aware* of the simulation, because then she will reject immersion in it. But it is possible that she was transported to another node while in a temporary state of more complete cryostasis."

Riordan thought he might vomit as he realized the next question he had to ask. "Could she be dead?"

"No. A consciousness can continue in Virtua even if the body requires complete life support, but the brain must still function. I suspect this was the primary reason her overseers embedded her in Ur Virtua. It was insurance, to keep her mind active even if the rest of her body continued to decline."

Exhausted, swaying on his feet, forgetting how malevolent Kutkh could be, Riordan mumbled, "So what do I do now? Where do I go?"

"Records housed in this facility will indicate who took your mate's body and their intended destination." Kutkh stared into the distance for a moment. "The transfer records have now been relayed to your ship. We are finished. You must leave."

Riordan nodded. Or tried to. He discovered that once his head dropped forward, he could not lift it easily. When he tried, the world spun.

He reached out to steady himself against the rim of the hexagonal hatch.

"You look ill, human. The stimulants are wearing off sooner than I expected. Can you move? Do you require assistance?"

"I do not," Riordan responded defiantly.

Even as the floor rushed up at him, bringing abrupt blackness.

"Caine Riordan, I understand that you are fatigued, but please, attempt to focus."

Caine blinked, realized his eyes had already been open but couldn't remember what, if anything, they'd been seeing. At the moment, they showed him an unfamiliar ceiling. He raised up on his elbows.

Hsontlosh was uncomfortably close, blocking his view. "Has the nausea passed, Mr. Riordan?"

"Must have. Can't remember experiencing it or anything else..."

Elena!

Caine jerked upright. His head swam; he fell back.

"Please, Mr. Riordan, move slowly. We had to increase the stimulant dose to inadvisable levels. But before you can commence your actual recovery, we must report what has occurred in your absence and set our course."

"More stimulant? I don't remember—"

"After the shock of discovering that Elena Corcoran was not on Leltlosu-shai, and the node keeper's stimulant wore off, you slipped into a semiconscious state. The new dose we administered will not last long. This time, sit up slowly."

Riordan felt simultaneously exhausted and jumpy. He was shivering even though he wasn't cold. "Okay. Update me."

"*Dios mio,*" said a familiar voice. "Hear that? He's giving orders already."

Riordan frowned, searched his memories for that distinctive accent. "D-Dora?"

"Who else?" Pandora Veriden replied with a twist of trademark sass. She smiled crookedly as Hsontlosh backed away from Riordan and revealed the rest of his surroundings.

He was in a Dornaani sick bay. And it was lined with smiling faces he hadn't seen in four years. Bannor. Peter. Duncan. Dora. Newton Baruch. Miles O'Garran. Even Yaargraukh. And, most surprising of all, Ayana Tagawa. Eku stood off to one side, very much by himself, looking...furtive?

Riordan's body quaked involuntarily. He couldn't be sure if it was from the drug, surprise, relief, or joy. But alongside those feelings rose a less pleasant sensation. "What the hell are you doing here? You can't just travel—"

"Correction, Boss," Miles O'Garran almost sneered. "Since we're here, we obviously *can.*"

"Little Guy, I am glad to see you, every one of you. So glad that I won't even try to explain it. But what about the Lost Soldiers, the Cold Guard, the rest of the crew?"

"Still hiding, still safe," answered Bannor with a lazy smile. "Alnduul is trying to work out a deal for them."

"Alnduul? Making a deal on behalf of hundreds of renegade humans?"

Newton murmured, "It is a brave new world indeed, Commodore."

Riordan shook his head, wondered if he was still in a semiconscious state and if it might include bouts of delirium. "Ms. Ayana, while I am glad to see that you made it off Earth—"

"Explanations should wait until time permits, Commodore. For now, you must heed Hsontlosh's warning."

Riordan nodded, turned his attention to the face that was much higher than, and radically different from, any other. "Yaargraukh, I am guessing that matters back on your homeworld have not improved."

The Hkh'Rkh simply inclined his head-neck.

Riordan returned the nod, leaned back. "Where are we?" he asked the room. "And where is Irzhresht?"

Uncomfortable looks crisscrossed the space behind Hsontlosh, whose lids lowered slightly. "I am saddened to report that Irzhresht was killed four days ago."

"Killed? How?"

"She was electrocuted."

Damn. "Doing what?"

Hsontlosh's gills tightened. "Apparently betraying us. She triggered a security countermeasure while seeding coded messages into our communications stream. The routing data indicate that they were to be carried out-system."

"And you killed her for that? She could have been sending confidential updates to Alnduul, for all we know." And which Caine rather expected: Alnduul had clearly intended for his various assistants to keep surreptitious watch upon each other.

Hsontlosh blinked. "I was not aware she might be involved in authorized back-channel communications." He seemed ready to glance at Eku, but stopped himself. "At any rate, no one sought her death. It was she who attempted to bypass my own ship's automated protection systems. Unfortunately, they were still calibrated for loji space, where criminals are rarely dissuaded by anything less than lethal force."

"Have you been able to determine who she was sending to?"

Hsontlosh snapped down the fingers of both hands; they resembled clusters of stilettos. "She was sending messages to a powerful Patron—the term translates literally as 'Apex'—who dwells upon the First Ring. But we have been unable to break Irzhresht's code."

Riordan's brow grew cold. "You suspect she meant to sabotage us?"

"Yes, or simply undermine your mission." Seeing Caine's puzzlement, Hsontlosh added, "The mishandling of your mate's transport and care has been perpetrated solely by loji. This may indicate a concerted effort on their part."

"But why?"

Hsontlosh's burble was exasperated. "The Rings may assert they are loyal to the Collective, but old resentments still turn with them. To many there, whatever injures Dornaan is as succulent as new-hatched smelt."

Ayana's eyes were very bright. "Then I am at a loss to understand why Alnduul risked entrusting the Commodore's safety and mission to loji."

Eku's eyes were lowered, his tone clipped. "Necessity."

Hsontlosh's fingers rolled through the air. "Our continuing search will require that we examine private data compilations, consult cooperatives that specialize in illicit activities, interact with violators of numerous prime statutes, and possibly visit worlds that are interdicted or 'cordoned' from contact. Alnduul foresaw this."

"And that's where you come in."

Hsontlosh wagged a finger. "My credentials as a ship's master and pilot are more crucial than my familiarity with the illegal activities of lojis. Indeed, I am not an optimal representative to my own people."

Newton lowered his head slightly. "And why is that?"

Hsontlosh turned to look at the human. "They consider me a traitor."

Dora's tone was incisive. "Are you?"

"From their point of view, I am collaborating with their traditional adversary and constant oppressor: the Collective."

Ayana nodded. "And from *your* perspective?"

Hsontlosh's speech became more constricted. "I am a Dornaani, first and last. The bigotry of both sides belies our claim to be an enlightened species. Few know this better than I. Only because I am regarded with suspicion by *both* societies am I allowed to operate in them. That is why Alnduul selected me; no matter where the search may lead, I can expedite it. Also, when he learned that he might be prevented from doing so himself, he needed a pilot. Accordingly, he provided me with the necessary authorization and contacts to acquire this shift-capable ship. I returned with it from system HR 4084 A five days ago, just before Irzhresht's demise."

Riordan nodded his approval at the unfamiliar bulkheads. "So exactly whose ship is this, then?"

Eku spoke before Hsontlosh could. "It has been indefinitely requisitioned under Alnduul's authority as a Custodian. His request invoked an obscure and archaic provision for furnishing a small starship to 'diplomats, dignitaries, or important visitors.' However, shift-craft can only be operated by government personnel or by licensed pilots." He gestured without looking. "Such as Hsontlosh."

Hsontlosh tapped his control vantbrass. The image of a ship appeared over Riordan's bed. It was narrower than *Olsloov*, more of a spearhead than a delta-shape. "It is among the smallest shift-craft the Collective ever built. Its overall length is one hundred and seventy meters. Its smart hull enables dynamic optimization of aerodynamics. It is also equipped with a self-energizing grid."

Riordan raised an eyebrow. "Which means...?"

"That, despite its small size, this ship can conduct a standing shift. Furthermore, the lifting body's leading edges, the prow, and the stern all have extendable EM emitters for extra radiation shielding. However, the habitation modules rely on physical shielding alone when they are in rotational configuration."

Riordan scanned the ship's smooth, flowing lines for any sign of hab mods. "Uh...I don't see any modules."

Hsontlosh tapped his vantbrass. Just forward of where the airframe widened into sharply swept wings, the hull retracted, revealing two pods. They extended outward from a rotational collar sleeved around what looked to be the ship's formidable spine.

Riordan leaned back. "How long was it in mothballs?"

"In what?"

"In storage," Peter furnished mildly.

"Approximately nine centuries."

Riordan's and Eku's were the only human eyes in the room that did not widen; Yaargraukh's black, knob-ended eyestalks tucked back under his cranial shelf.

Hsontlosh was studying Caine. "You seem less surprised than your crew, Mr. Riordan."

"I ought to be. Even *Olsloov* is three centuries old." He nodded at the floating image. "When was the hull laid down?"

"Just over fifteen centuries ago, at which point it was already a somewhat dated model. It is one of the last of its class in such excellent condition."

Riordan nodded. "So where are we heading?"

The loji burbled once again. "What little data and documentation we were able to glean from the biohousing facility indicate that we should visit four systems between Leltlosu and the Collective's main naval reserve facility in L 1815-5A, which we call Ygzhush."

Duncan Solsohn folded his arms. "Which translates as...?"

"Depot. The first world along that route requires caution. It does not enjoy full Collective membership. It is what you would call a protectorate."

"It has a large loji population. Two rings," Eku added in response to Caine's frown, but without looking at him.

Riordan folded his arms. "And why do we need to go there?" *And what the hell is eating at you, Eku?*

"The protectorate system is a major hub for loji traffic," Hsontlosh replied. "Your mate's module is likely to have passed through it. And, as I intimated before, it is in just such systems that we must search for additional leads, since your mate is not being transported by officially sanctioned carriers." His concluding tone was almost challenging, as if he expected someone—Eku?—to contradict him.

Dora nodded. "So Elena is black cargo, requiring private transport. Your equivalent of a tramp freighter, no questions asked or answered. Cash and carry."

Hsontlosh had to work to keep up with her colloquialisms. He finally waved two tentative fingers. "Yes. It is as you say. I think."

Duncan frowned. "If that's true, then why is Depot such a crucial waypoint for us? Sounds like the kind of place loji would avoid. Probably a lot of Collective bureaucracy and patrols."

Eku's voice was flat. "Over ninety-five percent of Depot's security and processing, both shipboard and spaceside, is provided by advanced semiautonomous systems. Also, it is the largest legitimate source of spare parts and repairs in the Collective. It is a natural gathering point for spacefarers of all backgrounds."

Hsontlosh trailed a languid finger in Caine's direction. "More importantly, though, it is the astrographic gateway to Elena Corcoran's likely location: the Border Worlds. If her overseers are using illegal medical technologies and an illicit Ur Virtua node to sustain her, they require a location that is not only secret, but quite remote."

Riordan nodded. "So, even the Border Worlds have nodes of their own? Or could that just be a rumor?"

Eku shook his head grimly. "Mr. Riordan, consider what you have learned about the Collective. There are scores of illegal virtuality models with millions of users. There are gray and black markets for almost every conceivable illicit commodity or service. There are thousands, possibly millions, of disaffected loji who emigrate to systems that Collective ships rarely, if ever, visit. Correlate these facts and conjecture: where will one most readily find working access to, and support of, these activities?"

Riordan nodded. "Somewhere near the Collective, yet beyond ready scrutiny. The Border Worlds." Which, from the sound of it, was an interstellar outback where he and his companions would be unwanted and unwelcome. Except, perhaps, as unsuspecting targets of opportunity. He sighed. *Well, if that's what it takes...*

Hsontlosh possibly sensed Riordan's withdrawal from the conversation. He drifted toward the door. "One last matter, Mr. Riordan: your assistive recovery therapy. I need your express consent before I commence treatment."

Riordan sat up. "What does it entail?"

"A mixture of pharmaceuticals and brain destimulation that ensures up to twenty hours of deep, dreamless sleep daily. This, in alternation with four hours of daily exercise and nutrient intake, will promote rapid and maximum recovery."

"Did you say brain *de*stimulation?" From Newton's tone of voice, it sounded more like he was reaching for a gun than asking for medical clarification.

Eku raised a palm. "It is simply an outgrowth of the technology used in our control circlets and virtuality interfaces."

Miles O'Garran frowned. "You mean your cure is to put Caine back in never-never land? What is this? Hair of the dog?"

Eku shook his head. "No. The interface eases the brain into more quiescent states, so the subject spends more time in deeper sleep." He moved abruptly toward the iris valve. "Hsontlosh and I should depart. The stimulants will wear off quite soon."

As he and the loji exited, there was an exaggerated amount of space between them.

Chapter Sixty

JULY 2124
DEEP SPACE, BD+75 403A

The moment the iris valve closed, Riordan nodded at his team. "I need your best guess. Have either of those two been eavesdropping on you?"

Dora shrugged. "No way to tell."

"Figured. So we need to work out a method for written exchanges. Now, what the hell is the real story behind Irzhresht's death?"

Duncan shook his head. "Damned if I know, sir. From the moment we arrived three weeks ago, Eku seemed scared or suspicious of us. Maybe both. Hsontlosh went to get the new ship just three days later. A few days after that, Irzhresht started avoiding Eku."

Peter's shook his head. "Even before Hsontlosh departed, none of them were at ease with each other."

Riordan frowned. "Any idea why?"

O'Garran shrugged. "Didn't know the players well enough to even guess. But then again, they didn't seem to know each other that well."

Bannor nodded. "None of them are exactly sociable types. But I found it suspicious when Eku didn't take to us. Alnduul made it clear to him that we are trusted friends."

"Eku's a factotum. He doesn't always react like other humans."

Dora wagged a hand impatiently. "Yeah, okay, but can we trust him?"

Riordan considered. "I don't think he'd work against our interests. But that's not the same thing as his telling us the whole truth and nothing but the truth when it comes to what he knows or what he's up to."

Dora threw up both hands. "So the short answer about trusting him is, 'not really.'"

Riordan made his voice firm and level. "No, the answer is that we can trust him to a point. But he's not a de facto asset. Which is what you're *really* asking."

Dora grumbled, studied her nails, nodded evasively.

Riordan leaned back. "How did you find out about Irzhresht's death?"

Ayana Tagawa sat straighter. "Hsontlosh informed us. Eku was with him when he did, but did not speak."

Riordan rubbed his chin. "Did Hsontlosh show you where she died?"

"Yeah," grumbled O'Garran, "for all the good that did, staring around at a cockpit full of Dornaani fairy tech."

Ayana waited until O'Garran had finished grousing. "The chief is correct. However, Eku *is* familiar with the boat's systems and he did not question Hsontlosh's account, nor did his demeanor suggest that he had unspoken reservations."

Duncan shook his head. "Frankly, I think Eku has reservations about everyone. Except you, Commodore. Maybe he'll open up if he gets an opportunity to meet you alone."

Riordan shrugged. "Maybe. But if Eku suspected that Irzhresht's death put me at imminent and greater risk, he would have told you."

"That assumes," Yaargraukh added in reluctant tone, "that Eku is indeed a loyal servitor. However, his present attitude seems at odds with assumption. So let us imagine for a moment that he is not. If he suggested that Hsontlosh baited Irzhresht to her death, Eku would rightly anticipate that his accusation could be perceived as an attempt to deflect suspicion from himself."

O'Garran nodded. "And even if Eku is Alnduul's man Friday, what do we really know about him?"

Riordan shook his head. "We know that he's been traveling with Alnduul for centuries and that Alnduul trusts him."

Yaargraukh's small ears flattened slightly; he did not like what he was about to say. "If that is true, then should we not have trusted Irzhresht also? She, too, enjoyed Alnduul's trust."

Riordan shook his head. "Irzhresht's loyalty is more problematic than Eku's. Not only was she with Alnduul for a much shorter period of time, but even the most trustworthy loji might still be vulnerable to extortion by others of their kind."

Dora's eyes were grim. "You mean, by having relatives held hostage, that kind of thing?"

"That and much worse."

O'Garran shrugged. "But boss, that brings us right back where we started. Everyone's still a suspect."

Bannor unfolded his arms. "I can't see any way to settle this here and now."

"No," agreed Duncan, "but every day we don't may put us at greater risk."

"Of waking up on the wrong side of the airlock?" muttered Dora.

"No, of not knowing who to trust while we're almost totally ignorant about where we are, where we're going, and what we might have to do when we get there."

Riordan nodded. "Which means, that if we have to take a chance, we reach out to Eku." Seeing hesitation in several faces, Riordan leaned forward. "Look, if Irzhresht was a traitor, then the problem is behind us. On the other hand, if she was a victim, then we've got two suspects. And no, I don't know why he's being so distant all of a sudden, and I don't know him well enough to trust him. But I *do* trust Alnduul's confidence in him."

Yaargraukh pony-wagged his head. "There is merit in that deduction."

O'Garran sucked at his teeth. "Yeah, but if Mr. Eku is smart, that might also be the way he figured it would all play out when we compare our options on who to trust. Because the path to preferring him over Hsontlosh does seem pretty inevitable, doesn't it?"

Riordan nodded. "So even if we are provisionally prepared to rely on Eku, we can't completely disregard the possibility that he's the murderer. Now, how and where is the rest of the group?"

Bannor leaned against the bulkhead. "We were forced to activate our final contingency: bring everyone together in Zeta Tucanae. But they're all fine." Seeing Riordan's bent eyebrow, he added, "Really."

Duncan nodded. "Best morale in years."

"Why?"

"Because Alnduul is searching for a way to bring everyone over the border."

Riordan started. "*That's* the deal he's working on? To bring them all into the Collective?"

O'Garran's voice was a hiss. "Keep it down, Boss, or you might as well put it on the intership. But yeah, that's the plan."

"Okay, but how does he—?"

"Alnduul did not explain," Yaargraukh said quietly. "Which was, I think, prudent."

Duncan rubbed his chin. "Yeah, the longer we've been here, the more I get the feeling that Alnduul's plan must involve bending some rules. The Collective makes Beltway bureaucracy looks speedy and minimal. There's no way their, uh, Senior Arbiters would give official approval within a useful timeframe. Assuming they'd ever give our people asylum at all."

Approval notwithstanding, that sounds like a great option for us—but not so great for Alnduul. Riordan sat up as straight as the cocoon bed allowed. "Now, the most important question: why the hell are *you* here? You're supposed to be looking out for everyone else."

Bannor folded his arms. "Yeah, about that. Once we agreed to Alnduul's plan for complete extraction, we realized there was a leadership issue that needed settling. Specifically, that if we left the CTR, you had to be the CO."

Riordan wasn't sure if his breath was short because the stimulant was wearing off or because of the heavy responsibility that Bannor had dropped on his chest. "No. That's your role, Colonel Rulaine. You're career military. And you've been the commander for four years."

"Which almost everyone has spent in cold sleep," his friend replied. "So not a lot of commanding got done. But here's the real point: we're not a conventional unit and we sure as hell don't have a conventional mission. Yet I'm a conventional officer with conventional training.

"That's why everyone still thinks of me as the XO. Including me. Because given who we are and where we're going, our commander has to be more than a conventional CO." He didn't give Riordan the chance to rebut. "We also need a diplomat, a first contact expert, and yeah, a polymath. We're out where no humans have ever set foot, so we have nothing but each other—which all started with you. So"—he grinned and held out the letter of marque Caine had given him four years ago—"you're stuck with us again. Commodore."

Riordan shook his head. "If this journey takes us into the Border Worlds, it's a total unknown. Anything could happen."

"Yes," Duncan said with an assessing gaze, "it could. And that's why it's also a unique intel opportunity. We'll go to worlds that the Dornaani aren't bothering to police. Or over which they've lost control."

Dora's eyes widened. "Yeah. Nothing will show us the Collective's state of play as honestly as the places they don't want us to see." Her smile matched the one on Duncan's face. "*Coño,* talk about killing two birds with one stone."

Newton was frowning. "We should be mindful of aggravating the Collective's authorities. Had they foreseen the turn of events that brought us all to this point, they might have declared the Border Worlds off limits."

Caine shrugged. "Yes, but they've also renounced any responsibility for Elena or for my return to Terran space. So I can expect benign neglect in my further travels, just as long as I don't break any laws."

"You keep saying 'I,' Commodore," Peter murmured, "when you should be saying 'we.'"

"That's because, despite all your well-rehearsed rhetoric, I cannot let you come along."

Miles O'Garran pushed forward. "All due respect, sir, we didn't come out here to put the letter of marque back in your hand and then wave goodbye as you go solo on this crazy quest of yours. We wouldn't be together if it wasn't for you. And now that we don't have a home anymore, well, it's like Colonel Rulaine says: all we've got is each other. So staying together is what counts. And *keeping* us together is what you're good at. So you're leading. And we're coming. End of story. Sir." O'Garran looked as surprised at his outburst as anyone else in the room.

Bannor smiled faintly. "Caine, before we got on board *Olsloov,* we all promised each other that we were going to see this through. Not just for you, but for Elena."

Riordan managed not to show how desperately glad he was. "Sounds like I don't really have a choice."

Bannor shook his head. "No choice at all." He grinned. "Commodore."

PART FIVE

The Border Worlds and Beyond
November 2124–March 2125

TERRA INCOGNITA

(Unknown/unexplored regions.)

Chapter Sixty-One

Riordan, hand on his vac suit's tether, turned away from the closing airlock hatch and looked starward. The incandescent red-orange ball that was L 1815-5 A raged silently against the blackness of space. Off to one side was a small sickle of vermillion: the main world, a sliver of its sun-blasted bright-face limning its unlit bulk. In the middle ground, a small patch of the deep dark was marked by faint, intermittent glitters: ships of the immense depot that gave the system its name.

Caine checked the heads-up display inside the lightly built Dornaani helmet. The rads were still well beneath the suit's tolerances. Every other indicator was teal, the color of optimum functionality for the vacuum suits that Eku had brought from the *Olsloov*. Like most objects of Dornaani manufacture, they either never experienced mechanical failures, were self-repairing, or both. And the semiautonomous assistant invariably anticipated and displayed the wanted information at just the right moment. Extremely helpful, but also a bit eerie.

Riordan had organized and ordered a training rotation with their various suits, most of which had been brought by his crew. It was particularly helpful to Murray Liebman and Craig Girten, the Lost Soldiers from the twentieth century. They had never been EVA before, although Liebman insisted on calling it a "space walk," for some reason. Even after weeks of training, they exited the airlock with exaggerated caution, but without their initial white-knuckle hold upon the tethers.

However, broadening everyone's qualifications on diverse EVA gear was not why Riordan had initiated the training regimen. Partly, it had been to get away from the mindless routine of sleeping twenty hours, exercising aggressively, cramming special foods into his mouth and then exercising again. Space was a good place to think, to get outside of himself by getting outside of the ship.

In the distance, he spied a tiny flare of blue-white. It lasted ten seconds, then was gone. That was Hsontlosh and his primary proxrov, counterthrusting as they returned from finalizing the ship's maintenance arrangements. They had also surreptitiously canvassed the civilian highport to confirm the lead they had picked up seven days ago in the LP 36-181 system. Specifically, that the ship that had taken Elena's medical cryopod from the biohousing facility on Leltlosu-shai had passed through Depot only a few weeks later. Without even stopping to refuel. Clearly, that ship was going someplace in a hurry.

Hsontlosh's imminent return meant that it was also time to finish the plan that had necessitated Caine's instigation of the EVA program, since that made his access to space a routine rather than notable event. He released the smart flap on the suit's right leg pocket and removed a small matte black sphere: the emergency beacon that Alnduul had given him the day *Olsloov* set course for Leltlosu IV.

Riordan considered its featureless surface, wondered if he was being prudent or paranoid by deploying it here. So far, the greatest danger he or anyone else had experienced was the anxiety of living on a ship operated by so small a crew: Hsontlosh, Eku, two proxrovs, and a handful of repairbots.

But Depot was the end of Collective space. The enigmatic Border Worlds lay beyond. Hsontlosh was mostly unfamiliar with them, Eku wholly so. So this system was akin to that line delineating the far margin of an ancient explorer's map, marked with the legend *terra incognita*: the last place to leave a message in a bottle. Or to discreetly deploy Alnduul's beacon.

Riordan squeezed the sphere, felt it pulse three times: activated. With one steadying hand on the hull, he lobbed it into the black, felt the perpetual muscle soreness in his chest and shoulders as he did. Happily, that ache would soon decrease. This was his last day of treatment and incessant exercise. Less happily, he still had one last set of free weights to push through.

Both Hsontlosh and Eku agreed that Caine's post-Virtua recovery had not merely been successful, but remarkable: almost no degradation of memory and full recovery of his original mass within the first thirty days. However, he had continued to boost his weightlifting regimen. His reflexes were still wired for the additional muscle he had accrued in Ur Virtua, which had saved his virtual life on a few occasions. No reason not to have it here in the real world, too.

Riordan turned his back upon the red dwarf star, reentered the airlock, cycled it, and opened the inner hatch.

Eku was standing directly in front of him, less than half a meter away. With one hand pushed deep in the pocket of his duty jacket, he gestured for Riordan to back up. Back into the airlock.

Riordan balked. Neither Eku's expression nor posture were threatening, but—

"Quickly," Eku muttered urgently, "before the autonomous surveillance subroutine decides to record us."

So, this isn't an ambush. I hope. Riordan remained facing the factotum as he reentered the airlock.

As Eku stepped forward to follow, he yanked his hand from his pocket, stuck it out toward Riordan.

Who aborted his reflex to parry in mid motion. Eku was holding what looked like an oversize remote control fob.

"What is it?"

"Take it!" Eku whispered. As Riordan slipped the fob into his own pocket, Eku explained, speaking more rapidly than Riordan had ever heard. "Alnduul instructed me to give this to you if our safety ever became uncertain. It is a universal access and override—a backdoor passkey into all Custodial systems. Including every one on this ship."

"Can it—?"

"Be silent. It can also leave behind a hidden signal in any system that has a communications network." He turned to leave.

Riordan grabbed his arm—it was surprisingly muscular. "Eku, why are you giving this to me now? Has something happened? Do you no longer trust Hsontlosh?"

"Mr. Riordan, I have not trusted anyone except you since Alnduul left me on Leltlosu-shai. I did not even trust Irzhresht, at the last. I suspect she did not trust me either. Nor does Hsontlosh, now; he has denied me access to certain parts of the ship.

There have been, and continue to be, too many unknowns for my comfort. But if we encounter trouble in the Border Worlds, use this universal access key to leave a signal for Alnduul. It will help him find us. You have already taken the first step by deploying the beacon just minutes ago. He will use that as the marker from which to begin his search."

"Wait: how did you know that I just—?"

"Did you truly believe I would *not* know when you activated the beacon? Now, come. We must reenter the ship before we are missed."

Chapter Sixty-Two

JANUARY 2125
INNER SYSTEM, BD+37 878

Sweaty and six weeks post-therapy, Caine jogged toward the one iris valve that always seemed reluctant to get out of his way. But as usual, it did so just in time, revealing the outsized compartment that his team had repurposed into a human common area.

Seeing it was full, Caine wondered if he should hit the showers first. Bannor was already there, and they'd spent the morning sparring. After which Rulaine had worked out with the archaic dumbbells that he took everywhere and were some kind of family heirloom. Riordan suspected that their combined reek might even be too much for Dornaani air filtration to handle. On the other hand, this was certainly one way to test its limits.

Dora nodded gruffly in Caine's direction. She, like Riordan, had just been roused out of two weeks of cold sleep. Tagawa and Bannor, who were about to return to their cryopods, greeted him more sociably. Yaargraukh looked up from rebrewing the Dornaani equivalent of tea at the all-purpose and mostly automated refectory station. Given the Hkh'Rkh preference for strong tastes, he had to brew it three times.

As soon as Riordan sat, too tired to even get a bulb of water, Dora leaned toward him. "You get the memo from Hsontlosh about wanting our permission to stop at a cordoned world?"

Riordan nodded. The Dornaani captain had made the inquiry when Riordan and the rest of first watch—Dora, Duncan, and Craig—were still in cold sleep. It was becoming a trend; Hsontlosh didn't seek permission for anything potentially hazardous until Riordan was in cryo. "Other than it being isolated from Collective contact, is there anything particularly noteworthy about the planet?"

Bannor shook his head as he bit into one of the many mystery sandwiches that had been transferred from *Olsloov*. "No intel either way."

Riordan looked away from the sandwich. The bread looked normal, but the fillings, while agreeable, were enigmas best left unexamined.

Bannor mercifully made the rest of the sandwich vanish. "I understand why Hsontlosh minimizes how often we go dirtside. But not being materially involved in the search? That irks me." He stretched his arms. "Of course, we don't know the language and the locals consider us boors or vermin. Or both."

Dora snorted. "Don't forget, we're cretins, too. And pinheads."

Which, Riordan had to admit, was an accurate summary of how they'd been treated on the few occasions they'd made planetfall, usually to search for human-edible provisions. After six weeks of travel, they'd gone through more than two thirds of all the rations that *Olsloov* had transferred. The only way to significantly reduce the rate of consumption had been to split into three watches, two of which were in cold sleep at any time. "What about you, Ms. Tagawa? What are your impressions about Hsontlosh's latest request?"

She set down her own post-workout beverage: weak tea. If she perspired at all, it was a faint sheen. "I observe two trends. Firstly, Hsontlosh provides admirably detailed summaries of what transpires during his visits. But secondly, no matter how long his report, and no matter how much activity he undertook on our behalf, we never spend more than a few days inactive in any system. Whether this is because he is able to swiftly determine that there is no further profit in tarrying, or some species of urgency, I cannot discern."

Riordan nodded. Technically, their journey was turning out to be exactly what Hsontlosh had predicted: a lot of monotony until they found a good lead. But since they hadn't found one yet, they spent a great deal of time reading and training. And there would be even less to do after Rulaine, Tagawa and Newton rotated back into cold sleep after dinner, so maybe... "How about another match, Bannor?"

His friend glared at him. "Caine, I promised myself I wouldn't ask, but now I've got to. What the hell were you doing in Virtua? Fighting barbarian hordes?"

"Actually, we never faced off against barbarians. Just about everyone else, though." Riordan glanced meaningfully at the Dornaani version of PVC pipe that they kept in the commons as training swords.

Bannor shook his head. "I'm done. Dora?"

She tilted her chair back. "I kicked the Commodore's ass first thing this morning with short blades. Well, short pipes. But with the swords? Nah, I'll let D'Artagnan here bruise someone else for a while." She glanced evilly in Yaargraukh's direction. "What about you, Grendel? Bet he won't be so eager to close in on you." Dora smiled at her brand new nickname for the Hkh'Rkh.

Which was evidently not as private a joke as she had anticipated; Yaargraukh's eyes retracted. "You seem to forget, Ms. Veriden, that my other human language is German. Narratives from related and origin languages were required reading."

Dora's response was one Caine had never witnessed before: she looked abashed. "So, eh, you got the reference?"

"I did," Yaargraukh rumbled. "As for sparring with the Commodore, I have already had the honor."

"And?" she pressed.

Yaargraukh's neck swiveled around its axis: a Hkh'Rkh shrug. "It is in the nature of our two species that I am stronger, run faster, and leap farther. The commodore is more agile and dexterous."

"And?" she pressed.

"I have more bruises, but his are larger. Now, if you will excuse me..."

Before Yaargraukh could take a step toward it, the iris valve whispered open. Hsontlosh stood on the threshold. "May I enter?"

"It's your ship," Dora muttered, looking the other way.

Even the loji was able to decipher her reaction; his tattoos darkened slightly.

Riordan rose. "Please, come in. Some of us"—he cut sharp eyes at Veriden—"are getting frustrated with the lack of progress. Particularly since Eku tells us we're nearing the end of the Border Worlds."

Hsontlosh's eyelids cycled slowly. "I share your impatience for more promising results. That is the reason for my visit. We must soon choose whether or not to chart a course that leads to Psi Tauri III, one of the cordoned worlds I mentioned at the start of our journey. If we elect not to go there, our path forward becomes more uncertain."

Riordan gestured to the one saddle-shaped Dornaani chair in the room. "Let's discuss that."

"Very well." Hsontlosh looked around at the other faces, perhaps trepidatiously, but then slid into the chair. "What are your concerns?"

Riordan's crew had grown very quiet, focused. "You said at the outset that cordoned worlds are high risk, that you wished to avoid them if possible. But now you're telling us we should go to one. Why?"

Hsontlosh shifted uneasily in his seat. "In several recent systems, there have been rumors of special services that might be available on Psi Tauri III, or at least contacts who know where they are offered. However, the gray marketeers in *this* system insist that Psi Tauri's access to these services is not mere rumor, but fact. If they are right, this cordoned world may provide an answer that leads to the successful completion of your quest." Seeing Caine sit up sharply, he waved temporizing fingers through the air. "I emphasize: it may provide *an* answer."

Riordan worked to keep the annoyance out of his voice. "Hsontlosh, I appreciate you are trying to manage my expectations, but right now, I need you to be direct."

Hsontlosh touched his index fingers together; Riordan noticed they were trembling. "Let us begin by acknowledging that finding Elena Corcoran is but the first of many steps in restoring her to you. Agreed?"

"That's always been understood as the probable situation, yes."

"Now let us recall the possibility that, due to neglect or inoperability, her body cannot be healed. Even in that dire circumstance, there may now be a means of reclaiming her that is available on, or through arrangement with, this cordoned world."

"And this means of reclaiming her is... what?"

"Recarnation."

Dora scowled. "What else are you offering? Voodoo?"

Hsontlosh ignored her, kept his focus on Caine. "Not *rein*carnation. *Recarnation*. To furnish her mind with a new body."

Riordan was confused. "But her mind would still be trapped in her original body."

Hsontlosh's long exhalation fluttered his gills. "That statement may not be completely accurate." He folded his hands. "It has always been legal for the minds of the dying to remain embedded in Virtua. Factotums have long availed themselves of that option. So do an increasing number of Dornaani who are no longer able to rejuvenate their bodies."

"Wait, are you saying that when their bodies die, their minds *do* live on?"

Hsontlosh's fingers flapped erratically. "That debate continues. However, there are new, albeit secret, developments that suggest that true consciousness may persist. My contacts in this system intimated that well-resourced Dornaani have had their minds linked to cloned bodies in the same way that bioproxies are slaved to their owners."

Caine leaned forward. "So *maybe* a mind can exist after its body dies, and *maybe* it could operate a clone-puppet by remote control. That's still a long way from the recarnation you mentioned. There's got to be more."

"That is precisely what I said to my sources, Mr. Riordan."

"And?"

"And their answers became cautious, oblique. They included a very long overview of the Collective's ambiguous legal attitudes regarding attempts to fuse achievements in cloning with those of machine consciousness. I will spare you the details."

"*Gracias a Dios*," muttered Dora.

"Specifically, there are no laws against combining the two technologies, but nor are there approved procedures for experiments or testing. Consequently, practitioners in the Collective avoid involving themselves in such unconventional researches."

Bannor leaned back. "But anything that the Collective avoids, the loji gray market sees as an opportunity."

Hsontlosh rose two affirming index fingers. "Yes, and they may have achieved a breakthrough. Using a machine-contained consciousness and a cognitively inert clone of the original body, they have reportedly developed an interface that enables a mind-to-body transfer."

Riordan forced the skeptic in him to move well in front of the hopeful lover. "Even if what you're describing is possible"—*Could it be? Really?*—"we are no closer to finding Elena's body. And without that, none of this matters."

"That may not be entirely accurate either, Mr. Riordan. Consider the following facts. Elena Corcoran's mind exists within the most sophisticated mind-machine interface—and retention facility—of all: Ur Virtua. Samples of her blood and tissues have been taken and stored by numerous medical overseers. Psi Tauri III is either the location of, or gateway to, a mind transfer facility." Hsontlosh paused, letting the facts sink in. "She can be recarnated, Mr. Riordan. Healthy and whole."

He rose. "There is another factor to be considered. If we pursue this option, we will necessarily dive much deeper into the Border Worlds' underworld of illicit enterprises. Ironically, though, that may also put us in contact with persons who can locate her *actual* body." He waited. "Mr. Riordan?"

Caine was still trying to control his breathing, keep his thoughts ordered. "Yes?"

"As you required direct answers from me, I require a direct answer from you: do I have your permission to plot a course that will ultimately bring us to Psi Tauri III?"

Riordan nodded. "You do."

Hsontlosh was already halfway through the iris valve before he flared his fingers in an abbreviated version of the Dornaani gesture of farewell.

The common room was quiet for a long second.

"There's no way that's gray market tech," Bannor muttered. "That's black as a shark's eye."

Riordan nodded. "No doubt."

Dora was staring at the floor. Hard. "Caine, we came along as muscle to take Elena back by force if her abductors didn't comply. But with this cloning plan"—Dora shook her head—"you don't just need muscle. You need money. Uh, 'resources.' And you'll need lots."

Again Riordan nodded. "One problem at a time, Ms. Veriden. One problem at a time."

Ayana's voice was quiet, wistful. "I suspect our uncertainties would be fewer if Alnduul were with us." Solemn and unanimous nods approved her observation.

Riordan sighed. "I agree, Ms. Tagawa. And I suspect that, right about now, Alnduul would be far happier sharing our problems than dealing with his own."

Chapter Sixty-Three

With some effort, Alnduul focused on the blue-on-blue horizon beyond the broad window, where the sky and sea seemed to converge upon the towering Elder structure in the middle distance. Glamqoozht's most distinctive and iconic structure, it was a silent reminder of the regional capital's power and antiquity.

When Alnduul was sure his voice would not quaver, he asked, "How did Glayaazh die?"

"A shift failure. On the way here." Heethoo's voice was constricted, mournful. But then again, she had always been unusually expressive.

"A shift failure." Alnduul repeated. "That is almost unheard of. Is there any indication of a cause?"

"Nothing definitive," Suvtrush replied brusquely. "There may have been a slight navigational correction just prior to the event, but even that is uncertain."

The dispassionate recitation of the facts, or rather, the lack of them, calmed Alnduul, helped him focus. Which was essential if he was to emerge from the hearings with anything vaguely like an acceptable existence. He turned to face the room.

Four members of the investigatory board had been at the meetings with Caine Riordan: Heethoo, Nlastanl, Suvtrush, and Laynshooz. His eyelids flicked involuntarily when he regarded the latter. "I was not aware you had become a Senior Arbiter, Laynshooz."

"I am here as an acting Arbiter."

"Ah. To sit in place of Glayaazh." *Handpicked to ensure my downfall, no doubt.*

Laynshooz's reply was so indolent that it bordered on smugness. "No other suitable individual was able to respond in time."

Alnduul let his gaze drift into the far corners of the Communitarium. "I am even more surprised to see you here, Menrelm. I presumed the Custodial appointee to the board would come from the Audit Group, possibly the Senior Auditor himself."

"And so I have," Menrelm replied stiffly. "I am the acting Senior Auditor."

Alnduul cycled his eyelids very slowly. "You must be gratified at the felicitous change in your position. I heard that you had been removed from your position as Senior Mentor of the Arat Kur oversight group." *Hardly a surprise, since Menrelm's utter failure to detect the preinvasion preparations of the Wholenest was arguably the most spectacular case of Custodial incompetence in living memory.*

Menrelm became as stiff as his voice. "I was invited to serve directly under the Senior Auditor. Who is replacing Glayaazh as the Custodians' Senior Arbiter."

Which moves the Collective just that much further down the path of political disengagement. "And Vruthvur approved this?"

"Elder Custodian Vruthvur was traveling on other matters when the summons to this board arrived. He has not yet responded."

Alnduul lifted a single finger in acknowledgement, considered the faces in the room. Only Heethoo's was friendly. Nlastanl's was impartial. While scanning the rest, he did not allow his gills to ruffle in exasperation or misgiving. *And so the predators have swarmed me in deep water.* "Let us proceed."

"We have been ready to do so for almost a week," Suvtrush scolded. "What is the cause of your lateness?"

And so the shadow of the largest predator swims across the sun. "I was completing an errand of mercy that may have diplomatic benefits pleasing to both this board and the Collective. But that is a side matter. I am ready to begin."

Suvtrush raised himself high in his chair. "Alnduul, I am told you are familiar with the rules governing this board of inquiry."

"I have sat on many. Just not as their object of scrutiny."

"Long overdue," commented Laynshooz.

Suvtrush stared sharply at Laynshooz. "Personal invective has no place in these hearings."

Laynshooz's voice was stubborn. "That was not invective. It was a legal opinion founded upon a thorough consideration of the subject's career."

"Many voices on this board recommended against your inclusion, Laynshooz. More remarks of that nature will prove their reservations were well-founded."

Laynshooz shrank back slightly. "I shall alter my interactions appropriately."

"See that you do. Alnduul, we shall start by articulating those actions of yours that demonstrate the pattern of behavior evinced in the allegations, but are not under investigation today. Unless you have questions, we shall proceed."

Alnduul swished a finger toward the floor: no questions.

Heethoo recited the events that ostensibly established Alnduul's predisposition to ignore both proper procedure and his superiors: his siding with human and Slaasriithi ships against Ktor attackers at Homenest; his failure to censure the same forces for trespass when they rescued the Lost Soldiers from Turkh'saar; his unauthorized alteration of the Corcoran-simulacrum's source data; and lastly, his decision to use Custodial medical assets to save the lives of both Caine Riordan and Elena Corcoran.

As Heethoo finished, Menrelm leaned forward. "I should add that many on this board were disposed to include these actions in the list of charges against you."

Alnduul managed not to show any amusement. *Of that I am quite sure, Menrelm.*

Nlastanl commenced his part the proceedings—stating the actual allegations—with some reluctance. "Alnduul, based upon your own reports and records, which have been corroborated by accounts you neither deny nor contest, we determine that your following actions may warrant disciplinary measures.

"Firstly, after the most recent Convocation, you traveled to Earth without final authorization and implanted virus transmitters in humans to disable the Arat Kur data links.

"Secondly, you failed to recover three of the five viral transmitters that you implanted.

"Thirdly, during the counterattack upon the Arat Kur Whole-nest, your insufficient security precautions allowed the humans to learn how to conduct deep space shifts.

"However, it is the judgment of this board that your fourth and earliest violation was the most severe, since it was the root from which the others grew. Specifically, that you acted without authorization when you sent a factotum to introduce a medical biot into Nolan Corcoran to mediate the coronary damage he suffered during his intercept of the Doomsday Rock. In doing so, you preserved the one human who, more than any other, enabled their rapid and highly destabilizing interstellar expansion." Nlastanl spread his hands flat on the table and stared out toward the bay.

"This concludes the allegations," Suvtrush announced. "In summation, your mismanagement of the Custodians' human oversight initiatives makes you personally culpable, should war erupt between Earth and the Ktor."

Alnduul remained silent. The only way to handle such an outrageous statement was to politely ignore it.

Suvtrush's eyes narrowed slightly. "You have nothing to say?"

"I am prepared to allocute, if that is what you are asking."

Suvtrush leaned back slowly, his eyes hard upon Alnduul. "You may proceed."

Alnduul signaled his gratitude with two air-drifting fingers. "I shall deal with the last allegation first, since it is indeed the root of all that followed.

"Several years after his mission to the Doomsday Rock, Nolan Corcoran's cardiac instability increased without warning. The biot's implantation, which was pending final approval, required that the factotum be in position prior to any surgery. When Corcoran's condition continued to decline dramatically, we could no longer wait for authorization.

"If Corcoran had died, the humans would have been defeated or far more severely damaged when they were invaded over two decades later. So all my subsequent actions do indeed originate with the implantation of that biot. Including a further action you have not even bothered to mention."

Suvtrush's eyelids snicked audibly. "Indeed? And which is that?"

"My decision to carry out Corcoran's final request: to be buried in space."

Heethoo's gaze was steady, intrigued. "And how is that a violation?"

"I made the offer without prior authorization."

"That is a matter of no consequence," Suvtrush declared.

"I cannot agree. By doing so, I preemptively derailed a human investigation that would have been as damaging as revealing the existence of the Lost Soldiers."

Laynshooz's riposte was more sneer than statement. "If you are suggesting that Corcoran's body had to be removed to prevent closer forensic study, then you are compounding your past incompetence with present lies. The biot in Corcoran denatured into normative human biochemical compounds. It left no durable evidence."

"Correct. So you are also aware that the humans' forensic review detected the biot before it had completely vanished."

Laynshooz's voice became cautious. "If you are contending that the forensic damage had already been done, then there was no reason to remove Corcoran's body."

Alnduul trailed a patient finger in the air. "Laynshooz, your pursuit of a single smelt blinds you to the school in which it swims. As long as the humans possessed Corcoran's corpse, they might resume inquiries into his mysterious death. But without it, they would have no evidentiary basis for reopening the case. *That* is why Corcoran's body had to be removed."

Heethoo's breath went out of her gills in a warble of surprise. "Of course. Because a deeper investigation would have led to the factotum."

Alnduul swept two approving fingers upward. "Precisely. If the humans ever resumed asking questions about Corcoran, it would not be long before they ceased wondering *what* had been inside him, and instead began to ask *how* it got there. A cursory examination of his treatment records would show that just a week before the surgery, an individual with impeccable credentials was added to the postoperative team. But as their investigation went deeper, they would have discovered that every record pertaining to that person was not only electronic, but had since unwritten itself."

Heethoo's lids nictated once, very slowly. "Our factotum."

Nlastanl exhaled slowly. "And with the humans' postwar panic over Ktor-aligned infiltrators, the investigation would have been elevated to the highest priority. It would have engendered a paranoid outcry: just what we are trying to prevent by working to suppress disclosure of the Lost Soldiers."

Menrelm raised all his fingers. "Alnduul, it is perplexing that you were so careful to remove Corcoran's corpse and yet were so cavalier regarding the much more important matter of retrieving the virus transmitters you embedded in humans. That technology could destabilize not only their own polities, but the Accord itself. Yet the transmitters remain unrecovered."

Nlastanl's eyelids widened. "And do you have evidence of this ongoing dereliction of duty?"

Alnduul closed his eyes. "He does."

Suvtrush spread his fingers wide, turned to Menrelm. "Show us."

Menrelm complied. A holographic recording brightened at the center of the table. "This is the secure Communitarium on board *Olsloov*, just after the Arat Kur surrendered. Alnduul, I, and Vruthvur, then a Senior Coordinator of the Custodians, are present. This was the discussion."

The frozen figures began speaking. Alnduul heard the measured tone in his own voice. "Sabotaging the Arat Kur command and control on Earth was effected by a single human agent fitted with a viral implant. However, there were four others in place to perform the same task, if required."

"What of those other four devices? Have they been retrieved?"

"Not to my knowledge."

Menrelm's image sat suddenly erect. "Are you not responsible for these devices?"

"I am. However, we lost track of these operatives when we were compelled to accompany the humans to Homenest. We had no assets to leave behind for monitoring events or operatives on Earth."

"So you *chose* to leave four highly sophisticated cyberwarfare devices behind? In human hands? Unacceptable." Menrelm turned toward Vruthvur. "This operation has ever paddled beyond the edge of control and accountability. From the start, I have not liked it."

Alnduul's image raised a finger. "With respect, Menrelm, we had little choice. Without a Custodial flotilla to shield the humans, the only way to give them parity was by crippling their enemies. And since I received no authorization to make my presence known to the invaders, the virus had to be conveyed to the target by humans."

"And once they had liberated themselves, the implants should have been removed."

"Menrelm, had you ever known war, you would appreciate the axiom of the human strategist von Clausewitz: in war, even the simplest thing is very difficult. So it was in this case. Only one operative, Richard Downing, was even aware that he had an implant in his body. However, he was the senior intelligence officer for the Terran forces; we had neither the time nor seclusion to effect a surgical removal. Of the other four, two—Riordan and Elena Corcoran—came into our care after the Battle of Jakarta. Riordan's implant was removed while he underwent surgery. Elena Corcoran's condition was so critical that further surgery was likely to be fatal.

"The other two were inaccessible. One operative, Opal Patrone, was killed at the end of the Battle of Jakarta. Without a factotum in place, we could not infiltrate their casualty clearance services and gain access to her corpse. The other implant is in Trevor Corcoran, who remained on active duty. Again, we had neither access nor opportunity."

Menrelm waved the hologram away. "The implants are still unrecovered."

"True," Alnduul confirmed, "although I have sent over a dozen warnings to the Senior Assembly that, so long as the Collective eschewed communication with Earth, we had no way of correcting that situation. Of course, had we protected Earth as we promised, this war, and all the sequelae that you attribute to my incompetence, would not have occurred."

"Perhaps," Suvtrush allowed. "Yet, the combination of Corcoran's strategic foresight and our computer virus did not merely defeat Earth's invaders: it paralyzed them. The humans acquired a treasure trove of intact Arat Kur technology for analysis and emulation." He paused. "Or perhaps that was your intent all along."

Swim slowly and carefully, Alnduul told himself. *Here is where the sharpest teeth lurk.* "With respect, Suvtrush such a formulation relies entirely upon hindsight. The success of Corcoran's deception strategy, the cultural frictions between the Arat Kur and Hkh'Rkh, and Riordan's serendipitous presence at the enemy's command hub: none of these were foreseeable."

Suvtrush slashed the air with an accusing finger. "And yet you have not responded to, let alone denied, my assertion that Terran ascendance has been your undeclared objective for a century." He leaned forward. "You have been wildly intemperate in your support and admiration of humanity from your earliest years as Custodian and, as these allegations show, you became willing to break any rule on their behalf. You have even touted the humans' primal reflexes toward violent action as a virtue, have drawn parallels between it and the modus operandi of the Custodians themselves."

Suvtrush pushed back from the table, gills fluttering in disgust. "All opinions imbibed from your alarmist mentors, Thlunroolt and Glayaazh, no doubt. Their exhortations that we 'reclaim our proactive integrity' by swimming away from 'moral relativism' is as recidivistic as it is naïve."

When he was certain that Suvtrush had finished, Alnduul sat high in his chair. "You asserted that my first loyalties lie with Earth. You tasked me to reply. May I?"

Suvtrush waved an impatient but affirmative finger.

Alnduul discovered that he was suddenly, mysteriously, calm. "Do I admire humans? Yes. Is that why I undertook the actions I did? No. And most pertinently, was I emulating them? Only to the extent that, in the face of crisis, I will choose unauthorized action over disastrous inaction."

Heethoo's eyelids flickered twice in affirmation. Nlastanl's slow gaze suggested he was considering Alnduul's counterassertions as valid, possibly exculpatory. The other three were expressionless, impassive, their judgment a foregone conclusion.

Suvtrush leaned back. "Alnduul, inasmuch as you have not denied any of the allegations against you..."

The best I may expect is a three-to-two vote. Which gives me the right to appeal.

"...nor provided evidence that your superiors' orders were unclear or contradictory..."

But if either Nlastanl or Heethoo vote against me, I am lost.

"...and since your one defense has been unproven 'extenuating circumstances'..."

What was Glayaazh's final warning? To retain freedom of action at all costs?

"...this board of inquiry will now vote to determine—"

"Wait," said Alnduul.

Suvtrush halted, eyelids narrowed to slits.

Alnduul stood. "I believe that I can resolve the matter of the Lost Soldiers in such a way that it meets with the approval of this board and convinces the Ktoran Sphere that war is unnecessary."

The board of inquiry sat silent for several long seconds. Their gazes turned toward Suvtrush. Who said, "Explain."

Alnduul waited until he was once again as calm as his external demeanor suggested. "You asked me at the outset why I was late. I deferred answering. I offer that answer now. Anticipating that the matter of the Lost Soldiers remained crucial, I crossed back into human space to search for them, based on Caine Riordan's accounts of how they were initially hidden. Given our knowledge of Terran cyphers and security protocols, I was able to discern how they coordinated their changes of location. That led me to their current base, where I learned that they remain in constant fear of discovery by certain Terran authorities whose mandate includes their extermination."

"This is just another example of—" started Menrelm loudly.

Alnduul spoke over him even more loudly. "Foreseeing that the outcome here might end my ability to accompany Caine Riordan, I brought a small group of these refugees over the border to assist and protect him. In so doing, I gained the trust of their command staff. They are desperate to leave Terran space, and the great majority of the Lost Soldiers—over ninety percent—are still in the Ktoran lifepods."

The board was still silent, but the mood had changed from sullen condemnation to intense interest.

Alnduul took a deep breath. "This is the solution that I propose. I shall go over the border once again. I shall offer the remaining refugees from the Turkh'saar campaign complete exfiltration from CTR space along with their materiel, including all the Ktoran lifepods still in their possession. You will be able to assure the Ktor through back-channels that all the problematic personnel, both Lost Soldiers and Cold Guard, have been removed from human space. The Consolidated Terran Republic will logically presume that these groups simply remain hidden someplace within their borders, or have slipped undetected into the new 'land-grab' systems.

"The Collective will necessarily need to negotiate with the

Ktor to establish mutually acceptable means of verifying that the removal of the Lost Soldiers has been effected. This is unlikely to be difficult. Both sides seem far more motivated to find a solution than they are to waging an all-consuming war."

Suvtrush's eyes narrowed. "And where would you propose to deposit these refugee humans?"

Alnduul waved desultory fingers in the air. "Zhaashgleem."

Laynshooz's eye rims pinched tightly. "The last of the factotum worlds?"

"Where better? It is now almost completely untrafficked."

The five Dornaani glanced at each other, almost furtively. Suvtrush expelled a rattling rush of air, seemed both irritated and relieved. "There is promise in this plan, both to avert war and salvage what is left of your reputation, Alnduul. You have our leave to undertake this mission. Indeed, much may be forgiven if you can accomplish what you project. But if you fail..."

"I have no delusions as to the circumstances under which I would then exist."

"Even that phrasing is unwarrantedly optimistic." Suvtrush stood. "This board of inquiry is adjourned, pending the outcome of your mission."

Chapter Sixty-Four

Riordan rubbed his eyes again. Although Dornaani-manufactured cryocells enabled humans to revivify almost immediately and with minimal side effects, Caine had crawled out of his only three hours earlier. The shakes had passed, but it was still hard to focus.

Unfortunately, focus was exactly what he needed most. Whatever Hsontlosh had told the team of the second watch—Peter Wu, Miles O'Garran, Katie Somers, and Murray Liebman—they had unanimously decided to awaken the other two watches for a community decision.

Which is why he was perched on a chair in Hsontlosh's briefing room when he'd rather have been nursing a warm cup of... something. Anything. Instead, everyone in his self-styled "Crewe" was either tense or groggy, and Eku was sitting off by himself.

In contrast, Hsontlosh appeared unruffled as he stood and took in the room with a wide gesture of his hands. "I believe we have come to a crossroads in our journey. For those of you who have just reanimated, we arrived at Psi Tauri three days ago."

Riordan did the mental math: *so about three weeks since we gave him the green light to travel here.*

"I made planetfall two days ago and expressed interest in the mind-to-clone transference procedure. Within twenty-four hours, I was put in contact with persons who revealed information regarding your mate's condition, Mr. Riordan."

Caine leaned forward, wasn't sure the shakes he was suppressing now were due to his recent reanimation. "What did you learn?"

"First, a caveat: her name was not used. The sources merely
related reports involving a comparatively young human female
who required unusual medical services. It strains credibility that
this description could refer to anyone else."

"Okay, so you're not one hundred percent sure. What did
you learn?"

Hsontlosh held up two didactic fingers. "Months ago, offworld
exchange agents—you would call them 'middlemen'—acquired
biostimulation nanites of loji manufacture. A prerequisite for the
purchase was that the nanites could be modified for use in the
human female matching Elena Corcoran's description.

"This may be why they came to the Border Worlds in the first
place. They may have foreseen needing not only a circumspect
Virtua node but one where this black market nanite therapy
could be openly applied and monitored."

Riordan leaned forward. "Do your sources know where she is?"

"No, but they report a request for additional regimens of the
nanites, as well as for experts in remediating their side-effects."

"What side-effects?"

"Understand, Caine Riordan, these nanites are derived from
two ancient series. One was designed to rejuvenate the body. The
other protected it from genetic damage or oncological mutation.
However, when this imperfect hybrid begins to lose function, it can
revert into an oncological 'hunter-killer' and become become...
woefully indiscriminate in its targeting."

Riordan put a hand to his head. "So are you saying that the
very therapy they're using to jump-start Elena might now be
consuming her from the inside?"

"It is possible. This may be why her abductors have moved
her to the very edge of the Dornaani border. Possibly beyond."

"Beyond? Into neutral—unclaimed—systems?"

Hsontlosh's lids closed and opened very slowly. "Yes. These
nanites, as well as their most skilled practitioners, originate from
such worlds."

"I thought we were already out of the Collective. For weeks, now."

"Technically, that is correct. But these worlds are farther still,
beyond those where the Custodians can still exert nominal influence if they must."

Riordan frowned. Concern for Elena was still at the forefront of his mind, but now something else was drawing up alongside it: wariness. "So what is it about these farther neutral systems that keeps even the Custodians out?"

"They are but one or two shifts from another species' border."

Riordan suddenly felt as if he were entering a lightless cave, checking the floor with an outreached toe. "Whose borders?"

"The Ktor. Which is why I must ask, Caine Riordan, that you reconsider your resolve to find your mate. While there is no indication that the Ktor have ventured into this region in centuries, it is not impossible that they might do so. And I would be ingenuous to pretend ignorance of the unfortunate encounters you and your crew have had with them. That is why I encourage you to take careful counsel on whether this quest is worth proximity to such a daunting species."

Riordan nodded. "We'll talk about it over dinner and let you know." *Assuming I'm not too busy vomiting up everything I eat.*

No one else seemed to be thinking about dinner, either, as they huddled around the table in the commons room. Katie Somers had tricked the Dornaani commmplex into playing multiple raucous music selections simultaneously, while two differently modulated layers of white noise ran underneath. Unlikely to defeat determined eavesdropping, but it was the best she could do.

Their conversation was not the one Hsontlosh had advised, however. It was clear from postures alone that there was no thought of abandoning the search for Elena just because the danger had increased. Even Girten, Liebman, and Somers were committed to that journey. The only issue to be considered was the one Craig Girten articulated as they crowded around the table. "Look, this guy Hsontlosh could be a shyster."

"Aye," Katie Somers admitted, "but he just warned us away from pushing on. Twice."

Duncan shook his head. "That could be part of his act."

Miles frowned, nodded. "Yeah, he's had plenty of time to look us over and figure out that our unspoken motto is 'all for one and one for all.'"

Dora nodded. "Hsontlosh knows that if he says, 'It's too dangerous! Abandon the quest!' then we'll only be more determined than ever."

Bannor glanced at Riordan. "So what's the play?"

Caine put his right hand flat upon the table. "We go forward and play along. For now. If it's a trap, he'll see us doing what he expects. That might make him less careful than he should be. In the meantime, we have to weigh a risk."

Ayana's tone was blithe. "Do you mean the risk of attempting to take this ship?"

"No. Of letting Eku into our full confidence."

Dora's frown was pinched. "And why do we need to do that?"

"Because if we don't, there's no way I can ask him to dip into the ship's computer and find out if Hsontlosh is telling us the truth about where he's taking us. And why."

Peter's left eyebrow had risen. "And just how is Eku able to 'dip into the ship's computer?'"

"You let me worry about that." As Riordan said it, the universal passkey fob suddenly felt heavier in his duty suit's pocket. Only the other watch commanders, Bannor and Peter, were aware of it. Which didn't sit well with Riordan, but the more people who knew and might whisper about it, the more likely that Hsontlosh would overhear. "For now, we go back to business as usual."

Duncan was glum. "Which means most of us will be going back into cryocells. Can't say I like that much."

"Can't say I like it either," Caine agreed. "But any change to our routine could alert Hsontlosh that we're becoming suspicious. And we can't afford that, because if we have to take matters into our own hands, surprise is the only effective weapon we're likely to have."

Just over three weeks later, Caine sat down at the same table, recovering from cold sleep again. It had been a typical reanimation: exercise and a full day spent choking down various restorative cocktails. Others leeched out traces of the chemicals that would keep the water in his cells from freezing if the cryocell's temperature sank to zero Celsius.

Caine's incoming watch and Bannor's outgoing watch gradually gathered for their one shared meal. Someone in the Crewe had dubbed it the Changing of the Guard: that period of congenial overlap when the old watch briefed the new watch on whatever had happened while they lay undreaming in cryogenic stasis.

As Caine began picking at a white mass that might have been a puree of cauliflower, celeriac, potatoes, or all three, Bannor drawled, "I've been toying around with a plan for mixing up the watch structure. We're getting too comfortable working in the same teams all the time." Which was a preset message that translated as: *I've got something you need to read, because it's too sensitive for conversation.*

Riordan nodded. "You have a list of the new watches?"

Bannor nodded, pushed a folded sheet of paper across the table. "Just a first pass. I expect you'll want to tweak it a bit."

"I might," Caine agreed as he unfolded the sheet. He was able to hold it at a normal angle since he had purposely seated himself in the corner where the two blank bulkheads met. Riordan read:

> February 22, 2125 – Ship arrives in system ADS3321C. Immediately initiates standing-start shift.
>
> February 23, 2125 – Arrives in BD+14 831. Ship moors to spinbuoy so that maintenance robots may work on drives. Upon completion, another standing-start shift: the second in two days.
>
> February 24, 2125 – Arrives in BD+19 872. Same as yesterday. Ship moors to spinbuoy for full cycle of drive maintenance. Then a standing-start shift. The third in three days.
>
> February 25, 2125 – Arrives at unknown destination. Ship moors to spinbuoy. Post-shift drive maintenance normative. Refueling begins.
>
> February 26, 2125 – Refueling operations continue at twice normal speed.
>
> We're going somewhere fast, and not being told why or where.

After the others on Riordan's watch had craned their necks to get a look at it, he refolded the sheet, nodded. "Looks good. Bannor. And I think you're right about adding Eku to our watches. Like Yaargraukh here, he never goes into cold sleep. He could be a full-time asset."

Bannor took back the sheet. "Okay. So when do we put Eku to work?"

Riordan nodded. "Soon. I'll go tell him after dinner."

Chapter Sixty-Five

Eku slipped into Caine's quarters without appearing furtive. His eyes were wide. "The diversion you staged—the sparring accident with the Hkh'Rkh—was quite convincing, Commodore. But it did not last as long as we hoped. Hsontlosh nearly discovered me accessing his files."

"But he didn't. What have you learned?"

"Hsontlosh cannot be trusted. Our present location is the system you know as BD+13 778. I could not access the future shift-plot, however."

"What about the logs?"

"They are also sealed, along with the ship's comm records. However, Custodial hulls automatically retain archived copies of all comm traffic. He is probably aware of them, but they cannot be removed. Access to them is by code, which can only be changed by a Custodian."

Riordan smiled. "And you have knowledge of that code?"

"Alnduul entrusted me with it." Eku looked away. "Giving me that code was a profound violation of Custodial directives."

Riordan shook his head. "It was also a profound compliment. So, who's Hsontlosh been talking to since we started on our journey?"

"Actually, the important information is who he was speaking to *before* we left. Even before he acquired this ship."

Caine frowned. "The ship has a record of his comm traffic from before he took possession of it?"

Eku smiled faintly. "Any authorized crewperson may retroactively update the comm record. Hsontlosh added his prior records. Probably for improved security."

"I don't follow. Copying his records to the ship's computer *improves* their security?"

Eku nodded. "Hsontlosh's earlier communications were likely stored on his control circlet. That is risky. If apprehended, a full record of his illicit actions and arrangements would be on his person. By storing them in the ship's records and erasing them from his control circlet, he eliminates that risk."

"Okay, so what's in the archive?"

"I recognized three comm codes. Two are those of Regional Arbiters Yaonhoyz and Laynshooz. The other is that of the Seventh Senior Arbiter, Heethoo."

Riordan didn't respond right away. "That can't be right. The two Regional Arbiters I understand; they hate my guts. But Heethoo? Connected to Hsontlosh? She was one of the few Arbiters who was sympathetic to Alnduul. And to me."

Eku shook his head. "When Hsontlosh arrived at HR 4084 A to take possession of this ship, Alnduul's requisition for it had been appended so as to permit it to travel beyond Collective worlds. And to retain its weapons."

Riordan nodded. "And I'm guessing that this addendum required authorization from either a Senior or Regional Arbiter."

"Precisely. Hsontlosh's records show that he contacted Yaonhoyz for that authorization and received it two days later."

Riordan smiled. "But I'll bet it was issued by Laynshooz."

"How did you know?"

Riordan shrugged. "A classic firewall. Never more than a single, one-way communication, and never with the same person. So how did Heethoo's name come up?"

"When Laynshooz sent Hsontlosh the authorization, he neglected to remove earlier coded messages in the thread. Although I cannot decipher the content, two of the other comm addresses were Yaonhoyz's and Heethoo's. I am puzzled that Hsontlosh retained this message at all. It clearly incriminates him."

Riordan shook his head. "Actually, that message may be the most valuable thing that Hsontlosh possesses."

"Why?"

"Because Heethoo's comm address is Hsontlosh's only insurance that they won't get rid of him as a 'loose end' later on. With that message, Hsontlosh can prove a covert relationship between three Arbiters who not only made sure that he got a Custodial ship with all its armaments, but with inappropriate travel permissions. That suggests collusion, even conspiracy. And if the message is set for timed release, Hsontlosh has to be alive to keep resetting it."

"But early on, the possibility of its discovery would have been a threat to him, as well." Eku's eyes widened. "So he must have *baited* Irzhresht into illegally accessing his system, to get rid of her before she had a chance to find the comm record on her own."

Riordan nodded. "He probably left just enough false signs to get Irzhresht to hack his system and get herself killed. It wouldn't have been difficult, since she was already watching for a loji double-cross."

"Eminently logical conjectures, except for this: the three Arbiters have no reason to help—let alone *know*—Hsontlosh. Indeed, the only thing they have in common is a record of utter contempt for loji. It is a conundrum."

"So much so that it can't be chance. Whatever Hsontlosh is up to, it must advance those Arbiters' hidden agenda. But without them getting their hands dirty."

"And what agenda would that be?"

"We don't have enough information or time to figure that out. Besides, we've got bigger problems."

Eku frowned. "Such as?"

"When Hsontlosh recently made three successive standing shifts, Bannor didn't have any safe opportunities to use the fob. So the trail of signals that Alnduul could have used to follow us has been broken. Badly." Riordan leaned back, knew his smile was crooked. "Sorry to have gotten you mixed up in this, Eku."

"It is a gratifying assignment, and I am honored that you and the others have taken me into your confidence."

"I'm just glad you're on our side, Eku."

"I was from the outset, Commodore."

"Then why were you so distant when I returned from Virtua?"

Eku sighed. "Because although I had no reason to doubt Hsontlosh's account of Irzhresht's death, the circumstances left me uneasy. Irzhresht might have been the traitor, but if it was Hsontlosh instead, then I could not show a strong affinity for you or your personnel. He might have perceived that as a sign that I suspected him and was attempting to recruit you to the same perspective."

Riordan nodded. "Now all that matters is finding a way to tell the others and make a plan. Can we use the fob to create a blind spot where we can talk?"

"That would be too obvious. However, I can cause an innocuous circuitry failure that will compel the repairbots to cut the power—and with it, any surveillance feeds—to my stateroom."

"Then that's where we'll meet. Ten minutes?"

"Give me fifteen."

Chapter Sixty-Six

MARCH 2125
DEEP SPACE, BD+13 778

Despite a life that spanned many centuries and historical events, Eku sat among Riordan and his companions as if he were a bookish new student unexpectedly invited to sit at the popular kids' lunch table.

"So Hsontlosh is getting suspicious?" Tagawa asked Eku.

The factotum nodded. "He feels an urgent need to get to the next destination. He is preparing for another standing shift. But even if it does not damage the drive and capacitors, the outcome is likely to be dire."

Bannor nodded. "You mean, we might be unable to seize control and get back home?"

"That, too, but I was referring to our probable destination."

"Which is?" Yaargraukh asked.

"In official Ktor space."

Ignoring the stares exchanged among his crew, Riordan leaned toward Eku. "What do you mean by 'official' Ktor space? Is there any other kind?"

Eku shrugged. "Legally speaking, no. Practically speaking, yes. For weeks now, we have been traveling in what the Ktor call the Scatters: an outback inhabited by their Exodates and other renegades. But I am almost certain our next destination is 13 Orionis, a member system of the Ktoran Sphere."

Duncan crossed his arms. "Do you think Hsontlosh has been heading there all along?"

"If so, then the path he charted through the Border Worlds and Scatters is mystifyingly circuitous."

Craig Girten frowned. "Then what's he been doing? Kinda strange for a grifter to go sightseeing before he's completed his con."

Dora's smile was crooked, knowing. "Nah. He's not sightseeing. He's been trawling for a fence."

"For a 'fence'?" Yaargraukh's small black eyes extended far out of his head. "Hsontlosh is searching deep space for a vertical barrier?"

"No, no. A fence is . . . is a go-between, a person who finds buyers for a thief's stolen goods." Dora smiled. "Saw this all the time in Africa. If you're dealing in contraband, you don't go straight into a new port. You watch the traffic, then hang just offshore, maybe send someone to drop a few hints in a dockside dive. In a few days, you're contacted by a local fence. Far safer than doing business with the primary customer. If you're stupid enough to deliver the goods to them directly, they're likely to just take you out of the equation and walk away with the merchandise."

"Okay," Craig said, "but if that's true, then why has Captain Treefrog *stopped* looking for a fence? Why suddenly rush straight into the very place he's been trying to stay out of?"

Duncan's eyes narrowed. "Because we've spooked him by changing our routine. Bannor's watch should have gone back into cold sleep last night, but here we are, still awake. We've also started interacting with Eku. And now we're in a room where Hsontlosh can't see or hear us because of a suspiciously convenient electrical failure. He knows we've started asking questions, the kind that could ruin his big score."

Newton sighed. "Yes, but *what* is his big score?"

Eku touched his index fingers together: a Dornaani gesture signifying rumination. "It has been speculated that some loji go over the Ktor border to acquire the ancient technology that is still discovered in the Scatters."

All eyes turned toward the factotum.

Riordan folded his hands patiently. "I think you should tell us more about that, Eku."

"Of course. Many believe that the comparative rapidity with which the Ktor regained spaceflight after the Final War indicates that they had limited access to ancient devices. If prospecting for such items is ongoing, loji might acquire these artifacts from the Ktor renegades who reside in the Scatters."

Duncan sighed, leaned back. "Well, now we know how Heethoo and her allies mean to expose Hsontlosh, and why."

Yaargraukh pony-nodded. "It would prove that the loji have been trading with a hostile polity in order to procure technologies that would enable them to challenge the Collective's supremacy. The Senior Arbiters would have no choice but to preemptively eliminate the loji threat.

"At the same time, Hsontlosh's own actions will rid the Senior Assembly's isolationists of a more recent, yet particularly vexing problem."

"What problem?" Caine asked.

Yaargraukh turned to look at him. "You, Commodore. Or, more specifically, the provocative issue for which you have become the symbol: the fate of the Lost Soldiers. If Hsontlosh delivers you into the hands of the Ktor, they acquire a new source of political leverage. Or classified information. Or both."

Duncan shook his head. "Shit, the Ktor could spin the narrative around one hundred and eighty degrees. Once they have the commodore, they could claim he hired Hsontlosh to sneak him over their border to spy, to seed a plague virus, or just sow discord in the Sphere. But whatever story they might cook up, you can be sure of this: they'll use every method at their disposal to get all the intel between his ears."

He turned to Riordan. "Sorry, sir, but no one can hold up under that forever. You'll almost certainly reveal that Alnduul has, with a nod from Collective officials, violated the CTR's borders to exfiltrate the Lost Soldiers. If that's made public, it means the end of any moral or legal authority associated with the Collective or the Custodians. The Accord would be finished."

"But then Heethoo and Laynshooz *can't* be behind what Hsontlosh is doing," Dora almost shouted. "If the Ktor reveal that the Dornaani can't or won't control their own Custodians or loji, that's a black eye for the Collective. So what do three highly placed Arbiters get out of *that*?"

Riordan smiled. "They get everything they want, Ms. Veriden. Firstly, if Alnduul does go over our border to bring back the Lost Soldiers, you can be sure no one will have *ordered* him to do it. He'll have been given verbal encouragement to 'work out the particulars' on his own. Meaning the Senior Arbiters can wash their hands of it later, claim that Alnduul went rogue.

"But implicating Alnduul is only a means to an end for Heethoo and her conspirators. They're hunting much bigger game."

"Like what?"

"Like political transformation. The debacle involving me and Hsontlosh will vindicate all their accusations. I'm the exemplar of intemperate humanity, constantly disrupting peace and balance. Alnduul's assistance proves that Custodians will break every rule to help Earth. The more moderate Arbiters who supported him will be called irresolute and blamed for threatening the peace and tranquility of all Dornaani. Hsontlosh's actions prove that the loji are working to overthrow the Collective by actively cooperating with the Ktor."

Eku's breath was shallow. "So, a coup d'état."

Riordan shrugged. "But probably without a drop of blood spilled. A 'firmer' Senior Assembly will replace the current one and come down hard on the loji... with lethal force, if necessary. They'll resolve the Lost Soldier issue by putting both our people and Alnduul in detention cells. Or graves. And finally, they can point to our actions as proof that Earth is the loose cannon they've always claimed, that it can't control its own forces. We'll no longer be a protected species; we'll be on parole. The landgrab will be shut down, by force, if necessary. And the new isolationist Senior Assembly will do it all in the name of saving both the Collective and the Accord."

Riordan leaned back. "No, Ms. Veriden, Heethoo and her cabal stand to get *everything* they want. Just by letting us continue along our merry way."

Ayana nodded. "I believe your analysis of Heethoo and her allies to be accurate, Commodore. However, you may be overlooking one of the motivations of the Ktor. Arguably, the one that is most important to them."

Riordan raised an eyebrow. "You certainly have my attention, Ms. Tagawa."

"The Ktor will want you, personally, Commodore. They would also be gratified to capture your staff—collectively, you have frustrated several of their stratagems."

Bannor frowned. "Are you saying they want us for interrogation or for revenge?"

"Neither, Colonel. I am saying that they want you for analysis."
Dora guffawed. "Ending with dissection, I'm sure."

"Or what might be worse," Ayana admitted. She waited for several seconds of uniformly wide-eyed silence to pass. "The Ktor admire strength, success, those who surprise them. It teaches them how to improve their own performance. It is also how they screen for genetic qualities they wish to appropriate." She looked around the table. "Do not underestimate the Ktor determination to perfect themselves by integrating others' presumed traits into their own genecode. Be assured, this is part of their motivation." She sat back in her chair and sipped at her glass of water.

Riordan exhaled. "Well, at the risk of monstrous understatement, that is certainly food for thought. But right now, we need a plan."

Bannor nodded. "We have two primary objectives: get rid of Hsontlosh's robots and get access to the bridge." He leaned toward Eku. "The robots—how dangerous are they?"

Eku stammered. "I ... I do not know if they are armed. I have never seen either model before. The repairbots came with the ship, so they are very old."

Not what Bannor asked, Eku. Riordan made sure his voice radiated patience. "Okay, so let's assume the robots are not armed. How dangerous could they become?"

"Usually not very. Dornaani robots are programmed to reject any orders that would injure sapients." Eku paused, then added, "However, there are both built-in overrides and gray-market work-arounds that can alter that."

Like pulling teeth. "And if the robots' programming has been altered or overridden as you just outlined, *then* how dangerous are they?"

Eku shrugged. "They will be impervious to any physical force we can generate ourselves. Unless an unusually large individual were to be wielding a very heavy hammer or pick-ax." He glanced briefly at Yaargraukh.

Duncan leaned toward Eku. "How good are their sensors?"

Eku's small Adam's apple cycled rapidly. "The two proxrovs' sensors are quite acute. Those on the three maintenance bots are rudimentary: audio, basic visual with IR and low light. Image resolution will be limited except in their primary activity range:

one to two meters. However, Dornaani robots are quite robust. I doubt you would succeed at disabling their sensors."

Duncan smiled; Caine could see the impatient grimace behind it. "So, if the sensors can't be knocked out, is there any way to obstruct them?"

Eku thought a moment, then nodded. "The ship's paint supplies are not restricted. Dornaani paint is, to use your term, 'smart.' It can be programmed to spread in a radially symmetric pattern, and accrete in user-defined layers. Hull paint is particularly sophisticated. With the proper settings, it could be preprogrammed to completely cover the visual light sensors and seriously degrade the infrared. However, control over the robots' movements would then default to the ship's main computer, using the interior sensors. That's how the bots are deployed to the systems they must service: the ship shows them where to go."

"And the two proxrovs?"

"More agile, more autonomous, but less heavily built."

Newton's eyes were hard. "Weak spots?"

Eku nodded. "The neck. But unlike a human, the back is more vulnerable than the front."

Dora's grin was mirthless. "Good to know."

Ayana put down her glass of water. "It seems inevitable that, at some point, we must take the bridge. But how?"

Eku shrugged. "The ship's welding kits can cut through the bulkhead and expose the door controls. But all heavy tools are stored in engineering. Which is also sealed."

Yaargraukh's neck shook as if suddenly chilled. "Even with torches, we lack the time. If Hsontlosh is readying the ship for a standing shift, he may risk engaging the drive early, rather than waiting while we breach the doors."

Bannor shrugged. "I don't disagree, but what's the alternative? Use the fob to get on the bridge? Hsontlosh keeps those two proxrovs with him all the time. They may not have any built-in offensive systems, but if Hsontlosh has weapons, he can arm them."

Miles sighed. "Yeah, and last I checked, our own packs are stored in the hold, behind the same bulkhead as engineering. So we'd have to go against them with whatever clubs we can scrounge. Anyone up for that?"

A chorus of negative grumbles was the only response.

Eku cleared his throat and said, "I have a firearm." Again, he became the focal point of every pair of eyes in the room.

He rose and removed the weapon from a secure panel beneath his bunk. It was an antique that had probably started life as a military sidearm, but—its brass cartridge design eclipsed by caseless and then dustmix and liquimix ammunition—it had obviously been decommissioned for sale on the civilian market. "A nine-millimeter, I believe it is called. Manufactured by a firm known as... Ruger?"

Bannor smiled. "How many rounds?"

"Forty-two. And three, er, clips?"

"Magazines," Craig Girten corrected irritably.

Ayana nodded approvingly at the weapon. "That is an excellent addition. But there are two matters we have not yet addressed. Firstly, what prevents Hsontlosh from disrupting any plan by detaching from the spinbuoy and putting us all in zero gee?"

Eku shook his head. "He will not do that. Dornaani robots have a precautionary design limitation: they have no zero-gee capability. They would become useless to him."

"Reassuring," agreed Tagawa. "Secondly, let us say we use the fob and enter the bridge. What is to prevent Hsontlosh from taking all the ship's systems off-line before we can retask the fob to override them. And if he does so, can we restore those systems if he refuses to cooperate?"

"Or if he's dead?" O'Garran added.

Eku frowned. "Eventually. But not all of them. And it would take a long time."

"How long?"

The factotum shrugged. "Weeks. Months. Maybe longer. It depends upon three factors: the encryption; the intricacy of the software; and, most important, if Hsontlosh installed failsafes that require biometric overrides."

Craig Girten blinked. "What the hell does that mean?"

Newton began explaining before Eku could start. "Some of the ship's controls might not respond without Hsontlosh's fingerprint, retinal pattern, or genetic sample."

Riordan leaned forward. "So we've now identified three tactical approaches that won't work.

"Crashing the whole system ourselves might paralyze both sides at first, but Hsontlosh is the only one who can bring up the life support systems quickly enough to keep us from asphyxiating, freezing, or both. So he wins.

"Crashing a smaller number of key systems isn't any better. Hsontlosh can stop us simply by crashing all the other systems, too. Once again, he comes out on top.

"And although we can use the fob get on the bridge, we've only got one old pistol and a bunch of improvised clubs to take on two tough proxrovs. So, even if we eventually disable them, Hsontlosh will have had plenty of time to, again, crash the system. Hell, if the proxrovs are holding us off, he might have enough time to summon the repairbots to come in behind us.

"And it doesn't matter if we target engineering, instead. Same problems, same outcome."

Dora pushed back from the table. "*Madre!* I thought we were trying to come up with a way to win, not ways to lose!"

Riordan smiled. "It's easier to see the path to victory when you've eliminated all the paths that won't take you there."

Ayana nodded. "However, all the paths end at this quandary: how do we overcome the robots and gain entrance to the bridge at the same time?"

Riordan stared at Ayana for a long moment and then smiled. "Thank you, Ms. Tagawa."

"For what?"

"For helping me see a solution." Riordan glanced around the table. "We don't use the fob to overcome Hsontlosh. We use it to trick him into both opening the bridge's iris valve and putting the robots in vulnerable positions."

Yaargraukh leaned forward slowly; his shadow blacked out half the table. "Intriguing. How do you propose to do this?"

"First, we don't go after the robots; we bring them to us. Second, we have to enter a place Hsontlosh doesn't want us nosing around, but doesn't have anything crucial, nothing that would prompt him to crash the ship's systems."

Bannor shrugged. "Okay, but if we're not breaking into engineering or the bridge, what's left that will get a rise out of him?"

Riordan nodded toward the stern of the ship. "Near Airlock Two, there are three midship compartments that he's locked against entry. Ostensibly, they're for storing maintenance spares, emergency stores, and fragile cargo."

Duncan frowned. "Well, that's pretty standard. You don't want passengers messing up your supplies or vice versa. Breaking into those compartments might not get a rise out of him."

Riordan smiled. "Except for the one compartment where he hasn't just locked out passengers; Eku doesn't have access either."

The factotum nodded as their eyes turned to him. "As I told Mr. Riordan some time ago, my ID chip should have granted me entry, but it did not. When I asked Hsontlosh to authorize my access, he refused."

"You know," Dora observed in a sly tone, "that mystery room just might be where Hsontlosh keeps the weapons rack that's missing from his ship's locker. Or maybe it's where he stores other gear that could be used against him."

Duncan smiled. "Which sure does make it an especially tempting target."

Dora's lip curled. "True, that."

Bannor leaned back. "I think we've figured out where to use that fob, Commodore."

Riordan smiled. "So do I. Although we're going to have to task it to do a little selective data erasure at the same time." He looked at Eku. "Can the fob do that?"

"Quite easily, but if it triggers an alert, or otherwise attracts Hsontlosh's attention, he is likely to—once again—shut down the ship's systems. Except for the shift drive—he would isolate that to operate autonomously. That way, the fob cannot access and stop it."

Riordan nodded. "My plan will keep the fob under the radar."

Duncan hunched forward. "So exactly what is this plan, Commodore?"

Riordan leaned back far enough to see all their faces. "Here's what I was thinking..."

Fourteen minutes later, a tone began chiming in sync with a pulsing light that appeared on Eku's commplex. He stood quickly.

"What is it?" Riordan asked.

"Countdown sequence for standing shift! Hsontlosh may have detected our meeting, could be fearful that—"

"Forget Hsontlosh." Riordan snatched the Ruger off the table, tossed it to Dora. She caught it in midair, went low, led the way out the door. As she did, Riordan asked, "How much time do we have?"

"It varies. There could be—"

"Best guess, Eku. And right now." The room was already empty except for them.

"Ten, maybe twelve minutes. It—no! Wait!"

Riordan had grabbed Eku by the collar and was already dragging him out of his stateroom toward their first objective: the utility storage locker and its paint supplies. "No time to wait. Time to act."

"But we weren't finished. The plan isn't complete!"

"They almost never are, Eku."

"Then what do we do?"

Riordan smiled. "We improvise. As usual. Get moving."

Chapter Sixty-Seven

MARCH 2125
DEEP SPACE, BD+13 778

The final "ready" signal—sent by Ayana's assault team—chirped from Riordan's collarcom. He activated the fob's door override, muttered, "Go."

Two bounds and he was across the passageway separating the maintenance utility locker from the now-opening iris valve of the prohibited compartment. Duncan, Newton, and Eku—who, like Caine, were stripped down to their underwear—followed him into the compartment, paint sprayers in their hands.

Rather than the open space that Eku had told them to expect, they discovered twelve cryopods, six against both the fore and aft bulkheads, stacked in two layers on purpose-built racks. Covering the entirety of the far bulkhead were ten very narrow semitransparent doors. Although appearing like very compact shower stalls, they seemed to be storage units. Riordan ran to where the left-hand bulkhead met the back, and started scaling the cryopod rack toward his objective: the sensor cluster high in that corner, just where Eku said it would be.

Duncan, who was making the same climb toward the high right-hand corner, swore beneath his breath. "Just our damned luck. No tools or weapons."

"Maybe in the storage units," Riordan said as he raised his sprayer and coated the sensor in smart paint. "Check them when you're done."

He dropped to the ground as Yaargraukh entered the now-blind room, carrying an outsized paint canister in one hand

468

and a bulging duffel bag in the other. He set the duffel down, pulled out a belt—the tough, woven one from Craig Girten's old fatigues—and began lashing it to the canister's handle, which was already locked in the extended position.

An unmistakably Dornaani klaxon started groan-hooting.

Eku clambered down from one of the corners closest to the iris valve and stated the obvious. "Hsontlosh has discovered the breach, knows what we have seen."

As Newton hopped down from the last of the blinded corner-sensors and began scanning the cryopods, Riordan checked his wristlink. "How soon can we expect a response, Eku?"

"It is already on its way."

Riordan's collarcom emitted a quick sequence of three tones; they repeated. He spoke so everyone could hear. "Two repair bots just came out of the engineering section, heading forward along the starboard passageway."

"How quickly are they moving?" asked Eku.

Riordan shook his head. "Not part of the codes we set. But not fast enough to warrant a report over open comms."

Duncan put his face up against one of the lockers to get a glimpse of its contents through the frosted panel. "Some kind of standard pack in each one, along with a few personal effects. Probably for the coldsleepers."

"Any way to get in?"

"Nope. No handles or locks. Just a small black control tab that doesn't respond."

Eku halted in surprise when he saw the units, moved over to them with a growing frown. "They are activated by a dedicated fob. But..."

"But what?"

"I know these storage units." Reaching a locker, he peered inside. "And I know those packs. They are ours."

"Ours?"

He turned toward Riordan quickly. "Standard issue for factotums. What you would call a survival kit or go-bag. But that means..."

Riordan followed Eku's suddenly horrified gaze toward the cryopods, called out to Newton as the factotum approached them. "Are any of those 'pods our models?"

Newton was kneeling alongside the one nearest the iris valve, inspecting it closely. "No. The manufacture and writing is Dornaani, but the occupants—"

"Are human," Eku finished for him, staring through one of the fogged observation panels. "They're all factotums."

Duncan finished trying the last storage locker, crossed behind Riordan to join Yaargraukh, who was waiting and listening at the open entry.

"So what the hell is Hsontlosh doing with these cold cells?" Caine murmured, mostly to himself.

"I don't know, but they didn't come with the ship," Newton muttered. "Look at the dust pattern on the floor, around the rack. These cells were all shoved in here recently." He moved rapidly from pod to pod. "The occupants are elderly. Very. Advanced geriatric degeneration. They wouldn't last five minutes without full life support."

Duncan was helping Yaargraukh tie a hand loop into the loose end of the belt knotted to the paint canister; human fingers were faster and better at that job. "So why move these people around? What does Hsontlosh have to gain?"

Eku leaned back from one of the cold cells. "Factotum genetics are groomed to remove all congenital flaws, but they are otherwise unchanged from the first population, taken almost twenty millennia ago. The Ktor are said to have an intense interest in original human genecodes."

Riordan's collarcom chirped out a new sequence of tones. He relayed the message to the others. "The first two repairbots passed the airlock. ETA here is ninety seconds. The third bot just came out of engineering, following the same path."

Eku stopped as he passed the last of the cryopods, frowned at what he saw. He put his face close against its misty panel, and then started back, incredulous. "I know this sleeper! He...he chose to go into Virtua decades ago. What...why does Hsontlosh have him here?"

Riordan hadn't the heart to say what Newton blurted out. "This isn't about genetics. This is about information."

"But...?"

Riordan spoke rapidly; there wasn't time for anything else. "Eku, you factotums know Dornaani technology. You learn the Custodians' capabilities, their secrets."

Newton's voice was harsh as he added, "And this bunch is just another black market commodity that won't be missed. Which is perfect for Ktoran purposes."

"Movement at the bend in the corridor!" hissed Duncan. "Five seconds!"

Yaargraukh stepped back as the humans crowded behind the bulkheads flanking the iris valve, Riordan and Eku to the left, Newton and Duncan to the right.

As they did, a smooth hum of multiple roller-spheres became audible out in the corridor, grew rapidly louder. Without any pause, the first repairbot glided over the valve's threshold—

Riordan and the others swarmed it, spraying paint into its sensors at close range. The smart fluid worked like plaster amoebas; each blast cohered, clumped, and then rapidly hardened.

As it did, the bot thrashed in the direction of the paint streams, but the humans had jumped away. A moment later, they darted in again, smacking it with their chair-leg clubs, always from a different direction. Except from the extreme right flank.

That was where Yaargraukh stood, legs braced, both hands swinging the belt-leashed paint canister around his head. Two fast spins and it was already making a low, lethal moaning sound—right before the Hkh'Rkh stepped forward and stretched his arms further into the rotation.

The canister finished its arc by crashing into the top-mounted processing cluster that was the bot's head. Its arms twitched in unison, roved more wildly as Riordan waved the others back and Yaargraukh got the can swinging again.

Still in the corridor, the second repairbot attempted to press forward, but its damaged mate couldn't move aside quickly enough to let it enter the fray.

Yaargraukh grunted as a last vicious yank to the belt-handle added a pulse of extra force to the canister just before it smashed into the bot's head and disintegrated. Metal fragments flew everywhere. As did the paint, most of which splashed in a wave against the near wall and spattered across the lower chassis of the second bot.

But part of that wave sheeted across Newton's torso and legs. A torrent of smaller droplets sprayed Duncan. Riordan discovered few specks on his arm, felt them start to congeal...

Damn it, when the paint hardens... "Into the corridor! Next attack! Now!"

✧   ✧   ✧

Unit Three, the third repair robot, was running a self-diagnostic when a priority alert preempted all other functions. The passengers were endangering the ship's systems. Unit One was already disabled just beyond the ingress to compartment 17-B. Four humans were attempting to work around it to reach Unit Two, which was preparing to attack them with its actuators.

The ship's computer instructed Unit Three to support Unit Two, ordering it to follow the same route and relaying real-time images of the starboard corridor leading to the airlock and the left-hand turn just beyond it.

Unit Three sped forward and engaged its retrofitted defense protocol.

As it approached the deceleration point for navigating the bend beyond the airlock, the corridor video feed alerted it to an anomaly. The inner hatch of the airlock was ajar, as was a nearby suit locker. The airlock's interior sensor was functioning, but was apparently covered. However, Unit Three's own records indicated that the passengers had left the hatch ajar numerous times over the past three months. The repairbot dismissed the supposed anomaly as an established trend and remained focused upon reaching Unit Two.

As Unit Three drew abreast of the airlock, its audio sensors detected a faint sound from its rear right flank. An instant later, the corridor sensors showed the airlock hatch swinging inward, opening more fully.

Unit Three's threat assessment subroutine engaged, but was abruptly overridden by a priority warning from the ship's computer. The same instant the passengers acquired access to compartment 17-B, the security archive had ceased recording and the preceding 389.1 seconds had been wiped. In consequence, the computer lost prior locational data on the passengers. It instructed Unit Three to turn and attack one or more humans that were presumed to be approaching from the airlock.

Unit Three turned, arms extending in accord with its new orders...

...and its video sensors discovered a vac-suited female passenger—the one labeled Veriden—in contact range. Helmet open, the human's face was seamed in the expression known as a "smile," which was occluded as it raised an object to within fifteen centimeters of Unit Three's sensor cluster.

The object was a sprayer.

The last useful video data Unit Three received from its sensor cluster was a sudden, expanding bloom of paint.

As soon as the bot was blinded, Dora leapt back, just a moment ahead of the first defensive scissoring of its arms. Bannor raced out of the airlock, vac suit open, both hands wrapped around the straps of a rescue airpack he held cocked behind him. He sidestepped to the robot's far right flank, swung the pack as hard as he could.

The impact sent a jolt all the way up his arms and into his shoulders. A few pieces from the robot came loose as the pack rebounded and he hefted it for another attack.

The bot swayed in his direction, righting itself, manipulators extending. Stepping into the growing momentum as if he were throwing the hammer in the Olympics, Bannor put his full weight behind the second swing.

Yaargraukh dropped the remains of his makeshift flail, reached back into the duffel bag. Newton was cursing, limbs already sluggish as the paint stiffened. He wasn't going to be fast enough to slide through the narrow gap between the first bot and the side of the iris valve, not before the second robot smashed him or gutted him like a fish.

Riordan waved Newton back. "Duncan, take his place. We go together. It can't cover both gaps at once. Eku, you'll follow me—"

But Eku jumped forward at the sound of his name, not waiting to hear the rest of the orders. He misgauged the angle between the inert bot and the side of the iris valve, took a moment to angle sideways, and then slipped through.

Damnit! "Duncan, go!" Riordan yelled as he snaked through the gap after Eku.

The factotum's momentary pause had allowed the second repairbot to swing toward him, right arm pivoting outward as Eku raised his chair-leg club.

The robot's arm crashed into Eku's, mashing it against the chassis of its motionless mate. The chair-leg left flew out of the factotum's hand as he bounced off the first repairbot with a high-pitched groan.

But Duncan had already dodged through the slightly wider aperture on the other side of the dead bot. He whacked the active one with his own club.

It rotated toward Solsohn, just as Riordan slipped through on the other side, hopping over Eku to bring his own club down on the back of the second machine. When Duncan retreated hastily, it spun toward Riordan.

Whose cheeks were aching from a wide, savage grin as the robot came forward. *Ever play monkey in the middle, Tin Man?*

Bannor's second swing slammed the airpack directly into the third repairbot's sensor cluster, rocking the whole unit. A quick duck and roll as its arms flailed momentarily, and then Bannor was beyond its ready reach. It followed his movements awkwardly, now guided solely by images relayed from the passageway sensors.

For that same reason, it was unable to react in time when Dora leaped out of the airlock again, paint sprayer in one hand, asteroid pitons in the other, and a prospector's mooring hammer hanging around her neck. She slipped past the bot and tossed the sprayer to Bannor, who caught it and leaped toward the nearest bulkhead's sensor cluster. He set the sprayer to full power, raised it, and coated the passageway sensors with a blast of paint.

Dora, behind the reach of the bot's manipulators, jammed the point of a piton into the louvre of its rear exhaust vent. According to Eku, a slightly down-angled penetration there would reach the primary processor.

The repairbot was starting to roll backward, probably in an attempt to crush Dora against the bulkhead behind it, when she brought the hammer down. The bot quaked, then haltingly resumed its rearward motion.

Just as Dora drove in a second spike. The unit froze in place, inert.

She slipped out of the narrow space left between the back of the robot and the bulkhead, cursing.

"I thought you were all about one shot kills," Bannor quipped as she slid the hammer into a smart ring on her vac suit.

"Go to hell," she muttered. "Couldn't punch a hole in the processor until the first piton opened a gap."

Bannor thought she had lisped at the end of the last word, then realized it hadn't been her: a faint hissing sound was rising...

Dora looked up sharply. "Here comes the gas." She slapped her helmet closed and sprinted toward the second bend of the passageway's dogleg, where Caine and the others were probably still fighting the second repairbot.

Bannor ducked back into the airlock. Sealing his own helmet with a downward snap of his chin, he grabbed the waiting bundle of four more lightweight Dornaani spacesuits and ran after Dora.

Now, assuming Ayana remained alert for any sign that the ship's computer was beginning to compensate for the fob's erasure of its recent security data, this crazy plan just might succeed.

Ayana Tagawa, leaning over the commplex in Eku's room, saw a shuddering glitch in the ultrahigh-definition images being streamed by the astrography program she was running; the ship's computer had briefly shifted a huge part of its processing resources. "Jam the hatch!" she shouted over her shoulder.

Craig Girten triggered the iris valve and pulled a chair into the opening, just as the valve reversed into a high-speed contraction. Which it automatically aborted as soon as it encountered the obstruction.

Tagawa dragged another chair with her, heard a series of faint snaps along the corridor in either direction. "Security protocols," she said in response to Craig's perplexed expression. "The computer will lock every hatch it can until it reestablishes full control."

Girten leaned back into Eku's quarters, handed out the lead of a knotted chain of bed sheets and blankets. Ayana took it, nose wrinkling at the uniquely nauseating combination of odors: several different thinners and solvents from the maintenance locker mixed with sugar, syrup, and cooking oil from the galley. Girten picked up a wad at the middle length of that same string of sodden linens, glanced back to make sure that the last third was spread widely enough on the stateroom's floor that it would feed smoothly. "Ready," he said.

Tagawa nodded, turned, and sprinted up the passageway, unreeling the knotted band of cloth and linen in her wake. From well behind, a cacophony of clangs and flat crashes told her that the ambush on the robots was in full swing.

As if pushed on by that din, she ran harder, had a momentary vision of herself doing some bizarre sprinter's version of the *carmagnole*, unfurling tapestries of death and anarchy.

The line tugged her to a halt. She had played it out, the far end now in Girten's hand. Ayana went a few bounds further, as far as the linens still wadded in her hand would allow, then turned. The corridor behind—two thirds of the distance between the forbidden compartment and the bridge—was now decorated by the twisting braid of sheets and blankets. And still, no suppressive gas. As Eku had expected, the largely autonomous security system would be more likely to interpret her actions as some species of irrational biot behavior, rather than a threat.

Until now. Ayana reached into the utility pocket on her thigh, pulled out emergency flares harvested from the suit lockers. She snapped off the caps, suddenly had a handful of incandescent pink flames.

She sprinted back down the passageway, flinging them onto the accelerant-inundated cloth. Girten met her halfway, having done the same with his flares, just as a steady hiss rose above the breathy rush of growing flames. Fire retardant mist started jetting into the corridor, along with suppressant gas.

Ayana reversed direction yet again and ran toward the bridge, skirting the winding trail of flame.

Riordan dodged in to smack the back of the repairbot. The chair-leg wasn't going to do it any real damage, but it kept the machine occupied.

"Gas!" shouted Duncan as the bot rotated back toward Riordan and accelerated abruptly.

No more monkey in the middle, I guess. Riordan yanked out his soaked wash towel, clamped it over his nose and mouth, turned, and ran. Behind, he could hear Newton and Yaargraukh grunting on the other side of the open iris valve, laboring to pull the disabled bot out of the way. He glanced to check on their progress, discovered that the repairbot chasing him had halved the distance. *Shit! Dora, where the hell are—?*

Beyond the onrushing repairbot, beyond where Duncan had joined Yaargraukh and Newton to finally muscle the inert unit aside, a lithe, space-suited figure came sprinting around the corner. Through the visor of the helmet, Caine saw Dora Veriden's eyes widen. With her free hand, she yanked the Ruger from its shoulder holster and squeezed off three hasty shots, aiming low.

Only one of the bullets hit the bot chasing Riordan, but that was enough. As Eku had predicted, and Dora had gambled, the robot halted, spun back around, accelerated toward her. A firearm trumped any number of ineffectual, club-armed attackers.

Dora just grinned, backed up, pitons in her left hand, pistol in her right. Bannor appeared around the corner behind her, carrying the spacesuits and a sprayer.

Newton was slumping sideways; when the gas hit, his paint-frozen arm hadn't been able to reach his own soaked towel. Duncan had his cloth over the lower half of his face, wobbled slightly as he moved to the far side of the passageway and slashed his club weakly at the automaton. Since it was faster to dodge the human than run it over, the bot merely flinched away from Duncan's attack as it sped past the open iris valve.

Yaargraukh emerged from the compartment directly behind it. His left hand clutched a towel over the blunt end of his long head; the other was raised and ready.

And holding a thirty-five-kilogram dumbbell from Bannor's set.

Maybe it was the gas, but to Caine, it seemed that everything happened in a dreamlike ballet of simultaneity. Dora retreated a further step. Bannor jumped forward, a plume of paint reaching out toward the bot. Yaargraukh leaped at its back, his fist bringing the dumbbell down in a sudden arc. The sound of the impact wasn't like those typically heard in melees; it was as loud and metallic and ragged as a car crash.

Riordan's knees felt weak, started buckling as the repairbot veered sharply into the bulkhead closest to Bannor, just before Yaargraukh brought the dumbbell down again, this time over his head with both hands. Metal panels, parts, and sparks flew up as the weight crashed down into the top of the unit. It sagged and was still.

The world tilted. Caine felt passive pressure on his right shoulder; he'd slumped against the wall. Dora raced past, holding Bannor's sprayer. Bannor came running behind her, but seemed slow. He stopped to fit a helmet over Duncan's lolling head, rolled out one of the Dornaani spacesuits. Then he rose and came toward Riordan. Slowly. So slowly. Even as he loomed close, Bannor's face began to fade away...

Suddenly his face was back. Riordan was wearing a space helmet, had a rebreather jammed between his teeth, was groggily shoving his arms into the sleeves of a Dornaani-made spacesuit.

"We've gotta move," Rulaine shouted. "You ready?"

Caine's tongue and consciousness pushed up through layers of cotton and cobwebs. "I'm ready. Let's go."

Chapter Sixty-Eight

Dora raced up the corridor into an omnidirectional blizzard of fine, flame retardant mist. After taking five long, deerlike strides into the murk, her helmet's thermal imaging picked out two dim silhouettes slumped against the portside bulkhead: Tagawa and Girten. *So no reinforcements up near the bridge. No surprise. Still, have to get them out of the smoke ASAP. Assuming we live to do it.*

As she passed the last guttering blankets and sheets, Veriden switched the hammer to her right hand and muttered at her vac suit's smart system. "Seal in body heat. No venting." Which, in combination with the thermally opaque mist, would render her nearly invisible to the ship's IR sensors. Between that and the smoke, the video pickups wouldn't be faring much better. But she'd only know if it would keep her safe at the end of her sprint.

Which she finished, without incident, next to the bridge's outsized iris valve.

Crouching and flattening against the bulkhead beside it, she waited, body heat rising in her suit.

Riordan picked up his spray can as Yaargraukh approached, helping Duncan; his knees were still wobbly. Solsohn looked up the corridor; just ten meters forward, it was a gray mass of mist and smoke. "Bastard'll still zee uz through dat," he slurred. "Gotta shift to therm-thermal seal. No IR sign."

Riordan patted Solsohn on the shoulder. "Not the plan, Duncan. We *want* Hsontlosh to see *us* approach. Remember? Right now, the suits are just for protection."

Duncan's head sagged down, then raised slightly: probably the best nod he could manage. "Yeah. Right."

Riordan wondered if Duncan remembered *any* of the plan at this point. But at least he was up and moving. "You hang back with Yaargraukh."

The Hkh'Rkh's voice was muffled by the towel over his long nose. "Caine Riordan, one last time, I ask you to reconsider. Allow me to walk in the first rank. The proxrovs could be armed. They might kill—"

"Yaargraukh, every one of us is at risk. But you're the only one who's got the power to put our enemies out of action. Until you've got a target, you've got to stay screened in the rear." He glanced at Bannor. "Besides, Colonel Rulaine and I would get bored back there. Right?"

Bannor grinned. "You tell such pretty lies. You have your suit set for reactive resistance?"

"Just switched it on." Caine returned the smile, wondered if it would be his last. "Let's go."

As on most ships, the bridge's iris valve was so thick that it was impossible to hear anything going on behind it. Consequently, Dora had no warning before it whispered open.

But she knew what it meant: Hsontlosh was sending out his proxrovs. They would be as blind as the ship's sensors, but at close range, their audio would be unimpaired. Even though she was sealed inside a suit that did not even have its ventilator running, Dora held her breath as the first one exited. It was unarmed.

She suppressed a sigh of relief as the anthropomorphic robot walked into the mist. She continued to wait.

As expected, the second proxrov emerged a few moments later. This one stopped in the doorway, holding some kind of gun. Eku hadn't known if Hsontlosh actually possessed a personal weapon, much less what it might be. A brief glance wasn't any help. Dora didn't recognize anything except the barrel. But if she wound up looking down that part of the firearm, or whatever it was, she was pretty certain she was as good as dead. She felt sweat roll down from her brow, was suddenly struck by a pang of fear and misgiving. *Damn it, I should have holstered the Ruger, freed both hands for the hammer.*

But there was no time to make that change, or even fully process the regret. The proxrov moved one step forward, weapon carried at the hip. Or rather, the armature that passed for one. It surveyed the corridor. Its high-autonomy system decided to take another, bolder step into the wall of mist and smoke.

Riordan and Bannor stayed to either side of the corridor, sprayers at the ready, unable to see more than a dim silhouette of each other. Radios off, they had to rely on external speakers. Even though any sound would tell their enemy where they were, live radios would have been the electronic equivalent of painting bull's-eyes on themselves. Besides, the proxrov would know when contact was imminent—its own thermal imaging and the corridor's IR sensors would pick them out, despite their suits and the fog. So the humans' only reasonable strategy was to keep advancing until...

A faint sound—a footstep?—and then the grayness in front of Riordan darkened, hardened into an anthropomorphic shape.

"Contact!" Caine shouted, leaping back as far as he could. He lost his footing, fell backward.

The proxrov pursued, but not fast enough to catch hold of Riordan before another shape emerged from the murk: Bannor, who leaped across the corridor toward the robot's side, got his arms around its hip armature.

The proxrov didn't go down. Not a surprise: although well under two meters tall, it massed well over one hundred kilograms. Which was why Bannor dropped his grip and slid under the easy reach of the proxrov's powerful hands.

Riordan scrambled to his feet, but Duncan was already rushing past him.

Steadying itself with one hand against the bulkhead wall, the anthrobot raised its free fist, adjusting to hit Bannor...

Duncan crashed into the machine's upper torso, dragging it along the wall and backward. With Bannor's arms still locked around its legs, it went down.

Riordan rolled up into a sprinter's crouch as Yaargraukh's feet started pounding closer. Caine ran to where the three humanoid forms were struggling on the deck. The bot's left hand was now on Bannor's left arm, squeezing with almost as much force as a Hkh'Rkh. But the Dornaani suit's reactive hardening compensated against that grasp. Even so, Rulaine grunted in pain as Riordan found an opening and jammed the sprayer down into the proxrov's face. He squeezed the trigger, moving the flow down into the neck articulation.

The proxrov didn't seem to react for a moment, was probably calculating and weighing options, then threw Duncan off bodily, freeing a hand to wipe at its sensors.

Caine yelled, "Yaargraukh!" and stepped quickly to the side.

Just as the proxrov's somewhat crude hands cleared its video sensors, a hulking shape loomed out of the mists behind Riordan. Its right arm flashed down, capped by what appeared to be a double-headed hammer of immense proportions.

The dumbbell missed the proxrov's head, caught its shoulder instead. The arm holding Bannor's arm went limp. Duncan rolled up to his feet, unsteadily preparing to dive back at the machine. Riordan prepared to do the same—

But was stopped by Bannor's voice. "We've got this one. Go! Take the bridge!"

As the armed proxrov stepped past her, Dora didn't stop to think. She acted.

Knowing that the proxrov's audio sensors would detect her instantly, she stood and swung the hammer in one smooth movement.

The robot was already turning when the head of the hammer struck the side of its neck. The proxrov staggered to the side.

Dora flipped the hammer around, drew it back again.

The automaton righted itself, bringing up its weapon.

Veriden sidestepped to stay on its flank and swung the hammer's sharp, curved back-spike into the rear of its neck. It penetrated the thinner, articulated metal. Fluid—coolant?—jetted out as the proxrov continued to pivot, firing the weapon as it tracked after Dora, each projectile digging a divot out of the bulkhead. Dora waltzed along with the faltering machine, got further around its turning flank, struck again.

The pick-end lodged in its neck. The proxrov froze and began to topple.

Veriden grabbed its weapon arm as it tilted toward the deck, swinging her weight against the direction of robot's fall so that it landed just where she wanted it.

Across the threshold of the bridge's open iris valve.

Bannor shifted his grip, slipped behind the damaged proxrov, but it rolled out of his double-armed hold. Duncan, who was now holding its thighs, could hardly keep from being bucked and sent flying. Again.

"Yaargraukh," Bannor grunted as the proxrov squirmed into a position where it could use a knee against him, "any time now."

The Hkh'Rkh's reply sounded tight, anxious—a tone completely unfamiliar to Rulaine. "I could miss."

"And we could die." A sudden inspiration. "I'm going to help Duncan with the legs." The proxrov's knee caught Bannor in the gut, winded him, might have ruptured something.

"Understood."

Bannor didn't try to speak, didn't try to coordinate, didn't know if he'd survive another blow like the last. He opened his grip just long enough to slip his arms down to join Duncan in grasping the machine's upper legs.

The proxrov, discovering that it had unimpeded range of motion from the hip up, spun quickly, jackknifing to bring its good arm into striking position upon the humans.

Yaargraukh slammed the dumbbell down into the machine's suddenly exposed center of mass. Its shell now partially caved in, the proxrov changed tactics. Rather than striking the humans, it was trying to extricate itself.

Another hammer blow fell, this time hitting the juncture between its neck and its head. The proxrov flinched, faltered.

"Get clear," Yaargraukh rasped, snout fully exposed to the gas.

Bannor turned his head, saw the immense torso of the Hkh'Rkh rise up, the dumbbell held in both hands.

He dove aside, shouting for Duncan to do the same.

The smoke thinned so suddenly that Riordan barely saw the yawning iris valve in time to slow down before charging straight into Dora.

She rose up from the proxrov she was straddling. "Can't figure out the pocket cannon this proxrov was using. So all I've got is this." She drew her Ruger.

Riordan nodded, said, "I'm sure that will do," just before the ship plunged into darkness. A moment later, amber-colored emergency lights flickered to life. Having lost control of the ship, Hsontlosh had crashed its systems.

Caine popped his helmet, glanced at Dora. "You ready?" She nodded. He stepped over the remains of the proxrov. Dora followed.

Hsontlosh was standing at the navigation console, more interested in the readouts than in them. Behind the loji, the shift-chronometer was ticking down steadily. Caine knew enough Dornaani to read it: five minutes left. "Terminate the shift, Hsontlosh."

He seemed genuinely unconcerned. "I shall not. On the other hand, if you lay down your weapons, I will consider concealing any two of your party from the Ktor when I meet them. Those two will be allowed to return to the Collective."

Riordan shook his head. "Even if I believed you, we stick together."

"So you choose collective suicide, then. A pity. I realize that you might have considered the offer more favorably if I could have made you one of its beneficiaries. However, I'm afraid that's not possible, Commodore Riordan. You are, after all, the commodity in which my buyers are most interested."

Dora raised the gun into a two-handed grip, fixed on the point directly between the loji's eyes. "You'd better start thinking about cutting a whole new deal. With us. Who knows? *We* might even let *you* live."

"Ms. Veriden, your bravado is not only entertaining, but proof that homo sapiens' reflex toward barbarity is matched only by its capacity for self-delusion. I will not make any new arrangements. This exchange has been almost a year in the planning. Its success ensures me lavish resources in perpetuity. Conversely, disappointing the independent agents with whom I have made my arrangements would lead to an outcome far more grim than any with which you might threaten me. But lastly, I will not terminate the countdown because I have no need to do so.

"Eku may have explained that the shift cannot be halted unless I manually enter a code that will reconnect the drive to the ship's systems. Without that connection, the drive remains isolated from all controls. Including, therefore, your universal override key. If you attempt to disable or destroy the drive, the capacitors will still discharge on schedule and vaporize the ship.

If you attempt to tamper with the capacitors themselves, again, the system breach discharges them. So you are without recourse."

Dora shook her head. "Doesn't look that way from where I'm standing." She leveled the Ruger meaningfully. "I see two knees and two elbows that I can blow apart. Unless you are a whole lot tougher than you look, you'll be begging us to let you enter that code before I can fire a third shot."

Hsontlosh folded his hands patiently. "You seem to be unaware of the position in which I am standing, Ms. Veriden."

Riordan raised his chin. "I know where you are standing."

"Of course; Eku would certainly have informed you."

"I also spent the better part of a year on another Custodial ship. The bridge layout is not dissimilar. Including the location of the navigation console."

Hsontlosh backed up until he was brushing against the controls behind him. "Then you know that if Ms. Veriden should miss and hit the console..."

"I won't miss, asshole."

"...or the projectile penetrates my body and, again, damages the navigation system, you will be committing suicide."

"Actually, according to Eku, we will mis-shift."

Hsontlosh's mouth curled half around its axis. "And has the factotum told you what that means?"

"He was about to explain when you started that countdown clock." Riordan nodded at the shift chronometer's steadily decreasing numbers. Three minutes remained.

Hsontlosh cycled his lids slowly. "This is what happens during a mis-shift. You will transition out of this volume of space-time successfully, because your commencement coordinates are fixed. But the damage to the navigation system will corrupt your terminal coordinates, and so, your reexpression into normative space-time shall be uncontrolled.

"You might come out as a spray of energetic particles. You might reexpress in the void between stars, your drive and capacitors burned and useless. Or you might never emerge at all, dissipating as a wash of energy so diffuse that it cannot be discerned. A hundred other outcomes are imaginable, but all equate to this: to mis-shift is to die."

"So is crossing over into Ktor space," countered Riordan, "or being stuck here on the ragged edges of it."

The loji's gills burbled in open derision. "Low odds of survival are better than no odds at all, human."

A new voice—Bannor's—responded. "True. But you've got the odds backward, Hsontlosh."

Caine turned, saw that Bannor, Duncan, and Yaargraukh had survived.

Hsontlosh's lids flickered. "Why do you say that I 'have the odds backward,' Colonel Rulaine?"

Duncan's voice was still hoarse from the gas. "He means that at least our odds of surviving a mis-shift are better than zero. So they're better than our chance of surviving captivity under the Ktor."

"You might escape, even from the Ktor."

"Maybe. But you know who won't escape?" Duncan jerked his head aftward. "Those ancient factotums. The Ktor will find a way to tear every last secret out them. Secrets that might enable them to destroy Earth, the Collective, even the loji Rings."

Hsontlosh's eyes opened wide, turned toward Riordan. "I have studied you, Commodore. You, at least, have an enlightened understanding of the axiom that where there is life, there is hope. But to mis-shift is to *abandon* all hope."

Caine crossed his arms. "If you think that hope only gives you a reason to live, then you don't really understand hope. Sometimes, in order to preserve it for others, hope is what gives you the courage to die."

Hsontlosh turned away abruptly. "There is no point in commending the use of reason to beings that lack it. So I simply repeat my offer: the first two who surrender shall be concealed from the Ktor. You have half a minute to contemplate the alternatives: bondage or oblivion. At least one of you will succumb to your reflex for self-preservation; do not be among those who miss that opportunity."

Dora leaned her head sideways, peering down the Ruger's sights. "Do I take him, Boss?"

"Only if he's still in your line of fire when that countdown clock hits three seconds." There were twenty seconds left.

"I thought honorable humans refused to shoot their adversaries in the back."

Bannor stepped forward so that he was next to Riordan. "This time, we can live with it."

"If you destroy this console, you will not live at all."

"You'll forgive the irony," Caine said, "but we can live with that, too." He glanced at Dora, then at the timer: three seconds.

Riordan nodded.

Dora's grim smile widened; she squeezed the trigger three times in rapid sequence.

Each round hit, leaving splashes of maroon blood and orange lymph fluids among the constellation of circles and whorls that spread away from Hsontlosh's spine like still-born wings. The first bullet lodged in the skeletal cage that protected his heart, killing him instantly. The second and third bullets fully penetrated his torso, hitting the panel behind him. Flakes spalled outward as the impact-resistant surface ablated, slowing the rounds. But not enough.

The second bullet, by some freakish quirk of fate, managed to hit only one inactive backup coupling before it embedded in the rear of the console. But the third bullet tore into the neofiber-optic coordinate relays less than half a second before the shift engaged.

Unlike typical Dornaani shifts, Caine did not plummet down into nothingness before rising back up. Rather, he felt his body being ripped apart, his mind stretching as though it might tear. And then he felt—

Nothing.

Chapter Sixty-Nine

Caine could suddenly see again, feel again...

The instant he realized *I'm alive!* was also the instant he vomited.

The rest of his crew were doing the same, simultaneously discovering the mis-shift's improbably coherent outcome and their own profound nausea as they floated in darkness. The emergency lights had failed and the ship was no longer connected to a spinbuoy.

The ragged chorus of retching almost caused Riordan to begin a second bout of his own, but he swallowed against it and turned on his helmet lights. "Sound off."

Everyone did, although Yaargraukh, not being familiar with all human military commands, lagged a moment behind. Other helmet lights shot sudden, bright beams through the darkness.

Riordan stretched a magnetic sole toward the deck, got his footing, and slow-walked down to the navigation station. He leaned a hand on the twice-punctured, and now completely dark, console and surveyed the bridge. Not a single control was illuminated. Caine hadn't expected any different, but—as Hsontlosh had so eloquently expressed the truth he had so poorly understood—there was always a reason to hope.

"Where the hell are we?" groaned Dora.

"No way of knowing," Duncan groaned back. "Need to retract those cockpit, er, bridge covers."

"We don't have the juice to do either, Duncan," Riordan said, crossing his arms. "And no way we're going to get enough from these suits, or the bots' power cells, to make that happen. Besides, keeping power in these suits is the first order of business. So shut down their primary systems."

"What?" It was the first time Dora had ever said something that ended on a high, rising pitch. "Why?"

"Because that extends our survival time. Not only did Hsontlosh crash the ship's systems, but it looks like the mis-shift has fried or drained everything that still had any juice in it. So we're not just without life support. We don't even have a way to filter the air or concentrate higher O_2 levels in a smaller section of the ship.

"That gives us two days. On the third, we'll get woozy, then stupid. On the fourth, hallucinations, hypoxia, then death. But there are still ways to extend that time." He tapped his life support unit. "Our personal supplies give us another twelve hours. Plus we can tap whatever O_2 is in the repressurization and refill tanks in the airlock, one of the few parts of the ship we can still reach." He started toward the yawning hole of the iris valve. "Now, let's help the others."

Noradrenal response and mental exhaustion had Riordan longing for just fifteen minutes to sit and decompress, but neither he nor the rest of his team could afford that luxury. Not until they knew more about their situation.

Once Eku's right arm was splinted, he pointed out a small access panel in the bridge that provided manual access to an array of primitive analog meters. Their sole intended purpose was to provide reactivation teams a quick look at the onboard levels of primary consumables, even if the ship had no power.

As expected, the ship's main tanks were entirely out of fuel. However, what Eku called a restart tank—fuel that was isolated from the main power-generation or thrust systems—was approximately half full. Normally used to facilitate the jump-start of the main plant after long years, or centuries, in depot storage, it could provide a few hours of regular power or a few minutes of thrust before being exhausted. The capacitors and reserve batteries were drained. And although the bioactive and water reclamation elements of the life support system were well stocked, it was all just so much inert matter without electricity.

Riordan reported the findings when the crew regathered on the bridge, asked if there were questions. Craig Girten, whose fear was magnified by his lack of knowledge about the machines and skills upon which their slim hopes of survival depended, asked, "Is there any *good* news?"

Caine smiled, waited until Craig had finished coughing. The smoke had not been kind to his lungs or Tagawa's. "Actually, yes, one bright spot. According to our suits' dosimeters, REM accumulation is quite tolerable. Either the ambient radiation is low, the ship's own passive shielding is keeping it out, or both. So, for a change, rads will be the last thing that kills us."

The seasoned space travelers in the group grinned at the black humor. The others did not.

The only other question came from Dora. "I already know the answer to this, but someone's gotta ask: when do we wake up the other four?"

Riordan nodded. "Until we get the final data point we need, we don't know if the Second Watch is better off in their cold cells living on the integral emergency battery power, or out here with us, increasing our oxygen consumption by almost thirty percent."

Newton nodded. "And when do we get that final data point?"

"Right now." Riordan stood. "I'm sure all of you would like to be involved, but that's not possible. We don't have enough equipment and we can't spare the oxygen. So it's going to be four of us, chosen on the basis of relevant experience and fitness for duty." Caine tapped his chest, then pointed to Bannor, Duncan, and Dora. "Let's go."

Riordan insisted on being the first through the airlock's outer hatch, not because it was the privilege of rank, but because it was the curse of being the commander. Whatever they saw when they emerged would irrevocably determine their fate. And he wanted one moment of advance warning to shape his reaction. And if necessary, orders.

Caine emerged into darkness, the flank of the ship as lightless as the space that surrounded it. The distant stars were sharp points of light: motionless, solemn, even ominous. Here, they did not twinkle, did not excite sensations of timeless and titanic majesty. In space, the stars were as cold and pitiless as nature itself.

Riordan held his breath, examined the heavens that he could

see: nothing except those ice-bright chips in the deep black. As the others followed him out, he triggered a set of puffs from the compact Dornaani maneuver unit. Turning slowly and heading toward the upper surface of the ship, he kept his eyes aft, waiting for the first stabilizer to rise into view.

When it did, it was a whitish shark fin against the surrounding dark. Riordan managed not to gasp or cheer. "Join me," he said quietly into his radio. He drifted higher.

A moment later, he cleared the top of the ship's slight ventral hump and was blinded by the most wonderful and improbable sunrise he had ever seen. As he did, the others spied the light reflecting off the stabilizer. Caine heard their suppressed sighs.

Against all odds, against every prediction or reason for hope, they had arrived near a star. And where there was a star, there were likely to be planets. That didn't mean they'd survive. Most planets were lethal, and the great majority of the remainder were savagely inhospitable. But a star meant hope, whereas to have discovered themselves stranded in the trackless void of interstellar space would have been the grimmest of all prospects.

"It's a G-class star," muttered Riordan, "if you can believe that."

"Jesus, Caine," Duncan breathed as he rose up into the full light, "I'm not sure what's harder to believe: how bad our luck can be, or how good."

Riordan smiled, was about to agree, but then noticed that as he continued to rise, the leading edge of the far wing was also lit, albeit dimly. *My God, it can't be.* Riordan boosted higher.

"Caine," shouted Bannor, "are you okay? What are you doing?"

Riordan watched the ship drop away beneath him, knew he'd come to the end of his tether any moment, watched the far wing-rim.

And was unable to suppress a gasp when a planet appeared over it, seeming to rise up before him. It was awash in blue oceans and the white whorls of marine storms. The continents were daunting, however: expanses the color of sand and rust, riven in many places by sharp black mountains. The ice caps were small, and the barren land marched right up to their limits. But still...

"Holy shit!" Dora shouted as she rose into position to see the planet. Although her face was invisible beyond her helmet's active screening, Riordan had the impression that she was staring back defiantly. "Tell me you didn't think the same thing!"

"I thought it," Bannor agreed as he and Duncan floated closer. "I just didn't pierce everybody's eardrums with it."

"Okay, okay, but..." She began to mutter something under her breath. Was it... a prayer?

Duncan, in contrast was chuckling. "Y'know," he said, "I'm actually feeling the tiniest bit better about our chances of survival, now."

Bannor sounded like he was smiling. "You're just a crazy optimist, Solsohn."

"No, Rulaine, we're just crazy lucky."

"No," interrupted Caine quietly as he realized the significance of what they were seeing. "We're not."

"Uh... what?" asked Duncan.

"It's too much good luck. First, we don't emerge in deep space, but near a star. Then we find out we're near a planet. And it turns out to be a planet with water. Which, along with those clouds, means probably enough of an atmosphere, and maybe enough oxygen, that we've got an outside chance of being able to breathe it, filtered or otherwise." He turned to face the others, even though they couldn't see each other. "This isn't luck."

Duncan was the first to break the silence. "Er... you never struck me as the religious type. Commodore."

"I'm not. That's not what's at work here."

Dora sounded a little spooked. "Then what is?"

Riordan sighed. "I'm not sure. But here's what I do know: our part of the galaxy was populated by unthinkably advanced beings up until twenty millennia ago. Who knows what they left behind? Who knows what kind of—I don't know, rescue system—might have been designed for ships that mis-shift?" He looked back at the planet. "What are the odds that we would just happen to pop out of shift here, out of all the cubic light-years of nothingness that surround every tiny star? No, this isn't chance."

He motioned toward Dora. She drifted forward. "You may have the best eyes of any human being I've ever met, Ms. Veriden. Tell me what you see down there. Take your time. What you spot, or miss, could determine all our fates."

"*Coño*, no pressure, hey?" But she went silent, her head forward slightly.

As she stared at the world, Bannor turned slowly in every direction. "Granted that we could be turned upside down and around, but..." His voice trailed off.

"Yes?" Riordan urged.

"Caine, this starfield doesn't have a single feature I recognize. None of the deformed constellations that you can still make out, even if you're fifty or a hundred light-years away from Earth. None of the close pairs of big stars that should be visible from almost anywhere in our cluster."

Duncan exhaled slowly. "I was wondering that, too. Not that my familiarity with starfields is as good as the colonel's, but... damn, nothing here looks familiar."

Riordan nodded, discovered he wasn't surprised. "See anything interesting, Ms. Veriden?"

"Yes. Look there, that archipelago a little bit below the equator. Look at the biggest island."

Riordan saw it at the same moment that Bannor said, "It's... it's got some green on it. I think."

"Yeah, that's green alright. I've also been checking near the banks of all the rivers I can see. I can't tell for sure—maybe it's just wishful thinking—but I think I see little specks of green along them, too. Some are surrounded by a darker ring, I think."

"A scrub margin?" Duncan wondered aloud.

Riordan nodded. "That's as good a guess as any. Of course, it could all be a misread, at this range. Maybe we're seeing a big tidal pool that makes water look green from orbit. Or maybe the color comes from crystalline clusters, bouncing the light in just the right way to charm our hopeful eyes."

"Sounds like we need a closer look," Bannor murmured.

Caine couldn't help smiling. "Sounds like someone's eager to burn that little bit of fuel we found."

"You got someplace else to go...Commodore?"

Riordan surprised himself by laughing. "Not just this minute." He stared at the cold, unfamiliar stars again. "We may not know where we are, but we know we can't stay out here for long."

Solsohn's voice was hushed. "Then I guess we're going down there."

"I guess so, Duncan," Riordan answered. He turned his back on the planet, headed toward the airlock and the hard, hasty work ahead. "I guess we *are* going there," he repeated, attempting to drown out the deafening qualifier in his mind:

Assuming we get down in one piece.

Appendix A

Dramatis Personae

Humans and Allies

Angus Smith: technical specialist (covert) for ODINS

Ayana Tagawa: Former XO of SS *Arbitrage*; former Japanese Intelligence

Bannor Rulaine: Colonel, crew of UCS *Puller, former US Special Forces/IRIS*

Caine Riordan: Commodore, USSF (ret.), former IRIS

Connor Corcoran: son of Caine Riordan and Elena Corcoran

David Weber: Director of ODINS; Captain USSF (Reserve)

Dora Veriden: crew of UCS *Puller*

Duncan Solsohn: Major, crew of UCS *Puller, former CIA/IRIS*

Elena Corcoran: anthropologist, diplomat

Enis Turan: Compliance Officer, Procedural Compliance Directorate, IRIS

Ed Peña: covert operative for ODINS

Eku: factotum in the service of Alnduul

Gray Rinehart: Associate Director, IRIS

Karam Tsaami: Pilot and Flight Officer, CSSO; crew of UCS *Puller*

Kim Schoeffel: Captain, SS *Down-Under*, ex-UCAS naval officer

Kyle Seaver: Lieutenant, USSF, Operations liaison between JAG and IRIS; covert operative for ODINS

Larry Southard: analyst (covert) for ODINS

Lorraine Phalon: Commander, USSF; JAG

Miles O'Garran: Master CPO, former SEAL/IRIS; crew of UCS *Puller*

Missy Katano: Lost Soldier; civilian contractor

Newton Baruch: Lieutenant, Benelux/EUAF; former IRIS; crew of UCS *Puller*

Peter Wu: Captain, ROCA/UCAS; former IRIS; crew of UCS *Puller*

Richard Downing: former Director of IRIS

Ryan Zimmerman: analyst (covert) for ODINS

Trevor Corcoran: Captain, USSF; SEAL/IRIS

Dalir Sadozai: Associate Director, Procedural Compliance Directorate, IRIS

Yaargraukh Onvaarkhayn of the moiety of Hsraluur: Exile from the Hkh'Rkh Patrijuridicate, former Advocate of the Unhonored

Yan Xiayou: Director, Procedural Compliance Directorate, IRIS

Simulacra

Antanas Voldermaras: leader, resistance movement

Bram Prins: leader, resistance movement

David Lawrence Weiner: Earl of Greater Connecticut, industrial magnate of the CCC and avatar of Kutkh

Nolan Corcoran: Deceased Admiral, USSF; Director (and creator) of IRIS

Rebecca: niece of Pip Robinson

Steven "Pip" Robinson: veteran of the Coal War; leader, resistance movement

Dornaani

Alnduul: Senior Mentor of the Custodians of the Accord, Dornaani Collective

Glayaazh: Third Arbiter (Senior) of the Dornaani Collective

Heethoo: Seventh Arbiter (Senior) of the Dornaani Collective

Hsontlosh: loji liaison and expediter retained by members of the Collective's Senior Assembly

Irzhresht: Custodian; loji under Alnduul's protection

Laaglenz: Virtua expert; "The Speculator"

Laynshooz: Regional Arbiter of the Dornaani Collective

"Kutkh": Keeper of Virtua node of Leltlosu-shai

Nlastanl: Fifth Arbiter (Senior) of the Dornaani Collective

Menrelm: Acting Senior Auditor of the Custodians

Oduosslun: former Academician of the Collective; "The Observer"

Ssaodralth: journeyman Custodian

Suvtrush: Fourth Arbiter (Senior) of the Dornaani Collective

Thlunroolt: Warder of the Rooaioo'q Conservancy, former Custodial Senior Mentor

Uinzleej: Caretaker of Issqliin, Park of Antiquities; "The Historian"

Yaonhoyz: Regional Arbiter of the Dornaani Collective

Appendix B

The Accords

1. The Accord is a democratic council comprised of politically equal member states. Membership is conferred through a process of mutual assessment and determination. Attendance at all Convocations of the Accord is mandatory; absences are treated as abstention and warrant the censure of the Accord. Accord policy and arbitration outcomes are determined by simple majority votes. However, changes in the accords themselves (additions, deletions, emendations) require unanimous approval (abstentions are construed as rejections). Issues addressed by the Accord include:

   - Accord policies and actions toward non-Accord powers, races, objects, or phenomena;

   - interpretation and application of the accords;

   - proper procedures for administering the Accord, including first contact, meeting, and communication protocols;

   - reassessment and periodic alteration of the current pathways of allowed expansion for Accord member states.

2. A member state's membership in the Accord requires, and remains contingent upon, truthful self-representation in

all disclosures of data or statements of intention: lies of omission or commission are expressly forbidden. If it is found that a member state misrepresented itself upon application for membership in the Accord, its membership is annulled.

3. One member state of the Accord is designated as the Custodian of the accords. The Custodians are charged with ensuring that all member states comply with the accords, that lack of compliance is corrected, and that disputes are resolved by arbitration commissions.

4. The Accord and its individual member states are expressly and absolutely forbidden from interfering in the internal affairs of any member state. The only exception to this is articulated in the Twenty-first Accord.

5. All entry into another member state's space must comply with territorial transit agreements negotiated between the member states in question. If no such agreements exist, a member state may declare any intrusion into its territory as illegal and may require the Accord to convene an arbitration commission to seek redress. The race designated as Custodians are excluded from these constraints when acting in their capacity as Custodians. However, they are expected and enjoined to use all possible restraint and to secure prior permission wherever and whenever possible.

6. No violence of any kind or on any scale is permitted between the races of the Accord.

7. No espionage is permitted between the races of the Accord, nor are other clandestine attempts to subvert or circumvent the autonomy, prerogatives, or secrecy constraints of another member state.

8. No agreement (legal or personal) made between individuals or collectives from two (or more) member states may ever explicitly or implicitly encumber or abridge the absolute indigenous autonomy of any of the parties to the agreement. Therefore, any member state (or inhabitant thereof) may terminate any agreement with any

other member state (or inhabitant thereof) at any time for any reason, contractual obligations notwithstanding.

9. Disputes between member states and violations of these accords may only be resolved by a Custodian-appointed arbitration commission. Member states involved in a dispute may not serve on arbitration commissions convened after the commencement of their dispute until said dispute is resolved. All arbitration commissions are chaired by Custodians, and must follow the same determinative protocols as the Accord itself, as outlined in the First Accord.

10. Member states which are found to have violated an accord are instructed by the finding commission how to make amends for this violation. If the member state finds these instructions unacceptable, they may propose an alternate means of making amends, may request a reconsideration, or may appeal for clemency or exoneration (if there are suitably extenuating circumstances).

11. Member states which flagrantly or willfully violate one or more accords forfeit their membership in the Accord. The same applies to member states which choose to ignore or reject the final determination of arbitration commissions. Former Accord member states may reapply for membership.

12. Members of the Accord must agree to restrict their use of interstellar-rated microwave and radio emissions to dire emergencies (such as distress calls, or in the event that all other communication systems have malfunctioned).

13. All Accord ships must be equipped with a transponder that, upon inquiry from any other Accord ship, will relay its member state of origin, its name or code, its master, and any special conditions under which it is operating.

14. All Accord ships must be furnished with multiple crewpersons who are conversant in the Code of Universal Signals and, if requested, must use this Code to initiate and respond to any and all communiqués.

15. All member states must maintain strict compliance with the Accord-prescribed pathways of allowed expansion. A single race may petition for a revision of its own expansion pathway: this is handled as an arbitration.

16. New races are contacted by the Accord only when they achieve routine interstellar travel, whether of a faster-than-light or slower-than-light variety.

17. The time and method of contacting a new race is determined by the Custodians of the Accord. Prior to contact, new races are designated as "protected species."

18. Monitoring of nonmember intelligent species is the responsibility of the Custodians. Routine supporting tasks may be assigned to one other member state that possesses sufficient technological and exploratory capabilities.

19. An outgoing Custodian member state selects the order in which member states are invited to succeed it. FTL travel is the prerequisite for Custodianship. The minimum duration of Custodianship is 24.6 Earth years. Minimum advance notice of resignation from Custodianship is 4.1 Earth years.

20. If no race is willing to accept Custodianship, the Accord is considered dissolved, as are all agreements previously made and enforced under its aegis.

21. Extraordinary circumstances: the Custodians are to intervene as soon as is practicable, and unilaterally if that is most expeditious, if:

   • any member state's or protected race's homeworld is invaded or otherwise attacked;

   • if any member state or protected race takes action that is deemed likely to result in the destruction of a planet's biosphere.

   The Custodians may undertake this intervention without soliciting Accord consensus, and may, if necessary, violate other accords in order to ensure that the intervention is successful.